# The Bank Robber's Daughter

# The Bank Robber's Daughter

## Steve Love

With thanks to Alex Brummer, City Editor of the
Daily Mail, for his encouragement and his book 'Bad
Banks' which gave me the idea for my own,
and to Barbary Love for all her editorial help,


With appreciation for the police officers of Bethnal
Green and the District 7 Major Crimes Unit
who took me under their wing back in the '90s,


And with acknowledgement of the bad bankers
who brought us the banking crisis and the credit
crunch and without whom this story would
not be told.

# CHAPTER 1  THE MONEY PROBLEM

Like all successful bank robbers, Janie Laker had a problem. A money problem. What to do with it all. In Hollywood movies a briefcase can hold a million tightly-packed dollars, but Janie found it a struggle to get even just twenty thousand pounds in used notes into a pillowcase, so a million would be fifty very full pillowcases. And she lived in a one-bedroomed flat in Bethnal Green, with barely enough space for herself, let alone her money.

Then there was another problem. Not only is money difficult to hide, but if you do hide it then other people will try to find it. Janie knew plenty of criminals who would happily rob a fellow robber, secure in the knowledge that they are hardly likely to be reported to the police. Or the police themselves may turn up with a search warrant, in which case the best to be hoped for is that they help themselves without leaving a receipt. But the more likely outcome is that the money becomes the evidence that sends you to gaol for a very long stretch.

Or you can just spend as you earn. Many robbers do this, but their expensive lifestyles, mansions, cars, gambling and drinking eventually give them away, and their downfall is never far behind. That did not appeal to Janie either. So she decided to open a bank account. Her Dad told her she was crazy, but she did it anyway.

So there she was, aged 19, on the pavement outside Royal London Bank's branch in Hackney, with a holdall full of stolen money, no visible means of support, and an appointment in a false name to see the manager at eleven. Janie paused, took a deep breath to steady her resolve, and pushed open the door. In those days, back in the nineteen seventies, every High Street had a bank, every bank had a bank manager, and every manager saw every new customer in person. It was a Tuesday, she chose that day to make sure that there would be no chance of the place being robbed while she was inside. All robbers know that banks are light on money on Tuesdays because last weekend's shop takings went away on Monday, while next weekend's payrolls don't come in till Wednesday.

At eleven on the dot she was whisked through the 'PRIVATE – STAFF ONLY' entrance and into an office whose door was marked "MR M. PHILLIPS MANAGER". She was expecting an oldish, tubby, bespectacled Captain Mainwaring character from 'Dad's Army', her own father's favourite TV show, so she was surprised when Mr M. Phillips turned out to be only a year or two older than herself. Tall and slim, in a smart three-piece suit, clean-shaven with slicked-down blond hair, he leaned back in his chair and beckoned Janie to sit facing him, then looked her up and down. When he spoke, he managed to combine formal politeness with unspoken contempt for the skinny 'Befnall girl' who was spoiling his view of the other side of his large and uncluttered desk.

"What can I do for you?" he asked, taking a long look at his watch. "We'll need to be quick, I've another client due in five minutes."

"I'd like to open a bank account," Janie said.

"What sort of account?"

"I don't know, Mr Phillips, I've never had a bank account, nor has anyone else in my family. I thought maybe you could help me."

Mr Phillips sighed and glanced at his watch again. "There are lots of different types of account, I'm sure we can give you a leaflet. Then maybe you can come back when you've read it. Thank you for your time, now if you'll excuse me, I'll see you out."

He stood and stepped towards the door. Janie rose too and slung her holdall over her shoulder. Its weight threw her off balance and the bag caught Mr Phillips squarely in the chest, knocking him two steps backwards.

"Oh I'm really sorry, Mr Phillips." She wasn't sorry. "Are you alright?"

"I'm fine thank you, but that's a heavy bag you've got there, what's in it?"

"The money."

"Money?"

"To open the account with."

"How much money?"

"Ten thousand pounds."

He let go of the door handle without turning it.

"I think we'd better sit down again, don't you?"

They sat down again, and it is fair to say that from then on Janie detected in Mr Phillips an interest in her that had not previously been apparent.

"What can I say? I do rather owe you an apology, I'll get us coffee, then I'll tell you about all the accounts we can offer you."

"Don't you have a client due, Mr Phillips?"

"Oh that's just a thing I say to get rid of people who I think are going to waste my time," he replied. "You'd be amazed how many people pull that trick. Doctors are the worst. Followed closely by bank managers, I'm sorry to say. You aren't wasting my time, I assure you."

Janie was rather charmed by his candour and his willingness to let her in on his trade secrets. 'Maybe I can work with this guy', she said to herself, and she listened attentively while he told her all about how bank accounts work, deposits, dividends, interest rates and the rest. She had the feeling he was enjoying trying to impress her, and she admitted grudgingly to herself that she was rather enjoying feeling important.

"So, would you like me to open a high interest savings deposit account for you, in the sum of ten thousand pounds?"

"Yes I would please."

"Then bear with me, I'll need some details."

From his desk he took out a form headed 'Royal London Bank', and said, "Your full name please?"

"Jennifer Marie Harding." Mr Phillips didn't lift his head, but raised his eyes to hers for just long enough to convey the message 'I know that's not your real name'. But he wrote Jennifer Marie Harding down anyway.

"Thank you, and may I call you Jennifer? Call me Mike, by the way."

"Of course Mike."

"Your date of birth, Jennifer?"

"Eleventh of January nineteen fifty-five." Not true either.

"Address?"

"116 Curtain Mansions, Bethnal Green, London". That was a real address, just not Janie's. It was where Maxie Martens lived, a friend of her father's. Maxie would pass on Janie's mail while denying her existence. Janie pushed across the table a sheaf of false documentation, procured for the price of a few drinks from another of Dad's mates. The papers confirmed that she was indeed Jennifer Marie Harding, born 11/1/55, of 116 Curtain Mansions, Bethnal Green, London. Mike Phillips pushed it back.

"That won't be necessary," said Mr Phillips. "Occupation?"

"General trader." Mr Phillips glanced up again, but Janie had chosen an occupation that he could neither verify nor disprove. And an occupation where cash transactions would be the norm. She smiled back at Mr Phillips, and he understood.

"Now, your deposit," he said, and Janie took twenty bulky rolls of banknotes from her holdall and laid them out them on the desk in front of him. "There's five hundred in each roll. Is cash OK?" she asked him.

"Cash is always OK," he said, as he undid the first roll and started to count it.

Janie watched in silent surprise. In the underworld of London's East End it was then, and still is now, the custom that when you give someone money you are careful to ensure that it is the exact right amount, and the recipient takes it from you without counting it. If you were ever to short-change anyone, even just once, your reputation as someone who can be trusted to do business will be gone forever. And if you count out money in front of the person who has just given it to you, you are insulting them by showing that you do not trust them. Banks, Janie concluded, do not share the code of honour that East End villains have taken for granted since before anyone can remember.

Anticipating that Mr Phillips' next question would be about where a nineteen year old girl from Bethnal Green lays her hands on ten grand in twenty pound notes, Janie checked her jacket pocket for the bundle of fabricated betting slips, provided by a helpful bookmaker nephew of Maxie's, that purported to show how a run of fortunate bets on obliging horses and dogs had multiplied an original £100 stake a hundred-fold. But to her surprise the question never came.

Another surprise was that he counted out all the money himself. She thought that as a hotshot bank manager he would give that grubby task to an underling. Used bank notes are not the cleanest of things, Janie always washed her hands after a share-out of the loot from a robbery. But while she watched Mr Phillips at work, the thought struck her that there may be certain transactions that he preferred not to be observed even by his own bank.

She watched in silence until he had finished counting. "Well done, Jennifer, it's spot on. Ever considered a bank job?"

"Now there's an idea," Janie said, "But if you don't mind me being nosey, Mike, I thought bank managers are all posh and old, but you seem like a regular bloke and not a lot older than me, how's that?"

"Since you are going to be my favourite customer, Jennifer, I'll tell you. I'm just an Essex boy who quit school to make some money. I talked my way into a job as a junior in the local bank, then worked flat out to get on the management track. A month ago they made me the youngest branch manager in the whole of Royal London Bank and sent me out here to Hackney."

"Why Hackney?" Janie asked.

"Hackney isn't exactly the richest part of London and our Hackney branch was losing money hand over fist. My director sent me here, he said if it makes any more losses then I'm out of a job, but if I can turn it round to a good profit he'll get me promoted and swing me a bonus. And you, Jennifer, are my biggest new account to date, which is what makes you my favourite customer." Janie decided that Mike Phillips was a man she could trust. It took her thirty years to change her mind.

He took an illegible scribble of a signature from her and stamped the forms in green ink from a pad in his desk drawer. "Thank you, that's all set up. Here's your account number."

He passed her a slip of paper with an eight-digit number on it, and a receipt for ten thousand pounds. From then on, most of the money that came to Janie over bank counters at gunpoint went back over Mike Phillips' counter and into her savings account. She put the word around that in Royal London in Hackney there was a bank and a manager who were not too fussy who deposited money and where they got it from, and a number of her associates started to put their nest-eggs there too. That did not stop her father robbing it a couple of times, but Janie made sure she was out of the way when he did.

# CHAPTER 2.  THE BANK JOB

Next day, back to work.  There were five figures in the stolen car that pulled up outside Williams and Glyn's Bank, now long gone, on Catford High Street in South London.  The getaway driver and the Guvnor were in the front, Janie and two men behind them, there was plenty of room in those big old Ford Granadas.

The Guvnor was Janie's father, but people called him 'Guvnor', even Janie when they were out at work.  In those days in London's East End there was no so-called social mobility, and if a daughter was not off to get married or find a job in a local factory, she went into the family business.  So that is what Janie did - she quit school at fifteen and went to work for the Guvnor, robbing banks.  There was no Mum around to stop her from going or him from taking her.

In the square mile that contains all the life, bustle and people of Bethnal Green, the Guvnor was a well-known and respected figure, a professional, and Janie was a very proud daughter.  He was not one of the Great Train Robbers, though he helped them to plan their job and declined their invitation to take part only because if successful he knew that they would be hunted for the rest of their lives.  He once hinted to Janie that he knew where the money went, but if he did he took that secret and quite a few others with him to the grave.  He steered clear of the Kray family, but they had the good sense to keep out of his way too.

Janie never knew her grandfather Frank, who started the family business using guns that soldiers brought home as souvenirs from the First World War and then sold for food money in the Great Depression.  A diligent father, Frank Laker taught his son the trade just as the Guvnor in turn taught her.

The Guvnor looked up and down the street, then across to a teenage girl who was idling at a bus stop across the road.  With a petite figure, a stud-encrusted jacket, and a small round face topped with an eyebrow ring and a green punk hairdo, she did not look much like a bank robbers' lookout, which is precisely why he chose her. This was Minnie, and between these work assignments she used to hang around with Janie and her pals without ever spoiling things by becoming anyone's serious girlfriend.

Minnie gave the Guvnor a discreet nod, that was enough. He took his pistol out of the glove compartment, clicked off the safety catch, pulled on his mask, and looked over his shoulder

"Rudy, Nutter, Hulk, all ready?"

"Ready Guvnor" came three replies.

"Then it's time, take 'em!"

As always the Guvnor was first out of the car, gun in hand, to take up position in the bank doorway, with a good view into the lobby and a clear line of fire up and down the street. "Go!" he shouted, and the crew all knew what to do, the Guvnor had drilled and rehearsed them to the second.

Rudy - not his real name - was across the pavement and straight into the bank as the rest of the crew scrambled out behind him. One of the Guvnor's many rules was that everyone had a nickname so that nobody ever gave away a real name on a raid. Rudy was short for Rudolf, in honour of his nose, which went red when he was pumped up with adrenalin, which happened whenever he was robbing a bank. He was two years older than Janie, already a seasoned criminal by the time she joined the gang, a big man whose powerful voice and bulky presence could be relied on to send everyone cowering. If the voice and size didn't do it, the sawn-off shotgun did. Even from outside, Janie could hear Rudy yelling "Get down! Now!" and sense the commotion as customers threw themselves to the floor.

Nutter was right behind him. While Rudy kept the customers down, it was Nutter's job to intimidate the bank staff into instant and total obedience. Pointing a gun at someone only works if they think you will fire it. Anyone who tried to look into his blank expressionless eyes peering out from the depths of his black balaclava would conclude, quickly and correctly, that not only was he capable of pulling the trigger, but that he would not mind at all if he had to.

Nutter was not Nutter's real name either, but everyone called him that, and Janie followed suit. He was the same age as Rudy, and was at school with him for as long as they actually went to school, which Janie gathered was not very long. At first she thought he was merely a slightly odd friend, who would terrify bank staff at gunpoint and then stop to feed the pigeons and talk to the stray cats in the park on his way home afterwards. Later on, she found out about psychopaths in a magazine she was reading, and reflected what good bank robbers they can make.

Nutter rotated his gun slowly round the bank, from one teller's chest to the next, as he ordered them to remain standing at their stations with their hands away from the alarm buttons, and take all the notes out of their tills ready for when the bagman came round. "Do it now," was all Nutter needed to say, and they all did it now.

The bagman was Janie, known by the gang as Hulk as a joke because at the time she was short and scrawny, with thin bony arms and short-cut boyish tousled mousey hair. With just a pistol in order to keep one hand free, it was her job to step over the prostrated customers and go round to each window filling the bag until it could hold no more or the tills were empty, whichever happened first. The robbers were lucky that day, the manager was at one of the counters, so Janie started with him because the Guvnor maintained that the boss types were always the least heroic, and once they capitulated everyone else would follow their example.

Forty-five well-rehearsed seconds later and Janie was out, with Rudy and Nutter covering her exit and then the Guvnor covering theirs, into the car, and away via two changes of vehicle to a disused warehouse where they shared out the loot over tea and sandwiches laid on for the hungry crew on by Maxie Martens. Maxie was a lady of around Janie's father's age whom he called his goalkeeper, and she was always the first name on his team sheet. She and the Guvnor went way back, and she never called him 'Guvnor', she just called him George, which was his real name.

Every gang had a goalkeeper, back then and even nowadays. The goalkeeper's job is to rescue the gang if the job fails and they all have to flee with the police in hot pursuit. The gang make for the keeper who in turn makes them disappear. This is nothing glamorous, like a flight to Brazil with a suitcase of money and a new secret identity: it means going into hiding in an attic, drain, the back of a van in a breakers' yard, anywhere that the police manhunt might miss, with a bucket for a toilet and knocked-off army iron rations for sustenance.

Then when the heat is off, the goalkeeper has to get the fugitives away to wherever they are going, alone unless someone is crazy enough to want to go with them and spend the rest of their life as an outlaw.

Maxie was Minnie's aunt, and her main line of work was running a brothel. Brothels can be handy hiding places because the police are wary of raiding them for fear of finding a politician, judge or one of their own chiefs in there. The Guvnor's gang were so good at what they did that they only ever used Maxie's goalkeeping talents once, when their very last job went so badly wrong. Janie liked Maxie, who made a big fuss of her whenever she called round in her red Cortina to collect Minnie for a girls' day out to Southend. Janie could tell that Maxie was fond of her father too.

So there Janie was, walking home with her share, £4000, a lot of money in those days. But the Guvnor made sure there was absolutely no celebrating afterwards.

"You wouldn't believe how many gangs have given themselves away and gone to gaol because they don't follow my 'no celebrating' rule," he would say to Janie over his pint of mild and hers of blackcurrant-and-lemonade.

"And I'm not buying you alcohol", he would always add, "You're under age and it's against the law."

16

"I'm old enough to rob banks", Janie would always argue.

"There's no legal age limit for that," the Guvnor would always reply.

The Guvnor started every raid the same way - "It's time, take em!" It was his lucky catchphrase. He did not believe in luck, only in meticulous planning and preparation, but he still had a favourite lucky catch-phrase. Year after year he, Rudy, Nutter, Minnie and Janie swept back and forth across London and the Home Counties, emptying out banks and security trucks. Twenty, fifty, sometimes a hundred thousand pounds in cash for a morning's work, counted and divided up the same afternoon. Dad was the Guvnor and Janie worshipped him. And there was no Mum to be fretting about them, she had gone long ago.

And all the while the money piled up in her bank account in Hackney. There was nothing Janie particularly wanted from life other than her Dad's affection and Rudy's, Nutter's and Minnie's company, and she had no boyfriend to waste money on, so she called in at the bank every month to offload her takings. Mike Phillips always said hello if he was around, and a couple of years later he took her out for a long lunch to tell her he was being promoted to a big new job in head office and that she was still his favourite customer. He gave her his card with his new number 'in case there's ever anything I can do for you'.

## CHAPTER 3  THE AMBUSH

The seventies were the golden age for bank robbers. Back then, most people were paid their wages weekly and in cash, which meant there were bulk payroll deliveries going in and out of banks all the time, just waiting to be harvested. And the police could not even get close. A few of the police were bent and helped robbers out with tip-offs in return for a cut of the loot, which caused a succession of police commissioners to lose their sleep, or their temper, or their jobs. But that was not the police's real problem. Their real problem was that the robbers were just too good for them.

Bank robbers had Jaguars and Rovers, the police drove Minis and Marinas. The robbers had hoods and disguises, the cops had grainy black-and-white bank camera images of unidentifiable masked figures. The robbers lived among communities who would shelter them, and had informants who would tell them everything that was going on, while all the police had was non-cooperation and a wall of silence. Even when the police managed to put together enough evidence to go to court, the juries were nobbled. But best of all, the robbers had guns and the police did not. Britain's proud tradition of unarmed policing worked very much in the robbers' favour. For the Guvnor's gang and many others, business boomed.

Then there was an occasion when the Guvnor needed a stolen safe-box opened and Janie found that she had nimble fingers and a natural talent for figuring out how cogs and levers work, so between robberies she became a free-lance burglar and taught herself how to open every type of bolt, case and safe that mankind's ingenuity has invented. Jennifer Harding's bank account prospered accordingly.

Janie was never caught, whether burgling, safe-cracking, or robbing. She had respect on her own patch and was anonymous when off it, which is how she wanted things to be. She lived well but she was not greedy, she had money in the bank and cash in her pocket but she was not flash, she had a flat of her own and a nice car, she had job satisfaction and plenty of time off, she had true friends in Rudy, Nutter, Minnie and Maxie, and though she had no Mum she had her Dad and she was happy.

But she knew even then that it could not last. Times were changing. Pickings became slimmer as employers started to pay wages direct into people's bank accounts. Banks improved their cameras and installed hidden alarm buttons that went direct to Scotland Yard. There was still plenty of cash being driven around town, but much of it belonged to drug dealers and other very bad people from whom even the Guvnor had no wish to steal.

And the police were getting their act together too. They drove Mercedes and BMWs and bought themselves helicopters, and set up teams of sharpshooters who studied robbers' tactics and trained endlessly to overcome them. They paid informants to infiltrate gangs and then, equipped with inside knowledge, came at robbers 'across the pavement', that is, with their own guns drawn and in broad daylight. In a single swoop they would capture a whole gang red-handed with their weapons, disguises, vehicles and loot, and all on film so that even the most nobbled jury would be overwhelmed with evidence and would have to put in a Guilty verdict.

When the Guvnor brought the gang together urgently for another planning session in the room above the bar in the Oak Barrel in Bethnal Green, they had no way of knowing that for all of them this job would be their last. It was short notice but everyone was there, the Guvnor, Janie, Rudy, Nutter, Minnie, Maxie and two of the best getaway drivers in the business. Over soft drinks and tea - there was no boozing before, during or after the Guvnor's raids - he told them the plan.

"Lads, ladies, this is the big one we need, and it's going down this afternoon. We've had a tip-off and it's good.

Barclays' main London cash store has a broken main nearby and there's water pouring in. While they fix it they've got to get all the cash out quick to somewhere dry till after the weekend. Their Lewisham branch has a big vault, so there's a huge pile of money coming over this way, all high value used notes and untraceable. It's a risk for them, but they reckon it's only till Monday and nobody knows. Or that's what they think."

The gang absorbed the significance of what the Guvnor was telling them. Get this one right, and it could be their biggest payday of a year when they had had to work harder than ever just to make less money than in any year in the previous ten. Get it wrong and - well, Janie preferred not to think about that.

The Guvnor continued. "Because it's short notice and they think nobody knows about it, the money's going to be in an unmarked truck with no police escort. One option is to ambush it somewhere along its route, but the run's today so we don't have enough time to plan a job like that." If the Guvnor had said they were going to take the truck out that way they would have done it, such was their faith in him. They knew what to do, they had all done it many times and invariably profited well.

Taking out a vehicle on the move is risky and takes time to plan. On one occasion the gang had managed to bring their target to a halt right under the bucket of a carefully placed mobile crane. Then they dropped the bucket onto its roof and the sides of the van just popped open sending money bags spilling out onto the road. Happy days, but there was no time for that degree of planning today.

"Or we could wait until the money's in the bank and then make them fetch it out again for us at gunpoint. Eh, Nutter?"

Nutter grinned. He liked the idea of making people do things they didn't want to do. "Sure, Guvnor."

"But that would take too long," said the Guvnor, "And we'd have to leave some of the money behind, and why would we want to do that?" Why indeed. "Their weak point is when the truck pulls up in front of the bank to unload. So for this one we're going to go across the pavement."

Janie knew he was working up to this. The only way money can get from inside a locked vehicle to inside a locked bank is for the guards to open the van doors and the bank doors simultaneously and then carry it all in. For just a few seconds, all the doors are open and all the money is exposed. Even better, the security guards have to be able to carry it, so it is all packed into portable cases. That is the time to strike.

"The truck gets to the bank at four. That means there's a lot less planning time than we normally have, but there's nothing here we haven't done before, and you people are the best. Are you all in?"

They were all in.

"OK, here's the plan. Maxie, goalkeeper. Minnie, Boots' doorway across the road, lookout. Rudy, pistol, take the truck driver. Nutter, sawn-off, bank doorway. Hulk, pistol, pavement, get the bags, smallest ones first, they'll be the ones with the fifty pound notes in them . . ." and so the briefing got under way. It lasted two hours and even though they had all done jobs like this many times before, the Guvnor covered every last detail, as he always did. Then they moved out to take up their positions.

After she was arrested the police let Janie see their whole video of how they ambushed the raid. They played it over to her so many times that she suspected they were rather proud of it. The truck pulls up outside the bank right on schedule and three hooded figures jump out of a car parked nearby and run to the truck, guns in hand. The truck doors swing open and there are armed officers waiting inside. One of them has his gun pointed at the Guvnor and shouts "Armed police, drop your weapon!" The Guvnor does not drop his weapon, he lifts his gun hand up, the police officer shoots twice in rapid succession, the Guvnor falls back still holding the gun and hits the pavement, and that is it, all over in a second.

Janie did not know why Dad raised his gun at the policeman. Maybe he was going to surrender, but he was not the type. Or hand his gun over, possible but also unlikely. Could it have been a reflex, out of surprise? She could certainly see how that could happen. Or was he going to try to shoot his way out? She did not know and she never will. But as he falls, the video picks up another masked figure who has just jumped out of the same car. That figure drops a gun and sprints away down the road with the police in hot pursuit.

George Laker died on the pavement. Janie should have been there with him, but she was running very fast down Lewisham High Street with an armed policeman close behind her. The Guvnor's last living words, as they all piled out of the car, had been "It's time, take'em!"

Janie made for the crowds and away to the goalkeeper and from there into hiding. The police pulled in her friends, who all denied knowing her. They turned her flat upside down, but found nothing because there was nothing there to find. They ripped up her mattress and all they found was springs and fluff. Her pillowcases contained only pillows. They would have dug up her garden, but her flat was on the seventh-floor.

Her mind was made up before she was home from the funeral, and a week after that Janie was gone. Saying goodbye to Bethnal Green was not as hard as she expected, because everyone who knew her understood.

# CHAPTER 4   THE FUGITIVE

Janie chose Brighton for her new life for the simple reason that it was about the only town within fifty miles of London whose banks she and the gang had never got around to robbing. She watched her reflection walk by in the shop windows outside Brighton railway station, a twenty-four year old retired bank robber with all her worldly possessions packed into two small suitcases, heading for the address of a cheap bedsit a couple of streets back from the seafront. She knew nobody in the town, had never been there before yesterday, and she was tired, hungry and lonely, and missing Rudy and Nutter and Minnie and Maxie, and especially missing Dad, and missing her Mum too even though she never knew her.

Apart from the few clothes and bits and bobs in her suitcase, she had brought nothing with her to start over again, but she did have two things going for her.

One of those things was her practical knowledge of security equipment, so the next morning she took herself down to the High Street where Hodge's Hardware shop had a card in the window advertising for a junior assistant. "Apply within" it said, and she applied within.

She told Mr Hodge, the founder and owner, that she had experience with security hardware. He was sceptical until she took his most expensive tamper-proof lock off its display shelf, stripped it down, changed the combination, reassembled it and challenged him to change it back again. He could not, she did, and he gave her the job, starting just as quickly as he could dig her out his previous assistant's brown shop coat from the back room. On the Friday, he gave her a pay packet containing twenty pounds and seventeen pence.

Two ten pound notes, a ten pence, a shiny little five and two pennies. Janie turned the notes over in her hand and studied the pictures of the Queen. She even read the inscriptions round the edge of the coins, then put them in her pocket and jingled them to hear the noise. It was the first honestly earned money she had ever held in her life. It felt good, and at that moment she knew that she never again wanted money that she had come by in any other way.

The other thing Janie had going for her was Jennifer Harding's bank account, which by then contained close to a million pounds of very dishonestly earned money. She did not want it, but she had no idea what to do with it, so she just left it all in the bank and lived frugally on her twenty pounds and seventeen pence a week, plus extra when Mr Hodge and she did stock-taking on a Sunday.

Mr Hodge and Janie got on well. She worked hard and used her practical knowledge to secure some big new orders. He took her under his wing and taught her all about the business. Janie had no Dad and Mr Hodge had no children, and within a few weeks it was clear to them both that a kind of father and daughter relationship had emerged, though they never expressed it that way. Within a year Mr Hodge made her his assistant manager. He was sixty-six and feeling his age, and increasingly left her to run things for him. Then when he was ill and off work for three months, she took charge of the shop for him and it thrived.

When Mr Hodge came back to work he walked Janie across the road to the Shipman's Arms for his usual pie and pint lunch. What he said next changed her life.

"Janie, my wife has been telling me for years that it's time I retired, and I think it's time I listened to her. Do you want the business?"

"The business?"

"The shop. I've nobody to leave it to. If you want it, it's yours. You can buy me out."

"I've got no money, Mr Hodge." Except for the million in the bank account in Hackney, but that was not for buying shops with.

"You can pay me off in instalments when you turn in a profit, as I'm sure you will with your talents."

At twenty-five you do not think about things for too long. Janie certainly did not.

"OK Mr Hodge, I accept. Shake on it?"

"No Janie, I won't shake on it. Not till you ask Sam."

Sam was Sam Lockwood, Janie's boyfriend. They first met on the weekend after Janie arrived in Brighton, when she was Mr Hodge's new girl and he was his Saturday help. Sam was twenty-three and working towards his accountancy exams. Trainee accountants don't earn much, Sam told her, and Mr Hodge's Saturday money came in handy.

Sam was fun and he was smart. Tall, five feet ten, slim, dark hair cut short around a lively round face and twinkling brown eyes, he dressed well and with care, and had passes in all his accountancy exams to date. They were Mr Hodge's youngest employees by far, and they made sure everyone knew it. They hit it off straight away, larked about in the shop, played pranks on the other staff and on their better-natured customers, flirted in public and fondled in private, and Janie fell completely and totally in love with him. She still is.

It was in the shop that they made love for the first time, on a Sunday morning while Mr Hodge was away and they were supposed to be doing a stock-take, in an out-of-sight alcove in Timber Treatments, with the aid of some cushions from Soft Furnishings. Afterwards they put the cushions back on their display rack and, their guilty secret, sold them all at twenty percent off.

Janie found it hard to lie to Sam. She felt that to lie to someone you love is to betray that love. But Sam could not know about her past, so Janie told him she was an orphan brought up in East London, and that she had learned her hardware skills odd-jobbing with one of her foster parents who was a locksmith, and that aside from Mr Hodge's pay she had no money. To her surprise, Sam believed her.

Janie gave notice on her bedsit and moved into Sam's flat. Four months later she was pregnant. Sam told her he wanted to marry her but she said not yet, they weren't settled enough. But on the subject of Mr Hodge's kind offer, he said 'Yes' and Mr Hodge and Janie shook on it the following morning.

## CHAPTER 5  THE MAN IN JERSEY

One evening Janie was watching Sam's little black-and-white TV when an item on the BBC News caught her attention. The government were bringing in new powers for the police to look for secret bank accounts owned by criminals and freeze them until they could confiscate the money and arrest and convict the owners.

Janie was, to put it mildly, quite concerned. With interest the balance in her bank account was now over a million pounds, and though she did not want to touch 'her' savings, neither did she want anyone tracing them back to her and unravelling her new life with Sam.

Royal London Bank, employer of Mike Phillips from Essex, had merged with a number of other banks to form the biggest bank in Britain and was now just called RoyalBank. Janie wondered if he was still around, so she phoned RoyalBank's switchboard to find out and was pleasantly surprised to be put straight through.

"Mike Phillips, Head of London Group, how can I help you?"

"Hello Mr Phillips, I don't know if you remember me, I'm Jennifer Harding, I was one of your customers at Hackney?"

"Jennifer, of course I remember you!  How could I forget my favourite customer!  But call me Mike.  How are you keeping?"

"Good, thank you, Mike.  And you've made it up to head office now, I take it?"

"I have indeed Jennifer, Hackney did well for me, I've got the whole of London now.  We must have another lunch next time you're up this way.  But was there something I can do for you?"

"I don't know if there is, but you did say to contact you if there might be something . . ."

"Jennifer, I said that and I meant it.  What would you like?"

"A bit of advice, maybe. My account's done well, it's now got over a million pounds in it, but sitting in Hackney it feels a bit, well, exposed, it you get my drift. I've nothing to hide, of course, but I just wondered if there was any way of, sort of, moving it out of sight a bit?"

"Aha Jennifer, I know the problem, I have the same trouble with my own money, especially at bonus time when the tax man's sniffing round. Do you have a pen and paper handy?"

"I do."

"Well then, jot down the number I'm going to give you. It's a pal of mine called Gordon, he's in RoyalBank's personal banking section, it's a sort of club that looks after our millionaire customers, which includes you and which one day I hope to join too! I'll let him know you'll be calling him. I'm sure he'll sort you out."

"Is that Mr Gordon, or first name Gordon?" Janie asked.

"Both. His actual name is Gordon Gordon but everyone just calls him Gordon, that keeps it simple."

Mike Phillips gave her Gordon's number, and after wishing each other good health and fortune she rang off.

Janie phoned Gordon three days later. He was expecting her call and invited her up to London to meet him. She did not want to tell another lie to Sam, so she had to wait until he was going to be away on a training course, then took a day off work and caught the fast train north.

Gordon had arranged to meet Janie at his club. Now when she lived in Bethnal Green her father had a club too, though he had only taken Janie there once. It was down some narrow steps, Dad rang a bell on an ill-lit door, someone peered out at him through a spy hatch, and then the door opened just long enough to let them in and was locked swiftly behind them. Inside, the only lights were those of the bar. Everywhere else was in semi-darkness, as figures, all men, no women, hunched over tables, talked, ate pie and mash or fish and chips, and drank plentifully. There was more business transacted in that club than in all the markets in Bethnal Green put together.

Gordon's club was not a bit like Dad's club. The entrance steps were wide and went up from the pavement, not down, and a commissionaire met Janie on the steps and showed her in. A hat-man whisked away her coat and bag and a waiter threaded her through to a corner table whose occupant rose to greet her, shook her hand vigorously, introduced himself as Gordon, and bade her to be seated. Gordon was a couple of years older than Janie, tall enough to tower over her, a little overweight, suave, pinstripe suit, gold signet ring, charming and condescending all in one flourish of his cuff-linked sleeve.

The menu being in Italian, Janie let Gordon choose for them both. As they ate, Gordon and she spoke plentifully without either of them giving away much about themselves. Only over the post-dessert brandy did Gordon get down to business.

"Jennifer, I hope you don't mind, I had a peek at your account this morning. You've been doing rather well if I may say so. And you haven't touched a penny of it?"

"No, it's a long term investment. But I'd like to keep it safe, if you know what I mean. As I said when I called Mike, I could do with some advice."

"Well Jennifer, it won't surprise you to know that you aren't our only client who's asking the same question just now. We need to move you abroad. Offshore, we call it. Less scrutiny. Less tax too, which can't be bad, can it?"

"I wasn't thinking of leaving the country, Gordon."

"Oh, you don't have to go anywhere, it's only your money that we put out of sight. But to do that we need to register you as domiciled overseas, that's what we call it. I'd suggest France, nice and easy. Here's how." He spent the time it took him to work through a second brandy to give her a list of instructions, to which she listened carefully.

Janie wanted to make a note of what Gordon was telling her so that she would not forget anything, and took a pen and a scrap of paper from her pocket, but he stopped her and shook his head. "Bad form in here, old girl, sorry. And against club rules, you'll get me thrown out." She looked around the other tables, and sure enough nobody was making any note or record of any of the many intense if muted conversations. "Sorry Gordon." She put her pen away, embarrassed at her social gaffe and hoping nobody else had spotted it.

Then he passed her a card which bore the RoyalBank crest above an address in Jersey, and that was it, they turned back to chatting and sipping, the day's work done. And looking around Gordon's club, Janie could see that it was not very different from her Dad's after all. People were sitting at tables, consuming, imbibing and doing shady business deals in dark corners. And also, just like the club in Bethnal Green, all men, and nothing ever put in writing.

Back in Brighton that evening, Janie was going round the flat finding things to tidy and dust and polish, which is how she relaxed then and still does, when Sam came home to report that he had just passed his latest exam and that they should celebrate. Janie decided that this was the right time to tell him some news of her own. She was expecting his baby. That night they made it a double celebration.

When Sam was next out of the flat, Janie fished out the card that Gordon had given her and called the Jersey number it bore.

"Charles Borden here." It might have been Jersey, but the accent was Scotland.

"Hello, Mr Borden, my name's Jennifer Harding. Gordon from RoyalBank in London suggested I should see you."

"Ah, Miss Harding, how nice to hear from you, Gordon did tell me to expect you. You need to come and see me here in Jersey to sign some papers that I've drawn up for you, why don't you let me arrange a trip for you. Tell me when you're free and RoyalBank can sort out your flights and a couple of nights in a nice hotel we know. You can make it a romantic break if you like, bring your feller. Or someone else's feller if that suits you better, confidentiality guaranteed. On us, of course."

"The best time for me to come is next week, when my boyfriend is up in London doing some exams."

"Let's do that then. Bringing a different chap?"

Janie did not bring a different chap, or any chap, nor even stay overnight. So as not to rouse Sam's suspicions she asked Mr Borden for a day return flight on a day when she knew Sam would be away, then headed into town to get the items Gordon had advised her to take with her.

Early the following Tuesday Janie saw Sam off to London then made straight for the airport and Jersey. On arrival she only had a couple of hours between flights so she took a taxi into Saint Helier and was dropped off outside a glass-and-concrete block with a view over a bay of blue sea and white yachts. Time was short so she went in and asked for Mr Charles Borden, and once in his office they settled straight down to business.

"Well Miss Harding, Gordon tells me we need to make it look like you're moving to France?"

"Yes, I've found a house I could say I'm going to live at, would you like to see it?"

"I'd love to," said Mr Borden. "My wife's French, so we really do go there all the time. She gets to see her family and I get to shoot boar, hunting is my true passion you know, you can't beat the thrill of the stalk and the kill. But I shouldn't imagine guns are quite your thing."

"Sorry, not really."

"You should try it, you might find you like it, quite a few women go shooting these days. Anyway, tell me about this place?"

From her bag Janie produced an estate agent's brochure for a very dilapidated farm cottage near Calais. Tucked inside was a receipt for a deposit of £200 made out to J. M. Harding. "I can say I'm going do it up once I'm over there," she said, "Calais would be handy for my business."

"Which is?"

Her original Royal London Bank account application said she was a general trader, and Janie thought she ought to stick to the same line. "I'm still trading, but we could say I'm moving into imports, French antiques, end-of-line Paris fashions, whatever sells." This was all from the script that Gordon had given her, and Mr Borden was nodding. She continued. "And branching out into wine. Would you like to see some?"

"Rather," Mr Borden said. From her bag Janie produced two bottles of vintage Champagne. Another of Gordon's ideas.

"These are the samples," she said to Mr Borden as he picked up one of the bottles and read the label. "Perhaps you'd like one as a thank you for your work?"

"Oh no, Miss Harding, it's good stuff but the bank doesn't allow us to take gratuities. Besides, I haven't done any work for you yet."

So he did some work, and by the time she was ready to leave his office, Miss Jennifer Marie Harding, born 11/1/55, was recorded as officially domiciled in France and registered for banking and tax purposes on the island of Jersey. For an annual fee for the bank and presumably a handy commission for Mr Borden, her money was to grow vigorously and tax-free for the next thirty years.

Her two 'sample' bottles of fine Champagne had cost her £49.99 each in Calverly's Fine Wines of Brighton. Over the brandy in his club, Gordon had told Janie that in Jersey her task was not to convince Mr Borden that she was actually moving to France, but merely to provide him with enough evidence to enable him, if challenged by the bank regulators, to be able to say he genuinely believed that she was. 'Nod's as good as a wink', he had said. Her Dad used to use the same phrase.

Just to make sure of Charles Borden's co-operation, as she left his office she put one of her bottles of Champagne on the sideboard by her chair, which he saw without feeling the need to remind her that she had left it behind.

Janie threw the estate agent's brochure into the waste-bin at Jersey Airport as she boarded her plane home. This was because she did not want to have to explain to Sam that on Gordon's advice she had put down a £200 deposit on a ruin of a farmhouse in one of the 'Properties Abroad' shops that were then springing up along the south coast. The next week she called in and told them she had changed her mind, and they were even kind enough to give her the deposit back.

She had also changed some money into French francs so that if she happened to open her wallet Mr Borden would see further evidence that she must have been to France recently, but the opportunity never arose. Those all went into the airport bin too.

Janie managed to get back home just before Sam. They were both exhausted and neither of them wanted to cook supper. Calverly's Fine Wines of Brighton do not take returns so when Janie produced the remaining bottle of Champagne she told Sam she had bought it on special offer at Sainsbury's, and over a Chinese takeaway she allowed herself one small glass while Sam demolished the rest at around a fiver a swig.

# CHAPTER 6  THE ACCOUNTANT

Janie gave birth to a baby girl, named Helen after Sam's favourite aunt. Helen Laker was just six weeks old and in her mother's arms when Sam and she married quietly at Brighton Registry office. Under Sam's strict management they were saving hard to pay off Mr Hodge and there was no money for a proper wedding, which they promised themselves they would have one day. Given her past Janie did not feel able to invite any of her old pals from Bethnal Green, so Mr Hodge gave her away, with a tear in his eye.

After that, things moved along at quite a pace. Mr Hodge was as good as his word, and one Saturday afternoon Hodge Hardware closed for the last time, then the following Monday morning it reopened as Lockwood Hardware. As the new proprietor, it fell to Janie cut a ribbon with a pair of her best £6.99 wallpaper scissors before going to the back office to serve tea and cake for the staff.

The name 'Lockwood Hardware' was Janie's idea. It used Sam's surname, and given its evocation of ironware and timber, there could be no more fortuitous name for a hardware store whose owners had big ambitions. Janie also decided that as a businesswoman she should be a 'Janet' and not a 'Janie', and surrendered her maiden surname to become Mrs Janet Lockwood. Any distance that she could put between her new self and an armed robber named Janie Laker had to be good.

Mr Hodge went to Devon and his retirement, while Lockwood Hardware prospered. Janie ran the shop and Sam looked after the books. Before long they were searching the south coast for a second branch. Sam, Helen and Janie moved out of the flat into a little house with a third bedroom: she was expecting again.

While Sam studied for his final exams, Janie was working so hard at the shop that Sam did not know where she had found the time or energy to get pregnant again, but she did. She rolled up enormous on Sam's arm at the prestigious

Institute of Chartered Accountants annual graduation ceremony, with a 'Twins On Board' badge on her lapel and with Sam in a new suit clearing the space in front of her in case anyone really could not see either her badge or her bulge.

The ceremony took place in the Institute's great hall with gold chandeliers, red curtains and marble balconies. The graduating accountants sat alphabetically in rows, waiting to be called up to the platform to be presented with their certificates by the gowned President of the Institute and the Lord Mayor of London in dress uniform with plumed hat and sword. The guests sat in rows further back. No cameras please, if you wanted a photograph they had to be bought from the Official Photographer at £50 each unframed, £100 framed. Janie ordered four, all framed.

When it was Sam's turn to be called to the stage, Janie pulled herself to her feet for a better view, and was the last one left clapping, until the guests behind her encouraged her to sit down.

Afterwards they all headed for the reception hall and Janie let Sam escort her round to make polite conversation with his President, tutors, and fellow graduates. As he worked her round the room, they came to a woman a little younger than Janie, who had just concluded a deep conversation with the President and who, on seeing Sam, surged towards him with outstretched arms with which she made a great show of embracing him without actually making any contact. "Yuck" thought Janie to herself.

"Sam, darling, congratulations! You must be so pleased. And you . . ." - she turned to Janie to allow Sam to introduce her - ". . . you must be a very proud wife too. Sam has been an absolute star on our course!" Janie's dislike deepened instantly, and she took a step back.

"Janet, this is Melissa Campbell," said Sam to Janie, "She's the actual star of the course, she came top in the country."

"Congratulations Melissa," Janie said, "I saw you on the platform when that was announced."

Janie had indeed noticed her. Most of the graduates were men, which Melissa Campbell very clearly was not. Her tall and elegant figure was further elevated by high heeled shoes and covered but not much concealed by a sharp dark blue jacket and matching short skirt that she gauged to have been very expensive.

"What's the prize for coming first, may I ask?", said Janie, a little more bluntly than she had intended. "Money, or silverware, or just a top job?"

Melissa didn't rise to the bait. "Well actually Janet it's none of those, it's just a framed certificate on gold parchment." She held it up for Sam to admire. "But as it happens I have just been offered a rather good job, with PCMG," She nodded discreetly in the direction of the President, who was still nearby but was now in another conversation, "So I should have enough money to buy my own silverware if ever I run short of it." Janie knew it was the put-down that her facetious question had invited, but she still did not like it, or Melissa Campbell.

"PCMG?" she asked.

"Only one of the top accountancy firms in the world, Janet, the ones called 'The Big Four'" said Sam. "I won't tell even you how much their accountants get paid, because you'd never believe me anyway. Eh Melissa?"

"More congratulations then, Melissa," Janie said, but Melissa ignored her and turned her attention back to Sam.

"But Sam, you've done so well too," Melissa gushed, "And with a wife and baby to look after and now two more on the way. It must take so much out of you. Such strength."

"We just have to be organised," said Sam. Janie knew him well enough to know that he was getting prickly, though maybe only she would notice.

"Yes but still, Sam, "said Melissa, "People who want careers don't usually tie themselves down if they can help it, I do admire your courage." Sam really did now look upset.

Melissa did not notice, or more likely did notice and did not care, and ploughed on, "And how's the job hunt going? There are some accountancy jobs up here in the City if you'd like me to ask around for you? Long hours though," she added, "And with the children and all that . . ."

"That's very kind of you, Melissa, but I'm not in the running for a job just yet." Sam glanced down at Janie's bump and then back up straight into Melissa's eyes. "We've got more important things to do first."

Melissa's lips tightened as she looked straight back. "Of course you have, Sam. Well, it was lovely to meet you Janet, you both must let me know any time you're up in London." And with that Melissa Campbell was gone, towards a knot of suited men in a tight circle which opened to absorb her before she even got there.

"Bitch!" said Janie. "Stuck-up bitch! Sam, let's go home. Right now."

They did, and Sam seethed in silence with his arm round Janie as she cried all the way from London Bridge to Three Bridges.

The Lockwoods did not go much to London after that, and when they did, they certainly did not look up Melissa Campbell. Janie has seen her since though, most recently when she was lifting her, bound and gagged, into a large wooden trunk with Nutter's gun stuck up her stuck-up nose.

# CHAPTER 7 THE MILLENNIUM

There was so much going on in Brighton that weeks and then months and finally years went by without Janie really thinking about her former life, her past haunts and her old friends. Other than when Maxie sent her Jennifer Harding's annual bank statement, Janie gave no thought to RoyalBank either.

Just a year after having Helen, Janie gave birth to twins, a boy and a girl. She and Sam called the boy David, the name of Sam's grandfather, and another way of distancing her children from her own past. The girl they named Jessica, for no better reason than because they both liked the name. They started visiting estate agents to look at bigger houses near the Downs with views of the sea.

Meanwhile Lockwood Hardware rose on the crest of the DIY frenzy of the eighties and nineties, fuelled by a craze for home-and-garden make-over TV shows. In order to be ready for the weekend rush, Sam and Janie watched each episode as it went out and the next morning she placed wholesale orders for whatever paint, gadget or gizmo it featured, and usually sold out by Sunday afternoon.

When the children were old enough to go to school, Sam took a job in the finance office of a group of care homes, of which there are many in Brighton, and in the evenings he still did the books for Lockwood Hardware.

Lockwood Hardware expanded into all the south coast towns and in due course Janie had another bank account with a million pounds in it, but this time it was money that she had earned honestly, and Sam knew all about this account because his name was on the cheque books alongside her own.

Being a businesswoman now, Janie kept an eye on the financial pages in the newspapers, and names she knew cropped up occasionally. Melissa Campbell was announced as PCMG's youngest-ever female Partner, Mike Phillips had a mention as a high-flyer and potential future chief of RoyalBank, and Gordon and Charles Borden were also in the news from time to time, blowing their own trumpet or talking up their bank.

The children grew up, as children do. David took after his father, good with numbers and always top of maths at school. He seemed to be wired differently from other children of his age. While they were watching TV or out playing on the beach, he would be reading a book of football statistics or train timetables or astronomy data - anything with numbers - and finding things to figure out and connect together. Except for spy stories where he was fascinated by all the technical spy-craft details, he had no time for fiction.

Sam and Janie worried that David never had many friends, but he was a happy child, trusted everyone, and was always wanting to please. Then before they knew it he was seventeen and off to university a year early to do yet more maths. Sam had high hopes for him there. Janie just worried and fussed and packed and wrote him lists of instructions, and then the day came when she drove him up to his digs and left him there to fend for himself.

Helen, David's senior by a year, was quite different. To her, school was just a means of having fun until the school day was over when she could then go out and have some more fun. She was sociable, chatty and friendly. She treated "Don't Talk To Strangers" as a challenge not a warning, and was at everybody's birthday party which was a nightmare for her parents because all these friends then had to all be invited back to her own celebrations.

Helen did not excel in school, except at computers, though her interest in those stemmed mostly from their potential, as the internet developed, for keeping in constant touch with all her friends, but she took it seriously enough to get some good marks.

She left school for temping work while taking secretarial and computer evening courses at Brighton College, and was the Saturday girl at Lockwood Hardware, though given her out-going nature Janie had the layout modified to remove the out-of-view alcove in Timber Treatments. Armed with her night-school certificates, Helen was taken on as a counter clerk at the Brighton Building Society. She carried on living at home, though she was rarely there in the evenings.

Then there was Jess. At last, one who took after her mother. As a toddler Jess followed Janie round the shop helping her to empty boxes and fill up shelves, whether it needed doing or not. In the school holidays she came out with Janie in the van all day to make deliveries and collect supplies. She sat on the front seat next to Janie and they chatted all day about anything and everything as Janie drove, and taught herself to read using Janie's order book and delivery notes.

Later when she was old enough Jess took over from Helen as the Saturday girl and did a much better job of it, and at twenty she was assistant manager of one of the Lockwood Hardware stores along the coast in Lewes. Janie and Sam agreed that if Lockwood Hardware had a future beyond their eventual retirement, it would be with Jess Lockwood at the helm.

Janie picked up from the newspapers that back in London the police were rounding up some of the old-time robbers, using newly acquired 'supergrasses', who were criminals facing long sentences who did a deal to spill the beans on everybody they had ever worked with in return for their freedom and a new identity.

But mostly the robbers and the cops who had chased them had moved on or retired, and Janie did not spot the names of any of her old comrades in the high-profile robbery trials that the papers reported. By now the police presumably had other more pressing priorities. Janie harboured an ever-present fear that one day she would get a knock on the door from a policeman who had found Jennifer Harding's money in Jersey and joined the dots back to her, but her only personal encounter with a policeman was to be two decades later, with the officer who checked off her name on his admission list at the gates of Buckingham Palace on her way in to meet the Queen.

On Millennium night, Sam, Janie, Helen, David and Jess all had a family meal together and at midnight Sam made a champagne toast to "Our Future". Janie added something about maybe giving her some grandchildren, and got the expected "Oh Mum!" treatment from her offspring. Janie was looking forward to seeing what "Our Future" would bring for their son and two daughters as they stepped out into adulthood and the new Millennium. She did not have long to wait.

# CHAPTER 8  THE TAKEOVER

When Helen returned to work after the New Year weekend she found that the Brighton Building Society had been bought up by the ever-expanding RoyalBank. Within days, all the old Brighton Building Society signs were taken down and replaced by new RoyalBank signage and corporate colours, and a new manager was parachuted in. He took a shine to Helen and picked her to go on a week's training course at RoyalBank's head office in London.

It was the first time Helen had been out from behind the counter and she was excited to be going. She was not quite as excited when she got back.

"It's rubbish, Mum," she said, on the Friday evening that she was home from London. "When RoyalBank took us over I thought we'd be doing things like improving customer service and having better facilities in our branches, but it isn't, it's all just about making them more money."

"How do you mean?"

"One of the bosses came in to open the course. His name was Gordon Gordon but everyone knew him as just Gordon."

Janie made no comment.

"Anyway," Helen continued, "Gordon told us all that old fashioned banking as we knew it is now ancient history. 'So last millennium', he called it. He said we're now all part of RoyalBank, and from now on each and every one of us has to justify our own jobs by getting new business for the bank. He said that whatever our role in the bank is, our number one job is to sell the bank's products, sell, sell, sell!"

Helen rolled her eyes, and continued.

"He said that every time a member of the public walks into a branch of RoyalBank, even just to see the time on our clock, they are a potential purchaser of the bank's products. He wants us to be pushing loans, insurance, bonds, mortgages, or whatever, to everyone and all the time."

"Yes," Janie said, "I must say I've noticed that myself. And they are always phoning up, trying to sell me things I don't need."

"Exactly, and he said he knew that some people wouldn't want to make the change, he said they are free to leave any time, just go. Three did, the same day, just packed their bags and went. He also said we would all would earn commissions on everything we sold. That caused quite a stir, we've never had commissions before. Anyway, other people came in and gave us talks on all the products we have to sell and how to sell them. There were all the things you'd expect, like loans and mortgages and investments, but then towards the end there was a new one I've never heard of before, called Payment Protection Insurance, PPI for short."

"I've never heard of that either," Janie said, "What is it?"

"If you take out any sort of loan, you can pay extra for PPI and then if you're ill and can't make your loan payments they are covered for you."

"That seems sensible enough to me. What's wrong with it?"

Helen pulled a face. "To start with it seemed a good idea to me too, but by the time the trainer had finished trying to explain PPI to us we all had so many questions that he had to go and fetch Gordon to come back and answer them for us."

"And?"

"Well, Gordon got us all together and said that PPI is new so he's not surprised that there are some questions, and as he designed the product himself, he's the best person to answer them. He told us to ask anything we want but take no notes, he said it was all 'off the record' as he put it. So to help me remember what he said I put my notepad on my knee under the desk and used my shorthand from night school."

"Smart girl. And?"

"I'll read it to you."

*Q: Is there anyone we shouldn't sell PPI to, Mr Gordon?*

*A: Just call me Gordon, please, we're all colleagues here at RoyalBank. PPI is for any customer at all who's borrowing money in any way. That means no-one is off limits. The key thing to remember is that you get cash commission on every PPI you sell.*

*Q: What if someone's in a job where they already get sick pay and benefits.*

*A: Sell them PPI anyway. A lot of people don't realise what benefits they get from their work. And then if they're ill we don't have to pay out because we deduct anything they are due to get from their own employer.*

*Q: Will PPI cover people who are self-employed?*

*A: No, but there's no need to mention that. Remember, commission, right?*

*Q: What if someone is long term sick or has an accident and gets badly injured and can never work again?*

*A: That's covered in the small print. However long the illness or injury lasts, PPI only pays out for a year. And not at all for bad backs or stress, which just happen to be the two most common causes of long term sick absence from work. But there's no need to tell the customer. Just say 'For only pennies a day, this insurance policy gives you security against illness and injury and being unable to repay your loan.' That's usually enough, people mostly don't read small print.*

*Q: What if someone does insist on reading it?*

*A: Let them, and tell that they should to take all the time they need to read it. That way they'll trust you and quite likely give up part way through. Which is why we've put all the real limitations at the end.*

*Q: Can we sell PPI to people who don't speak English?*

*A: A signature's a signature and a commission's a commission. Even if they can't read at all. And nobody ever checks whose hand actually held the pen that signed the form, if you get what I'm hinting at there.*

*Q: Can people get loans and mortgages from us without taking out PPI at the same time?*

*A: Technically they can, yes, but there's no need to tell them if they don't ask. The smart move is to sign them up for the mortgage or loan they need, then drop the PPI in on top. You know, 'Have you thought about how you'll you pay this if you're ill, we'll cover that for you too?' That sort of thing. PPI's optional, but just don't tell them that. Or just tick the 'PPI required' box yourself and rely on them not noticing, and apologise for your mistake if they do.*

*Q: Are there any upper age limits?*

*A: There are no upper age limits for buying PPI policies, and our market research shows that older people worry most about not being able to pay their debts. It's actually in the terms and conditions that they don't get any payouts if they are over 65, but if you don't tell them they aren't going to know, are they? Think of it as a tax on stupid old codgers, after all they get their bus rides and TV licences for free.*

*Q: Even with all these restrictions in the small print, quite a lot of people do get sick, so how is the bank going to make a profit on PPI after all their pay-outs and our commissions?*

*A: Excellent question, with a simple answer. There's a company called PCMG who we are paying to deal with claims for us, and they've got a razor-sharp partner there called Melissa Campbell who is going to make it as difficult as possible to get a pay-out. They'll demand written evidence, forms, doctors' letters, medical examinations that the claimant has to pay for, and so on. Most people will just give up and abandon their claim.*

*Q: So nothing can go wrong with PPI?*

*A: It's cast iron. We're looking at eighty percent profit for the bank. In fact, we calculate that we'll often make more money on the PPI than we do on the loan. Good for the bank, good for me, and good for you. Remember the three magic words - commission, commission and commission - and you can't go wrong. No further questions, goodnight and go sell."*

"Interesting," said Janie, "Remind me never to buy any PPI. But how did the other people on the course take it?"

"Like I said, a few resigned there and then, but I was a bit shocked by the rest of them to be honest Mum, they thought it was great."

"Great? How is any of that great?"

"Commission, commission, commission. In the bar after the PPI session, a lot of people were working out how many PPI policies they need to sell to hit the commission targets and getting very excited about it and all the things they are going to buy with the money. I guess the idea of being able to double your salary in a year excites quite a lot of people."

"Maybe," Janie said, "But it worries me."

"Me too," Helen replied.

Helen went back to her desk at the bank a little despondent, but she quickly settled into the hustle and bustle of customers, colleagues and friends. A few weeks later Janie brought the subject up over breakfast.

"How's that dodgy PPI thing going, Helen. Are you selling any?"

"I am, Mum, yes, otherwise there's grief from the management, but I'm only selling PPI to people who will actually benefit from it, and only then after making sure they understand all the terms and conditions first."

"Then from the sound of it you'll be the only one who is."

# CHAPTER 9  THE GOLD SWINDLE

Janie and Sam generally had an idea what Helen and Jess were doing because they were living at home, but what David got up to was a mystery. They knew he went to university, because Janie took him up there and Sam paid his bills, but he rarely came home, scarcely phoned and never wrote.

"He hasn't fallen out with us, or anything like that," Janie explained one day to a colleague at work. "It's just the way he is. He's different."

"How do you mean, different?"

"Well he never rests, he's always active, constantly working or reading or doing complicated things in his head or on his computer. He's awkward with social contact but he gets on fine with other people where there are boundaries and structures and tasks to perform. He never tells us how he's doing, I only saw his university report because it was posted to our Brighton address, his professor says he has an unusual ability to spot patterns in numbers that his fellow students and even computers can't see. Our doctor says he has a form of Asperger's Syndrome, but I don't like to give people labels so to me he's just my son and special."

Sam and Janie did not even know that David had quit university to take up a job with RoyalBank in London until Helen spotted his name on an internal bank newsletter. They had to piece the details of his story together long afterwards, from the conversations they had with David years later on his prison visits.

For his second-year university summer break, David fixed himself up with an internship at RoyalBank, sitting alongside their analysts to learn on the job by looking over their shoulders when he was not being sent out to fetch their sandwiches and coffee. His only pay was the knowledge he acquired along the way, plus anything else the analysts told him on the frequent occasions when they all trooped off to the pub after work.

The bank must have seen something in him though, because they offered him a job as a temporary trainee analyst in their investment division, on a short-term contract. The deal was, "Do really well and we'll make your appointment permanent, do anything less than that and you are out by Christmas." It turned out that his boss was one Charles Borden.

David had only been at work a few weeks when Borden called him in to his office and closed the door behind him.

"David," he said, "I've been following your progress since you were an intern here. You've been impressing people."

"Thank you, Mr Borden."

"And how are you finding it? Enjoying it?"

"Yes, Mr Borden." David was not one for conversation.

"Well, David, there's a little job I'd like you to do for me. Confidentially, not telling anyone else. Can do that?"

It is part of David's condition that he is very trusting of people in authority. Mr Borden had no need to be concerned about David's discretion: he was the boss and he only had to ask and it would be assured.

"Yes, Mr Borden."

"OK, David. What do you know about gold?"

"Rare heavy metal, symbol Au, atomic number 79, adjoins platinum and mercury on the periodic table, chemically unreactive except . . ."

"Very good David, but that's not quite what I meant. What do you know about gold trading?"

"Nothing, Mr Borden."

"Good, because I have a problem with our gold trading that none of our gold trading experts has been able to solve. I need someone who will come at it completely fresh."

"Who?"

"You."

Borden set out the problem. "RoyalBank trades a lot of gold on the international markets. The world price of gold is always moving up and down, and anyone who makes the right bets on changes in the gold price stands to make a lot of money - or lose a lot of money if they call it wrong."

David said nothing, he was listening and learning. Borden continued.

"RoyalBank has some of the highest-paid gold traders in the world, yet we're consistently making losses on our gold trades. Which is bad for the bank's profits, and more to the point it's playing havoc with my bonuses. So I need you to do a special job for me."

"What job?"

"Without telling anyone else what you're doing, I want you to read up on everything that's ever been written about gold trades, study every gold transaction RoyalBank makes and every price movement in the world precious metals markets since the year dot, and then come back and tell me the answer to just one question - what the hell are we doing wrong?"

"Are we doing something wrong?"

"If we're losing money then we're doing something wrong. That's my definition of doing something wrong. So yes, we are doing something wrong and I want you to find out what."

"I'd like to do that, Mr Borden, thank you," David said. "How long have I got?"

"Not long, David, we're losing a million pounds a month on our gold trades."

"Of course, Mr Borden, I understand."

"But remember, David, nobody except you has to know what you're doing. This work is top top secret. Got it?"

David got it. He threw himself into the task, and six weeks later was back in Mr Borden's office.

"You asked me to find out what we're doing wrong, Mr Borden."

"I did, David. And what is it?"

"Nothing. I can't find anything that we're doing wrong. I picked a thousand loss-making gold trades that RoyalBank has made in the last year, and dug into each one to look at the prices of all the other commodities on the same dates, and all the related stock market activity and fluctuations in exchange rates. And as far as I can see every one of our gold trades was made on the best possible prediction of the most likely movement in that day's gold price. It's just that our predictions all turned out to be wrong."

Borden seemed displeased.

"That can't be right David, otherwise we'd be making money, not losing it hand over fist. So how do you explain that?"

"Well, if we're doing nothing wrong, then it can only be because somebody else is doing something wrong. It's logical. That's the only possible explanation."

"What do you mean by that?"

"Well as you know Mr Borden, every day a panel of all the world's major banks and gold brokers make a conference call and agree that day's gold prices. That becomes the price at which gold is traded until they re-set the price the same way the next day."

"I know it how it works, David. So what?"

"So, if RoyalBank is doing everything right yet still losing money, it follows that somebody else at another bank must be fixing the prices to our disadvantage. It's logical."

"Let me get this right, are you saying someone is swindling us?"

"Yes, Mr Borden."

"Who?"

"Well Mr Borden, I've been through hundreds of trades made by all the other banks in the world, and there's one that stands out. It's NationBank in New York. Each time we make a loss on a gold trade, they make a corresponding gain. Their gold trader must have found some way of rigging the gold price to their benefit, and he's made us their dummy."

"David, that's very interesting. Very interesting indeed. Well done, by the way. Excellent work."

David left Charles Borden's office glowing with pride. His respect for structure and hierarchy includes a love of praise from on high. He was very happy again a few days later when Borden called him back in.

"David," he said, "I've been thinking about what you told me last week."

"So have I, Mr Borden. I told you I've worked out who it is in New York who is rigging the gold rates against us, but I haven't been able to work out how he's doing it. If it's OK I'd like to spend a few weeks seeing if I can figure out his system."

"Then what, David?"

"Well then we could report NationBank to the United States government so they can take action."

"That's an interesting idea, David. But it's not what I'd like you to do. Have you ever been to New York?"

"No, never."

"Well it's time you did. I want you to go over and see this Yankee clown from NationBank and tell him we've rumbled his little game. Anyone could go, but you're the only one who can carry it off because you're the one who knows how he gave himself away. And keep it all completely hush-hush, remember."

"Yes, Mr Borden, I'd be happy to do that for you. And shall I tell him that we are reporting him?"

Charles Borden laughed. "No, no David, for goodness sake don't do that! We banks do our best to avoid reporting each other for bad behaviour, think where that would lead! No, just give him this." He handed David a sealed plain white envelope which David put in his pocket. "Aren't you going to ask me what's in it?"

"What is in it, Mr Borden?"

"A letter to tell him that we're onto his little game, and that if he doesn't pack it in straight away we'll have no choice but to shop him to the FBI. That should do the trick."

David learned very much later that the letter said nothing of the sort. But as he left Charles Borden's office with the envelope and his hush-hush assignment, he was feeling bathed in his boss's appreciation and very proud of himself. His New York trip went as intended, and a letter of permanent appointment as a RoyalBank analyst, signed by Charles Borden, was waiting for him on his desk on his return.

It was around this time that a note reached Janie from Minnie. The handwriting looked like a man's, and Minnie told her later that because she struggled with reading and writing she had dictated it to a helpful neighbour.

Its purpose was to tell her that Maxie had passed away. By the time it reached Janie the funeral was already a week past, though she would not have gone anyway - it was twenty-three years since she had left Bethnal Green, and she rarely thought about her past life, not much even about Dad. But in her note Minnie asked if Janie still wanted to receive letters addressed to a J. M. Harding.

Jennifer Harding. For years Jennifer Marie Harding had been living in the place to which Janie had banished her, which was a dark recess in her mind where Jennifer didn't trouble Janie if Janie didn't trouble Jennifer. Janie left her there without thinking about her, except when the envelopes from Jersey arrived via their roundabout route to finish their journey, often unopened, in the Lockwood Hardware office shredder. Minnie's reminder of Jennifer Harding's existence jolted her.

As a bank robber, finding somewhere to put cash away safely had been a problem solved by Jennifer Harding's bank account, but the bank account itself was now a much bigger problem. Even in Jersey and after all these years Janie knew that it was a time bomb ticking away alongside her life, primed to explode the minute some curious investigator took an interest, found there is no such person as Jennifer Harding, and then traced the money back to Hackney and Janie Laker and from there to Janet Lockwood and the destruction of her, her family, and all they had worked for.

Janie had thought about getting rid of the money but she could not come up with a way of eliminating a sum of that size that would not draw attention to its existence. So the money just sat in Jersey and in that recess in her mind, while the tax-free interest piled up every year.

In any case, even if there had been a way to retrieve the money undetected, Janie did not want it. Ever since she held those two ten pound notes, the ten pence, five and two pennies that made up her first week's pay from Mr Hodge, Jennifer Harding's money just felt dirty to her - physically dirty, as if touching it would stain her hands and her life and taint everyone else she touched too. She wanted Jennifer Harding's money to stay well away from her life and to go nowhere near anyone she loved. She feared and hated the money, but she had no idea what to do with it, and dealt with it as far as she could by ignoring it. But she could not ignore Minnie's note.

Minnie's phone number was at the top of the page, and when Sam was out of ear-shot Janie called her. When Minnie answered it was the same familiar voice, and for the first time Janie felt the tiniest twinge of nostalgia for the old times and old places. She needed to deal with the matter of the letter addressed to J. M. Harding and suggested they meet up somewhere neutral. A week later Janie was at Liverpool Street station, in the little self-service café up the stairs by the entrance, at a table with a good view of the door.

Minnie walked in, not a teenage punk any more, but a petite and smartly dressed middle-aged woman with neat dark grey hair in a bun, a round face, and welcoming smile. She bounded across the room and hung around Janie's neck with her feet off the ground long enough to plant a huge kiss on her cheek, then they collected tea and crumpets from the counter and settled down to business.

The way Maxie sent Jennifer Harding's annual bank statements to Janie was to sellotape them into the inside of a large jiffy envelope, then add some random item of hardware from a local store - a bag of paint-brushes, for example, or a three-pack of screwdrivers - and post it to Lockwood Hardware in Brighton, where anyone opening it might think it was a trade sample.

In the week when she was expecting the envelope, Janie would make sure she was in the shop when the post arrived so she could be on hand to open any jiffy bags until she found the right one. Not quite James Bond, but it worked just fine for years, and when Maxie's hands became too arthritic Minnie had taken over the task for her, so Janie asked her to carry on.

"Who is J. M. Harding anyway?" Minnie asked her. "Should I remember her?"

"You never met her. More tea?"

"I've got a bit of time till my train, yes please." Janie fetched more tea.

"So, how are you keeping, Minnie?"

"Good, Janie, good. Maxie gave up her business years ago, but she taught me a lot and I took on some of her girls, and that's what I still do. Only nice girls whose mothers I know, and good class clients. I don't want my girls out on the streets or getting beaten up or being given drugs. And you won't believe it, I own a house! It cost half a million pounds! It's in a little new estate where that shoe factory used to be, remember it?" Janie did. "It's not really mine, of course, I bought it on a huge mortgage, but even so, fancy me having a house!"

Minnie pulled some well-used photos from her bag and showed them off proudly. Kitchen with big table. Lounge, sofa. Bedrooms one and two. Little garden with herbs in pots and flowers in tubs. It was actually very sweet, Janie agreed.

"And do you ever see Rudy, Minnie?"

"Several times a week, as it happens. He got twenty years, I don't know if you heard, did twelve with his remission, he kept himself sane in the clink dreaming about buying his own pub and making lots of plans in his mind. But when he got out and retrieved his stash, all the notes were in old types that you can't use any more. The only place you can change old notes is to go to the Bank of England in person and he couldn't very well do that could he? So he burnt the lot out back, he invited all of us round and called it 'the bonfire of my dreams'. It was quite a party actually, people still talk about it." She poured the tea.

"Anyway," Minnie continued, "He did all sorts of jobs, built up some savings, and eventually, I don't know how, it took him eight years, but in the end he managed to get a business loan from the bank. He bought the Oak Barrel, remember it Janie?" She did. The last job. The upstairs room. Lewisham High Street. Dad.

"Well anyway, that's where he is, and he's doing fine. It's a proper old fashioned East End pub, about the only one left, with a piano in the corner and a happy crowd there every night, and Rudy behind the bar knowing everybody's names and what they like to drink and telling all his funny stories about the old days."

For a moment, Janie wanted to be back in that pub. She shook herself out of it. "And how about Nutter?"

"Oh, Nutter's moved away. He went straight after that last job with you and your Dad. Really sorry about your Dad, by the way Janie, if it's not too late to say so?" Janie shook her head.

"Anyway, Nutter's moved over Dagenham way, he's got a job at the car factory. I've only seen him once since then, I was taking Maxie to see her sister who lives out there, we popped in to the Co-op to get her some things and Nutter was in the queue in front of us. He looks older of course, don't we all, but you couldn't mistake that face. Or those eyes."

Janie nodded in agreement.

"We had a quick chat, Nutter never was one for long conversations was he, Janie, and it turns out he's as happy as pie. He's on the production line making the holes they put car doors in or something like that. He says he likes the routine and prefers working with machines because they leave him alone and don't make him get angry."

"I wouldn't want to be the foreman having to tell him he's doing something wrong," Janie said.

"No, Janie, nor me. But anyway, he'd bought his own place, done it up nice he says, got a cat, and a shed where he keeps pigeons, he seemed fine and said he gets paid well and he'll get a good pension when he retires at the end of it all, so he's OK." She glanced at the big clock over the counter. "Ten minutes till my train, I'd better be going."

Janie walked Minnie down to the ticket barrier, got another kiss for her trouble, and headed for the tube back to London Bridge and Brighton.

# CHAPTER 11  THE DINNER

Thursday is feasting and drinking night right across London's financial districts. David usually joined the crowd touring the pubs on those evenings, not for fun but because he took it to be part of his job and he took his job seriously. So he was surprised to get a message on a Tuesday inviting him to join one of the senior managers for a meal at the Stripes Tavern after work the same day.

The Stripes wasn't far from RoyalBank's head office, but rather more upmarket than their usual Thursday dives. David made his way there and arrived at exactly the appointed time to find his host and a dozen other invitees already there and well into their second drinks.

His host greeted him warmly - "You must be David Lockwood, I'm Mike Phillips, call me Mike."

"Thank you for inviting me Mr Phillips."

"It's Mike."

"Sorry, I mean Mike."

"I've heard good things about you from my colleague Charles Borden, David. I'm looking forward to getting to know you, what'll you drink?"

Drinks in hand, Mike Phillips' group was ushered through to a small private back room which contained one large dining table and no other diners. Phillips had pre-ordered a lobster starter and a steak main course for everyone - "No time for dithering over the menu, we've got work to do" - and instructed the waiter to leave several opened bottles of wine on the table and then clear off and shut the door behind him until the next course was ready. Then he got straight to the point.

"Gentlemen," he said - RoyalBank didn't employ many women on its trading floors and there were certainly none present in this party - "Unless you've spent the last two years in a hermit's cave, you will know about the sub-prime frenzy that's going on across the pond in the USA." He took a sip of wine and looked around the table.

"As we sit here, armies of salesmen are fanning out across the tenements, trailer parks and backwoods cabins of North America, selling mortgages on big commissions for brand new homes, to people who have never been able to afford a mortgage and who never will."

He had everybody's attention at the word 'commissions'. He continued.

"NINJA loans is what they call them over there, it stands for 'No Income, No Job or Assets'. There are no income checks or credit score requirements. No deposits either - in fact they'll lend you more than the price of whatever home you are buying, so you can pay off your other loans or credit cards or take a holiday or buy a nice truck or some more guns or whatever you want." He eased some lobster meat out of its shell, then picked up his thread.

"These sub-prime NINJA mortgages come with teaser rates, a really low interest rate for the first couple of years, often lower even than the rent of the cheapest trailer home. There are building firms throwing up whole towns of shoddy houses out in the deserts just to sell to all these sub-prime mortgage buyers. There are stories making the rounds, like a Mexican strawberry picker in California with a $750,000 mansion, and a part time Las Vegas night club hostess who's bought a row of five new build detached houses. Then after two years the interest rate shoots up and there's no way any of the poor suckers will ever afford it so they'll get repossessed and evicted. It's gone crazy." He stopped for a sip of wine.

"Sounds a mess, Mike," said one of his audience, "How's a bank supposed to make any money out of that?"

"Well, it turns out the banks over there are lovin' it," Phillips continued, "They're doing a roaring trade buying up all these junk mortgages, lumping them together thousands at a time, converting them into investment bonds, and then flogging them for a profit through Wall Street to anyone who wants them - pension funds, insurance companies, savings trusts, foreign banks, whatever. If you've got money in an investment anywhere in the world, some of it is probably in this junk without you even knowing. And it is junk, because it's all based on mortgages that are never going to be paid and which are going to default within a few years."

"If it's junk then why are investors buying them?" asked the diner seated opposite David.

"The investors aren't just buying these bonds, they're fighting each other for them," said Phillips. "In fact we're one of the few banks who aren't selling mortgage-backed bonds, and we're getting grief from some of our clients who want to buy them." He spread his arms.

"But to answer your very good question, the reason they all want them is because these bonds give a much better rate of interest than any other investments and the American banks have conned their ratings agencies in to giving them a triple-A rating, which is the best safety rating any investment in the world can have." He paused, sipped, and looked around the room.

"That all sounds pretty bad, Mike," piped up a diner seated next to David.

"Not just bad, terrible," said Phillips, "And do you know what's the most terrible thing of all?" Blank faces round the room.

"Go on, what's the most terrible thing of all?" he repeated. "You are the cream of your generation at RoyalBank and you can't tell me what's most terrible of all?" Still blank faces.

"Then I will have to tell you," he said. "The most terrible thing of all is that those big American banks are making an absolute killing out of sub-prime, while we here at RoyalBank are sitting on our backsides making diddley-squat out of it. Nothing. Not a penny. That's what's most terrible, my friends." Another sip, another mouthful of lobster.

"And that," he continued, "is the reason why I've brought all of you together in this room. I've hand-picked each one of you because you are the smartest guys in the whole of RoyalBank." He looked over to David and nodded to him in acknowledgement. David flushed with a mixture of embarrassment and pride.

"Well as of now RoyalBank is going to get a slice of that sub-prime action. We're going to be the bank that brings sub-prime to Britain's doorsteps. And you are the people who are going to make it happen."

He topped up his glass and waited for the other diners to do the same, even David who does not usually drink much but who was keen to conform.

"Gentlemen, six weeks from today we are going to launch the RoyalBank All-In Mortgage. No deposit, no proof of earnings, no credit history, and 25% cashback which makes it a 125% mortgage, the biggest excess there has ever been in the history of British mortgages. On the same day we'll launch our new mortgage-backed investment bond, to get all these iffy mortgages off our hands pronto and out to investors and turn a nice profit in the process." Sip of wine, more lobster.

Phillips pushed back his chair, stood, and then with his glass walked slowly round the table placing a hand on the shoulder of each diner as he told him what his assignment would be.

"Here's who's doing what. Marketing, you're doing the adverts and brochures for the All-In Mortgage. Sales people, get the sales force trained and stack up a commission scheme that really gets them salivating. Lawyers, make sure the small print on the mortgage forms ties down everyone but us. Bond desk, get the new bonds ready to sell and whip up investors into a frenzy so that they fly off the shelf."

He reached David, who tensed as he waited for the boss's hand on his shoulder, but no hand came. Phillips moved on past him to the next diner. "Insurance division, make sure the mortgages come with lots of PPI. Compliance, see to it that there's no trail for the regulators to find . . ." And so on, round the rest of the table.

The steaks arrived. David looked up a little anxiously at Phillips, who caught his eye and winked back at him. David had to wait for the port before he got to find out what his own job was to be.

"OK, everybody," said Phillips, "Let me introduce David Lockwood. You won't know him as he's not been with RoyalBank long, but this boy can sure do numbers. David, everyone on this project has a difficult task but yours is going to be the most difficult of all." All eyes turned to David.

"We're going into sub-prime, and RoyalBank, and I, and everyone here, are all going to rake in a lot of money. But it won't last, it's a bubble and bubbles burst, from that Dot-Com bubble in 1999 right back to the Dutch Tulip bubble and the South Sea bubble three hundred years ago. I tell you, gentlemen, sub-prime is the biggest bubble there's ever been, and when it bursts there will be carnage." At the word 'carnage' he smiled.

"Other British banks are going in for sub-prime too, but they have no idea how much money they've got tied up in it and what risks they're taking, and when the bubble bursts, as it surely will, it's going to take entire banks down with it. We have to make sure we aren't one of those banks. We're going to get in quick, make some serious money while there's money to be made, then get out. We're going to be like looters in a jewellery shop in an earthquake, we're going to grab everything we can carry, then get out just before the building collapses on all the people still inside."

Silence around the table, all eyes on Mike Phillips. He picked up his port glass, swirled it around, sniffed it appreciatively, then put it carefully back in the same place beside his coffee cup.

"And that's where you come in, David," he said. "David, there's nobody in the world who truly understands the sub-prime phenomenon, not even me and certainly not the other banks. We need you to be the person who understands it better than anyone else on this planet. I want you to follow the figures, track the trends, pore over the prices, whatever it takes. And, David, I want everyone round this table to listen to what I'm about to say to you."

Everybody was indeed listening.

"David, your job is to tell us when it's time to stop."

David was not the only one to look puzzled.

"One day, I don't know when, that jewellery shop is going to collapse and crush everyone caught inside. David, when you tell us that it's time to stop and get out, we are all going to turn round and run for the door. As fast as we can. Neither I nor anyone else on this team will argue with you or try to second-guess or countermand you. When you say stop and get out, we stop and get out. There and then. Got that, David?"

"Got that, Mike".

"And have you got that, the rest of you?"

They all had.

The next morning Mike Phillips' dinner guests moved into a big suite with locks on the doors, on the same floor as his own office and away from prying eyes, and set to work. To keep the rest of the bank in the dark and blunt their curiosity, the sign on the door read 'COBALT INVESTMENTS STUDY PROJECT'. David set to work, as content as he could ever be.

# CHAPTER 12  THE LORD OF THE MANOR

Janie and Sam finally got around to having their proper wedding. They thought they ought to do it before any of their now-grown-up children stole their limelight by having one of their own. It was, as was reported in the Brighton Argus, a lavish affair, with a hundred guests joining them at the Grand Hotel. Jess and Helen were Janie's bridesmaids, David was Sam's groomsman, Mr Hodge shuffled on a walking stick to give Janie away for a second time, and they were the happiest family in town.

David used his bonuses from the bank to buy a flat in London, but he popped home most Christmases, on some birthdays, and even once on a Mothering Sunday which Janie thought very nice, though he didn't say much or stay long.

For the rest of the Lockwood household, life in Brighton settled down to a steady pace and a regular routine. Jess was out of the house first each morning to drive over to the Shoreham branch of Lockwood Hardware where she was now the manager. Helen went next, always in a rush and leaving just enough time to collect an elaborate and expensive coffee to take into the bank before it opened. Then followed Sam, who as finance manager for Brighton Care Homes had the privilege of setting his own start time. Janie was the last to leave, her day involving less time in the office and more time living the life of a successful businesswoman, meeting suppliers, having lunches, fundraising for local charities, and the occasional afternoon free to go walking on the Downs.

One of the people whom she persuaded to shell out for a good cause was a neighbour, Bill Stewart of Stewart & Co Estate Agents who were, according to their very glossy brochures, specialists in selling 'prestige country residences'. Janie twisted his arm into paying £5,000 a year for the privilege of being a trustee of a local homelessness charity on the condition, as he put it, that "I don't have to meet any of their bloody clients."

Janie was round at Bill's house one Sunday afternoon for a barbeque, and asked him how the prestige country residences business was going.

"Can't complain," he replied. "The latest fashion for all these city boys is to spend their massive bonuses on amenity farms, and they happen to be one of our specialities."

Janie had heard of arable farms, dairy farms, fish farms and health farms, but never 'amenity farms'. She asked Bill for enlightenment.

"Amenity farms are a sort of rich man's playground. A working farm but with woods for shooting, lakes for fishing, tracks for riding or more likely razzing round on a quad bike, and a house for weekends and guests, but they leave the actual work of farming to rent-paying tenants."

"And how much would one of those set someone back?"

"I've just sold one for four million over by Shoreham, two hundred acres with some old farmworkers' cottages that are now holiday lets, a stables and a ruin of an old manor house that will cost another million to put right if it doesn't fall down first. Some stockbroker fellow phoned me out of the blue, said he'd seen it on our website and wanted to buy it for cash. I said, when would you like to come and view it, he said he was too busy. I said what's your offer, he said he couldn't be doing with all that faff. He just wired us the asking price last Friday and we posted him the keys on Saturday. It's his now and I've still never met the man. Funny old world."

Four million pounds at five percent sellers' commission makes £200,000, which is how much richer John Stewart had become over that single weekend. Janie did not feel too guilty about taking his five thousand for her charity.

Mike Phillips and Charles Borden still cropped up from time to time in the banking columns of the financial papers, and on one occasion there was a spread about Melissa Campbell becoming chair of a new charity called Women In Business, complete with a photo of her in the USA meeting 'the world's most successful women'. But around this time it was Gordon who attracted the most media attention.

Amid a blaze of publicity, much of it generated by himself, Gordon had left RoyalBank to set up his own property investment company that he grandly titled British Care. According to the reports he had persuaded a group of wealthy investors to put up several hundred million pounds, money he would never otherwise have afforded even on his bank salary and bonuses. He was promising his investors a big return on their money, which he was using to buy up unprofitable care home businesses.

If Janie had known then what he was later to do to her husband and to her children, and what they would all have to do to him in return, she might not have turned so quickly to the crossword.

Janie first spotted the big new "All-In 125% Mortgage" posters in the window of Helen's RoyalBank branch when she nipped out of her shop for a sandwich. She asked Helen about them when she came home from work, and found her to be distinctly underwhelmed.

"Yeah, it's the latest Next Big Thing from head office. I've read the brochure and I can tell you I'd never sign up for one. Still, someone on high must like them, because there's one heck of a big commission for selling them."

When Helen was back from a sales conference later that month she had more to say on the subject.

"Hey Mum," she said, "I'm getting quite concerned about the way RoyalBank's going. When I joined Brighton Building Society we were just there to look after people's savings and help them to buy a house. Now it's all about selling stuff to people whether they need it or not, and whether they can afford it or not, and loading yourself up with commission in a race to get rich."

"How do you mean?"

"Well, take these new All-In Mortgages. After the conference we all went to the bar and I can't believe what the sales reps were saying.  In some of the poorest parts of the country, the North, Midlands, Wales, they're out day and night knocking on doors in run-down estates and tower blocks, cold-calling people and selling thousands of these mortgages." She shook her head in disapproval.

"They're cutting every corner there is - just a quick look at the buyer's credit, which they call 'lo-doc'.  Or no checks at all, they call that 'no-doc'.  They're getting people who can't even afford weekly rent to take out big mortgages by telling them that the interest rate is two percent without telling them that after two years it quadruples."

Janie winced.  Helen continued.  "I've even heard them boasting about selling mortgages to people who can't read, and to a lady who's blind where they read out the small print to her but left out the bits they didn't want her to know about.  They all thought that was a laugh.  And the buyers don't seem to care either, house prices in those areas are going up fifteen percent a year, and people are splashing their extra twenty-five percent on cars and holidays.  And every time the newspapers call them 'liar loans' it's like a free advert and there's another rush of people wanting to lie about their income and grab their own All-In Mortgage.  It stinks."

Helen stomped off upstairs to get dressed to go out. Janie heard her leave, and as usual was asleep long before she came back in.


In the interests of a quiet life Sam stayed well out of the love-lives of his adult children, and even Janie hovered at a cautious distance most of the time.  This was not difficult in the case of David, because he was in touch only sporadically, never invited his parents up to London, and never brought any sort of friend, male or female, back to Brighton.

Helen was the opposite. Janie struggled to keep up with her romantic interests, while Sam made a point of not even trying, to both Helen's and Janie's relief.  They were all glad he did, because nothing came of any of them.

As for Jess, not only did she appear to have no enthusiasm for the dating game, but she declared herself to be "far too busy running a business for all that lovie-yuckie stuff." And clad as she generally was in shop overalls, with her hair under a baseball cap and grease under her nails, she was not exactly dressed to thrill. So for a while it looked as though Sam's and Janie's wedding would be the last and only one in the family

Jess did concede that she might find a partner sometime in the distant future, and one day when she was out for a coffee with Janie she completed a 'Who Will Be Your Perfect Match?" questionnaire that popped up on the internet on her phone. The answer came back that he must be tall, young, dark, handsome and exotically foreign.

When a man did eventually show up in her life, he was none of the above. He was an inch shorter than Jess, ten years older, a shaggy blond, not handsome in any particular way, and so unexotically English that his name was Henry Spencer and he had been to Eton and Oxford.

The family's first encounter with Henry came when Janie was over at the Shoreham store with a delivery for Jess. He was browsing and Janie went over to ask him if he needed any help.

"As a matter of fact I do, thank you," he said in a round plummy English accent, and produced two halves of a large, old and very broken wrought iron window catch. "You don't have anything like this, do you?"

Janie put the broken ends together and said, "I shouldn't think anybody's stocked these for a hundred years. Where's it come from?"

"I'm doing up an old place. I'm going to need about fifty, it has a lot of windows."

Janie called Jess over and they and Henry retired to the back office where together they went through all the house restoration catalogues to see if they could find Henry's window catches, but they could not. He was about to go away catch-less when Jess saved the day.

"I think there's a workshop in Wolverhampton who still make ironware like this to order. If you can hang on I'll call them." She found their number, phoned them, then photographed Henry's window catch on her phone and sent the images straight off to the workshop, who replied five minutes later that if Jess sent them the old catch they could make as many new ones as she needed, to sell at a hundred pounds each. Jess told Henry, who was delighted. So was Janie, at the prospect of a five thousand pound order from a chance encounter with a walk-in customer.

"What sort of house is it?" Janie asked him.

"It's an old manor, Elizabethan originally. It was in my family for four hundred years and there was a title to go with it once, but that's vanished into the mists of time. Then it stood empty for years, until my grandfather sold it for next to nothing after the war and died a few years later," Henry continued. "I inherited some family money and went into stockbroking and I've done rather well, so I've bought the place to live in and restore to its former glory. It came with two hundred acres which is a nice bonus. Woods, lake, cottages, everything. It's just perfect, I didn't even bother to view it, I bought it there and then over the phone."

Janie was impressed, as was Jess. And when Henry suggested a visit to see what other items of specialised hardware would be required, Janie resolved to make herself unavailable so that Jess would have to go on her own.

A week later, Jess arranged a half day off and Henry called back at the shop for her. He escorted her across the road to a bottle-green Porsche that was sitting, engine running, on the yellow lines opposite. He gallantly opened and closed her door for her, made sure her seatbelt was comfortable, and whisked her noisily away. They spent the afternoon exploring his house, from the empty wine cellars right up to the leaky roof and lightning-damaged bell-tower, while he talked about his ideas and she made notes and took measurements and photographs.

When the house had been thoroughly examined, Henry invited Jess out to dinner. She pointed out that she was still in her working overalls. The first Janie and Sam knew of all this was when a green Porsche screeched up on the front drive of their house, and Jess dived out to give them her news.

There were then twenty minutes of pandemonium inside the house, as Janie and Helen set to the task of scrubbing Jess clean and rifling through their own wardrobes, make-up bags and jewellery boxes to fit her out for dinner with the millionaire owner of a manor house. Sam meanwhile fled for the calm and comfort of the passenger seat of the Porsche, where he and Henry got on amicably until a shiny-clean, discreetly made-up, and elegantly dressed Miss Jessica Lockwood took his place.

Over the next six months, Jess was entertained by Henry at all the best restaurants along the South Coast, and in Cannes and St Tropez when he took her off for luxurious weekend escapes. When he came to the Lockwoods' house alone and by appointment to meet Sam and asked for his permission to marry her, Sam told Henry that he thought that the admirable custom of asking the bride-to-be's father had died out long ago, and said 'Yes of course'. The wedding, in the garden of the part-restored manor house, put Sam's and Janie's into the shade for its size, scale and, presumably, expense, and Henry insisted on paying for it all.

Mrs Jessica Spencer moved into the manor house and drove to Shoreham daily to run her store, while Henry took charge of the work to restore the rest of the house, landscape the gardens, improve the neglected woods and fishing lake, oversee the cottage lets and clear land that he wanted as a paddock 'for the children's ponies'.

Some weekends they went up to the auctions in London to buy antique furniture for the rooms and paintings for the walls. Henry had the in-laws round for Sunday dinner once a month and showed them the progress he and Jess were making. He also reported that he was having some success in tracking down the long-lost 'Lord of Welby Manor' title with a view to restoring it to its rightful owner, namely himself. Sam, Janie and Helen were not a little amused at the thought that their least lady-like female family member might one day be a Lady.

# CHAPTER 13  THE LOOTERS

David spent the next three years of his working life in the doorway of the jewellers, listening for the first tremors in the ground, but he heard none.

He watched as tables, charts and lines of data rolled past his eyes on the four computer screens on his desk. He compiled data from the USA, Germany, Japan, France, the Gulf States, China and everywhere else where mortgage-backed bonds were being bought and sold. He studied house-building statistics, employment trends, credit scores, car purchases, loan defaults, anything that might help him to understand the monster that was sub-prime lending.

While he was doing this, RoyalBank's salesmen and saleswomen scoured the country, furiously signing up NINJA, lo-doc and no-doc customers for All-In 125% mortgages that many would never be able to repay, while back at head office Mike Phillips' hand-picked team were just as furiously bundling all these mortgages into investment bonds, taking the bank's slice of profit and then selling them on in huge quantities to an enthusiastic if uncomprehending global investment market. David did not discuss his bonuses with his parents, so they had no idea whether he claimed them or not - it would have been quite like him not to bother - but from what he later told them in prison about the rest of the 'Cobalt Investments Study Project' team, Henry Spencer would have had plenty of company in the Porsche showrooms around that time.

All the while, David sat at his desk in a corner of the Cobalt team's room down the corridor from Mike Phillips' office, reading, scrolling, and thinking. As a joke, his colleagues made up a big red button marked 'PRESS TO STOP' and glued it to the middle of his desk. David liked his red button and was proud of it but never touched it.

Until, three years in, and two days before Christmas, he phoned Mike Phillips. "Mike, it's time to stop."

Phillips was out of his office and along the corridor to David's desk in twenty seconds. Seeing his arrival, other members of the team gathered round to catch what was happening.

"So tell me David," he said.

"Mike, you told me to warn you when it's time to stop. Well, it's time to stop."

"And why do you think that, David?"

"I actually don't know, Mike. I can't point to any proof. I wish she could. All I can say is that I've been watching the sub-prime business for three years and I know it's time to get out. I can just feel it."

Phillips pursed his lips, nodded gravely, and said, "In that case, thank you David. Job done."

He turned to the crowd. "The All-In party's over, gentlemen. David says stop. So we stop."

The rest of the team clearly did not agree and Mike Phillips was besieged.

"RoyalBank's making serious money on this Mike, thirty million a day! Why stop now?" said one.

"How can you take David's word on it without him showing us any analysis? He's an analyst after all. Since when was one man's hunch the right way to do business?" said another.

"Come on Mike, it's Christmas. Our bonuses don't come out till March. Can't we at least carry on till then, so we don't lose out on three months' worth of bonus?" demanded a third.

Phillips held up his hand and waited for the clamour of dissent to die down, and then said, "I gave David the job of telling us when to stop, and he says stop. So we stop."

Then to spare David the opprobrium of the rest of the team, Phillips leaned across him and punched the 'PRESS TO STOP' button. It lit up and played a tinny 'Jingle Bells' tune from a device that some wag had put in it from a musical Christmas card.

Phillips laughed. "Very apt, because Christmas is cancelled. We're all going to be working through the holiday, me included and Christmas Day included, because we're going to make the All-In Mortgage vanish up Santa's chimney. We've got two whole weeks ahead of us when the banking world and the newspapers aren't watching because they're asleep in front of the telly. Make it happen boys, and you can have your Christmas holiday at Easter, with double bonuses all round as my Christmas present to you."

Mike Phillips' boys did make it happen. By the time RoyalBank's branches reopened in January, there were no All-In posters to be seen, the All-In brochures had been collected up and pulped, the All-In website deleted. Anyone with an All-In mortgage application in progress received a nice friendly letter telling them that owing to an administrative oversight by the bank their mortgage offer was withdrawn but here is a cheque for £1000 by way of apology. Very handy for paying off those Christmas debts, there were few complaints.

Any All-In mortgages that were still on RoyalBank's books were bundled up into asset-backed bonds and offloaded to the world's investors at a price discounted enough to sell quickly but not so low as to arouse suspicions. By Easter, sub-prime was ancient history at RoyalBank, and Mike Phillips kept his word - David and the other rising stars in his All-In team were all paid a double bonus, with double time off to enjoy spending it.

Then nothing happened, and over their Thursday night beers some of the former Cobalt team used to get together and tell David that he had called the stop too soon, and as the months went by even David was not sure. Then on Friday 14 September that year Janie and Sam were coming through the front door after work when Helen called from the lounge. "Mum, Dad, you need to get in here and watch this!" Janie headed her way just in time to catch the start of the BBC Six O'Clock News.

*"Hello and welcome,"* said the newscaster from behind his desk. The screen behind him said 'NORTHERN ROCK'. *"Thousands of Northern Rock savers have queued for hours at branches to empty their accounts. Many more have withdrawn cash via the internet. Despite reassurances from the bank over the safety of their savings, customers have now taken out well over a billion pounds. Many failed to access online accounts because of the massive demand and many branches were forced to extend opening hours. Our business correspondent Roy Cellan-Jones reports."*

The screen showed crowd scenes from a town centre street and a new voice said, *"For thirty-six hours now they've been told that their money is absolutely safe."*

Then there was a shot of a young woman in a bank-style jacket and skirt suit, standing on the steps of her branch and looking rather harassed. She was saying to the crowd, *"The Bank of England would not have lent us any money if we were in an unstable financial position. It's as simple as that."*

Sam called out to her, "If your bank was in a stable financial position then the Bank of England wouldn't have had to lend you any money in the first place, you muppet."

"Shut up Dad, I'm listening to this," said Helen.

The screen now showed long queues outside a succession of Northern Rock branches around the country. The voice-over was saying, *"At branches across the country Northern Rock customers have been queueing for hours to take their money out. Everyone from the Bank of England to the Chancellor has been telling them that there's no threat to their savings, but that doesn't appear to have made any impression."*

An interviewer was now talking to people in the queue. *"The Chancellor has said don't panic,"* he told a middle-aged woman, who replied, *"So did the captain of the Titanic. And that went down!"* and managed a cheery laugh. A more sombre man said, *"I'm not panicking. I'm being totally rational. I'm just moving my money somewhere else."*

The camera switched to a young woman who was sitting at a computer screen and tapping her keyboard, while the commentator said *"This is also a crisis for internet banking. Carol*

*Hill has been trying and failing to get access to her Northern Rock online account since Thursday evening. The bank says its website is now working a bit better, but this customer is having second thoughts about banking online."*

Carol Hill turned away from her screen to address to the camera, *"I have no means, absolutely no means, at this moment in time, of accessing my money, and that is an uncomfortable place to be, very uncomfortable actually."*

Janie turned the TV off and just sat looking at the blank screen in shock. She remembered from the history she did at school, the black-and-white photos of the collapsing American banks besieged by their customers during the Wall Street Crash, and people in Germany carrying their useless paper money around in wheelbarrows leading to the rise of Adolf Hitler. She never thought she would see such scenes on the streets of her own country and in her own lifetime.

Then in short order Bear Stearns Bank in the USA collapsed in a sea of its own sub-prime debt, followed by Lehman Brothers. Janie happened to be in London for a meeting the morning it happened and was shocked to see the street outside the Lehmans' head office filled with their workers carrying away their belongings in bags and boxes, or even carting off whole computers, or just sitting in the sunshine on the pavement crying into their mobile phones.

As the sub-prime banking crisis spread across the world, the government had to close down Northern Rock, bail out Lloyds, RBS and HBOS and take them over, and Barclays sold itself at a discount to a bunch of Qataris to avoid a similar fate. The government spent £86 billion of the public's money to dig the banking system out of the sub-prime hole of its own making, and in return the public got the Credit Crunch, austerity, and a recession that cost the country seven percent of its value and a million people their jobs.

But David had pulled Mike Phillips and the All-in looters out of the jewellery shop just in time, and RoyalBank came safely and profitably through the earthquake.

# CHAPTER 14  THE LOAN MEN

Helen clattered into the house late from work one evening. Janie was in the kitchen and came out to see what all the excitement was about.

"Guess what Mum, we've got a big boss up in London called Mike Phillips and he's sending out teams all over the country, there's one coming to our patch next month, they want meetings with everybody who's got a business loan from us. I've got the job of arranging the visit and then I'll be working with them for the week they are here."

"What's it about?"

"It's a new thing called Interest Protection Insurance, it means that if you've got a big loan and interest rates go up, you never have to pay the increase.  They want everyone to have it.  It's a whole week away from the counter, getting out and about, lunches, meeting people.  And I can get all the head office gossip while I'm at it, the girls at the branch will want that."

Helen was late plenty more evenings over the next month, making the arrangements for the head office team. Then when the week came, she met her visitors at the station and whisked them from place to place, making introductions, passing out files and taking notes.  In the evenings she had dinner with the team and then stayed up late completing reports for them to check when she went to meet them over breakfast at their hotel the next day.

Then on Saturday she took over the dining table to finish the reports that head office needed on Monday.  When Janie finally got her out of there on Sunday afternoon, one of Helen's Interest Protection Insurance brochures was on the floor.  She picked it up and, being nosy, started to read it.

Interest Protection Insurance, she learned, is a "Great Deal For Your Business!" which she took to mean, it's a great deal for RoyalBank's business.  It "Assures Your Profits" and also, no doubt, RoyalBank's profits.  So she read on.

RoyalBank's brochure offered what looked like a smart deal - swap your existing business loan for a new one that includes Interest Protection Insurance. Then if the Bank of England interest rate does go up, RoyalBank guarantees that your loan interest will not. Janie could remember when the Bank Rate reached fifteen percent in the early nineties, so a guaranteed cap was quite attractive. And best of all, there was no charge for making the swap, it was all free. Which immediately raised her suspicions.

"If it looks too good to be true, it isn't," she said to herself, and set about working through the small print looking for the catch. She found it, at paragraph 146b on page 12, in very tiny writing. If the Bank of England rate rises then the interest is indeed capped. But if the Bank of England rate falls, then the interest rockets. RoyalBank must be expecting the Bank of England rate to fall, she thought, otherwise why go to the trouble of swapping all these loans, and for free? No wonder Mike Phillips was being generous with his lunches.

Janie said nothing to Helen, but fished out from Helen's bag her list of local companies that the RoyalBank team had signed up for the swap. She saw the names of half the business community of the town - friends, neighbours, and competitors. She took a photocopy and put the original back in the bag.

Over the next week, she phoned them all, even her competitors, and suggested they turn to page 12 of the small print and read paragraph 146b carefully before the end of their two-week cooling off period. She wonders to this day whether Call-Me-Mike Phillips noticed most of his swap customers in Brighton pulling out of the deal, and if so whether he wondered why.

# CHAPTER 15  THE SPYMASTER

After his triumph on All-In Mortgages, David was granted possession of a pair of large desks making up the quietest corner of the noisy trading floor at RoyalBank's head office, where he set out his three computers and four screens. As an analyst he was there to help anyone in the bank who needed him to make sense of complicated data, and he had plenty of takers. He was working at his desk one Monday afternoon when he felt a presence behind him.

"Hello, David, what are you are doing this evening?

David turned round.

"Oh hello Mr Borden. Working late. The commodities desk need to know what's going on with lead, the price has gone up and nobody knows why."

It was David's birthday and he always worked late on his birthdays. Jess and Helen loved birthdays and both spent the best part of eleven months and twenty-nine days after each birthday planning their next one. David never showed any interest in birthdays, his or other people's, and he had long ago ceased coming home to celebrate them with his family.

Charles Borden dropped a slip of paper with an address on it onto his desk. "Forget the lead, as long as there's enough left in the world to make my shotgun pellets I'm not interested. Meet me at this place, eight-thirty tonight."

It was ten to eight before David got round to looking at the address on the paper and realised that it was on the other side of central London, a place called L'Escargot Jaune in Mayfair. He grabbed his jacket, rushed for the station, and reached the restaurant breathless at eight thirty-five. When his eyes adjusted to the low light he saw Charles Borden beckoning to him from a table in a booth at the darkest end of the room. Borden brushed David's apologies aside and told him he had already ordered for them both. Food and drink came and went as they sat and talked.

"A little birdie tells me you have a keen interest in spies, David," said Borden.

"How did you know that?"

"Well, I'm a bit of a spy herself. I was asking one of your colleague analysts about you the other day and he happened to mention it. The thing is, I need a bit of spy work done, and I think you might be just the man to do it."

David was flattered. And curious. "Like what, Mr Borden?"

"I need you to do a special piece of what I know you are best at - analysis. But this time, instead of looking for trends and forecasts I want you to look for people. Some very secretive people. I don't know who they are, but I'd like you to be my spy because I think you can find them without any of them knowing that you're even looking. Are you up for that?"

Deep down, David always fancied himself as the spy hero of his boyhood books. Maybe Charles Borden had worked that out. But in any case, he had David in the palm of his hand.

"Yes. Completely. So what's the mission, Chief?" asked David, getting into the spirit of the thing.

"Slow down, David, I'll come to that. Let's begin at the beginning. Now as you know, every time anybody in the world changes money from one currency to another, whether it's a few euros for a day trip to Calais or a hundred billion yen to build a power station in Japan, it goes through Foreign Exchange, Forex for short. But do you know how the Forex exchange rates are actually set?"

"No, I don't think I do."

"It's quite old fashioned really, David. Four times a day, people from all the main banks in the world talk to each other and agree what the exchange rate will be for each currency, and that becomes the rate for the next few hours, until the next ring-round. OK David, then there's Libor."

"The London Inter-Bank Originating Rate."

"Sure, originally it was just the interest rate that banks used when they lent money to each other, but nowadays Libor's used to set the value of trillions of pounds worth of investments all over the world."

"And how's the Libor rate set?"

"Same as for Forex, David. Every day, just before eleven a.m. London time, all the banks get in touch with each other and agree the world's Libor rates for that day. And therein lies a problem, and the reason why we're having this conversation. It's the worst kept secret in the banking world that the Libor and Forex rates are being rigged."

"Rigged? How?"

"Well in theory it shouldn't be possible. There are fifteen to twenty different banks involved in setting each rate, the idea being that no single bank can fiddle the rate on its own. But what really happens is that a group of traders and analysts from maybe half a dozen banks get their heads together and collude to shift a rate up or down. Then because they know in advance which way a rate's going to move, they can set up their deals so as to make a guaranteed profit. It's like going to a casino knowing in advance what number the roulette wheel's going to throw up."

"That's pretty smart," said David.

"These are pretty smart guys, David. There are different groups rigging different currencies but their system is always the same - a small cartel pushing the rate up and down and making a tidy profit for their banks and nice bonuses for themselves in the process."

"If they're making money, someone must be losing it," said David.

"Just so, David. Every time they win, someone has to lose. And that someone is RoyalBank. We're losing money because we're on the wrong end of a lot of the rigged deals they're doing. But indirectly everybody in the world loses a tiny slice of their money every time these clowns secretly get their heads together to fix the rates so that they win."

"Is RoyalBank involved in this, Mr Borden?"

"No, David, whatever else RoyalBank does, when it comes to fixing Libor and Forex rates our hands are clean. We decided to stay out years ago. Being honest is costing us a lot of money, but sooner or later someone's going to get found out and hung out to dry. The traders who are doing it are getting careless, I've seen copies of e-mails circulating round where they're boasting about their exploits and sending each other first class air tickets and holiday vouchers and cases of champagne to celebrate."

Mr Borden leaned forwards, lowered his voice, and continued.

"They're even paying off favours by doing 'wash trades' with each other - that's where one of them sells his pal in another bank a huge dollop of high price stock, then immediately buys it back again for the same price, generating two big  lumps of commission for his pal for services rendered without anyone being the wiser."

He topped up the glasses, and added, "When it all comes out somebody's going to go to prison, but it won't be anyone from RoyalBank and certainly not me or you. That's why we're having no part in it. We're sitting this one out."

David was enjoying this. He liked knowing how things work, and was basking in the confidence and trust that Borden clearly had in him.

"So here's your spy mission, David. I want you to burrow deep into the murky world of Libor and Forex, undetected of course, and find out who is in each of the rate-rigging cartels. Which people, which banks. I want their names. Get me names. That's your secret mission."

David went quiet, brow furrowed, and stopped eating. Borden watched him in silence for a few minutes, then asked him, "Are you OK, David?"

"Sorry Mr Borden, I forgot you were there. I was just working out what I need to do to get started."

"That's the spirit David, but don't start just yet. There are some more instructions. First, I want you to fit this in with your other work. Don't do it full-on or people will notice, just chip away at it when you get a bit of time, lunch breaks, evenings, so nobody knows. Got that?"

"Got it, Mr Borden."

"Second, no communication between us. Even this dinner tonight, I happen to know it's your birthday so if anyone asks it's just me taking you out to celebrate, okay? Then when you've got the names don't call me, just slip them to me when I'm doing my rounds on the trading floor, make sure nobody sees."

"Got that too."

"Third, don't keep copies. Not a thing. Delete any files you use, make sure there's nothing for anyone to find if they search your desk or computers."

"Check."

"And that's about it, David. Any questions?"

"Just one, Mr Borden. Is it OK to ask you what you need the list of names for?"

"Of course it is, David, I don't keep any secrets from you. When I know who the cheats are, I'm going to stop them cheating and make them play fair. Happy?"

"I'm happy. And thank you for my birthday treat."

"I'll go and pay for our meal, then I'll get us some more wine, the night is still young. Last chance to celebrate, you've got work to do, starting tomorrow."

Charles Borden and David finally left L'Escargot Jaune at ten past midnight. David, who notices details, was puzzled as to why Borden paid two bills, one when they finished their meal and another as they left, and why he ordered multiple single glasses of wine when buying by the bottle would have cost less. Some time later he heard from a colleague that this was standard practice, to get round the bank's daily expenses limits by splitting the bill into two across midnight, each bearing a different date, and evading the bank's drink limits by being able to claim if challenged that a number of the bank's clients had showed up unexpectedly and each had to treated to a glass of wine.

# CHAPTER 16  THE BOSSES

Helen came bouncing in from work one evening with a copy of RoyalBank's latest staff newsletter.

"We've got a new boss," she said, "Look."

Janie looked, and there smiling back at her was the face of Mike Phillips, formerly the shifty bank manager who took a no-questions-asked ten thousand pound deposit from a nineteen-year-old bank robber with a false name, and now, according to the caption above the picture, the new Chief Executive of RoyalBank.

So, Call-Me-Mike had made it to the top!  Fancy that! Janie stared again at his photograph.  Older, of course, less hair, put on some weight.  But definitely him.  The Essex boy who quit school to make some money was doing just that.

"What's so interesting, Mum?  Do you know him or something?"

"No, never seen him in my life.  I'm just reading what it says."

Janie read on.  There was the usual glowing career history, the early years of which were already familiar to her. Then a piece about the new Chief Executive's plans.  He intends, says the guff, to get out and 'break down barriers' and 'connect' with RoyalBank's customers and staff, and he wants everyone to 'call me Mike'.

She read that he had a new slogan for the bank - '*RoyalBank – Honest British Banking*' - to distance themselves from all the banks that got into trouble and lost investors' money in the banking crisis.  He's the new broom, the breath of fresh air, the man for the future, etc, etc.  It went on for several more gushing pages that she could not be bothered to read.

Janie noticed, down at the bottom of the page, another name from the past that merited a mention - Charles Borden, who was joining the board on promotion to Director of Investments.

"You can buy your own champagne now, Charles Borden, you don't need my freebie," she muttered to him.

"What's that, Mum?" said Helen.

"Nothing, just talking to myself."

"Well then, guess what, Mum? Mr Phillips is coming to our branch next week and wants to spend time with front-line staff. My manager went off sick with stress the minute he heard about it, so I've got the job of showing him round. He even wants to do a stint behind the counter, that should be fun!"

"Like counting out money that people want to pay in?"

"Of course!"

Helen laughed. Janie did not.


It took David a year to identify all the bankers who were rigging the Libor and Forex rates.

The task took that long partly because it was such a huge job, but also because he had to pretend that he was not doing it. For the first three months he made a file on each of the currencies that are used for Libor and Forex, and researched which banks contributed recommendations to each rate in each currency. He traced all their recommendations going back ten years, looking for patterns of groups of banks making matching recommendations at matching times, which is the footprint of a rigging ring.

He found plenty of these clusters, but some would just be coincidence, and even where there were rings at work, they did not try to rig every index every day. But three months in, David had at least narrowed the field down and felt he had a good idea of where to look more closely for rigging and riggers.

For the next three months, he monitored daily rate-setting minute-by-minute as it happened, studying the recommendations of the banks and groups that he suspected of rigging. From this, he was able remove from his list banks whose recommendations appeared on closer examination to be clean, and build up his data profiles on those that were confirmed as active in the rigging game.

But his lists only told him which numbers were being rigged and which banks were involved, not the identities of the riggers themselves. Charles Borden had said he wanted names. For those, David would have to penetrate the riggers' banks. From here on he really did feel like a spy.

Every bank was different. Some, helpfully, published the names and positions of the rate-submitters on their websites, though of course some of these individuals could be innocently submitting false rates that someone else was feeding them. Sometimes he could find banks' organisational charts or policy manuals lying around online, often out of date but still useful for figuring out who might have their hand on the rate-submitting process.

Professional development sites such as Linked-In gave him further clues. If you are a Libor or Forex rate-setter it could well be the sort of thing a banker might put on their profile to build themselves up for a potential future employer. But again, David had to be alert to the fact that people who want better jobs have been known to exaggerate their own importance and embellish their experience . . .

David knew that banks erect formidable anti-hacking defences around their customers' online accounts - good thing too - though experience shows that even these are not infallible. Their personnel systems tend to be less well protected, because many of their staff work from home or while moving around the world and need daily access to manage routine matters such as expenses and time off. David found that he could sometimes bluff his way into these systems and then on through to job descriptions and role profiles. At his trial he was described as a 'master hacker', which is not how he saw himself - he was just doing what Charles Borden asked him to do.

Slowly and painstakingly, David put names to the rate-setters in each cartel in each Libor and Forex index. That all took him another three months. But never once did Charles Borden chase or hurry him.

The whole task could have been finished in half the time if David had not had to follow Charles Borden's instructions to keep it secret. To his own discomfort, as he liked facing into his corner, he moved his desks round and had his back to the wall to make sure that nobody could get behind him and see his computer screens. He allowed no let-up in his work-rate on all the other tasks that managers and colleagues on the trading floor gave him. And he always had another job in progress on his computer so that he could quickly switch to that task if anyone came too close. For breaking into other banks' computer systems he took the extra precaution of only using his own laptop back at his flat.

All David did for the last three months of the year was check his own work. He took every name in turn and ploughed back through all his data to see if he could prove himself wrong on any of his conclusions. As a result, he deleted several individuals, which still left him with a list of fifty names of the world's most active and prolific rate-rigging bankers.

David ran off two copies of his list of names, deleted the computer file from which he had printed it, and then put one copy into a plain envelope and the other in in his jacket pocket. Back home at his flat that evening, he switched off the refrigerator in his kitchen and made himself a supper-time feast out of all the perishable fridge food.

Then the next day, as Charles Borden passed by on one of his walkabouts of the trading floor, David slipped the envelope into his hand. Borden pocketed it without comment and carried on with his rounds.

Back at his flat that evening David pulled his fridge away from the wall, checked that the motor pump on the back was cold, then took the piece of paper from his jacket pocket, folded it very small, and tucked it into the recess behind the motor. He poked it down out of sight, then blew fluff from the back of the fridge over his finger marks until they disappeared.

He switched the fridge back on, listened with satisfaction as the motor kicked in, and pushed it into its place against the wall.  In the unlikely event that someone should search his flat, the hot fridge motor would burn any fingers that got too close and discourage them from probing the recess behind it. He had read about this trick in a spy manual that his parents bought him as a Christmas present when he was nine.

Then he celebrated with a glass of room-temperature white wine.

# CHAPTER 17  THE WEALTH MANAGER

Janie thought she should keep Jennifer Harding's life simple and uncluttered.

"Are you married?  Partner?"

"No," she replied.

"Children?  Grandchildren?"

"None of those either," she said.

"Pity, they make my job easier."

Janie was of course married with three children and, since ten days ago, a little grandson, born to Jess and named Harry, weighing in at a very respectable eight pounds.  But to the 'wealth manager' who was asking the questions she was Jennifer Harding and he did not need to know any of this.

Janie had no idea such a thing as a 'wealth manager' existed until the arrival, via its circuitous route, of J. M. Harding's latest annual statement from RoyalBank in Jersey, accompanied by a letter headed 'PCMG Wealth Management' from 'Melissa Campbell, Managing Director' informing her that PCMG were RoyalBank's 'recommended wealth management advisers' and that all clients with over £5,000,000 on deposit were 'invited to take up a free confidential consultation'.

Annual interest and zero tax had indeed built Jennifer Harding's balance up to that amount, and if advice was being offered and it was discreet and free then Janie felt that she might as well take it.  She phoned the number given on the letter and found that as a five-times millionaire, Jennifer Harding could meet her wealth manager in person, anywhere she liked, and over lunch or dinner as PCMG's guest.

Remembering the nice lunches that Mike Phillips and Gordon once bought her, Janie was tempted, but in the end she plumped to meet for a late-morning coffee at an upmarket tea rooms overlooking the seafront at Southsea, far enough away from her usual haunts to avoid recognition but near enough for her to get there and back without Sam noticing her absence.

Her wealth manager was called Andrew Morgan, and with coffee and cake ordered she took the opportunity to ask him, "What actually is a 'wealth manager'?"

"Good question, Jennifer. As a wealth manager I can do three things for you. First, I can help your money to grow. Then I can help you pay less tax on it."

"Milk?" Janie asked. She did not feel that she had any need to grow her money or avoid tax.

"Then, if you need me to, I can make it disappear."

That was more like it. He now had her full attention. Janie put the milk down and sat forward, conspirator-style.

"Tell me more."

"OK, growth first. People get their wealth from all sorts of sources, often a source they choose not to disclose."

That's me, Janie thought. He continued.

"I can advise you on how and where to invest it to make the best returns. PCMG can offer you investment options that are somewhat beyond the scope of your average high street bank, if you get my drift."

She got his drift, and nodded.

Mr Morgan continued. "Then there's tax. The more money someone has, the more the taxman would like a slice of it and the less I as your wealth manager want you to have to pay. The wealth manager's job is to help you to minimise your tax liability or if possible eliminate it altogether. PCMG, who I work for, have access to a number of ingenious tax avoidance schemes, all certified legal by our own lawyers."

"What sort of schemes?"

"Take your pick. For instance, for a client I saw yesterday I have set up a registered charity in the Cayman Islands, he made a hundred pound donation to a non-existent kid's home there, then we put all his money tax free in the charity, which lends it all straight back to him and he just never pays it back. You don't pay tax on loans, you see. Or we can turn you into a business registered in Luxembourg, where you are the sole director and the only employee, then you employ yourself at a wage so low that you don't pay tax on it and you keep the rest off shore tax-free."

He must have picked up Janie's lack of enthusiasm. He tried again.

"Or a very popular scheme at the moment is films. The government gives big tax breaks to support the British film industry, but we've found ways to turn this into huge tax rebates without anyone making any films at all. Very popular with sports stars and celebs, that one. Anyway, those are just some of the things we can do at PCMG to keep the taxman at bay."

"Interesting," was all Janie could say.

"That's why I asked if you have children. They can be handy for keeping your tax down, you can set up trusts or name them as co-directors of your company and add their tax-free allowances to your own. On the other hand, in my experience kids cost so much money that even with the tax breaks they bring, you'll still be out of pocket."

"That's what people with families tell me, Andrew. It' nice outside, fancy a walk round?"

It was a bright sunny day. They set off for a stroll along the promenade.

"You were saying?" Janie said to Mr Morgan as they walked.

"The third thing we do is wealth concealment. If you have a lot of money there are likely to be practical reasons for not wanting people to know about it. You don't want begging letters from strangers. Or blackmail. Especially from your own family, they're often the worst. I can help you avert that sort of unpleasantness."

"I can see that," she said. They were leaning on a parapet, looking out to sea. A hopeful seagull hopped sideways along the wall towards them.

"And with the state of the world today, you need to think about hiding your wealth to protect you from criminals. Kidnapping for ransom is on the up and people are pretty worried, especially if they have children, which you don't of course. And I should imagine you wouldn't fancy being robbed at gunpoint either."

Janie shook her head. "Not really."

The seagull spotted a couple eating chips and hopped away in their direction.

"But some of the most important work we do is deeper concealment. Take divorce for example. The wealthier party needs to appear to be very poor by the time he goes into the divorce court, otherwise he really will be a lot poorer by the time he comes out. Or she, of course, if that's who has the money. If your aggrieved and litigious ex and his team of lawyers are going to take half of everything you've got, it's best if it looks as if you haven't got anything to take half of. We can see to that too. But since you aren't married, I don't suppose you'll be needing that service either."

"No, I shouldn't think I will."

"Or there could be any number of other reasons why someone has wealth that they don't want anyone else to know about . . ."

It was getting towards the time when Janie needed to head off back to work, so as they talked she walked Mr Morgan back to his car. He gave her his business card, they thanked each other for each other's time, shook hands, and parted. Janie thought he seemed a nice enough chap and she felt a little bit guilty that Jennifer Harding, having used up his day out of curiosity, would be sending no business his way.

# CHAPTER 18  THE FLY ON THE WALL

The visit of the newly anointed chief of RoyalBank to Brighton went well.  Helen, done up in her best business blazer, blouse, skirt and heels combo, was there to meet Mike Phillips at the kerbside as his chauffeur opened the door of his limo outside the bank.  She welcomed him to Brighton, took his coat and bag and ushered him inside.

She had researched how he took his coffee and what biscuits he liked, and both were waiting for him.  She made apologies for her still-off-sick manager and introduced all her colleagues with an ice-breaking remark or compliment for each to put them at ease.  She called Mike 'Mike'.  She showed him round the branch, then took him to her till position and gave him a quick refresher course in how to bank a cheque, and then let him do a real one for a somewhat bemused customer while the photographer from RoyalBank's public relations department took pictures from all angles to put in a press release.

Mr Phillips invited her to join him for another coffee before he left, and Helen asked about his 'honest British banking' plans, which he liked because he said it showed that she had read his newsletter.  He probed her about her background - secretarial college, computer courses, customer services training.  Then when it was time for him to leave he found she had put a pack of sandwiches and a piece of cake in his car for the onwards journey to his next destination, with another for his driver.  She waved him off from the kerbside and he waved back.

Helen was tidying up ready to go home that evening when a colleague called over to her, "Phone call for you, Helen, someone called Mike."

"Hello, Helen Laker, can I help you?"

"Helen, it's Mike Phillips here, calling from the car.  Lovely cake, by the way, I'm eating it now crossing the Severn Bridge.  My driver says thank you too."

There was a muffled 'Cheers Helen!' presumably from the front of the car.

"Thank you, Mike, I'm glad you like it, I made it specially yesterday. How can I help you?"

"There's a vacancy in my team in head office, I wondered if you might consider applying for it?"

"Thanks but no thanks, I couldn't work in London, have you seen the property prices there? I couldn't even rent a bedsit!"

"I think you'd find the salary covered a nice place to live. Especially as you'd qualify for one of our special interest-free staff mortgages."

"And anyway Mike, I hate interviews."

"You've already had the interview, Helen. You passed it today. So do you want that job or don't you? You've got till I finish this piece of cake to decide."

A month later, at the ripe old age of thirty, Janie's eldest daughter finally flew the nest and moved to a flat in Greenwich, four stops on the train from RoyalBank's front doors and the lifts up to her and Mike Phillips' grand offices on the tenth floor.

On the first morning of her new job, Helen underestimated how long it would take her to get through London's busy streets to Royalbank's head office and she did not arrive until nine., half an hour late. She hurried through the main door and was about to cross the crowded lobby when a security guard stopped her with a 'Sorry Miss, you need to wait there'.

Everyone else in the lobby was waiting too, leaving a passage clear from the front door to the lift. The lift was empty, and the security man was keeping it that way. An instant later his radio crackled, a Rolls Royce pulled up outside and the driver was out like a shot to open a rear passenger door. Mike Phillips emerged and strode across the pavement and in through the front door, then moved swiftly past the lobby to the waiting lift without acknowledging anyone en route, and was up and away.

While Helen joined the scramble for the remaining lifts, she looked around the lobby and counted no fewer than six posters proclaiming *"RoyalBank - Honest British Banking."* There were three more in the lift that she eventually managed to cram into, and another on the wall opposite the lift door when she disembarked at her destination.

Once she got the hang of getting to work on time, Helen settled in quickly to life on the tenth floor. Anyone who had business with Chief Executive Mike Phillips had first to get past his 'outer office' - the team of women who occupied a large vestibule that separated his door from the main corridor. Helen was now one of these women, albeit the youngest, newest, most junior and furthest from the boss's door.

The oldest, longest-serving, most senior and nearest to his door was called Judy. Judy had occupied that position since before anyone could remember, and did not take kindly to new colleagues, especially young smart ones. Helen, never someone to be put off her stride, got on well with everybody else and kept out of Judy's way while she learnt all the ropes, rules and customs of her new workplace.

One of those customs was an informal get-together of directors in the Chief Executive's office after work on Friday afternoons. It was just a wash-up of the week and did not usually run late: bankers work long hours then go out eating and drinking late on weekday evenings but they do like to get home on time on Fridays.

Another RoyalBank tradition, Helen was told, was to open a bottle of whisky at these Friday evening sessions - not just any old whisky, but fine old Scotch whisky. This custom went back to when RoyalBank was first expanding and won a bitterly contested hostile takeover of Findlays Bank, Scotland's oldest and proudest independent bank. When RoyalBank's takeover team arrived at Findlays headquarters in Edinburgh to see what they had just bought, they found in a vault a large cache of whisky intended to grace the tables of

Findlay's directors for decades to come. RoyalBank whisked the entire stock away, and ever since then it had reappeared at the rate of one bottle a week on the Chief Executive's side-table.

It was part of Helen's job to sit in on these gatherings, and Judy told her what to do - bring a notebook, sit quietly in the far corner, and if anyone asked her to make a note of anything, jot it down for them. In the same way that royalty never carry money, it seems that top bankers do not carry pens or paper.

"And whatever you do, don't call him Mike," Judy told her. Helen had already noticed that in the few weeks since his 'meet the people' visit to Brighton, Phillips was as no longer telling people to call him Mike, and nobody did, so she fell in step.

Mike Phillips' suite was, as befitted his status, spacious and on a corner of the building with tinted windows overlooking the city in two directions, and furnished with a vast desk, a meeting table and chairs for twelve, and then a section with armchairs around a coffee table which is where the week's bottle of Findlays' whisky was set out and where the Friday sessions took place.

Besides Phillips the most regular Friday attendees were Charles Borden and a woman Helen did not know. Judy told her she was a long-time friend of Mike Phillips and a big cheese at PCMG, named Melissa Campbell. After the session, when everyone had gone, Helen would tidy the office then type up Phillips' notes to have them on his desk when he arrived on Monday morning.

Things went smoothly for Helen for a few weeks, until one Monday morning Phillips was irritable about having to rewrite an important letter that he had asked Helen for at the previous Friday's get-together, and which Helen had apparently got wrong.

She apologised, but to make sure it did not happen again she bought herself a miniature audio recorder which she placed unseen behind an ornament on a shelf just inside

Phillips' door as she went in for each session, and then collected on the way out after clearing away the whisky glasses. From then on, any time she was in doubt as to what he wanted, she knew she could have a quick listen and make sure everything was just right for him.

Four years later, the device was among the clutter Helen threw into her black bin sack in the fifteen minutes she was given to clear her desk after Mike Phillips fired her.

# CHAPTER 19  THE SHREDDER

One of David's phones rang.  He picked it up and heard a woman's voice, brusque and efficient.

"Mr Lockwood, would you come up to Mr Borden's office on the tenth floor please, he'd like to see you."

The tenth floor!

The tenth floor held the whole of RoyalBank in a grip of mystery, fear and envy.  It was the home of the boardroom, where some of the world's biggest financial deals were thrashed out, and the directors' offices, where the bonuses were given out and the firing was done.  Other than those who worked there, most RoyalBank staff never set foot on the tenth floor or wanted to, except for the ambitious ones who dreamed of one day having one of the directors' offices for themselves, with the power, status and money that went with it.

"When?"

"Now of course, Mr Lockwood, he's waiting for you."

A swift lift ride later, David was knocking on a double door marked CHARLES BORDEN, INVESTMENT DIRECTOR in gold lettering.  Inside, three smartly dressed women were working at large desks with, beyond them, floor-to-ceiling windows which gave an uninterrupted view straight across to the office tower opposite and the River Thames beyond.  The woman nearest the door looked up.

"Mr Lockwood, thank you for coming up, I'm Ann, Mr Borden's secretary.  He's just had to take a call from Frankfurt, he won't be long, have a seat and I'll get you a coffee, how do you take it?"

Ann ushered him over to a sofa with a low table near the window and poured David's coffee just as Charles Borden opened his door, spotted him, and boomed, "David dear boy, come on in.  Bring that coffee with you."

Mr Borden held the door for David, then took him past his desk and a wall of hunting trophies to two comfortable chairs in a window bay.  He waved out towards the view.

"Not bad, eh? I suppose you saw I got promoted again, though I still only get the south-facing side which gets a bit hot in summer. The chairman and chief exec get the north side. Still, mustn't grumble, eh?"

David said nothing, he was a long way away out of his comfort zone, and Borden's joviality, though well intended, only put him more on edge. Realising this, Borden changed tack.

"Anyway, David, to business. My fellow directors and I are very impressed with the work you did to get us out of sub-prime just in time."

David started to feel better. He liked praise, especially from on high.

"We don't think you've been adequately rewarded. We feel we should do more to show our appreciation."

David was pleased, and curious.

"Since you made that 'stop' call for us, David, you will have seen how most of our major competitors have gone under, dragged down by all the sub-prime debt that you helped us to offload just in time. RoyalBank came through all that successfully, thanks to you."

"It was a pleasure," David said.

"The pleasure is ours. In fact we've actually done rather well out of it. When all the other banks were having to sell off their assets cheap out of desperation just to stay afloat, we snapped up some bargains. And a lot of their customers came over to us too. The whole world thinks it's got a banking crisis, but we've actually got record profits. As they say, every cloud has a silver lining."

David was silent, but even more curious now.

"The upshot, David, is that the board consider that you deserve a piece of that silver lining for yourself. We've decided to give you a RoyalBank stock option to the value of a million pounds. Your ownership certificate is over there on my desk."

"A stock option?" said David. "For a million pounds?"

"Yes, exactly that. You now have your own slice of RoyalBank, a million pounds worth. You can't sell it for ten years, but if the value of the bank goes up in that time, as it surely will, your stock value goes up too. Then in ten years, you can cash it in and be a rich man."

David had never thought about being rich, and did not react. Being rich is not his thing. Maybe Mr Borden realised that he was pressing the wrong button, so instead he turned to praise, which works better on David.

"It's almost unheard of for us to award a stock option like this, normally they're reserved for executives and directors. You are the exception, but then you are exceptional, David."

David was close to tears, proud tears. Mr Borden went over to his desk and collected an envelope, which he handed to David. "David, in here is your certificate, keep it safe, and don't lose it, we don't issue duplicates."

David finally found his tongue. "Thank you, Mr, Borden. This means a lot to me." He picked up his envelope and made to leave. Mr Borden stopped him.

"Don't go just yet, David, there's a bit more on that spy job that I need you to do. Sit back down and I'll give you your next briefing."

"It's just a matter of fairness," continued Charles Borden, resting his eyes on the horizon beyond the tower blocks and river before turning back to address David, "Fairness to the bank that employs us both. And even more importantly, fairness to our customers who have placed their trust in us."

David raised an eyebrow but said nothing.

"You see, David, you've confirmed what we've long suspected, that there are people at our competitor banks who are rigging the Libor and Forex rates. And that's not fair to our customers, who expect us to give them the best return on their investments. Each time one of our competitors tweaks a rate, they gain money and our customers lose money."

He drew out of his pocket David's folded list of rate-setters' names, opened it up and laid it on the coffee table.

"For instance, say you're a big customer who wants us to change a billion pounds sterling into dollars for you to buy a company in the United States, and some other banks have deliberately shifted the Forex rate so that you get a hundredth of a cent less per dollar than you should. They have now just made a hundred thousand pounds at your expense. It's stealing, simple as that. That can't be right, can it? Or fair?"

"No, I see that Mr Borden," said David, "Not fair at all. Things like that should be fair."

"And it's even worse with Libor, David," continued Mr Borden. "Half of all the investments that our customers put through our bank are linked to a Libor rate, so every time the other banks move that rate to their advantage, all our own customers lose out."

"That's wrong too, Mr Borden," said David, "Shouldn't someone stop it?"

"The truth is that no-one can stop it. We'd like to, but if we took your list of names to the banking authorities, the people on it would just deny it and their banks would cover up for them. They all have too much to lose. Maybe a few of the rate-setters might get moved on or quietly fired, but after the dust settles others will step in to replace them, and the rigging will just carry on as before."

"So what's the point of all that work you asked me to do?"

"Well, maybe there is something we can do for our customers. It won't be easy. But we're going to need a secret weapon. And that's going to be you, David."

"What do you mean, Mr Borden?"

"This is what I mean. I want you to find a way to get some of those dodgy rate-setters on your list to put in the rates you tell them to, on the days you tell them to. Build them into a network that you control. Then from time to time, no more than once a month, I will tell you which way we need you to move the Libor and Forex rates, and you will get your network to make it happen."

"Why?"

"Because if our own bank knows which way the rates will move and when, then we can make sure that we put our customers' deals through in a way that gets them a fair price. The other banks are moving Libor and Forex separately. We are going to move them both at the same time, nobody has ever done that and nobody will suspect us. That way we can correct the cheating that all the other banks are putting into the rates. And the great thing is that nobody will know we're doing it, not even the banks who own the rate-setters."

David sat in silence, looking distracted.

"Is everything all right, David?" asked Borden.

"Sorry Mr Borden, I was just thinking. Isn't all this against the law? You know, like, illegal? And going to get us in trouble?"

"You leave that to me, David. The key thing is that we're only doing it to protect our customers and make things fair for them. It won't ever get out and if it does, I'll take full responsibility. You are completely in the clear."

David went quiet again. Borden noticed.

"You've gone quiet again, David."

"Yes, sorry Mr Borden, I was just making a start on thinking about how to do it."

"That's what I like about you, David. There's no problem you can't figure out. But to help you along, let me tell you a few things. First, you can spend as much money as you need to, to get the other banks' rate setters onside - meals, drinks, cases of bubbly, sports tickets, holidays, whatever it takes. If they want money, don't give them cash, that looks too much like bribery, just run them a few big wash trades, I'll make sure nobody finds out."

"OK," said David. It sounded odd to him, but whatever the boss says must be right.

"Second, you can travel anywhere in the world, business class of course, you need to be alert and ready for action when you get to your destination."

"OK," said David again. He was happier with this instruction, as he'd enjoyed his trip to New York and liked the idea of going further afield.

"Third, don't contact me as you go along or mention this task to a soul. It must be done in absolute secrecy. Nobody is to know. Then when you have it all ready, just tell my secretary Ann that you want to discuss your stock option, that will be the code. Have you got all that David?"

"I've got all that, Mr Borden, yes."

"And I assume," said Borden, picking up David's list of rate fixing cartels "That you've got your own copy of this list?"

"I have."

Borden carried the list over to his shredder and dropped it into its jaws. With a 'bzzzt' the paper was no more. "Best place for that then," he said, as he led David to the door.

"It's been a pleasure talking with you, David. Now crack on."

# CHAPTER 20  THE OTHER WOMAN

It's an old story, and in the course of human history it must have happened to untold numbers of people.  And then it happened to Jess.

She took a call from Harry's nursery to tell her that he was poorly.  She picked him up to deliver him to Henry, who was at home that week fixing up the stables.  On her arrival he was not at the stables, so she went to look for him and found him in the house, in bed with another woman.

While the woman was dressing to leave and Harry hid under a sofa, Henry, confronted by a furious Jess, demanded equally furiously to know what business it was of hers what the hell he did as long as he put a roof over her head and fed her and her child.  He refused to give any undertaking to end the affair and challenged Jess to 'divorce me if you dare'.

Which is how Jess, the Lockwoods' family solicitor John Murphy and Janie came to be sitting round a table in Mr Murphy's office poring over divorce papers.  There was no question of Jess's application for a divorce being refused, because Henry's behaviour, which he admitted, passed the 'unfaithfulness' and 'unreasonableness' tests handsomely, and in any case he was not contesting the divorce or demanding custody of Harry.  He was, however, refusing to pay maintenance, on the grounds that he had no money and could not afford to pay Jess anything towards the cost of Harry's upbringing.

"But he lives in a bloody castle!" said Jess.

"I know he does," said Mr Murphy, "But his solicitors have sent the court a statement from his accountants which certifies that he doesn't own it."  He showed Jess a document from one of the stacks of files in front of him.

"Well then who the hell does own it?" she asked with incredulity.

"According to the deeds, and there is a copy here, it belongs to a company registered in Gibraltar, that is owned by a company registered in Bermuda, that under Bermudan law is not required to divulge its shareholders."

"But he bought it himself, for four million pounds. He even showed me the receipt, it was made out to his name and signed by that Mr Stewart from next door," she said.

"That's mentioned in the statement, but apparently he was buying it on behalf of the Gibraltar company who then leased it back to him at no charge to live in rent-free."

"And the furniture and antiques he bought?"

"They aren't his either."

"They must be! I was sitting next to him when he bid for them, we went to the auctions in London and he paid cash to make sure they'd be delivered the following week."

"Well according to these legal papers, they all belong to a Guernsey-registered charity to which he donated them and which kindly allows him to keep them in his house. Mr Spencer is the founder and sole trustee of the charity, of course."

"What about the income from the farm and the shooting woods, fishing lake, and holiday cottages? Can't he pay for Harry out of that?"

"Apparently not, Mrs Spencer. There is another statement from his accountants, showing that the total income from the estate is less than the cost of its upkeep, and that rather than making a profit he has been subsidising it from his own pocket."

"That's rubbish! He used to show me the accounts for the estate and I happen to know we were making a good profit. I can read a balance sheet, you know!"

"I'm sure you can, Mrs Spencer, but his accountants have done a few magic disappearing tricks and they now show a loss, and that is what they will tell the divorce judge."

"He's even got a Porsche, he could sell that."

"Not according to his solicitors. The Porsche is on lease and is being paid for by a holding company in the Isle of Man whose shareholders are, again, undisclosed. So it's not his to sell. Apparently."

"What about the money he's been living on all these years, and that he's now spending on his lady friend so I hear? Don't tell me that's not his either?"

"Well technically, according to his solicitors, it isn't. They tell us that what appears to you and me to be his income is in fact gifts, either generously made to him from trusts whose trustees seem to be lawyers registered in Panama, or from kind and well-to-do friends who don't live in Britain and who have declined to disclose their identities to us. Discretionary gifts don't count as income in British law, and are not shared with the other party when the recipient divorces."

"So are you telling me, Mr Murphy, that he can carry on living in our marital home, raking in the income from the estate, getting whatever money he wants whenever he wants out of his so-called trusts and imaginary friends, driving his Porsche and screwing his woman in the bed that I chose, while I get nothing for bringing up his son for the next twenty years?"

"It's worse than that, Mrs Spencer . . ."

"Don't bloody call me Mrs Spencer any more! Ms Lockwood will do just fine from now on."

"As I was saying, Ms Lockwood, it's worse than that. His solicitor is claiming that Mr Spencer is without employment, assets or income, while you are working full time as a manager and have a share in a successful business, so it is you who should be contributing to Mr Spencer's future support . ."

"What the . . ."

". . .but that if you agree not to press your claim for maintenance against him, he will call it quits and not go after your money."

"I can't believe this!"

Janie had to take Jess outside for a walk around the square to cool down, otherwise she could see Mr Murphy getting thumped for something that was not his fault. He got on with other work until they were ready to take their places round his table again.

"So, John," Janie said, "What do you suggest?"

"Well, it looks as though your daughter's soon-to-be former husband is one of the thousands of well-bred and well-resourced upper-crust Brits who live from cradle to grave protected by the best wealth management that money can buy, starting with offshore trust funds at birth and ending with off-shore avoidance of death duties. It's how they and all the other people in their world do things and have always done things. Though this chap does seem to be a particular git, doesn't he?"

Janie nodded. Jess stayed silent, sensing what was coming next.

"It has been my misfortune to have had to deal with a number of these characters over the years. If you apply for maintenance he will bring an army of expensive lawyers and accountants to court to prove to the judge that he is penniless and that his financial affairs are exactly as these letters here tell us. Mr Spencer is using a firm who are expensive but know everything there is to know about making money go invisible. You may have heard of them, they're called PCMG."

"I've heard of them," Janie sighed.

"Well you and your family will never have the resources to unpick the world-wide routes through which his money is flowing. Even the police find this sort of thing almost impossible. There's also a chance that he could turn nasty and make false claims about your own conduct, Ms Lockwood, and contest custody of Harry."

Jess was still silent. She just glowered at him.

"My advice, since that is what you are here for, is to take the divorce and custody but forget the maintenance."

Jess let out a sigh. "Can I think about it?"

"Of course you can," said Mr Murphy, "But not for too long, I have to respond on your behalf within the next ten days."

But Jess had already decided. She wanted nothing to do ever again with Henry Spencer, and the best way to have nothing to do ever again with him was to let him keep his house, land, Porsche, paintings, money and woman, and be content that she had Harry. The divorce was rubber-stamped a few weeks later, and Jess and Harry moved back into her old bedroom in the Lockwoods' house near the Downs.

## CHAPTER 21  THE BOSS'S FRIEND

One Friday there was an extra guest at Mike Phillips' Findlays session. Despite the passage of time, Helen recognised him immediately as Gordon and Judy told her that he liked to call in at some of Mike Phillips' Friday get-togethers to drink his Findlays whisky and catch up on what was going on in town. Arriving for his first session since Helen started work at head office, he clocked her straight away, strolled across to her desk and leaned over her for a better view down her top.

"Well, hello new girl, I'm Gordon, who might you be?"

"Good afternoon Mr Gordon, I'm Helen Laker, I'll be taking the notes for your meeting this evening."

"It hasn't been a good afternoon up to now, but it's just improved," replied Gordon, with what he must have thought was an inviting smile, but which Helen regarded as a disconcerting leer. "I'll see you in a few minutes then," he continued, "And I can tell you, I'm looking forward to it."

Gordon headed for the Chief Executive's office door, opened it and greeted the occupant cheerily. "Hello Mike, great to see you, just met your new girl, very nice, high score on the babe factor, well done!" and then headed on in to the sound of chinking glasses.

Charles Borden and Melissa Campbell joined them a few minutes later and Helen followed, slipped her audio recorder discreetly onto its shelf, and settled down into the chair in her usual corner, notepad ready. Gordon chose a seat facing her across the expanse of the office from where, when not engaged in the conversation, he could let his eyes rest on her legs.

After Helen was sacked and she was trying to prepare a defence for David's impending trial for international bank fraud, she retrieved her audio recorder from its black bin sack and, being out of work, passed some time going through her recordings and transcribing any sections that would give an idea of the type of people David was up against - as if by then they did not already know.   The extract from this occasion read -

*FRIDAY SESSION DATE 11 MAY 2012*
*Present: M. Phillips, C. Borden, M. Campbell, G. Gordon*
*Gordon: Your new girl's a bit of a looker isn't she?  Improvement on Judy, if you want my opinion.*
*Campbell: That's a bit sexist isn't it, even for you Gordon?  You do know I'm the founder of Women In Business, don't you?  We're there to promote the cause of women in business, which includes not making comments about their appearance.*
*Gordon: OK then, how many women do you have on your board at PCMG?*
*Campbell: One.  Me.  But that's one more than RoyalBank have got, or have ever had, hey Mike?*
*Gordon: Yes Mike, even my board is fifty percent female.*
*Phillips: Oh come on Gordon, that's because there's only you and your wife on your board, and she's only there because Melissa's outfit told you to put the company in her name to reduce your tax bill.*
*Gordon: OK then, if I'm the only sexist in town, how come every director I ever go to see, has a good-looking PA?  It can't be because a pretty one costs the same as an ugly one, can it?*
*Campbell: Pack it in, Gordon, for heaven's sake.  Anyway, my PA is a man.*
*Gordon: Yes Melissa, and I've seen him.  The handsomest hunk this side of a modelling studio.*
*Campbell: Look Gordon, just leave it.*
*Gordon: Just saying, that's all.*

After the banter the meeting settled down, but whenever he was not talking or refilling his glass, Gordon smiled across at Helen, which made her feel very uncomfortable.   Then when the session broke up and they were all leaving the room, Gordon moved to block the doorway so that she would have to squeeze bodily past him to get out, but she side-stepped him and took refuge in the ladies' toilet until she was sure the coast was clear.

Back at work the following week, Helen asked the other women about Gordon. They told her that whenever he called in to see Mike Phillips he would wander from office to office trying to find ways to bump into or touch the women, but nobody wanted to put their job at risk by making a complaint because he was one of RoyalBank's biggest customers and a friend of the boss. Instead, they each just developed their own strategies for avoiding Gordon's unwanted attentions.

Helen resolved to do the same. From then on, if Gordon was expected she wore a frumpy trouser suit and high-collared blouse to work, made sure she was busy on a fictitious but elongated phone call whenever he ventured into her office, then stayed behind after the meeting tidying up the glasses and chairs in Mike Phillips' office until Gordon had gone. It worked for a while.

*FRIDAY SESSION DATE 1 FEBRUARY 2013*
*Present: M. Phillips, C. Borden, M. Campbell, G. Gordon*
*Campbell: I've got a question for you, Mike. Why do you let your customers bank for free? Free current accounts, free cheque books, free cashpoints, free cards, free statements, free everything. Nobody gives anything away for free now, but the banks do. RoyalBank must have ten million free accounts, so if you charged ten pounds a month for each one you'd be earning a hundred million a month for doing no more work than you do now.*

*Borden: That's true, Melissa, but we actually make a lot more than a hundred million from our so-called free bank accounts. What we want people to do is write cheques, flash their plastic and empty the hole in the wall, because the easier we make it for customers to spend money, the more they will go into the red, and then they'll be paying us interest, overdraft fees and excess penalties. And that's where we cash in.*

*Phillips: To a bank, Melissa, the perfect customer is someone who's permanently overdrawn up to their credit limit and who's paying top whack interest on it every month.*

112

*Borden: And here's another interesting fact for you, Melissa. Our industry research shows that the typical person in Britain changes their bank on average only once every twenty-six years. And if they do change bank, it's usually either because they've moved away from a convenient branch or got married to someone who banks with someone else, it's almost never because they think they can get a better deal on their bank charges.*

*Phillips: So you see, our free banking customers are a bit like tethered geese, we can feed them whatever we like and they eat it all up while we take all their golden eggs.*

*Campbell: I'm sorry I asked now. Pass that Findlays over, Gordon, it isn't all for you.*

# CHAPTER 22  THE FIRM

Janie tried to avoid having to have family meetings. They generally degenerated into a big row, then when she and Sam made the final decisions and laid the law down everyone went away and did exactly as they pleased anyway.

But this time they were all there: Janie, Sam, Jess with Harry asleep on her lap, and Helen who had dragged David down for one of his infrequent but very welcome visits, sitting round the dining table for the meeting that Jess and Sam had called and made sure the whole attended.

Jess wasted no time getting the point. She passed round a sheet of numbers.

"What am she looking at?" Janie asked.

"Our future, Mum. Or lack of one. Unless we do something big, and quickly, Lockwood Hardware is going to go bust in less than a year. Dad and I have done the figures. Look at them, it's all there."

Janie looked, and it was indeed all there. She knew that she had been avoiding the issue and this discussion for some time, but Jess and Sam had shut themselves away for a month and been through everything, and then finally forced her to the table.

It was no surprise though. Lockwood Hardware were losing money hand over fist. Internet shopping was taking a big bite out of their sales. Low cost warehouses had set up on the industrial parks and were selling hardware at trade prices to their retail customers. Chinese-made products were cheap to buy wholesale but shipping costs ate into already slim profit margins. Younger people had less enthusiasm than their parents for Do-It-Yourself, and preferred Get-Someone-In, while the Lockwoods' loyal house-fixing customers of the nineteen eighties and nineties were getting a bit old for that sort of thing and were now worrying more about stairlifts and wheelchair ramps. Even their staff were, like Janie, mostly out of touch with the latest modern household gadgets and gizmos.

Jess and Sam's calculations showed starkly what all this was doing to Lockwood Hardware. Every month, more money was leaving the business than coming in. By this time next year they would run out of credit and be just another business that failed in the recession. It was not a pretty picture.

Janie surrendered without a fight. "OK Jess, what have we got to do?"

"Close our shops."

Janie had not expected that.

"Which ones?"

"All of them."

"All of them?"

"All of them. Even the one you first started with here in Brighton and where you met Dad."

Janie was shocked. She looked over to Sam for some support. She thought back to Mr Hodge, herself the new junior assistant in the second-hand brown coat, Sam the Saturday help, the Sunday stocktakes, the alcove . . .

"Oh, and Dad told me what you two got up to there by the way," said Jess. "That shop too, they all have to go."

Sam looked across to Janie, stony-faced. "You need to listen to what Jess has to say, Janet. You can't keep avoiding the issue and hoping it'll go away."

Janie turned back to Jess,

"OK Jess, go on."

"Mum, we have to change our business completely. Shut the shops. Take over premises on the industrial park. Then instead of selling over the counter, we can employ mobile teams of craftsmen to go out in vans and do work for customers in their homes."

Jess looked around to make sure that she had everyone's attention. She certainly had Janie's. She continued.

"We need to be getting into the 'Get-Someone-In' market, it's growing fast. Because of all those cooking and baking shows on TV, new kitchens are all the rage and people are spending thousands on them and we should be the people doing the work. Loft conversions. Games rooms. Home offices. Hardwood floors. There are loads of older people round here - no disrespect, Mum and Dad - and if they need stairlifts and ramps and special bathrooms, then we ought to be doing those too. Granny annexes. Log burning stoves. Hot tub rooms. All that stuff."

"Really?" Janie said. "Hot tub rooms? Do people have those?"

"Yes they do, and saunas and gyms, and basement pools," Jess said, "That's the sort of thing people are spending their money on these days, not putting up wallpaper and curtains and shelves like in the old days when you got started in the business, Mum. And none of it is work people can do for themselves, so there's a huge demand out there for good reliable fitters to do the work for you." Janie could not disagree with that, it was a regular topic of grumbles at her business lunches.

"And here's another thing," Jess went on, "There are lots of women who want work done at home but don't want a big hairy bloke hanging round their house for days on end, and there are plenty of competent women out there with building trade skills or keen to learn, but who traditional builders won't employ because they're women. So we'll employ them, and being women they'll work harder than the men and finish one job before drifting off to the next. And clean up after themselves."

"OK, OK," Janie said, "So if I buy that, what then?"

Sam passed a slim folder round to each of them. "This is the business plan for turning Lockwood Hardware round," Jess said. "Dad's been though all the costings and can confirm them, can't you Dad?"

"I have and I can."

Jess continued. "What this business plan says is that we need to borrow three million pounds now to buy and equip our new warehouse, workshops and vans and set up our first mobile teams of craftsmen and fitters. Then over the next three years we'll close our shops in a rolling programme, with the worst loss-makers first. Any staff who are due to retire can do that, and we can offer the younger ones re-training to work on the van teams to make sure nobody gets made redundant. On our projections, in three years we'll be back in profit and can start to repay the loan."

Sam added, "I've been through it all with Jess and the figures check out. Can I suggest we each take some time to read over the business plan to see if anyone has any questions?"

Janie leafed through the pages dejectedly, looking at the graphs and tables and trying to come to terms with her daughter's intention to dismantle her own life's work. Helen flicked through her copy in a minute, said cheerily, "Looks good to me," then looked up at the wall clock, she had places to go. David worked carefully through each page in turn, making pencil notes in the margins as he studied the figures and tables. Sam and Jess watched him anxiously and awaited his verdict.

His verdict came. "It stacks up."

They all sat in silence, waiting for someone to say something. At no previous family meeting had there ever been any time when at least one person was not either talking or shouting. It fell to Helen to break the silence.

"Well as I see it, I think Jess's plan makes perfect sense so I support it. Dad's done the sums so he must support it too. David's a total geek and he's checked everything and says it stacks up. And it's Jess's idea. So whether Mum supports it or not doesn't matter because there are already four votes in favour."

Janie protested. "Since when did we vote at family meetings?" But Helen was right, it was just taking Janie some time to come to terms with the facts.

"And since it's Jess's plan," Helen continued, "Jess needs to be in charge of making it happen."

Janie looked around the room again for support. None came. This time it was Sam who broke the silence. "Janet, the rest of us have been talking. We all think it's time you stepped back and let Jess take charge. She knows what has to be done and she can't do it if you're in her way."

Janie pulled a face. Sam was not to be put off. "You know I'm right, Janet. And don't look at me like that, it was you who trained her."

There are times to fight, and times to give in. Janie had no fight left so she gave in. She announced her retirement from the family business and Jess's elevation to managing director, bade everyone goodnight and headed off to the kitchen for a large glass of wine en route to the lounge to find a movie to watch. Helen, on her way out for drinks with her old pals from the bank, stopped her in the hallway, gave her an unexpected kiss, said, "Sorry, Mum, looks like you just got booted upstairs," and sashayed out of the front door.

By breakfast Janie had not only come to terms with Jess's plan, but was enthusiastic about it and wanted to play her part in helping Jess to achieve it. The following week, on Jess's twenty-ninth birthday, she and Sam sat down with their solicitor John Murphy and signed the whole business over to its new owner, Ms Jessica Lockwood.

It was a brutal end to Janie's thirty years in the driving seat of Lockwood Hardware, but there was a consolation prize. Monday's post brought an invitation to see the Queen.

Unknown to Janie, somebody had thought that her charitable efforts were worthy of an honour, and the letter contained an invitation to come to Buckingham Palace for an investiture on a date two months hence, with admission passes for herself and family.

There was an acceptance form to send back, and Janie noted that it allowed the recipient to turn down the honour but had no space on it for saying that the date proffered was inconvenient and asking for an alternative. The Queen assumes that you will come when you are called or not at all. Needless to say, she went.

The day was warm, sunny and delightful. Janie received her gong, a medal on a ribbon and clip, as number one hundred and eight in a procession of a hundred and fifty assorted recipients that day.

Afterwards, back out in the sunshine on the forecourt of the Palace, Mrs Janet Lockwood MBE lent her camera to a passer-by who took a photograph of the whole family all in a line - Helen, Jess with Harry in her arms, then Janie holding up her medal, then Sam, then David at the other end.

That photograph has been next to the alarm clock on Janie's bedside table ever since. It is the final thing she sees before she closes her eyes at night, and then the first thing she sees when she opens them in the morning. And to this day, thanks to Gordon, Melissa Campbell, Charles Borden and Call-Me-Mike Phillips, that is still the last time that her family has all been together in one place.

# CHAPTER 23  THE CONTROLLER

*FRIDAY SESSION DATED 18 OCTOBER 2013*

*Present M. Phillips, C. Borden, M. Campbell. G. Gordon*

*Campbell:* I saw the other day that the Americans have fined some of their banks a billion dollars for rigging electricity prices over there. What's that all about?

*Phillips:* Yes, we've been following developments on that very closely. We've even set a couple of people on to monitor it full time and report back to Charles and me.

*Gordon:* Why, are you lot up to it as well?

*Phillips:* No, whatever our other sins, rigging the price of electricity is not something we do here at RoyalBank.

*Campbell:* That's very noble of you. Why not though, since there must be money in it somewhere?

*Phillips:* There isn't much scope for rigging the electricity market here in Britain. If you want to make money from rigging energy prices, you need to be in a country where there are plenty of short-term power shortages that cause big fluctuations in the price. In Britain that doesn't happen, we have stable electricity prices, a government-regulated electricity market, and predictable weather.

*Gordon:* And in the USA?

*Phillips:* Just the opposite.

*Gordon:* So if the conditions are wrong in Britain, why are you following the story closely here at RoyalBank?

*Phillips:* Because Britain is changing. The electricity companies here in Britain are campaigning to reduce red tape, by which they mean less regulation. We're closing down old power stations and not building new ones to replace them, so the country's getting to the point of power cuts at peak times. We don't even make all our own electricity any more, we have to buy it from France who can cut us off any time they choose. And with this global warming, our weather here in Britain is getting more extreme. All in all, Britain's electricity supply is looking pretty wobbly.

*Campbell:* So does that mean you're now looking at fixing electricity prices?

*Phillips: You might think that Melissa, I couldn't possibly comment.*

The task that Charles Borden had set David was to build a network of people around the world who would, at his request, rig the world's most important financial rates to RoyalBank's advantage. David expected it to be difficult and was surprised by how easy it turned out to be.

David did not need to retrieve the list of names from its hiding place in his kitchen, because every detail was firmly embedded in his photographic memory. To maintain secrecy, he decided not to do any of the work while he was at the office, but waited until he was secure in the privacy of his own flat to do his research into the people behind the names. He started in the obvious place - Facebook.

Banks take a dim view of their staff disclosing confidential information about the bank's business or making unkind observations about their bosses on social media, but beyond that they make no particular effort to constrain their people from sharing whatever details of their private lives they feel the rest of the world would have an interest in knowing about. In fact, Helen told Janie, her bosses found it quite handy to be able to peruse the social media profiles and posts of prospective job applicants before deciding who to drop quietly from their interview lists.

David found that in every bank in the world, whether in the United Kingdom, Germany, Switzerland, the USA, Japan, Singapore, Dubai, even New Delhi, many of the people on his list of names were rather like himself - young, male, hard-working, bright, introverted, with a small circle of personal friends in their own locality, or even none, but with contacts and correspondents around the world united by a passion for some common if sometimes obscure interest. Model railways, superhero comics, coin collecting, sci-fi films, baseball cards, computer gaming, things like that. They are not offended to be called 'geeks' and often use that term with pride to describe themselves, as David did.

Language was no barrier to communication, because English is the universal tongue of money people the world over. David built up a profile for each name on his list, then selected a dozen who were on the most valuable rate-setting groups and who seemed to David to be the ones he might get on with best.

He established contact with each in turn, using his own phone and computer so as to maintain the secrecy that Charles Borden demanded. For each of his dozen chosen rate-setters, he read up on the subject-matter of their interests and became a fellow-expert. David's own obsessive nature helped him here. He was capable of taking any topic of which he had no knowledge or previous interest whatsoever - Australian-rules football is one example - and within a few of weeks would have absorbed every detail and actually developed a genuine enthusiasm for the subject.

He looked for opportunities to go and meet up with his new contacts. He guessed that they would, like him, not be terribly interested in material considerations such as cases of champagne, expensive free meals and wash-traded money. Instead, he arranged to meet them at venues and events that would cater for their area of common interest. With a Canadian model railway nut he went to a major railway modelling convention in Toronto; with a Mexican superhero fan to a Comicon in New Orleans; with the Aussie-rules enthusiast - he was Japanese - to a game in Melbourne. And so on, around the world and in and out of these and other young men's interests and obsessions.

So as to leave no trace of his secret mission for Charles Borden in RoyalBank's accounts department, he booked his own flights on budget airlines and paid all his other expenses using his personal credit card, intending to total it up and bill Mr Borden for reimbursement in due course.

Back on the trading floor, nobody queried David's absences. People at the surrounding desks knew he was clever and busy, but they did not worry about what David was doing because they were too busy thinking about how to make money for themselves.

David stayed in regular touch with all his new-found acquaintances and looked for opportunities to keep meeting up with them. When these opportunities came - and there are plenty of events that service every variety of geekiness - he headed off to renew and cement the friendships. He found that his contacts were always happy to talk openly about their work with a like-minded fellow bank analyst. Like David, small-talk was not their strength, but they would converse happily and all night to someone with a common interest in things they knew a lot about, such as moon flights, baseball cards or rate-setting. David had little difficulty steering them into promising that if as a favour he ever needed them to set a Libor or Forex rate, then as a friend he only had to ask.

When it was time for David the secret agent to report back to Control, he e-mailed Charles Borden's secretary Ann and asked for an appointment to discuss his stock options.

Next day he was back in Borden's office. He noticed that since his last visit there was a new photograph of Borden in hunting gear with a landscape of African grassland behind him, cradling a rifle and the head of a large dead antelope, and another in similar pose with a recently-killed and rather bloodstained zebra.

"David, good to see you, I was wondering how it was all going," beamed Borden as he rose to greet him "Are we ready?"

"All ready, Mr Borden."

"Well done. How many rate-setters did you manage to get lined up for us?"

"Just twelve, but they are all on the most important groups, dollars, yen, euros, remnimbi."

"All men?"

"They are, actually, yes."

"That's good."

"Why?"

"Men are less likely than women to have consciences and scruples. Now, have you got a pen and paper?"

"Yes, Mr Borden." Borden looked askance as David fished a biro minus its lid from somewhere inside his jacket and picked the fluff off its ball point, then from his side pocket retrieved a tatty notebook that he used for reminders and shopping lists.

Charles took a neatly folded sheet of paper from his own inside jacket pocket, frowned at David's tatty notebook, then said, "That'll do I suppose. Right, David, I'm going to read out a list of dates that cover the next three years, each one with two numbers and a currency next to it. The date is when I need you to fix the rates, the two figures are fixes I need for Libor and Forex respectively, and the currency is the currency you are to fix them in. I'd like you to write them down exactly as I read them. Is that clear?"

"Received and understood, Mr Borden."

"Good man. OK, ready to write? Here's the first one. July 16. Up 0.2. Down 0.3. Japanese Yen. Next, September 12. Down 0.25. Up 0.2. US Dollars . . ." And so he continued, until David had the full list. David put his notebook safely away in his pocket. He did not much like the idea of carrying this information around with him as it could breach the operation's security, and resolved that as soon as he got home he would invent a code known only to himself and transcribe the information from his notebook into a coded list that he could safely work from, then tear out and destroy the notebook page.

"That's it, David. Thank you for all your work on this. RoyalBank and our customers are going to be most grateful for what you are doing for us all. Now if you'll excuse me . . ."

David took the hint and headed for the door while Mr Borden made his way over to his desk with his piece of paper still in his hand. Just as he was closing the door behind himself, David thought he heard once again the characteristic 'zzzp' of Borden's' shredder.

# CHAPTER 24  THE MONEY

*FRIDAY SESSION DATED 24 JANUARY 2014*
*Present: M. Phillips, C. Borden, M. Campbell, G. Gordon*

*Gordon: Back when I used to work at RoyalBank I introduced commissions for staff to incentivise sales.  I heard you stopped all that, Mike.  Why?*

*Phillips: We had to.  After the banking crisis, the Financial Conduct Authority brought in new rules to stop banks paying commissions to staff, they reckoned it led to reckless and dishonest miss-selling, perish the thought.*

*Gordon: Pity, it worked well.*

*Phillips: It did, but we've replaced it with a new scheme which gets round it all rather nicely.  Charles designed it so it's best he tells you about it.  Charles?*

*Borden: Yes, it's called a 'staff appreciation scheme'.  So, there's 'a grand in the hand', that's where a manager can now give any of their staff a thousand pounds for meeting their sales targets.  So that's not a commission, it's just staff appreciation.  And every time anyone makes sales over a certain amount they go into a monthly draw for champagne or a voucher for a meal out or a holiday, so that's not a commission either, that's just more staff appreciation.  Also we now review everyone's pay every year and move them up the pay grades if they've met their sales target and down if they haven't.  So that doesn't count as a commission either, it's just a performance-related salary adjustment.*

*Gordon: And how much do you adjust their salaries by?*

*Borden: For ordinary front line staff, the adjustments can take them up to £85,000 a year if they keep hitting their sales targets, or down to £15,000 if they don't, but nobody gets down that low because they'd be fired long before they got there.*

*Campbell: So what you're saying is that you've complied with a ban on commissions by giving staff who meet their sales targets a grand in the hand, champagne, meals, holidays and eighty-five thousand a year, and you cut their pay and fire them if they don't, but none of that is actually a commission?*

*Gordon: Oh Melissa, what's got into you today!*

Jess was uncharacteristically nervous on the morning of her appointment with the man from RoyalBank's business loans department. RoyalBank's business loans were no cheaper or better than any other bank, but Jess liked the 'Honest British Banking' idea, and in any case thought she ought to be loyal to the company who employed her elder sister and twin brother.

In the event the loans man turned out to be even more nervous than she was. He was called Simon, a couple of years her junior in age, slim, short neat hair, thick rimmed spectacles, new suit, old car. He was just out of the bank's training school and this was only the third day of his first week at work. He met up with Jess on an industrial park on the edge of Brighton where she had chosen a suitable warehouse, while Janie waited at home with Harry. They took ages.

Then they came back to the house, and Jess and Simon commandeered Janie's study to go through her business plan while Janie fetched them coffee and cake and hung around the kitchen with Harry, it being her turn to be nervous. After a couple of hours they emerged and shook hands and Simon drove off to meet his next client.

"He seems a very nice young man, Jess," said Janie.

No reply from Jess. Janie tried again. "You two seemed to get on very well together."

Jess reacted this time. "Mum, just pack it in will you. I know what you're trying to do. I've got a business to run and a child to look after and no time for any romantic rubbish. So before you ask, no I do not fancy him. OK?"

The loan was approved. The bank's letter arrived a few days later, and Jess's credit transfer for £3,000,000 the following week. Jess bought her warehouse and was there fifteen hours a day, supervising the work to convert it into her new workshops and depot. Once this was coming along, she threw herself into recruiting tradesmen and women and buying and equipping their vans, and even before there was a sales office she had a member of staff sitting on a packing case at a makeshift desk in the least draughty corner of the building, taking orders for work.

Janie and Sam took a back seat. Sam could not spare any time anyway, his group of care homes was feeling the pinch of the recession and he was often putting in fifteen-hour days too. And Janie had been booted upstairs, even more so when Jess told her she was changing the name of the business to reflect its new ownership - it was now to be 'Jess Lockwood & Co'.

Jess's business plan said that she would reach break-even point after three years, following which the company would start to make money. The terms of her loan reflected this - she was to pay only the interest for the first three years, then start repaying capital when the company returned to profit at that point.

Through Jess's relentless energy her plan stayed on track, and by the end of her first two years her depot was fully operational and she had twenty van crews out at work and a full order book. She was on track with her shop closure programme, and through retirements and retraining she managed to keep her promise do all this without having to make anybody redundant. Janie was very proud of her.

RoyalBank kept a close eye on their three million. Simon called in at Jess's depot once a quarter to check on progress. He did not need to, he and Jess went out on a date most weekends and he could have just asked her then.

*FRIDAY SESSION DATED 3 OCTOBER 2014*
*Present: M. Phillips, C. Borden. M. Campbell, G. Gordon*
*Gordon: I read on the plane over that that one of those big American coffee chains only pays eight million in tax in Britain on a turnover of a billion. That's not much is it, I take it they're one of yours Melissa?*
*Campbell: Of course. We're the best.*
*Borden: How does that work?*

128

*Campbell: Well there are lots of ways of doing it, but if you don't want to pay tax on your business it always comes down to three things - where you put your headquarters, how you buy your materials, and where you put your brand.*

*Borden: Go on.*

*Campbell: Let me give you a hypothetical example. Charles, let's say you own a profitable distillery here in London, turning British water, British-grown grain and British-picked juniper berries into Borden's British Gin and selling it to British gin drinkers, but you don't feel like paying British tax. So you come to us, a British firm, to sort it out for you. The first thing we will do is move your headquarters out of Britain, maybe to Luxembourg or Guernsey, or Monaco even.*

*Gordon: Great, the gin in Monaco's rubbish.*

*Campbell: The gin won't move to Monaco or anywhere else, Gordon. Nor will you, Charles, you never have to set foot in the place. Your entire operation will stay exactly where it is on the banks of the Thames, but there will be a brass plate inscribed 'Borden British Gin' next to dozens of others, on a door to an office with nobody working in it, in a handy tax haven somewhere. That's now your headquarters.*

*Gordon: I've seen those when I take my yacht over to the Channel Islands, there are thousands of the damn things.*

*Campbell: Exactly. Now Charles, all your grain is grown in England but we'll set you up a subsidiary in another obliging tax haven and they will buy your grain for you at the normal market price, then sell it back to you at an artificially high price, which reduces your taxable profits in Britain while transferring your money abroad tax-free. For a fee to us of course.*

*Borden: Nice work if you can get it*

*Campbell: I'm not done yet. We'll set up another subsidiary for you in a different tax haven, this time maybe in the Cayman Islands or Bermuda, and transfer ownership of the Borden's British Gin brand name to that subsidiary, who will charge your company enough in royalties to wipe out all the rest of your profits. By the time we've finished, your profitable Borden's British Gin that has a*

Union Jack on the bottle and 'Made In Britain' on the label will never pay a penny of British tax.

Borden: I'll drink to that. With Scottish Findlays.

Campbell: Your Findlays may be Scottish, Gordon, distilled in Kilmarnock, but it is owned in Holland, as are a lot of our other British drinks.

Gordon: And this just applies to the drinks industry?

Campbell: Good heavens no, it's anything and everything. English-made crisps advertised by an England football star but owned in Switzerland. World-beating medicines invented and made in Britain but owned in Puerto Rico. The water in your tap comes from rain that lands on British soil but the water company is owned in Australia through a Guernsey holding company. Some of our most famous British high street shops are owned in the Cayman Islands and Switzerland, though you won't find too many branches there. Even the company that bought a lot of the government's offices in Britain and rents them back to us is registered in Bermuda and Jersey. And so on. Why pay tax if you don't need to?

Phillips: And your own bonuses?

Campbell: Panama, since you ask.

# CHAPTER 25  THE BILLIONNAIRE

Running old people's homes is not the most glamorous work, but like most of the rest of the staff, from the cleaners to the boss, Sam took pride in serving the community and making life comfortable, or at least a bit more bearable, for their residents in the later years of their lives.

Nor was it easy. As the finance manager for Brighton Care Homes, Sam had to juggle the money to keep a group of ten homes going, maintain the standards of care, and still try to make a bit of a profit for the boss. He found it harder and harder. Staff costs rose every year and ever-tighter regulations and inspection regimes necessitated expensive modifications to old and crumbling buildings, while income from local councils who paid for most of the residents fell as the Credit Crunch and austerity forced them to make spending cuts. But Sam held it all together, liked working for his boss, and looked after the staff and residents in every way he could. It was a very big part of his life.

Which is why he was upbeat when Brighton Care Homes was taken over. He rang Janie up to tell her all about it while she was at home one afternoon, catching up on some paperwork.

"It came out of the blue. The boss walked in at lunchtime, called us all to his office as he had something to tell us, and then he came out with it just like that, he's sold the company this morning and he isn't our boss any more. He said he didn't get as much as he'd hoped for, but the pressure of the business and making ends meet was getting to his health and the buyer was paying cash, so he took the offer."

"Who's the buyer?" Janie asked.

"It's a company called British Care. They're a big outfit, they're all over the country buying up chains like ours. The way they're going, they'll soon own half the care homes in Britain."

"So what do you think about it?"

"Honestly, I think it's the best thing that could have happened to us. We'll miss the boss, but he's right about making ends meet. Hopefully if British Care have all this money behind them, they'll be able to invest some of it in bringing our buildings and facilities up to scratch, better training, better pay, more nurses, all the things we've been neglecting for years."

"Are your jobs safe?"

"No guarantees, that's up to the new owners, but at least Brighton Care Homes' pension scheme is in good health which means we all have something to fall back on one day."

Janie went back to the bills and birthday cards.

She picked up the British Care story in the papers a week later. The company was indeed buying up struggling care home chains, using a £400 million pot of readies that investors had lent to its founder, one Gordon Gordon, known simply as 'Gordon' to all.

There was a profile of Gordon - son of a humble vicar, scholarships to Marlborough and Oxford, rising star at RoyalBank who then left to form his own business. He had put together a group of wealthy backers and was now intent on revolutionising one of the largest and least visible industries in Britain - care homes.

There was a picture of him posed at his desk, looking very pleased with himself, thought Janie, he's put a lot of weight on, he needs to watch that. She thought it best not to say anything about Gordon to Sam, in case he started asking her awkward questions about how she happened to know him.

In any case it did not take long for Sam's optimism to evaporate. Gordon's millions continued to go on buy-outs, and according to the papers he was getting a lot for his money. Brighton Care Homes was not the only chain that was being crushed by the jaws of austerity, and some owners reportedly handed over the keys for nothing, just relieved to get out from under the burden. But none of Gordon's millions came anywhere near Sam or Brighton.

Instead, as the months wore on, there came only cuts. Cuts to the building maintenance budgets. Jess had to lend Sam buckets to catch the rainwater coming through the roofs. Staff cuts, to levels Sam and everyone else though were unsafe for their residents. All refurbishment plans were abandoned. Gardening contracts were cancelled and once-neat lawns turned themselves into meadows, flowerbeds into jungles. Entertainments and trips for the residents were abolished. They could still have televisions, but only if they paid an extortionate rental a year in advance, no refunds if they did not live to see the year out.

And so it continued, and relentlessly. Sam and his colleagues struggled bravely on, forever finding new work-arounds, still committed to the old people who were entrusted into their care.

Then one day, they had a further surprise. On the front pages of several of the newspapers was another picture of Gordon, this time with champagne glass in hand, relaxed and beaming in knee-length shorts over the belt of which his belly sagged awkwardly, leaning back in a folding chair on the deck of his yacht with the Monaco skyline behind him.

The headlines varied, but the Guardian summed it up with "IS THIS THE RICHEST MAN (NOT) IN BRITAIN?" over a piece that told of how former banker Gordon, now the owner of the largest chain of care homes in Britain, had taken a dividend of £1.5 billion in cash out of the company, used £500 million to pay off his backers with interest, and taken the other billion with him to Monaco to avoid tax. The two hundred foot yacht was his celebratory present to himself. He'd named it 'Jubbly'.

*FRIDAY SESSION DATED 20 FEBRUARY 2015*
*Present: M. Phillips, C. Borden, G. Gordon, M. Campbell*
*Phillips: You were all over the papers last week I see, Gordon? How's*
*   Jubbly? Is she luvvly?*

*Gordon: She's very nice, thank you. You must come for a trip when she's ready. You can have a go driving if you like, but you crash it, you pay for it.*

*Borden: And how's Monaco?*

*Gordon: Sunny. Warm. And tax free, thanks to Melissa here. She fixed it all up for me. For a fee of course, eh, Melissa?*

*Campbell: You got us cheap, Gordon, mates' rates, we charge most of the super-rich a lot more than that, to make their tax liabilities disappear. And talking of the super-rich, how is your personal billion?*

*Gordon: Very nice, thank you. You should get one of your own, I recommend it.*

*Borden: What's the secret then, how did you pull that off? I'd love to know.*

*Gordon: It took a lot of arm-twisting to get investors to put up the money I needed, but the promise of a twenty percent return in a year helped. As did the strings you pulled for me to get them onside, Mike.*

*Phillips: Always a pleasure to help a friend. And anyway, it was only a few lunches and I like lunches, especially when you were footing the bills.*

*Gordon: Having hard cash to spend meant I could buy up companies cheap. Say a fellow owns half a dozen care homes. I offer him a million cash. They're worth a lot more than that for the properties alone, but it's too tempting, he can have the cash in his bank account tonight and retire tomorrow as an instant millionaire. So I got a lot for my money. Then on the strength of that I arranged for British Care to take out a loan for £1.5 billion, thank you again Mike for brokering that for me.*

*Phillips: No need to thank me, Gordon, you paid RoyalBank a fee for it. You don't qualify for free banking any more.*

*Gordon: I used £500 million to pay off the investors, which left a billion for me, and with Melissa's help it's now all safely tucked away in Monaco and in my wife's name to make sure there's no tax.*

*Borden: That still leaves the £1.5 billion loan though, Gordon. How's that going to get paid off?*

134

*Gordon: No problem, Charles, I've put a hand-picked bunch of cost-cutters in charge of the homes and told them to make whatever savings they need to pay off the loan, and then keep anything left over for their bonus. That should incentivise them nicely. From all the complaints I'm getting from residents and their families, I know they're doing a great job.*

From time to time when David had a few hours to spare from the many other projects that his bosses gave him, he took a peek at how RoyalBank's gold trading was going.  He was pleased to see that shortly after his trip to New York to deliver Charles Borden's letter to the price-fixing miscreant at NationBank, RoyalBank's gold trades returned to profit and had remained that way for every trading quarter thereafter.

It was only years later when David was in prison that he told Janie about this episode.  As she was then getting Helen to hack her way into RoyalBank's computer archives she asked her to see if she could find any trace of that letter.

It turned up in a computerised archive that had been marked for deletion but had somehow got missed.  Helen printed it out for her, and it read -

*My dear American friend*

*I am having this note delivered to you by hand to spare any risk of its being intercepted.  At my direction the young man who delivered this note to you has been investigating the rigging of the international gold trading prices for the past year, and I am now in possession of a comprehensive file of evidence that implicates you.*

*I now require your co-operation and you have a choice.*

*If you do not co-operate fully with me, I will provide a copy of my entire evidence to the FBI and to the United States Securities and Exchange Commission, together with a witness statement indicating that I am willing to testify against you in any United States court.  You will be aware that the penalty for your crime is thirty years to life imprisonment.*

*On the other hand, I am offering you the option of co-operating with me.  To indicate your willingness to co-operate, you will call the private United Kingdom number shown on the enclosed card, ask for Mr John Smith, a fictitious name of course, and tell Mr Smith that you wish to co-operate with him.*

*Thereafter, you will continue to manipulate the gold price as you have done to date, but you will telephone Mr John Smith the day before you fix the price, so that he may have advance knowledge and trade profitably as a result.*

*In your own best interests I do hope that you will take the option of co-operating.*
*With best wishes*
*Your new English friend.*

There was no practical reason why David could not have opened the envelope and read the letter at any time before he handed it over. It had been in a standard plain white envelope, easily replaced. But David is too honest to have done that sort of thing, and Charles Borden must have known it.

*FRIDAY SESSION DATED 3 JULY 2015*
*Present: M. Phillips, M. Campbell, G. Gordon*
*Gordon:* I saw PCMG got a mention in the papers this week, Melissa. Front pages too, congratulations! All those footballers and pop stars and TV personalities putting their money into films and then getting zapped with a whopping great tax bill. What's all that about?
*Campbell:* Most of our tax avoidance schemes work just fine, I'll have you know Gordon, but I'd be the first to admit that that one has unravelled a bit.
*Phillips:* A bit? More like hundreds of millions. How do you avoid tax by investing in films anyway?
*Campbell:* The British film industry has persuaded the government that Britain has a great future making money and jobs for Britain if only film-making could have a tax break. They said the result would be Britain becoming a mini-Hollywood with lots of new studios and films and jobs in the industry.
*Phillips:* I can't say I've noticed that happening.
*Campbell:* No, because what actually happened is that the government inadvertently opened up lots of new opportunities for tax avoidance schemes. We can arrange for you to invest in a tiny studio and make a couple of low-budget staff training videos, then wash millions of pounds through in such a way that it

137

*looks like you've made a massive loss and generate a nice big
tax rebate for you.*

Gordon: *That's handy.*

Campbell: *Or the one that you read about in the papers Gordon, is not
to make any films at all, but just to rent the rights to screening
a Hollywood movie in Britain, then rent it back to the movie
company. Once our tax experts at PCMG have done their
stuff, you will show a paper loss on both transactions and be
able to get a tax refund that's twice the size of the money you
put up in the first place.*

Gordon: *That sounds handy, Melissa, can I have some of that?*

Campbell: *Don't be a jerk, Gordon, you don't pay any tax anyway.*

Phillips: *How come it's only celebs who use these schemes?*

Campbell: *It isn't, there are thousands of people in them, including
bankers with big bonuses to take care of, it's just that celebrity
scandals sell papers and go straight onto the front page.*

Phillips: *So have the people on the British films tax scheme now got to
pay it all back to the taxman?*

Campbell: *Yes, and they aren't too happy, but they can't kick up a fuss
or it will only draw attention to how much money they've got
and the lengths they've gone to, to pay less tax than their most
humble fans.*

Gordon: *I picked that up. Did you see that spat where that famous
comedian was trying to explain why he only paid two percent
tax on his millions, then that other comedian told him it was
like making a childrens' hospital buy him a pool table? I loved
that bit. But PCMG must be pretty sore about it all. Has it
lost you a lot of money?*

Campbell: *It hasn't lost us a penny. We charged non-refundable fees to
everybody who put their money into the scheme, and now we can
charge another fee to take it out again. So no harm done
Gordon, but thank you for your kind concern. Where's
Charles this week, by the way?*

Phillips: *He's off on one of his big game shooting trips. He spends his
bonus on safaris to hunt something different each year, this year
it's giraffes, he wants to see how many he can get.*

Campbell: *Poor things. The giraffes, not Charles.*

*Phillips: There's a big old lion he's after in Zimbabwe that he's building up for next year if he can get a permit.  Or even if he can't.*
*Campbell: Well then I hope it gets him first.*

# CHAPTER 27  THE KNIGHT

Janie had not seen Minnie for a few years, but ever since their last get-together to settle the matter of redirecting Jennifer Harding's mail she had been unable to rid herself completely of little tugs of nostalgia for the people and places of her youth. In the end it became too much for her, and she arranged to meet Minnie for lunch at Liverpool Street Station.

Over fish and chips and after answering her barrage of questions about Sam and the children and life in Brighton, their reminiscing took them back to Bethnal Green and the time when Minnie had been with her in Maxie Marten's kitchen on the morning of her Dad's funeral.

Janie had asked Maxie, "What do you know about my mother?"

Janie and Minnie had been sitting on bar stools at the little breakfast table, and Maxie in her flowing dressing gown had put in front of Janie a big mug of tea and was now cooking up breakfast.

"What do you want to know about her, Janie?" she had said, without turning away from the cooker.

"Well, everything I suppose."

"OK, wait till I've got your breakfast done, then I'll do that."

Janie had been at Maxie's since the previous evening. Before that, she had been in an armed robbery that went wrong, then in the boot of a car, then in a dilapidated caravan in a field, and then for ten days in a police cell.

The car boot was what she jumped into when Minnie arrived at the goalkeeper's place in an old green Marina in response to Maxie's urgent call. With Janie bumping around inside, Minnie drove for a couple of hours to deliver Janie blinking in the last of the evening light into a small paddock surrounded with overgrown hedges, up against one of which stood several abandoned cars and an ancient caravan. The caravan was in the wilds of Essex and was to be her bolt-hole, and she was glad of it. It had a camp bed, a chemical loo, a tank of stale water and a cupboard filled with tinned and dried food and bottles of beer.

Janie knew her Dad must be dead, and she stayed inside the caravan wondering and worrying about him, Rudy, Nutter and the rest of the gang. She was resigned to staying there for the rest of her life when three days later Minnie was back with a short chubby man of about Dad's age in a black suit, waistcoat and glasses, who offered her his condolences for father and told her that he was her lawyer.

"I don't have a lawyer," she said, "I've made a point of never needing one."

"Well you do now," he replied, "On Maxie's orders. I'm a friend of your father's. Or was, I'm sorry about the news. You're coming with me to Lewisham police station to hand yourself in."

"I thought lawyers were there to keep people away from the police, not to do the police's work by fetching them in."

"I've done a deal," he told her. "They know who you are. They've searched your flat and they're rounding up your gang. They've already got the one you call Rudy and there's a big manhunt on for the one you call Nutter."

"Nutter won't talk."

"No but Rudy or one of the others might crack. If you stay in hiding they will either keep searching till they find you then lock you up for a very long time, or else you will be on the run for the rest of your life. Either way you won't get to be at your father's funeral. If you come with me now and hand yourself in, the police have guaranteed that whether you're charged or not, and even if you're in prison, you will be allowed to go to the funeral."

"What makes you think I'd want to go?"

"Maxie Martens told me that's what your father would have wanted. Now I haven't got all day young lady, please get in the car."

She did, and spent the next ten nights in police custody while they alternately grilled her and left her to stew. But, as is the law, they told her "You have the right to remain silent" and, on the lawyer's advice, she certainly did that. On day eleven, on the evening before Dad's funeral, they gave up and let her go without charge. Minnie collected her and took her over to Maxie's place.

Maxie the goalkeeper was, as ever, on top of all the arrangements. She sent Janie off to have her first bath for a fortnight, and when she emerged, a lot cleaner than when she went in, she had clean clothes her size waiting for her on the spare bed, and a black suit, hat and white blouse also in her size hanging in the wardrobe ready for tomorrow. She gave Janie supper and sent her to bed. "Busy day tomorrow, Janie." Minnie slept next to her to keep her company.

So there they were the next morning, Janie eating Maxie's bacon and eggs and fried bread and tinned tomatoes, Maxie and Minnie nibbling toast and marmalade, all of them sharing the big pot of tea.

"Your Mum," said Maxie. "OK. Well, everything I know amounts to not much. Didn't your Dad ever tell you the story?"

"No. I never asked and it never came up. I wanted to know, I thought he'd get around to telling me, and then all of a sudden it was too late to ask."

"Isn't that so often the case. Well, what your Dad would have told you," said Maxie over the rim of her mug, "Is that when he was de-mobbed from the army after the war, he was mobbed instead with girls, yours truly included. A lot of our young men were lost or disfigured in that war, so those who came back alive and in one piece were in high demand. He was a fit good-looking boy and always had money and was generous with it. He would have been quite a catch. More bacon?"

"No thanks, Maxie." She put more bacon on her plate regardless.

"Anyway, most of his crowd got married and were having lots of babies to make up for lost time. He didn't, he stayed single, though a few of us tried to change that, including me as it happens. Without success. Given what he was doing for a living, he said he didn't want to be responsible for anyone if he went to prison or was killed." She paused, sighed, collected her thoughts, then picked up again.

"One day I went round to his place to take him out dancing and there was a little baby there, in a cardboard box. I asked him what's going on, and he told me that a former girlfriend who he hadn't seen for a while had just turned up at his door, stuck the baby in his arms, said 'This is yours, you can have it' and cleared off. He wouldn't tell me which girl it was but he said the baby was definitely his. That baby was you, I'm sure you've worked that out."

Janie had.

"He had no idea what to with a baby and nor did I, but between us we figured out how to get you clean and fed and off to sleep. Then we talked all night about what to do with you." She stopped, and looked at Janie. Janie was surprised to see that Maxie was crying.

"Go on Maxie, it's OK, I need to know."

"The upshot is, he kept you and brought you up. I was round there to help every day. He took it very seriously, like everything else he did. Planned every detail, he was always very organised, as you know. He used to drop you off at mine on the night before his jobs, with money and instructions for what do to if he didn't come back, then pick you up the day after. 'I've got to go to work, we're going to Auntie Maxie's' he used to tell you."

Janie could remember those visits to Auntie Maxie. She had enjoyed them.

"As you grew up he didn't need my help, you started school, and he was just another father with a kid in tow. I was getting busy with my own business, so I saw less of you, but I still kept a watch over you to see you turned out right, which you did." Maxie tried and failed to wipe away her tears, then turned away to hide her face.

"Thank you, Maxie. I'm sorry if I upset you. But one more question. Did my mother ever come back?"

"Never, Janie. Come on, it's time to get ready."

They cleared the table together, then went to dress for the funeral. At the graveside Maxie had taken one of Janie's arms, and Minnie the other.

"Thank you Minnie, I enjoyed our lunch," Janie said, as she walked her to her ticket barrier. "One day I ought to visit Dad's grave, if you'd come with me?"

"Of course," Minnie said, "Let me know when."


*FRIDAY SESSION DATED 25 SEPTEMBER 2015*
*Present: M. Phillips, C. Borden, M. Campbell, Sir G. Gordon*
*Phillips: Well, who'd have thought it, arise Sir Gordon, congratulations are most certainly in order. How was it?*
*Gordon: Very nice indeed thanks. Met the Queen, tea with her afterwards, then off for a bloody great party to celebrate.*
*Campbell: I read in the papers that it was for services to employment. What services are those exactly?*
*Gordon: Employment. I employ fifty thousand people in my British Care Homes. And before you ask Melissa, most of them are women. Then I support at least another fifty thousand more jobs in local businesses doing maintenance, catering, cleaning, that sort of thing. The Queen was very interested actually, lovely lady, I thought about asking if she'd like to join my board but she might be offended that I've got a yacht and she now hasn't.*
*Phillips: I'd just like to say how nice it is to see a banker, or at least a former banker, back on the honours list. It's been a barren few years for knighthoods for our sort of people.*
*Campbell: I'm not surprised after the way most of you, RoyalBank excepted, led your banks to destruction and made a total hash of this country's economy. Mike and Charles, I'm afraid you've a while to wait yet.*
*Gordon: You could always try the other way.*
*Phillips: What's the other way?*
*Gordon: A nice big donation to one of the political parties. Or all of them, if you want to back all the horses. Political parties are*

*always short of money, elections cost a fortune, and getting one*
*substantial donation from someone like you is easier for them than*
*running months of fund-raising raffles and cake stands.*

*Borden: Is that what you did?*

*Gordon: As it happens, yes. Ten million. I flew the party chairman*
*over to Monaco and wrote him the cheque on the drinks counter on*
*my yacht and tucked it in his top pocket. He went home a very*
*happy man, if a little unsteady on his feet.*

*Borden: Aren't there rules about the size of individual party donations?*
*And banning political parties from taking donations from people in*
*foreign countries?*

*Gordon: There certainly are, my friend. The way round it is to make*
*them a loan. There are no restrictions on political parties*
*borrowing money, so you make them a loan and then just tell them*
*never to bother paying it back. Though I suppose if they are ever*
*thinking of passing a law that you don't like, you could remind*
*them how you could make life very difficult for them by calling in*
*your loan. You boys should give it a go, I'm sure there's a bit of*
*spare money sloshing round your bank somewhere. You too,*
*Melissa, women are very under-represented in the honours list,*
*you'd go straight to the top.*

*Phillips: Ten million is a lot of money, even for RoyalBank.*

*Gordon: Oh, it doesn't need to be that much, I just wanted to make*
*absolutely sure because of my Monaco thing, in case it made them a*
*bit squeamish. The party chairman told me half a million will*
*usually swing it, though you banker boys are in the country's bad*
*books just now so I should think you'd need to up it a bit. I can*
*get you in to see him if you like?*

Back home from a nice walk on the Downs, Janie found that
Sam and Jess were still out at work so she decided to treat
herself to a plate of sandwiches, a mug of tea and a long
undisturbed read of the newspaper, following her preferred
sequence - crossword first, then holidays and travel section,
then the actual news, then the business section last.

It was over an hour later that she read that the chairman
of RoyalBank was standing down and that Mike Phillips was

to take his place, with Charles Borden replacing him in turn as Chief Executive. The paper offered its congratulations to them both, not only on their promotions, but on their forthcoming elevation - Phillips to Lord Phillips of Kidwelton, Borden to Sir Charles Borden - for worthy but unspecified 'services to the community'.

One Friday night some months later, Sam and Janie had long gone to bed when Helen turned up at their front door without warning and without her key. Sam went down to let her in, while Janie turned over and went back to sleep.

About an hour later, Sam came back up, switched the lights on and threw Janie's dressing gown at her. The clock said 02:40.

"Janet, you need to come and hear what's happened to Helen."

Janie could tell from the tone of his voice that 'Can't it wait till the morning?' would not be an acceptable response so she followed Sam down to the lounge, where Helen was sitting eating toast and jam like her mother used to make for her when she got home from school. She was still in her office clothes, and looked tired. Her face was reddened as if she had been crying. She offered Janie the plate and Janie took a slice.

"I'm really sorry you got woken up Mum, I told Dad to wait till morning but he said it couldn't." She pulled a face at Sam, who pulled one back.

"That's OK Helen, what's happened?"

"Well I was working late this evening to get things ready for a boardroom meeting on Monday morning. I'd already worked a full day, then at five I had a glass of wine in the office with the other secretaries to celebrate with Judy, she's the boss's senior personal assistant, she's just announced that she's going to retire next month and one of the other women is going to be promoted to be her replacement. Then I went back to work."

"Just you?"

"Yes, everyone else cleared off home after the drinks. Then around eight this evening I was still in the photocopier room doing copies of papers for a meeting on Monday that people have left to the last minute as usual. It was late and I was rushing and some of the papers started to slide off and before I could catch them they fell down the gap between the wall and the back of the machine."

"Oops."

"I said something a bit stronger than 'oops' Mum. The copier was too heavy to move and the gap's really narrow so I had to reach over the top of the copier and stretch my arm down the back as far as it would go. By standing on tiptoes I could just about reach the papers and bring them up a few at a time."

"You couldn't just leave them there till Monday then get someone to help you?"

"Maybe, but I wanted to go home with it all finished. I was doing that when I heard the door open behind me but I didn't try to look up to see who it was because I was at full stretch face down across the copier, I'd got hold of some more pages that I didn't want to let go of. So I just said, 'Hi, whoever that is.'"

"And who was it?"

"That's the point Mum, I didn't know. I had my arm stuffed down the back of the copier and my face was squashed on the top facing the wall so I couldn't see. Then I heard a footstep close behind me and a man's voice said, 'Well who's a naughty girl then?' and then there was a sharp slap right across my bum. I recognised the voice as Sir Gordon Gordon, he's one of the boss's pals who comes in to see him on Fridays, he's a creep and I normally keep out of his way but I wasn't expecting him in today, he must have been using one of the spare offices. Anyway I tried to pull myself up but all I managed to do was jam my elbow between the wall and a sharp bit of metal on the back of the photocopier. He said, 'Well this is a nice surprise,' then I felt his hand go up the back of my leg under my skirt and onto my bottom and under my pants and he said, 'Hope that didn't hurt. Let me rub it better for you.'"

"I told him to get off me and kicked backwards at him but I couldn't reach him, then I managed to twist my elbow free and get my arm out and stood up and he was facing me with a big horrid grin on. I slapped his face as hard as I could, then tried again but I missed because he stepped back. He was grinning and waving his hand about and said, "I've been waiting a long time to do that sweetie-pie, I'm glad I popped by. Don't work too late." Then he just turned round and walked out of the room and headed for the exit."

Janie said nothing. It was a lot to take in. Helen continued.

"For a few minutes I just sat there on a stack of copier paper boxes, trying to calm down and thinking what to do. I couldn't stop shaking and I felt a bit sick. I still had all the papers to get ready for Monday, but I didn't feel safe bending over the copier any more in case he came back, so I just left the rest of the fallen down papers where they were and copied a fresh set to replace them. I put them in my desk for Monday, then I went home to my flat."

"Why didn't you phone us earlier?" Janie asked her.

"I thought I didn't need to, I told myself I could deal with it myself. But also I was confused. It sounds silly now, but at the time I sort of felt it might somehow be my fault or at least my stupidity to get into that situation. And a bit ashamed, it didn't seem the sort of thing to tell your parents about. But when I got back to my flat I threw up and got the shakes and decided I wasn't to blame and I needed to tell somebody and I didn't know what to do and in the end I just came home. Sorry if I woke you up, by the way, I forgot my key."

It did not take much for Janie to persuade Helen, her story now told, to go to bed with the promise that they would talk about what to do when they were all fresh in the morning.

And in the morning, they were all agreed that on Monday Helen must out of courtesy tell her boss Mike Phillips, then go straight round and report Sir Gordon to the police. Helen made her way back to London and seemed much happier when she and Janie had their usual Sunday evening phone natter.

"How did you get on with the police?" Janie asked Helen on Monday evening, with Sam listening too on the phone loudspeaker. "And how did Mike Phillips take it?"

"He's Lord Phillips now. I saw him, he was nice, and I didn't report Sir Gordon in the end," she replied.

"Why ever not?"

"Mike Phillips sort of talked me out of it."

"Did he? How come?"

"Well, I went in early this morning waiting for Mike to come in. Judy guards him pretty tightly so when he arrived I just pushed past her and stood in his doorway and said, "Lord Phillips, I need to see you right now." He looked at Judy, she does all his appointments and runs his diary pretty fiercely and even he has to check with her who he can see and who he can't. She said 'No way Lord Phillips, you've got people all day.'"

"So he said, 'Sorry Helen, busy,' and went into his office, but I just followed him in and I think he could tell I was serious because he stopped and asked me what I wanted. Judy came in too and was pretty annoyed and said, 'Excuse me, Helen, what do you think you're doing!' but Mike said 'It's OK Judy, Helen looks upset about something, what is it Helen?'"

"I told him it was personal and important and I needed to see him right away and in private. Judy was fuming. 'Right now, Lord Phillips,' I said, and all the while Judy was shaking her head and mouthing 'No!' at him."

"Anyway, Mike gave in and said, 'OK, right now it is, but only two minutes.' I could tell Judy was furious, she went back to her desk and sat down with a scowl on her face while Mike closed the door behind us. He didn't sit down or ask me to sit or even take his coat off, I suppose he just wanted me to say my piece and get out, but I sat down anyway. So he had to sit too."

"Then I told him straight out, I said, 'Sir Gordon indecently assaulted me in the photocopier room on Friday evening. I'm going to report him to the police as soon as I leave your office, but out of politeness I'm telling you so that you hear it from me first. That's all, I'll go now, thank you for your time.' Then I got up to go. Mike looked a bit surprised and said, 'What did he do exactly?' so I told him."

"What was his reaction?" Janie asked Helen.

"His whole attitude changed completely and he started being really nice to me. He told me I'd done the right thing coming to see him, and he appreciated how hard it must have been to do it. He said it was a serious matter and the bank should deal with it properly. He took his coat off and asked me to stay and talk some more about it, then moved us over to his comfy armchairs by his coffee table.

"He called Judy and told her 'no interruptions' and got her to bring in a tray of coffee and pastries, which she did with a sort of 'I'll be seeing you later' glare at me. Then he asked me to tell him the whole story. He was really sympathetic."

"So I told him what Sir Gordon's like and everything that happened in the photocopier room. He was a good listener, I'd been worried that he might not believe me, or make it out that in some way I was to blame, or try to defend Sir Gordon, but he didn't do any of those things. When I finished he told me he was grateful to me for having the courage to come forward. He said I'd done the right thing. That made me feel a lot better. I'd been so keyed up that I hadn't touched my coffee and it had gone cold, so he got Judy to bring us a fresh pot."

"Then he said that as I'd been frank with him, he owed it to me to be just as frank back. He said I was free to report Sir Gordon to the police if I wanted to, and he wouldn't try to persuade me not to, but he said it wasn't likely to lead anywhere. He said he'd seen cases like this before, where someone goes to all the trouble and inconvenience of reporting to the police and giving statements, then the police interview the other party, in this case Sir Gordon, who denies it completely, as I should think he will."

"He said that there are no video cameras in the photocopier room and no witnesses, it's going to be just his word against mine, and whatever the truth of the situation it's never going to get home in court. He said the police will know this from the outset so they'll hardly go about it with much enthusiasm. He said a year down the road I'd probably still be waiting for them to finish their case with it all hanging over me while nothing happens to Sir Gordon. I didn't want to believe all this, but the way he explained it he made it sound pretty convincing."

"Then he told me there's another way. He offered to arrange what he called an independent investigation. He said he'd appoint someone who doesn't work for RoyalBank, who'd interview me and also other women members of staff to find out about Sir Gordon's behaviour. He said he'd appoint a woman to do it, to make me feel safer and more comfortable."

"I asked him how long all this would take, and he said no more than two weeks from start to finish to make sure I wouldn't left hanging around worrying about the outcome. He said he'd make sure that in the meantime Sir Gordon stays away from the building so he can't walk in on me by the photocopier or anywhere else. Then when the investigation report's done, he said he'll do whatever it takes to make sure it never happens to me again."

"It sounds like he's pretty serious about it then," said Sam.

"Yes, I thought about it, and then I told Mike that I'll do it his way. I told him I love my job and I just want to get this whole thing put behind me so I can carry on with my work, only without that man Gordon anywhere near me or the other ladies."

"What happens now?" Janie asked.

"He asked me to give him twenty-four hours to find the right person to do the investigation. He said he'd got someone in mind, he'd call her this morning and set it up for me, and he told me again that I'd done the right thing reporting Sir Gordon to him before I went to the police."

"Then he stood up for me to go, so I did too, but I was all stiff from being nervous and sitting so long and I caught the edge of the coffee table with my knee and the coffee tray fell off onto the floor. It was really embarrassing, there was coffee and sugar and milk and crumbs all over his nice carpet and the coffee pot landed on the cups and broke them. I said I'm really sorry and started to clear up the mess, but Mike wouldn't have it and saw me out of his office. Judy had to go in and clear it all up, you should have seen her face, served her right for her attitude I thought."

"So you're OK then?" said Janie.

"Yes Mum, I'm OK now."

"And you trust Mike Phillips?"

"Sure I do. He's the head of the bank."

Janie was decidedly uncomfortable about Helen's decision not to tell the police about Sir Gordon, but it had been Helen's own choice.  Helen did at least agree that when she met her investigator, Sam would go with her to make sure she was treated properly.

The morning after her coffee tray accident with Mike Phillips, Helen was working at her desk when she took a call inviting her to meet the investigator at six that evening.  She phoned Sam who booked the afternoon off to go and accompany her.  Then at two Janie got an urgent message from Sam to say that he was delayed by more problems at work and Janie should go instead, and giving her the address to go to - PCMG headquarters in London.  Janie set off in haste and with considerable misgivings.

PCMG are housed in a twenty-storey block overlooking the tiny green space in the middle of the forest of tower blocks that Janie remembered as a girl being just another stretch of derelict bombed-out dockland called Canary Wharf.  Through the huge panels of smoked plate glass Janie could see potted trees as tall as buses, arrays of low-backed sofas in PCMG's corporate colours, and Helen standing looking nervous just inside the revolving doors.  Janie revolved in.

"Hi Mum, I thought Dad was coming."

"Crisis at work."

"Again?"

"Again.  He sent me.  Who are we seeing?"

"One of their top bods, she's called Melissa Campbell."

Janie tried and failed to hide her surprise.

"What's up Mum?  Do you know her or something?"

"Your father and I met her once a long time ago.  I don't think we took to her."

"Well she rang me this morning," Helen continued.  "I know her from work, she seems OK and she was really nice to me on the phone.  She said we could meet here where we can be confidential, and if I can make six today she can get started straight away. I told her Dad was coming but I'm sure she won't mind if it's you."

"I hope so. I'd be interested to meet her."

They went to present themselves at the reception desk. Waiting for them was a well-groomed young man with the build of someone who frequents a gym, wearing designer stubble and a slim-fitting suit over a black tie-less shirt.

"I'm Kyle, Melissa Campbell's PA," he said, offering Helen a handshake, "And this is?" he said, offering Janie his hand in turn.

"My mother, she's coming with me."

"Janet Lockwood," Janie said, still on her guard. "Mrs."

Janie received the firm grip of a muscular handshake from Kyle, and he took them to the lifts and pressed for the fifteenth floor.

"I do apologise," he said on the way up, "Melissa's been delayed, she won't be long, I'll take you to her office and perhaps you'd like refreshments?"

On reaching the fifteenth floor, Kyle showed them in to a spacious office with a corner desk, a round table with chairs, photos and certificates in frames all along the back wall and a magnificent view of the terraces of windows that comprised the office block opposite. Helen sat by the table and watched as her mother browsed the photographs and mementoes. A framed certificate caught Janie's eye.

Kyle came over to join her. "That's her award from when she first qualified, you see it's got gold edging, that's real gold leaf, you only get that if you come top in the country, which she did."

"Well done her," Janie said.

She continued to browse photographs of Melissa in the company of captains of industry, shaking hands with celebrities, and launching prestigious women's events in Britain and the USA, Michelle Obama here, Hillary Clinton there, until sounds in the outer office indicated that Melissa was back. Kyle shot out to catch her as she came in though her office door.

"Hello Melissa, Helen Laker's here, and this is her mother Janet Lockwood who's come with her."

Melissa came straight over to shake their hands. "Hello Helen, I'm sorry to be late. And it's a pleasure to meet you too, Janet. Do sit down, please." She did not recognise Janie, which suited Janie fine, so Janie said nothing.

Melissa Campbell indicated the table in the window. Kyle left, the door closed, and she sat down facing Helen across the table.

"So, Helen, thank you again for coming. Let me tell you what I know. Your boss Lord Phillips rang me yesterday to say that you were assaulted last Friday evening on RoyalBank's premises. He said it was a serious matter and that he wants it investigated thoroughly and independently. He told me that he's come to me because I've done similar investigations in the past, which I have, and because I'm independent of RoyalBank, which I am."

Janie had her doubts on that point. She kept them to herself.

"And he wants a woman on the case, in case you'd feel uncomfortable discussing your personal experiences with a man. Lord Phillips tells me that the investigation is going to be about Sir Gordon Gordon, who I know but with whom I have no personal or business connections."

"Excuse me asking," Janie said, "But I've invited myself along to this meeting to make sure that Helen's interests are properly taken care of. If you know this man Sir Gordon, how can you be independent?"

"That's a fair question, Mrs Lockwood. It's a small world and there probably isn't anybody who doesn't know Sir Gordon in some way. So it's a matter of my own professional integrity, and I hope that what I've done for the cause of women in the man's world of business tells its own story. I don't have anything to do socially with Sir Gordon, and I don't even particularly like him. Do I Helen?"

156

Helen turned to her. "I sit in on their meetings, Mum, and it's true, Melissa sometimes has to be pretty sharp with him. I'm OK to work with her on this." She turned back to Melissa who smiled and continued.

"Lord Phillips asked me how long it would take and I told him that including seeing everyone I need to see and writing my report, I can get my investigation back to him in two weeks if I start today and cancel a bit of time off that I was going to take."

"Gosh, you'd do that!" said Helen. Janie could see that Helen was warming to Melissa Campbell. "I'm happy to go ahead, Melissa," she said, "And thank you, I appreciate what you're doing for me, I really do. What happens now?"

"Well, Helen, why don't we get started straight away. Are you free for me to take your statement this evening?"

Helen was. She packed Janie off to a wine bar nearby - there are no ordinary pubs in that part of town - and over the next two hours Melissa probed Helen patiently about Sir Gordon's past conduct towards her and anything else she had heard about him or seen him do. She took notes of everything Helen said.

When they reached the incident in the photocopier room Helen surprised herself by crying but Melissa offered her a box of tissues and reassured her that by re-living the experience she would feel better afterwards. She did.

It was dark outside when Melissa and Helen came to collect Janie and they walked together to the Docklands Light Railway station. Melissa thanked Helen for her help and gave her a friendly hug, and they went their separate ways.

A week later, Helen came back from an office lunch to find the corner of a note poking out from under her keyboard. It read -

*Helen, someone called Melissa Campbell is asking some of the girls here re Sir Gordon. She's not giving much away but there's a rumour that you've made a complaint about him. If you have, good luck to you, it's about time someone did, the lech needs to be nailed. He raped me three years ago but I was too scared to tell anyone. I've heard he's done it to other women too. But go carefully darling, nobody will tell her anything, you know how worried people are about keeping their jobs these days. Good luck anyway, from a well wisher and fellow victim.*

Helen sent it to Melissa Campbell to back up her complaint, and received a reply from Melissa that she had nearly finished her investigation and would have it on the chairman's desk by Friday. Helen carried on with her work and looked forward to never having anything to do ever again with Sir Gordon Gordon.

Jess had finished organising the day's tasks for her van crews when she found a missed call and a voice message on her mobile phone. She played it over. "Hey Jess, it's Simon. I don't think I'm supposed to tell you this, but there are three guys down from head office going though all our business loans and they're going to call you in for a meeting. I don't know what it's about, but you know that saying that goes 'we're from head office and we're here to help you' - well I don't think they are here to help you.  Just so you're forewarned. Hope it all goes OK, let me know, bye."

Sure enough, later that day Jess took another call, telling her to present herself the next afternoon at some RoyalBank offices in Croydon in south London for an urgent meeting to discuss her loan.  In view of Simon's warning she phoned Sam and asked him to come too, but he was tied up with yet another staff shortage crisis at one of his care homes so Janie had to go in his place.

Jess and Janie arrived at the appointed hour and were shown into a meeting room, where three men were seated at the far side of a large conference table.  None of them stood up, and Janie noticed they all had coffee but offered their guests none.

"I'm Mr Brading from RoyalBank," said the man in the centre.  He was in his forties, tall, broad, unbuttoned pinstripe suit, chunky gold watch.  "This is my colleague Mr Sandy."  He indicated the man on his right, mid thirties, leaning back in his chair, tie off, and who had Jess Lockwood & Co's loan file and a smartphone in front of him on the table.  "And this is Mr Patrick, from our partners at PCMG." He indicated to his left, a man who looked too young have left school, slim-fit suit buttoned up tight, with tousled boyish ginger hair over studious-looking black rimmed spectacles, who was tapping at an open laptop computer.

Jess and Janie said "Good morning."  The men didn't.

"Sit down." They sat down, facing the men across the table and waiting to see what Mr Brading had to say.

"We're from RoyalBank's Local Business Support Unit, which has been set up to offer practical help to local businesses that have loans from our bank, and who are running into difficulties. We're here to help your business, Mrs Spencer."

"It's Ms Lockwood now. And we are not running into difficulties and I don't need any help," said Jess.

"We believe you do, Ms Lockwood." he said, "We have assessed your business and there are a number of risk factors which it would be irresponsible of us to ignore."

"Such as?" asked Jess.

"Your loan repayments. Two years ago you borrowed three million pounds from our bank. How much of that has Ms Lockwood paid back, Mr Sandy?"

Mr Sandy was scrolling his smartphone and said, without looking up, "Zero."

"Excuse me!" said Jess. "Read our loan application, I can see it there right in front of you on the table, it says we'll be making just the interest payments for the first three years while we restructure the business, then we start paying off the loan in year four. Look at it, it's on page ten."

Mr Brading did not look at page ten, or even open his file.

Jess pressed on. "Your bank had my business case when you gave me the loan so you knew about it then. And I haven't missed a single interest payment, just check and you'll see!"

"That's as maybe," said Mr Brading, "But the fact remains that you owe the bank three million pounds and have paid nothing off. Next problem - your staff salary costs."

"And what's wrong with those?" asked Jess.

"Much too high. You're running at a loss, people cost money, and you've got too many people."

"That's all in the business plan too," said Jess. "Page eight. We're employing exactly the number of staff that we projected in the business plan. We have a big payroll just now because we still have people working in the shops that we haven't closed yet, while in the meantime we've had to recruit extra people to build up our new fitting business. And by the way, we employ women, you ought to try that sometime."

Mr Brading pursed his lips. "Well you need to do better. Then another big problem is the valuation of your business. This recession has reduced the value of a lot of local businesses. Customers now have less money to spend."

"Not ours," said Jess. "Most of our customers are retired or quite well-to-do and haven't been affected too much by the recession."

"Also," continued Mr Brading, "The recession has pushed property prices down, which means your shops and depot are worth a lot less than when they were valued for your loan."

"That's rubbish too," said Jess, "Commercial property prices along our part of the south coast have held up and whenever we sell a vacant shop we are getting the price we expected."

Mr Brading pushed on regardless. "The upshot, Ms Lockwood, is that we have revalued your business. What's the new value, Mr Sandy?"

Mr Sandy, without lifting his eyes from his phone, said, "Was three million, now one million."

"Well then as I see it, Ms Lockwood," said Mr Brading, "You own a local business that owes RoyalBank three million but is only worth one million, your payroll is much too big and you haven't paid us a penny back in two years. We are the Local Business Support Unit, and that's why you need our support."

"Mr Brading, that is absolute rubbish," said Jess. "We are exactly where our business plan says we should be, we've paid our interest on the nail every month, and in a year's time we'll be in profit and starting to pay off our loan. And as for your new valuation, you've got to be joking. I'll find another bank to value it properly, get a loan from them, pay yours off and never go near RoyalBank ever again." Jess was not going to give up easily.

"You can try if you like," said Mr Brading, "But you'll be wasting your time. Mr Sandy?"

Still without acknowledging Jess, and sounding a little bored, Mr Sandy said, "Because any bank that is thinking of lending you money will of course check with us first, and we will naturally be obliged to share with them all of our concerns about the poor state of your business."

Mr Brading picked up again, leaning forward over the table as he did so. "As a result of which they won't touch you with a bargepole. Do I make herself clear, Ms Lockwood? Now, let's get back to the point, we are the RoyalBank Local Business Support Unit and you are going to have our support."

Jess sank back into the seat beside Janie. "What sort of support?"

Mr Brading replied, "Mr Patrick here is a business consultant for PCMG, who are a very big accountancy firm who I am sure you have heard of. He will review your business and tell you what you need to do to turn it round."

Jess was deeply unimpressed. "And what can he tell me about my own business that I don't already know?"

She turned on Mr Patrick and pointed a finger straight at him. "Go on, why would I want any recommendations on how to run my own business from you or anyone like you? Well?"

"Because," said Mr Brading, "If you don't accept our help then we will have to conclude that you have rejected professional advice about how to rescue your failing business, and RoyalBank will cancel your loan with immediate effect. Then, unless your family has three million in its back pocket, the bank will take over your company and you will join the rest of your staff at the back of a very long queue at the

Brighton Jobcentre. Do I make herself clear, Ms Lockwood?"

Jess turned to Janie with a look of appeal. Janie actually had five million in her back pocket, or at least in Jennifer Harding's back pocket, but it was going to stay there, come what may. To produce it now would surely invite curiosity, then investigation, then discovery and then ruin. Nor did she want this tainted money anywhere near her family or Jess's business, however desperate the situation. In the back pocket it would have to stay.

"I think you're going to have to take the business review," Janie told her. "If you don't you'll lose your loan. Besides, who knows, PCMG might come up with some good ideas that you haven't thought of, you never know."

Jess reflected for a while, Mr Sandy read his phone messages, Mr Patrick made notes on his laptop, and Mr Brading just drummed his fingertips impatiently on the table and studied his watch.

"OK, I'll have the business review," she said.

"There's a good girl," said Mr Brading.

"You pat- . ." Janie put her hand firmly on Jess's shoulder, which is probably all that stopped her from leaping over the table and strangling Mr Brading. Nobody has called Jess Lockwood a 'good girl' since she was ten, but Janie felt that if she completed her sentence - "-ronising bastard" - then the meeting might come to a premature and unconstructive end.

Mr Brading, unruffled by his close escape, continued. "How much is the consultancy fee, Mr Sandy?"

"Ten percent of the loan value, three hundred thousand pounds. In advance, please. Payable to PCMG, not RoyalBank, they're independent of us of course."

"What!" said Jess. "That's ludicrous. All that just to sniff around, ask a few questions and then tell me everything I know already. And there's no way I've got that sort of money, you've already pointed out that we're running at a loss just now."

"If you don't think it's worth three hundred thousand to save your business, then just tell me," said Mr Harding, making a point of checking his watch again, "And we'll know what to do."

"Jess," Janie said, "I'll get you the money. Mr Patrick, can you give us a month to arrange a second mortgage on our house?"

He nodded, but just then Janie's mobile phone buzzed. She glanced down at the missed call message. It was from Helen's number.

Helen never rang Janie in work time. So when she saw Helen's number on the screen, she stopped listening to the meeting and started worrying about Helen.

"Agreed," said, Mr Brading, "But I must say Mrs Lockwood, I seem not to have your full attention just now." A bit rich, for someone whose colleague had not lifted his eyes from his own mobile's screen for the entire meeting.

"Excuse me," Janie said, "I need to make a call, if you don't mind." Mr Brading looked at his watch yet again and she got the impression that he certainly did mind, but it was too late, she was already heading out of the door. She rang Helen from the corridor. When Helen answered there was traffic noise in the background and she was crying.

"Mum, they just sacked me."

"What?" A car horn beeped near to her.

"They sacked me, Mum. Just like that."

"Where are you, Helen? What's going on? What's all the noise?"

"I'm on the pavement outside the bank. A security man marched me down and dumped me out here. With all my stuff in bin bags. People are just stepping over me like I'm a leper or something. Mum, they lied to me and threatened me. Then they sacked me. I don't know what to do."

"I'm coming, right now. Where will you be?"

"Mum, are you sure? There's a cafe called Coffee Exchange across the road, I can drag my bags that far."

"Wait there Helen.  I'll be with you in an hour.  And don't forget, I love you."

# CHAPTER 31  THE SACK

Janie supposed it would have been polite to have gone back to the meeting room to explain her sudden departure to the men from the Local Business Support Team, and it might have saved some trouble later when RoyalBank claimed that she had 'walked out of the meeting without even the decency of an explanation or apology and never came back', but it did not affect how things turned out in the end.

By the time she reached the Coffee Exchange it was still only late morning and she found Helen at a corner table for four. Three of the seats were occupied by bulging black bin bags and Helen was in the fourth, so Janie had to take a chair from another table. Helen was no longer crying but she had let down her hair to hide her face and was sitting with her elbows on the table and her head in her hands to avoid concerned glances from other tables. This café being the nearest point of refuge to RoyalBank's front door, its staff and regulars had seen the same scene plenty of times before, but Helen was still a matter of interest, curiosity and sympathy.

Janie ignored the onlookers and fetched coffee.

"Do you want to tell me what happened?"

"Not really, Mum, but I will anyway. When I got to work this morning I was called straight in to Mike Phillips' office, he was sitting at his big table with two other men, one on either side of him. He's usually nice to me but this time he was really cold and officious, he just said 'Sit down, Miss Laker' and introduced the other two men, one was Mr Halliwell who's our head of HR, the other was Mr Irving from our legal department. I asked him what was happening."

"Mike Phillips told me that he'd received Melissa Campbell's investigation report and had read it, and so had Mr Halliwell and Mr Irving. I told him I hadn't seen it yet, he said, 'That doesn't matter, to save everyone's time here's a copy of the most important part which is the conclusions' and he gave me just one page with a section highlighted, then read it out aloud. Here it is."

She took a crumpled sheet of paper from her handbag, unfolded it and passed it across the table to Janie, who read the highlighted section -

*"In summary, the allegations made by the complainant Helen Laker as recorded in her statement to the independent investigating officer are entirely unsupported by the evidence. It is the firm conclusion of this investigation that she is a mendacious individual who has fabricated her story for the purposes of her personal advancement and financial gain. In doing so, Helen Laker has placed herself entirely at variance to the values and ethical standards of her employer, RoyalBank. Formal disciplinary action for gross misconduct is recommended.*

*Signed Melissa Campbell, Managing Director, PCMG, Independent Investigator."*

"What!" Janie said. "How can that be right?"

"Well that's what it says," said Helen, "Then he just said, 'Mr Halliwell, over to you' and Mr Halliwell said 'We are now formally constituted as a disciplinary panel to hear the case against Miss Helen Laker.'"

"What! I don't believe . . ."

"Then Mr Halliwell said he'd reviewed the independent investigator's report and drawn up a statement of charges against me. He gave me this sheet." Another crumpled page emerged from Helen's handbag. Unfolded, it read -

*"You are charged with gross misconduct in that you did*
*1. On Friday 5 February of this year, while under the influence of alcohol, physically assault Sir Gordon Gordon.*
*2. On the same date, threaten and attempt to blackmail the said Sir Gordon.*
*3. On the same date, by your negligent loss of board papers, cause a serious breach of company security.*

4. *On Monday 8 February, threaten and attempt to blackmail Lord Phillips.*
5. *On the same date, display abusive and disorderly conduct towards the said Lord Phillips.*
6. *On Tuesday 9 February, make a dishonest and untruthful statement to the independent investigator Ms. M. Campbell.*

"Then he asked me if I had anything to say in my defence."

"This is absolutely ridiculous. They've got no right to do any of this!"

"Well that's what they did."

"It's all made up! Why are they doing this to you?"

"That's what I asked them, but Mr Halliwell said 'This is a disciplinary hearing and we are following due procedure, and I must warn you that you are facing dismissal' and asked if I had any questions. I said 'Shouldn't I have a lawyer?' and he said it's an internal hearing not a court so I don't get a lawyer."

"But they had a lawyer," Janie said, "You told me, it was Mr Irving."

"I pointed that out to them too, but Mr Halliwell said Mr Irving was there for a different reason which they'd come too later. I said 'What about a trade union rep?' and he said 'You're not in the union.' Then he said 'Do you have any explanation for your behaviour?' and I could tell he was getting ratty with me. That's when Mike Phillips butted in and said 'Can we all get on with this please.'"

"This is just unbelievable, Helen."

"Maybe, Mum, but it's what happened. Anyway, Mr Halliwell then told me that I was being dismissed for gross misconduct with immediate effect, unless I chose to accept an offer which Mr Irving was going to make me."

"What offer?"

"Mr Irving asked if I'd heard of such a thing as a Non-Disclosure Agreement and I said I have, in the newspapers, footballers having affairs, TV stars with secret families, that sort of thing. He said, 'That's right, Helen, well I'd like to offer one to you.'"

"But you aren't a film star or a footballer, you're a bank secretary."

"Thanks Mum, not since two hours ago. Anyway, he said I'd have to sign to agree never to disclose anything at all about what he called 'this unfortunate business' to anybody. Not the slightest detail. Not to my family, or my friends, or the police, or an employment tribunal, or the newspapers, not to anybody. Not ever, for the rest of my life. He said that in return I won't be sacked, they'll let me just resign quietly, and I'll get a good reference. Oh, and they'll give me five hundred thousand pounds, transferred to my bank account this afternoon."

"And what if you sign the agreement and then don't stick to it?"

"I asked him that. He said I'll go to gaol for contempt of court.

"I hope you didn't sign it."

"Like hell I did! I told him to stick it up his arse." Customers from nearby tables turned to look. "Sorry Mum."

"Don't apologise, Helen, I'd have put it a bit stronger than that. What did he say to that?"

"Nothing, Mike Phillips just said 'This meeting's over' and pressed his buzzer and a security man came straight in, he must have been told to wait outside the door. He just said 'This way, Miss, if you please' and took me over to my desk, he said I had fifteen minutes to clear it out and leave the building. None of the other office ladies were there, the security man said they'd all been told to make themselves scarce to spare any embarrassment, 'It's normal procedure' he said."

"Very considerate of them."

"He'd brought a roll of black bin sacks, he said he's done this before a few times but never on the tenth floor. Anyway you'd be surprised how much clutter you build up over the years. It took three bags and he had to help me carry them down the corridor to the lift. People were staring at me out of their office doors. He held the street doors open for me, put my bags on the pavement next to me, said 'Good luck Miss, you're not the first and not the last, chin up,' and then he was gone. That's when I phoned you."

The café was starting to fill up for lunchtime.

"It's time we went," Janie said, and shouldered two of the bags, leaving Janie to struggle with the third. They lugged them onto the tube and then the train back to Brighton, where Sam was waiting to run them home from the station. While Sam took Helen to the kitchen to hear tell the story over again, Janie unloaded Helen's bin sacks from the car and stacked them at the back of the garage, then pottered about in there distracting herself by half-heartedly tidying things while she pondered what had just happened, and why. And what she could do about it.

# CHAPTER 32  THE BARRISTER

Janie and Sam never found out how the FBI discovered David's rate-rigging activities, but somehow they did.

Until then, in the two years since his last meeting with Charles Borden, things had run like clockwork. David was actually enjoying the company of his set of new friends around the world, and at his orchestration the international Libor and Forex rates twitched up and down when he needed them to, never by so much as to attract attention but always by enough to land RoyalBank a tidy profit on its trades.

But unknown to David, the United States authorities had penetrated his network and one afternoon when he phoned his three US-based rate-setters the day before a Libor fix was due, his calls were traced and every word was recorded. The three American rate-setters were then hauled in, admitted everything, made statements, and named David as their ringleader.

The FBI put all this in a file of sworn evidence and sent it, accompanied by an international extradition warrant, via the United States embassy in London to their counterparts in the City of London Police Fraud Squad.

The first Janie and Sam knew of all this was one morning when Janie took a call from John Murphy, their solicitor in Brighton.

"Do you need any help?" he asked.

"Help with what?" Janie replied.

"With David, of course."

"What about David?"

"You do know he's been arrested don't you?" he said.

"No, what for?  When?"

"Put your telly on."

Janie switched the television on just in time to catch the nine a.m. news, and there was her son David being led in handcuffs from the front door of his apartment block in London to a police van in the road nearby.

She watched in horror as the newsreader told them *". . . the man is believed to be David Lockwood, an analyst who works on the London trading floor at RoyalBank, Britain's largest bank."* Figures in pale blue head-to-toe coveralls were carrying boxes encased in plastic wrappings from his apartment to a van marked 'CITY OF LONDON POLICE FORENSIC SUPPORT'.

*"Since six o'clock this morning, specialist police officers have been coming and going at the arrested man's flat where he is believed to live alone. A neighbour described him as a nice quiet young man who always keeps himself to himself, and other local residents told reporters that they are shocked that there is an international criminal suspect living among them."*

The picture changed to Sir Charles Borden, speaking from the front steps of RoyalBank's head office, looking sombre beneath a big 'RoyalBank - Honest British Banking' sign and reading out a statement - *"This arrest has come as a complete surprise to us. Given RoyalBank's worldwide reputation for honesty and integrity, we will of course be giving the police the fullest possible co-operation at all levels, and if it turns out that there is a rogue criminal in our midst, we expect the strongest possible punishment for him. Beyond that I have nothing further to say at this time."*

The image changed to a view down Wall Street in New York. *"There is speculation that this case involves the manipulation of key banking and currency exchange rates around the world, and if so then it is likely that the United States will seek extradition of any suspects to stand trial in an American court."* By now Janie was registering little of what was being said, she was in a trance as the words on the red banner line scrolled across the bottom of the screen: "BREAKING NEWS : LONDON BANKER ARRESTED FOR INTERNATIONAL FRAUD, USA EXTRADITION TO FOLLOW"

Janie and Sam spent the next four days desperately trying to find where David was and what was going on. They hit brick walls whichever way they turned. From the City Police desk sergeant all the way up to the Assistant Commissioner, the answer was the same - "Your son is an adult and we neither confirm nor deny the identity of adult persons who may be in our custody assisting with our enquiries and there is nothing further that we can tell you"

John Murphy, being a solicitor, was a little more successful, and managed to extract grudging confirmation from the police that David was indeed in their cells. He managed to get through to someone in authority to make the point that David has tendencies towards Asperger's syndrome which made him a 'vulnerable person' who, according to the police's own rules, should have an 'appropriate adult' to look after him whenever he was being interviewed.

But despite all their efforts, the Lockwood family found out nothing more until it was reported on the news that David had been charged with currency fraud and remanded to prison to await extradition proceedings. But at least they could now go and see him.

Wandsworth Prison is a grim place, even if you are just a visitor. To a remand prisoner, it must be even more ghastly. Sam drove in silence while Janie wept the whole way there and all the way to the visitor wing, where she stopped and tidied up for David's sake. John Murphy accompanied them.

David was still wearing the jeans and sweater that he had thrown on while the police waited to take him out from his flat, and he told them his story - Charles Borden's task, the special assignment, the network, his arrest and interview. He told them that the arresting officers explained all his rights to him but he did not ask the police to let him use the phone because he knew he had not done anything wrong and did not want to put anyone out. He had turned down their offer of having a solicitor present for the same reason.

He told Janie and Sam that at all his interviews there was a nurse present, who was very nice and who said she was there to make sure he was not confused or put under pressure, so at least John Murphy's message must have got through. He said his police interviewers were kind and did not touch him or raise their voices, they just asked questions and patiently tape-recorded his answers, however long, without interrupting or hurrying him. He said he told them every detail that he could remember, which is why the interviews went on for so long, and that he had explained how to find everything they needed on the computers they had taken away from his flat and desk.

He even told the police about the paper in the recess behind the fridge motor - they had missed it in their search of the apartment - and decoded for them his encrypted list of Libor and Forex fix dates that was among the papers that they seized from his cabinet on the trading floor.

All the interviews complete, he had been led out of his cell to the charge desk expecting to be released, and was instead charged with twenty-three counts of fraud, one for each of his monthly interventions in the Libor and Forex rates. He was given a copy of the charge sheet, then brought here to Wandsworth in a cubicle in a prison van.

Visiting time was up. David gave Mr Murphy his charge sheet, to which was stapled another document headed '*Notice of Application for Extradition to the United States of America*'. Janie hugged and kissed David and for his sake kept back her tears until they were out of his sight, while David trailed obediently after a prison officer back towards his cell.

John Murphy is a sound local solicitor with the wisdom to know that David's case was going to be far too big for him, so he put the Lockwoods in touch with lawyers' chambers in London and they engaged a barrister named William Clarence QC to fight David's case. Over the ensuing months Mr Clarence and Janie made many visits to David to piece together his story and prepare Mr Clarence to defend him at his trial. Sam came with them as often as he could, but his work back at British Care was getting to be overwhelming and some weeks he had to miss visits, which tore him apart. On those days, Helen or Jess took his place.

Mr Clarence was not cheap. His fee was £1000 an hour, but when he found out that Sir Charles Borden was to be the main prosecution witness he dropped his price to £500.

"I was at school with him," he told Janie. "He was a nasty piece of work then and I've heard on the grapevine that he hasn't much changed since. I've been wondering all these years if I might face him in a court one day."

And Mr Clarence earned his crust. He fought the extradition on the grounds that if any crimes had been committed, which he was of course disputing, then in view of David's Asbergers' tendencies he needed to be tried in his home country in order to have the care of his family during his trial. The United States authorities contested this and lost, and David's trial for fraud was listed for the Old Bailey in London six months hence.

# CHAPTER 33 THE CASE FOR THE PROSECUTION

"Members of the jury, the defendant has pleaded not guilty to twenty-three charges of fraud. I will now present the case for the prosecution."

In her youth the Old Bailey was a place which Janie Laker, as she was then known, made it her business to avoid, so she had never been there before the opening day of David's trial. The jury had been sworn in. The press gallery was full. There was a long queue for the public gallery, but as David's mother and for court purposes his 'appropriate adult' she had a special pass which secured her a seat at a desk behind David's legal team, with uninterrupted sight and hearing of the proceedings. Mr Cannon QC, for the prosecution, was on his feet.

David, pale from lack of fresh air but looking uncharacteristically smart in the suit Janie had brought in to Wandsworth for him, was seated in the dock with a prison officer behind him. He was spared handcuffs, his guard understood him well enough by now to know that he was not going to run away. In front of Janie sat Mr Clarence QC in his large wig and gown, several of his assistants in smaller wigs and gowns, and the ever-attentive John Murphy who like Janie had never been to the Old Bailey and who was taking detailed notes of everything said and done.

"Then Mr Cannon, please continue," said the judge, whose wig was bigger and gown more colourful than even Mr Clarence's.

"The prosecution case," said Mr Cannon QC, turning away from the judge and towards the jury, "is that the defendant David Lockwood solely and of his own accord, and for his own selfish financial gain, manipulated key international banking rates repeatedly for almost two years, through a world-wide network of associates that he personally groomed, recruited and master-minded for that specific purpose."

Janie jolted upright. What! John Murphy scribbled faster.

"In the course of this trial you will hear evidence," Mr Cannon continued, "That Mr Lockwood was a rising star of RoyalBank, where he was employed as an analyst."

He paused, to make sure the jury were keeping up, then carried on.

"Mr Lockwood was a member of a team that was analysing mortgages in the period running up to what we now all know as the Credit Crunch. The senior management at RoyalBank were pleased with his work and decided that he should get a million pounds reward. This sounds a lot of money, but he had saved the bank from making very big losses and they felt this reward was merited. They put his reward in the form of what is called a 'stock option'."

Another pause. He wanted the jury to stay with him all the way.

"RoyalBank stock options are linked to the profits of the bank. If you have a million pound stock option and the bank doubles its profits, your stock option doubles too, to two million pounds."

He paused for a sip of water and for the jury to absorb this detail, then he continued.

"Mr Lockwood, already richer to the tune of a million pounds, then hit on a criminal scheme to increase his money still further by inflating the value of his stock option. All the world's banks trade with one another and with other investors all the time. Mr Lockwood decided to rig some of those trades to RoyalBank's advantage, bringing in more profit for the bank and thereby boosting the value of his own stock option. To do that is completely illegal, it is fraud, and as a bank employee he would have known that, so he had to act with the utmost secrecy."

He paused to give the jury an opportunity to hate David for being a rich and dishonest banker, then went on to explain Libor, Forex and the rate-setting process - all in layman's terms for their benefit.

"Mr Lockwood's criminal master-plan was to build a secret network of rate-setters in other banks around the world, who at his direction would send the Libor and Forex rates up or down whenever he wanted. He worked on the trading floor at RoyalBank, so he knew when RoyalBank was due to make its largest international transactions, then he used his network to move the rates in the direction he wanted just at the right time to make the biggest profit on those trades. His bank did well out of the trades, unwittingly and innocently, but as a result Mr Lockwood's own personal share option did well too, because that was the whole point of the fraud."

His introduction complete, Mr Cannon took a minute to line up the papers on the desk in front of him, then resumed.

"Members of the jury, having summarised the case against Mr Lockwood, I will now turn to the evidence against him." He spent the next hour introducing his exhibits and passing them round the jury. The stock option certificate, made out to Mr David Lockwood for a million pounds. The list of names of rate-setters recovered from the recess behind the motor of his fridge. Incriminating files from David's desktop computer at RoyalBank, which David thought he had deleted but which forensic computer analysts had been able to recover. David's phone records showing all the rate-setters he called on the days when he fixed the rates. David's credit card statements for the past three years, showing the charges for all his trips to meet his network.

"You will note," said Mr Cannon, "That although his employer provides free business class travel for its staff and covers all legitimate work-related expenses, Mr Lockwood chose to pay for everything himself. There is no possible explanation, other than that he could not allow his bank to know what he was doing."

There were yet more incriminating exhibits to come. David's notebook with the torn-out page, and the results of forensic tests of the impressions in the blank page that followed it to reveal that the missing page contained a sequence of dates, numbers and currencies. A sheet of letters, numbers and symbols, in David's handwriting and all apparently meaningless but which David told the police was in code, and which he had translated for them back into a set of dates, numbers and currencies which exactly matched the impressions in his notebook.

Then there were the FBI transcripts of intercepted phone conversations between David and his three American rate-setters, in which he told them which rates to fix and when to do it, and their signed admissions to setting rates for David whenever he asked them to.

He put these exhibits back on his table and picked up one last bundle of papers. "And this, members of the jury, is my final exhibit. When the time comes I am going to take you through it word by word, because it is in Mr Lockwood's own handwriting and is signed by him on every page. It is Mr Lockwood's full confession."

It took Mr Cannon QC three weeks to present the case for the prosecution. Mr Clarence QC told Janie that that for a fraud trial this is a very short time indeed, and that merely to present the prosecution's case at a trial like David's would normally take at least six months, by which time the jury is tired and confused and has lost interest. He told Janie that this did not bode well for David – the last thing David needed was a keen, attentive and alert jury.

A week before the trial was due to start, Janie had been up to London with John Murphy to see Mr Clarence for a last run-through of David's case. Afterwards, with Mr Murphy heading for the train back south, Mr Clarence invited her across Essex Street for a drink at the lawyers' local pub. He said he wanted to talk to her without Mr Murphy around.

The Edgar Wallace was not quite what Janie had expected for a pub in the heart of London's legal district. There were no comfy old leather armchairs, carpets on the floor, portraits of distinguished judges on the walls or old law casebooks on the shelves. Instead, there were bare planks for the floor, the furniture was creaky wooden chairs and wobbly old tables, the walls were adorned with chipped old metal tobacco adverts, the windowsills looked as if they were shelves in an overstocked second-hand bookstall, and every inch of the very high ceiling had somehow been covered in beermats.

Settling into a corner booth, Mr Clarence drained half his pint, banged his glass down clumsily on the table next to his beer mat, and leaned back against the well-worn oak-panelled wall. Janie could see that he was angry.

"What the blazes was that boy of yours thinking of, Mrs Lockwood? He confessed the lot. Didn't he hear the police tell him 'You are not obliged to say anything' at the start of each interview? I know they said it, because you can hear it on the interview tapes."

"You've met David," Janie said, "He's very trusting. He didn't think he'd done anything wrong, so he just told them everything." But she felt guilty for never having taken a minute of his upbringing to teach him one of the very first things her own Dad the Guvnor taught her - "Don't tell 'em nuffing!" - words of advice that had saved her own skin in the Lewisham police cells all those years ago.

"I don't suppose you can get his interview ruled out of play, on the grounds he has Asbergers?"

"That would have been good," replied Mr Clarence. "If I could get the judge to throw out his interview and confession then I'd be free to attack the prosecution case. But it can't be done."

"Why not?"

Mr Clarence gripped his now-empty glass so hard that his knuckles went white. Janie was worried that it might shatter in his fist.

"Because your Mr John bloody Murphy from Brighton doesn't know how the big boys do things up here in the real world. When he warned the City of London Police that David was a vulnerable person who needed special treatment they went straight out and got that nice nurse to sit in on

180

David's interviews. She'll be able to tell the court that David was treated properly from start to finish, which to be fair he was. Which means now I can't get his admissions thrown out. Thank you Mr Murphy. Not good, Mrs Lockwood, not good. Murphy meant well but he screwed up big style."

Janie had to hand it to Mr Cannon QC, he played his hand well. Alert to the hazards of losing a jury's attention, and with Mr Clarence own hands tied by David's confession, he found a very effective way to present his case.

Instead of burying the jury in impenetrable detail and confusing them with numbers, he told them stories. He took David's twelve rate-fixers one at a time, and for each of them in turn gave the jury the tale of how David found them, how he befriended them, and then how he corrupted them. He did not give the jury bundles of papers and statements to wade through, he just told his twelve stories, each one illustrated from start to finish with pictures on the big screens around the courtroom.

His presented his evidence as if he was giving a true-life crime show on TV. He even put on a voice that sounded more like a television presenter than a courtroom lawyer.

Take, for example, how he dealt with Dirk Krueger, from Chicago. Krueger was BankCorp USA's rate-setter for the Euro/Dollar Forex rate, and one of the traders whom the FBI had trapped and taped.

First Mr Cannon gave the jury a short profile of Krueger, illustrated by photographs lifted from Facebook. Then he showed Krueger indulging his passion, which was ancestry research. Krueger had traced his ancestry back to the earliest Dutch settlers in North America, and was now obsessed with tracking and documenting every line of the Krueger diaspora all over the world.

Working from David's own Facebook pages he showed the jury how David first contacted Dirk Krueger. Their communications started as no more than mutual 'likes' but David was soon telling Krueger about his own life-long interest in the settlements in the Dutch colony which later became New York, and discussing recently published archaeological work and settler's diaries. Janie could see that David had made himself an expert on all this in a very short time.

"This was Mr Lockwood's system for grooming his contacts," explained Mr Cannon to the jury. "First he found a rate-fixer, then he created a shared interest. Now I will now show you how he turned that shared interest into a close friendship."

Facebook messages showed David telling Dirk that he was coming over to Washington to view a collection of early Dutch settler artefacts, and did Dirk fancy joining him? Dirk did, and next up were images of David's travel reservations, plane tickets and credit card bills, and then David and Dirk's Facebook selfies taken in the Smithsonian Museum and in front of all the city's best-known landmarks.

"Having made a new friend, Mr Lockwood then turned him into his agent," said Mr Cannon to the jury. "I shall demonstrate how."

Next came a sequence of graphics demonstrating that for all the dates on David's coded list, his itemised mobile phone bill showed an international call to Dirk's mobile number just before RoyalBank launched several big transactions on the global markets.

The court screens only went blank when it came time for the most telling evidence of all - the phone call from David to Dirk that the United States' authorities had bugged and recorded. David's voice played out around the courtroom, clear and confident and in his English accent, while the other male voice was unmistakeably American. The call was short, and while it was being relayed over the courtroom speaker system the actual words appeared in large black lettering on the plain white screens.

KRUEGER: Hello David, how are you?

LOCKWOOD: Fine Dirk, hey can you do me another rate?

KRUEGER: Sure buddy, fire away.

LOCKWOOD: Eleven hundred hours your time, Libor up zero point two three, Forex up one point six four, both US Dollars to Euros.

KRUEGER: Got that buddy, consider it done.

LOCKWOOD: You're a good pal, Dirk, speak soon. (Rings off).

Then the words on the screen melted away to reveal a blown-up image of the relevant entry on David's decoded list:

*July 27  1100  +0.23  +1.64  $>E*

Mr Cannon left that image on the screens while the voices were played over again. "Eleven hundred hours your time, Libor up zero point two three, Forex up one point six four, both US Dollars to Euros." "Got that buddy, consider it done"

After giving the jury time to let this sink in, Mr Cannon turned to the judge and asked for a short adjournment in order to change the discs to be ready for the next of David's rate-setters. Janie knew by now that this was his way of making sure the jury got a leg-stretch and a coffee before the next stint. There was no way Mr Cannon was going to lose his jury's attention or let them doze off. After the interval, it was the turn of the story of David and his Aussie rules pal from Tokyo.

In this way Mr Cannon took the jury through each of the twelve people whom he described as David's 'criminal accomplices'. By the third Thursday of the trial he was done. And from start to finish Mr Clarence had not risen or spoken once. He just sat and glowered in impotent silence.

The judge gave the court, and therefore himself, a long weekend off, with the defence to begin on Tuesday morning. Mr Clarence whisked John Murphy and Janie up the road to the Viaduct Tavern and bought six drinks because, he said, there would be a rush as soon as the other courts rose and he did not want to be scrumming at the bar. He was furious. He downed his own two pints with hardly a word, then headed off into the rush-hour traffic leaving John Murphy and Janie still only part-way through their first glasses and none the wiser as to how he would dig David out of all this, or if he even could.

There was a lighter side. The Sun newspaper, which prides itself on clever headlines, decided to call David 'Spiderman' because of his alleged web of accomplices and his supposedly sticky fingers. The other papers and TV news stations picked up on this and from then on gave their readers and viewers daily updates on 'The Spiderman Trial'. Sam, Mr Murphy and Janie did not think much of it, but Helen, Jess and Mr Clarence all thought it was quite funny.

# CHAPTER 34  THE FORECLOSURE

Janie made it home before Sam, who was held up at one of his care homes where the heating had broken down and the frail elderly residents were in some peril as sub-zero weather was forecast.  The heating contractors were refusing to do any work until they were paid for all the other unpaid jobs they had done for British Care, and British Care's head office was refusing to release any money because Sam had already spent his meagre maintenance budget.

It was convenient that there was no court sitting and that Janie was free the next day because Jess had another appointment with the men from the RoyalBank Local Business Support Unit.  In any case, as Janie and Sam had taken out a £300,000 second mortgage on their home to pay for PCMG's review, she was keen to see what they were getting for the money.  Janie went up to Croydon with Jess on the train.

The same three men faced them across the same table in the same room: Mr Brading centre, Mr Sandy left, Mr Patrick right.

"Ms Lockwood," began Mr Brading, without even a 'hello' or a 'good morning', "When we last met, you hadn't repaid any of your loan.  I see from our records that despite my pointing this out to you, you've still not paid off a penny."

"And I told you, Mr Brading," said Jess, coolly, "That it is not in our business plan to start repayments yet, and your bank accepted that business plan when you issued the loan."

"And then we turn to the matter of your business review . . ." said Mr Brading.  Jess cut him off again.

"Yes, the review.  Five of PCMG's finest came down for a week and went round upsetting my staff, pissing off my customers and getting in the way of our work.  For which they charged us three hundred thousand pounds.  That makes twelve grand per person per day.  How do you justify that?"

"That is the fee scale that RoyalBank's directors have agreed with PCMG's senior management," said Mr Patrick. "For that you get all of PCMG's wealth knowledge and experience."

"Knowledge and experience!" Jess was out her seat by now. "I followed some of your clowns around and they know nothing about our business except what my staff and I told them. I don't think any of them has ever set foot in a workshop or a fitter's van in their life. Talk about borrowing your watch to tell you the time, they bloody well stole the watch."

Mr Patrick didn't flinch. "That's as maybe, but I believe Mr Brading wishes to discuss the report's findings with you."

"How can he do that?" said Jess, "I haven't even seen it."

"Your copy must have gone astray in the post," said Mr Brading. Janie suspected that it had never even been as far as the post. "No matter, we have spares." He pushed a half inch thick ring-bound document across the table to Jess, and another to Janie who flicked quickly through her copy and saw that it contained fifty pages of text, photographs and charts, together with tables and graphs lifted from Jess's business plan.

"We need time to read this," Janie suggested.

"No need, and no time," replied Mr Brading. "If you turn to page forty-eight, you'll see a section headed 'Conclusions'. Mr Sandy, perhaps you will read that section out?"

Mr Sandy put down his phone for the first time in their two meetings, picked up his copy of the PCMG report, leaned casually back in his seat, and read, in a tone that managed to sound both bored and hostile at the same time:

"*Conclusion. The authors of this report, having reviewed the business of Jess Lockwood & Co, conclude that there is no realistic prospect of the company improving its trading results or its commercial value.*"

Mr Brading sat forward with his elbows on the table, his chin on his thumbs and his fingertips together. "No realistic prospect of the company improving its trading results or commercial value," he repeated. "Which means we are going to have to cancel your loan."

"You can't do that, surely?" said Jess. "Don't you have to give us time to get other funding? Sell off assets? Merge with somebody and at least save our staff's jobs?"

"You could have done all that six months ago after our last meeting, you had the opportunity then but you didn't take it," said Mr Brading. "You had your warning. Your time is now up." He took a sheet of paper out of his case and pushed it across to Jess. She read it then handed it to Janie. It was a letter bearing the RoyalBank crest, addressed to Ms J. Lockwood, Managing Director, Jess Lockwood & Co of Brighton. It was headed 'Notice of Foreclosure', and above Mr Brading's signature were three short paragraphs.

The first paragraph informed the addressee that in view of the fact that the business was worth significantly less than the value of its loan, RoyalBank was cancelling its loan.

The second gave the addressee a week to repay three million pounds to RoyalBank.

The third said that in default of this payment the business would be placed into PCMG's administration and all its assets would forthwith become the property of the RoyalBank Local Business Support Unit.

She handed the letter back to Jess.

"You bastards," Jess said. "You're stealing my business. The business that my mother built up for thirty years. A business that gives jobs to a hundred people. You're just thieves."

"And you, my dear," said Mr Brading, "Have a problem with your attitude. As does your mother, who I recall walked out of our last meeting without even the decency of an explanation. This meeting is over. We have another Local Business Support client waiting."

On the train on the way home, Jess did not want to talk so Janie did not make her. In fact Jess only spoke once all the way back. "I'm really sorry Mum," is all she said. Janie did not know how to reply, so she kept silent. Besides, she was too busy thinking.

# CHAPTER 35  THE WITNESS

At the Old Bailey Mr Clarence QC was waiting for Janie in the public lobby. He pulled her over to the quietest available spot, an alcove beside the pillars next to the main doors.

"I've been working on David's case all weekend, Mrs Lockwood," he said, his face close to her ear to overcome the hubbub of voices and footsteps as people crowded past, "And I've come to the conclusion that this whole case turns on Charles Borden. He's the lying piece of scum who set your David up from start to finish, used him to make himself and RoyalBank rich, and is now leaving him to hang for it."

"What does that mean for David?" Janie asked.

"It means that I'll call just one witness. I'm going to put Charles Borden in the witness stand. But by rights he's the man who should have been in the dock, not your David."

"What are you going to say to him?"

"I only told the court yesterday afternoon that I need him here this morning, which means hopefully he hasn't had time to prepare. He'll have to swear on oath to tell the truth. Then I'm going to get him to lie. One lie is all I need. If I can catch him out just once, then I can start to open him up and expose all his other lies."

"And if you can't?"

"If I can't, Mrs Lockwood, then quite frankly David is sunk. So wish me luck."

"Good luck, William," she said, as he moved off towards the lawyers' entrance, "But I hope you don't need it."

John Murphy scribbled furiously and continuously from the moment Sir Charles Borden took the witness stand to the time the judge discharged him. Here is what he wrote:

*Court usher calls Sir Charles Borden. Borden enters court, is shown to witness box. Usher gives Borden Bible and laminated card. Borden stands, holds up Bible and reads from card.*

*Borden: I swear by almighty God that the evidence I give shall be the truth, the whole truth and nothing but the truth.*

*Court clerk: Would you identify yourself to the court please.*

*Borden: I am Sir Charles Borden, Chief Executive of RoyalBank, based at the bank's headquarters in London.*

*Judge: Sir Charles, Counsel for the Defence will put some questions to you.*

*Clarence QC: Thank you my lord. Sir Charles, would you to give the court an outline of your career to date and an overview of your current responsibilities at RoyalBank.*

*Borden: I joined RoyalBank in 1979 and was first posted to the bank's Channel Islands business. I was promoted through a number of the Bank's investment divisions in the United Kingdom and five years ago I joined the board as Director of Investment Banking. Earlier this year I was appointed Chief Executive.*

*The Judge: Congratulations on your recent promotion, Sir Charles, I read about it in the Telegraph.*

*Borden: Thank you my lord.*

*Clarence: Sir Charles, in the dock you will see one of your former employees, the defendant Mr David Lockwood. Do you know Mr Lockwood?*

*Borden: Yes I do.*

*Clarence: And can you recall when you first met him?*

*Borden: Yes, I can. David Lockwood came to us some years ago for work experience and impressed his supervisors who recommended that we take him onto the staff, so I appointed him as a temporary trainee analyst in my division.*

*Clarence: And did you have a special task for Mr Lockwood?*

*Borden: Yes I did. At that time I was running the team who traded precious metals. The gold trading team was repeatedly failing to make deals at the best prices. I asked David to analyse our gold trading and see if he could spot anything that they could do better.*

*Clarence: Why did you choose David for this task?*

*Borden: He was new, and I thought his fresh eyes might be best for this task. Also, I knew that in due course I would need to either confirm or terminate his temporary employment, and this was an opportunity to test him out.*

*Clarence: Did you ask David to do this job in secret, without telling anyone else, and to report solely to you in person?*

*Borden: Yes.*

*Clarence: Is it normal for your bank to give its analysts clandestine tasks of this nature?*

*Borden: No.*

*Clarence: Then surely the jury would be entitled to find it highly suspicious that you operated in such a devious way?*

*Borden: I admit that it was devious but there was a good reason. It was because I couldn't rule out the possibility that someone in our own bank was trading dishonestly and I needed both David's fresh perspective and his secrecy if I was to find out.*

*Clarence: I see. And what did Mr Lockwood find out?*

*Borden: In the event he did a good job but he didn't find anything. Our rivals must just have been a bit smarter than us at that time. Banking is a highly competitive business.*

*Clarence: And what happened to Mr Lockwood?*

*Borden: I thanked him and he moved on to other tasks, but I was impressed by the work he'd done for me so I made his appointment permanent. Which I now regret, of course.*

*Clarence: Isn't there a rather important detail about David Lockwood and the gold trading task that you have not told the jury?*

*Borden: Not as far as I know, no.*

*Clarence: If I say 'NationBank of New York', will that jog your memory?*

*Borden: Not in any way, no.*

*Clarence: Then if you won't tell the jury, I will have to. David Lockwood did not come back from his task and tell you that he had found nothing. The truth is, he told you that he had worked out that a particular trader at NationBank in New York was rigging the international gold price and that RoyalBank was losing out as a result.*

*Borden: I have absolutely no recollection of that.*

*Clarence: And furthermore, you then sent David Lockwood over to New York to see this trader to threaten to shop him to the FBI unless he cut you and RoyalBank in on the deal.*

*Borden: That is totally untrue.*

*Clarence: As an analyst, David Lockwood has a particularly good memory for detail and he can recall your actual words, which were, "I want you to go over and see this Yankee clown from NationBank and tell him we've rumbled his little game." Then you gave David a sealed envelope to give to this American. That is the truth, isn't it, Mr Borden?*

*Borden: It is totally untrue.*

*Clarence: So what I am asking myself, Mr Borden, is what could have been in the envelope that you, RoyalBank's head of gold trading, gave to David Lockwood, and that David then gave on your behalf to an American banker who you knew was rigging the gold trading rate? Could it have been a Christmas card? Or a Marks and Spencer's gift voucher? Or was it some sort of note from you to him, with instructions on how to cut you in on his swindle? Which was it, Mr Borden?*

*Borden: None of those, because it didn't happen.*

*Clarence: The truth of the matter, Sir Charles, is that David Lockwood's account of what you said and did is true and shows that, notwithstanding your distinguished and senior position at the head of one of the world's largest banks, you are a liar.*

*Borden: On the contrary, this episode exposes Mr Lockwood as the liar, willing to invent whatever fairy tale he thinks will get him off the hook. For all the damage he has caused RoyalBank, I repeat that I now deeply regret hiring him, and I am only glad that in the interests of British justice and the good reputation of the bank I lead, he has now been caught and exposed for what he is - a dangerous and dishonest fantasist.*

*Judge: Thank you Sir Charles, the court will adjourn for fifteen minutes.*

From John Murphy's notes:

*Court resumes. Clerk reminds Borden that he is still on oath to tell the truth. Mr Clarence QC stands.*

Clarence: Sir Charles Borden, are you a liar?

Borden: No I am not. I have sworn on the Bible to tell the truth to this court. I do not tell lies.

Clarence: Five years ago, you took David Lockwood out for a meal, just the two of you. Do you recall that?

Borden: I do, Yes.

Clarence: Would you tell the court about that meal, please.

Borden: It was at L'Escargot Jaune, a restaurant in Mayfair that was a favourite of mine at the time. I don't recall what we ate, but I do believe Mr Lockwood and I had a good meal and a pleasant evening. I recall it was his birthday.

Clarence: Presumably it is too long ago to ask you to remember what the bill came to, but can you help the court with an approximate figure?

Borden: With pre-dinner drinks and wine, which I recall we both had, I should it imagine it would have been close to four hundred pounds.

Clarence: And who paid?

Borden: I would have paid the bill using my credit card.

Clarence: If I were to obtain a record of your expenses claims for the period in question, would I find an item on it for around four hundred pounds at L'Escargot Jaune?

Borden: Yes.

Clarence: And would your expenses claim for a meal and drinks for four hundred pounds indicate that your guest was a fellow member of your own bank?

Borden: No.

Clarence: Then what would it say?

Borden: It would say that I was entertaining corporate clients.

Clarence: And would you like to enlighten the jury as to why your expenses claim showed that you were entertaining corporate clients when in fact you were just having a very expensive birthday meal washed down with a lot of wine, with a colleague from your own bank?

Borden: It was because our rules state that bank staff can only claim expenses for legitimate entertainment of clients, not for meals or drinks bought for our own colleagues.

Clarence: So your expenses claim was false?

Borden: Yes it was.

Clarence: You admit that?

Borden: Yes. It was a false claim.

Clarence: And this was surely not the only time you wined and dined with colleagues, then put them down as 'clients' on your expenses claims?

Borden: No, I did it routinely.

Clarence: So when you regularly falsified your expenses claims, you wrote lies in them. Then you signed them as the truth.

Borden: I did.

Clarence: Earlier, Sir Charles, you told this court that you are not a liar and that you do not lie. But now we know that you lied, to your own bank, on your own admission, and not just once but repeatedly. I ask you again, Mr Borden, are you a liar?

Borden: It is quite true that I lied on my expenses claims. It was a custom that was widespread at the time, though I accept that that is no excuse. I am deeply embarrassed and regretful about my part in it. However, when Mike Phillips became our Chief Executive he launched a set of reforms across the whole of RoyalBank under the title 'Honest British Banking', and I reflected on my own conduct and decided from then on only to claim legitimate expenses, and to ensure that everyone under my authority does likewise.

Clarence: That's as may be, Sir Charles, but you still stand exposed in this courtroom as a witness who is a liar.

Borden: On the contrary, I have just shown that I will tell the jury the honest and plain truth, however painful it may be to me personally. I took an oath to tell the truth to this court and I will not waver from that.

(Court adjourned)

# CHAPTER 36  THE TRUTH, AND NOTHING BUT THE TRUTH

The TV and papers, already making the most of the 'Spiderman Trial', gave plenty of gleeful coverage to Charles Borden's admissions of serial expenses fiddling. Members of Parliament, who had recently been hauled over the coals on the same charge, must have enjoyed their respite.

However, it was not his expenses claims that really did for Charles Borden's public profile, but a dead rhinoceros. There appeared from somewhere a colour photograph of Borden and his latest kill. Initially it made its way around the internet but then it burst onto the front pages of the national papers. Under headlines that were all variations on 'BANKER MAKES A KILLING' there was Borden wearing hunting gear and a big smile, proudly sitting on the huge head and neck of the adult female rhinoceros that he had just killed, while its lifeless torso and legs lay slumped behind on the dust.

Such was the public outpouring of hatred and scorn in his direction that when the court resumed, the Judge had to remind the jury that they were duty-bound to disregard anything they had read about Sir Charles Borden and set aside any personal feelings they may have about him, and decide the case only on the evidence put before them. But from then on the fight to the death between 'Spiderman' and 'The Killer Banker' was daily headline news.

Taken from Mr Murphy's notes:

*(Court resumes. Charles Borden in the witness box. Mr Clarence QC examining for the Defence.)*
*Clarence: If you wanted to speak with David Lockwood, you could have just asked him up to your office. Would you tell the court why you took him out for the meal at L'Escargot Jaune?*

*Borden: Partly it was to get to know him better. I knew he was shy and I thought he might be more at ease away from the bank environment, with a meal and some wine to relax him.*

*Clarence: And the other reason?*

*Borden: I wanted to discuss a sensitive task with him, away from curious ears.*

*Clarence: What was this sensitive task?*

*Borden: I was hearing rumours that other banks were rigging some of the international Libor and Forex rates that we use to exchange currency and do business with each other. I wanted David to take a good look at all these rates and tell me if there was any foundation to the rumours. I needed him to do it confidentially, just in case, heaven forbid, anyone from our own bank was implicated.*

*Clarence: Why did you choose David for this task.*

*Borden: I knew him from his previous good work on gold pricing, and my colleagues told me that he had recently done an excellent job analysing mortgage markets.*

*Clarence: When he completed the task for you, what did he find?*

*Borden: He told me that on the basis of his work, he suspected that staff at a number of banks were indeed involved in rate-rigging, but that from the data available to him it wasn't possible to pin down who it was. He was able to reassure me however that there was no evidence of any malpractice on the part of any RoyalBank colleagues.*

*Clarence: What happened next?*

*Borden: I told David that I was grateful for his work, which I was, and he returned to his normal duties as an analyst.*

*Clarence: Around this time, you gave David Lockwood a stock option for one million pounds. How common is it for a bank to give stock options to junior staff.*

*Borden: Quite rare, I believe.*

*Clarence: Have you ever known it to happen before?*

*Borden: Not that I recall.*

*Clarence: Let us get this clear, Sir Charles. The bank gave a stock option to a junior employee, which is something you have never known before, and it was worth a million pounds. And you gave it to him just after he had undertaken a secret task that nobody but you knew about. That's very suspicious, isn't it Sir Charles?*

Borden: *No, there is a perfectly rational explanation for the stock option.*

Clarence: *I'm sure there is, and I am going to tell you what it is. David Lockwood was not, as you have told this court, unable to pinpoint the people who were rigging rates. The truth is that he identified all the operators in other banks who were manipulating the rates, and passed you a list of them as you walked by his desk one day. The court has already heard that a duplicate of this list was recovered from his apartment.*

Borden: *That is nonsense.*

Clarence: *Then shortly afterwards, you called David Lockwood up to your office, where you thanked him for his secret work on your task and gave him the stock option. Then you told him to set up a network of people who would rig rates on your behalf. At the end of the meeting you put his list of names through your office shredder to destroy the evidence. Sir Charles, would you explain to the jury why you did all that?*

Borden: *I don't have to, because I did none of that. David Lockwood's work on rate-fixing was useful but inconclusive and he gave me no list of names and I gave him no further instructions. Rigging Libor and Forex rates is a serious crime, and if Mr Lockwood had given me names of culprits I would have had no hesitation in reporting them to the authorities.*

Clarence: *Sir Charles Borden, you are lying. The only plausible explanation of the stock option is that you gave it to David Lockwood in order to link his future wealth to the profits of the bank so that you could make him the scapegoat if you and your fellow directors later got found out rigging the rates. That is the real truth isn't it, Sir Charles?*

Borden: *That is a preposterous accusation, and totally untrue.*

Clarence: *Then how else, Sir Charles, do you explain your extraordinary action in awarding a million pound stock option to an analyst who earns less than forty thousand pounds a year?*

Borden. *Gratitude and self-interest. Gratitude for his exceptional work on mortgages, which saved RoyalBank's shareholders from serious losses during the banking crisis. And self-interest, to stop other banks poaching our most talented analyst. The truth is as simple as that.*

*(Court adjourns for ten minutes. Resumes.)*

*Clarence: Sir Charles, did David Lockwood come to see you in your office some time later?*

*Borden: Yes.*

*Clarence: What about?*

*Borden: He wanted to see me about his stock option, for some advice about what to put on his tax form I believe.*

*Clarence: Sir Charles, that's not true is it? What really happened is that you arranged for David to tell you he wanted to discuss his stock option as a code for telling you he had your network of rate fixers ready. You called him up to your office and read out a list of the dates and times when you wanted him to fix the rates, and by how much and in which currencies. You got him to write these details out himself in his notebook so they'd be in his own handwriting, and you shredded your own copy to destroy the evidence that linked it back to you..*

*Borden: Not true.*

*Clarence: But it is true, Sir Charles. And then you ordered him to execute those fixes through the network that he'd set up for you. And on each of those dates you put through all the bank's biggest trades, at the highest profits, in order to boost your own and the other directors' bonuses. That's what really happened, isn't it?*

*Borden. It is not. None of that happened.*

*Clarence: Then how do you account for the fact that an encoded list of dates and fixes was found in David Lockwood's desk, and that on each of the dates on that list, RoyalBank made major trades that benefited profitably from exactly the rate shifts that the list specified?*

*Borden: There is a simple explanation. Working on the trading floor, Mr Lockwood would have been able to find out when big deals were imminent, and being the talented analyst that he is, he must have worked out what rates to rig in order to maximise the profits on those deals. Then he got his crooked contacts in the other banks to rig the rates for him. Our bank profited as a result, innocently, but so did his personal stock option, which it hardly needs to be said the bank now wishes it had not given to him.*

*Clarence: Sir Charles, that is all a fabrication. It was you personally who directed David Lockwood to fix the rates for you, and you gave him the stock option so that if it all came to light, you could blame him and let him carry the can. That is the truth, Sir Charles, isn't it?*

*Borden: The plain truth is that there is no way that I or the bank would ever want to rig the rates. It is clearly against the law and would also be entirely contrary to our ethic of 'Honest British Banking'.*

*Judge: Thank you for such a clear explanation, Sir Charles. I am sure you have no further questions, Mr Clarence. This court will adjourn until ten o'clock tomorrow morning.*

As the court rose, Mr William Clarence QC stood up and left without saying a word to Janie or anyone else. He did, however, phone her later than evening at the hotel where she was staying over.

"Sorry I dashed off, Mrs Lockwood, I needed to catch the judge to see if we can cut a deal, but he says no."

"What deal?"

"Some leniency in return for a guilty plea. But he says no, it's too late for that, just get the trial over with. The thing is, Mrs Lockwood, I have to be straight with you, this case is lost. I'm very sorry. I've been waiting all these years to get Charles Borden into a court and expose him for the crook that he truly is. And I've failed. Which means I've failed David. And you. And myself too. Charles Borden is going to get away with it and then carry on lying and stealing for the rest of his life. And he's so good at it that nobody is ever going to bring him down. I'm sorry, Janet."

"I was there in the court, William, I saw it all. And I know David's going to prison, I've already worked that out for myself. How long do you think the rest of the trial will take?"

"It could be all be over tomorrow. You'd better go home and prepare your husband for the worst."

# CHAPTER 37  THE SLAP ON THE WRIST

While Janie was listening to Charles Borden lying on oath to the judge and jury, Sam was taking a rare morning off, so the first he knew about the collapse of British Care was when his office phoned him to tell him that half his staff had not turned up for work. He called one of them and found her still at home and not happy.

"Hello Monica, it's Sam Lockwood, why aren't you at work just now?"

"Because we're not getting paid."

"Of course you're getting paid, I'm the finance manager, I should know!"

"That's not what it says on the news."

"What does it say on the news?"

"Like I just told you Mr Lockwood, that we're not getting paid."

"Why not?"

"Why don't you watch the news Mr Lockwood, then you'll see."

So Sam watched the news.

*"Tens of thousands of jobs are at risk of being lost, and a hundred thousand vulnerable and elderly people face homelessness as a result of the collapse of the giant British Care group, the Britain's largest residential care provider,"* said the presenter. *"Our economics editor brings us this report."*

A woman in an open raincoat and wind-blown hair stood in front of the closed front doors of British Care's London headquarters. Behind her a gaggle of British Care workers, mostly women, held hand-made placards reading "Who Cares? We Do!". The reporter spoke into her long furry microphone.

*"Following the announcement late yesterday evening that lenders have withdrawn their support from the stricken British Care group, care homes for the elderly across Britain are in chaos this morning.*

*With no money in the coffers, its head office behind me closed and the owner businessman Mark Shuffler apparently in hiding, some of British Care's staff have drawn their own conclusions that they will not be paid and have voted with their feet, though many have remained loyal to their residents and are still looking after them as best they can.*

*Mark Shuffler is the previously little-known businessman who just a year ago bought the entire British Care group for a pound from Monaco-based billionaire tax exile Sir Gordon Gordon. Sir Gordon has declined to be interviewed but has released a statement that reads. "I sold British Care a year ago in good faith and as a going concern and since then I have had no involvement in its affairs."*

*In addition to their concerns about their residents and their jobs, British Care staff are worried that their pension fund has gone the same way as the company and are calling on the government to intervene.*

*We now go over to Rita Shami who is in Manchester to tell us what the local councils there are trying to do to evacuate frail elderly residents from one of British Care's homes whose roof has, literally, fallen in overnight . . ."*

Over the next few days, the British Care crisis competed with 'Spiderman versus The Killer Banker' for the front pages. Sir Gordon had indeed sold the company for a pound a year before, and gave the press a copy of the previous year's auditors' report on British Care which stated that at the time he sold it, it was a 'viable and going concern'. PCMG, the authors of that report, issued a statement that their report was 'a correct assessment based on the information available to our auditors at the time'. Gordon referred all enquiries to the new owner and added that if Mark Shuffler was not up to the task he should not have bought the business in the first place.

Reporters soon ferreted out a copy of British Care's accounts. They showed that in his years in charge, Gordon had paid himself one and a half billion pounds in tax-free dividends but put nothing in the staff pension fund, which by the time he sold the company had a black hole of nearly six hundred million pounds. Once existing pensioners were paid, there would be virtually nothing left for any of the tens of thousands yet to retire, Sam included.

Sir Gordon's spokesman said that Mark Shuffler was told this when he bought the company, but when Shuffler was tracked down by the press he said it was hidden from him. Meanwhile Sam worked on at his homes, unpaid and unpensioned.

An enterprising news reporter managed to track Sir Gordon down and get aboard his yacht in Piraeus harbour where he was stocking up for a tour of the Greek islands, and confronted him on live TV.

"Sir Gordon," the TV news showed him saying, "What comment do you have to make about this dreadful crisis?"

"Crisis?" said Sir Gordon, standing on the deck and waving his arm towards the bright sun, blue sky and Greek islands, "Look. I'm on my yacht, it's a beautiful day, the ocean's calm, the breeze is warm and tomorrow I set sail round the Aegean. Now tell me my friend, who's got a crisis? Because I tell you, it's not me. Champagne?"


Janie was back at the Old Bailey the next morning, with Sam. It was David's turn to be sworn in. Then Mr Clarence QC rose and addressed him.

"Mr Lockwood, after you were arrested you were interviewed by the police for three days. You gave the officers a detailed account of your part in fixing the Libor and Forex rates. Then you wrote a confession in which again you owned up to everything you did. Is that correct, Mr Lockwood?"

"Yes sir, that is correct."

"And is everything you said in your interview and your written confession true?

"Yes sir, it is."

"And why did you do all these things?

"Because Mr Borden told me to?

"Sir Charles Borden told you to?"

"Yes sir."

"Then I ask you this, David," said Mr Clarence, very gently. "If Sir Charles Borden told you to do everything, and you did everything that Sir Charles told you to do, why is there no mention of Sir Charles Borden in any of your interview answers or anywhere in your confession?"

"Because he told me it was top secret, sir. I believed that if the secret ever came out, he would tell people that it was him who wanted me to arrange the rates to help our customers get a fair deal. I trusted him. I thought he was an honest man. I now know that he is not."

Mr Clarence turned to the judge. "I have no further questions, my lord, and no further witnesses to call." The judge told David that he could sit down. David turned to Janie, mouthed "Mum I'm sorry" across the courtroom, then took his seat.

The judge nodded to Mr Cannon QC, who rose and turned to the jury and said, "Members of the jury, before you retire to decide on your verdict, it falls to me to remind you of the case for the prosecution. Normally I would work late and long to prepare the material that I need for this purpose. On this occasion, my midnight oil has been spared. David Lockwood's own written confession sets out the case against him far better than I possibly could. I will therefore close the prosecution case simply by reading out to you, Mr Lockwood's confession, verbatim and in full."

And that is what Mr Cannon did.

The jury sat for two hours, transfixed, as they listened to Mr Cannon reading out what David had written in his own words about everything he had done, with no mention of anything Sir Charles Borden had done. Then after a short summing-up of his own, the judge sent the jury off to their sealed room to consider their verdicts.

Before the trial Mr Clarence had told Janie that juries in fraud cases usually take weeks to reach a verdict, and that the longer they deliberate the greater is the likelihood that they will fail to agree and will therefore be obliged to return a verdict of Not Guilty. David's jury sent a message out to the judge after just thirty-five minutes, to say that they were ready to come back with their unanimous verdict. There was panic in the courtroom as it appeared that several participants, including the judge, had underestimated the jury's decisiveness and drifted off for their lunches.

Once the court was reassembled the jury's verdict was 'Guilty' on all counts. The judge made a short speech about how evil David was and how much harm he had done to the good reputation of British banking. Janie could not listen and although John Murphy diligently wrote it all down, she has still never been able to bring herself to read this section of his notes. All she heard was David's sentence - sixteen years in prison, the maximum that the law permits - and then across the hushed court, the click of the prison officer's handcuffs before David called 'Goodbye Mum" and was taken away.

"KILLER BANKER SPLATS SPIDERMAN" is how the Sun headlined the next day.

Janie was home just in time to go with Jess to the meeting she was holding to tell all her staff that Jess Lockwood & Co was closing down. It was one of the saddest moments of her life. Not quite as bad as watching David being led off to prison, but worse, to her, than even the Guvnor's funeral. Janie was there as the founder of the company and the former boss who had personally recruited many of the hundred-or-so people who were now crowded into the loading bay of Jess's warehouse. Janie said a few words too, though there was not much she could add, and by then everyone knew about David so the sympathy went both ways.

The reporter from the Brighton Argus was waiting outside, scribbling her notes for the story to go under the 'Collapse of local hardware chain, hundred jobs lost' headline that would be on tomorrow's front page. Mr Hodge had died earlier that year and Janie was only glad he would not have to read it.

Janie was back in London the following week to visit Mr Clarence QC in his chambers and settle his bill with a cheque for four hundred thousand pounds, to be financed by a third mortgage on their house. She could see that he was busy and did not intend to stay, but he stopped her on the way out.

"Did you see RoyalBank in this morning's papers, Mrs Lockwood?" he asked.

"I haven't looked at any news since the trial, it keeps bringing back what happened to David."

"Then I'll tell you," he said. "The Financial Conduct Authority has fined RoyalBank a hundred million pounds over the Libor and Forex rigging job. They said that the only reason that it wasn't twenty times higher was because it was the work of what they said was a lone rogue trader whose activities were so cunningly concealed that his managers couldn't possibly have suspected anything."

"Still, that's quite a big fine," she said. "A hundred million's hardly a slap on the wrist, is it."

"You must be joking, Mrs Lockwood. RoyalBank must have made billions out of all the trades that they got David to set up for them. And I mean serious billions. Tens of billions, probably. That hundred million pound fine is going to hurt RoyalBank about as much as giving a speeding ticket to an armed robber's getaway car."

Janie would have preferred a different analogy, but she got his point.

# CHAPTER 38  THE EVIDENCE

Helen was too despondent to want to get involved in taking on RoyalBank over her dismissal but Janie decided that their solicitor John Murphy should know about it, so she went fishing through Helen's bin sacks in the garage until she found her gross misconduct sheet, then took it down to his office.

Helen would not come with her.  Since Janie brought her home from London, Helen had spent her time moping around the house, sleeping most of the day and watching TV rubbish all night.  She rebuffed all her friends who called to try to invite her out and cheer her up.

Mr Murphy read the sheet.

"That's quite a list, Janet," he said.  "Assault, deceit, blackmail, security breach.  It's a bit more than your routine 'late for work, unsatisfactory performance', isn't it?"

"Thanks for pointing that out, John.  I did know."

"Sorry Janet, it's just that I've seen plenty of these forms but never one like this.  RoyalBank don't like her much, do they?"

"Actually they liked her a lot until a few weeks ago, the guy who's now the chairman picked her personally to work for him and he was always fine with her."

Mr Murphy picked up the sheet.  "Well this doesn't look fine, Janet."

"So what do you reckon?  What are her options?"

"Well, option one is to give in.  Saves you and her time, money and hassle.  The downside is that she loses without a fight.  But it's cheap."  Mr Murphy was well aware of the family's business problems, not to mention the fee just paid to Sir William Clarence QC and the two extra mortgages on their house.

"Option two is to get a top legal team in and fight them all the way.  Expensive though.  Cost you half a million at least if you win, maybe triple that if you lose and RoyalBank get their costs awarded against you."

"That's not really an option then, is it." Janie said. "Are there any others?"

"Not really. Fight or flight. Law of the jungle. But if you put in an initial application for an Employment Tribunal it will only cost you a £1500 fee and for that you get to see all the other side's evidence, that should help you decide how to play it."

"That sounds good to me," Janie said. He showed her where to find the Employment Tribunals website and she left him to worry about all the other headaches that she seemed to be handing him almost daily now.

Janie hoped it might buck Helen up to get her involved in fighting her case, but Helen did not want to know. Janie worked through all the Employment Tribunal forms herself and, six weeks and £1500 later, had a call from Mr Murphy's office inviting her to drop round and pick up a package that was waiting for her there.

The package contained copies of the statements of all the witnesses that RoyalBank's legal department would be calling to defend themselves and justify Helen's sacking. Janie took them home but Helen refused to read them or even acknowledge their existence so she settled down on the sofa to read her way through the entire bundle herself.

The top paper was a short statement from Charles Borden, and it read -

*I am Sir Charles Borden, Chief Executive, RoyalBank, London.*

*On Friday 5 February this year I called in briefly at a celebratory drink being given by one of the secretaries who works in my division to mark her impending retirement and the promotion of her successor. She had invited all her colleagues to a glass of wine in her office at the end of work hours, and it fell to me say a few words and give her a card signed by her colleagues.*

*Helen Laker was present and I noticed that she refilled her glass at least twice in the twenty minutes I was present. I had been concerned at several indications of a fall-off in the previously high quality of her work in recent months, and I wondered if she might have some sort of a drink problem. I made a mental note to tell someone in HR the next time I was speaking to them, then I left to go home.*

*Signed Sir Charles Borden.*

Next in the bundle was Gordon's statement –

*"I am Sir Gordon Gordon, businessman, resident in Monaco.*

*On Friday 5 February this year I went to the London head office of RoyalBank to use one of their conference rooms for some meetings, and finished towards eight pm. There was nobody around and I was walking along the corridor to the lifts when I saw that the lights were on in the photocopier room.*

*I looked in the door and saw one of RoyalBank's secretaries, Helen Laker, whom I know from meetings I go to that she attends. She was busy at the copier so I stopped at the door to wish her goodnight. She turned to face me and said quite abruptly that she wanted a word with me. She proceeded to tell me all about how she and not a colleague should have been promoted as she was better and harder working than that colleague whose promotion she had had to celebrate earlier that evening.*

*I smelt alcohol on her breath and noted that she was a little unsteady on her feet, and concluded that she must have been drinking.*

*I told her that I am not responsible for staff promotions at RoyalBank and that if she had any issues she should take them up with her own management. She told me that I was one of the bank's biggest customers and that if I told the chairman Lord Phillips that he should promote her then he would do so. I said that I would not take her side with Lord Phillips.*

*She then told me that if I did not get her promoted, she would make an accusation that I had indecently assaulted her. I told her not to be ridiculous.*

*She reacted badly to this, addressed me by a number of expletives and then slapped my face with her right hand, and made a second attempt which I dodged. I felt I should terminate this discussion immediately so I said goodnight and made for the door. She tried to throw at me a bundle of the papers that she had been copying but they flew everywhere. I left her to it and made my way out of the building.*

*I thought about phoning Lord Phillips, but despite Helen Laker's conduct I am sensitive to the impact that stress and alcohol can have on an employee and had no particular wish to get her into trouble, so I resolved just to mention it to him in passing the next time I saw him.*

*Signed Sir Gordon Gordon"*

Janie had to put the papers down for a minute and take a few deep breaths to calm herself. She did not want to read any more, but she knew she had to, for Helen's sake. Next:

*"My name is Allan Forsyth and I am a Compliance Manager for RoyalBank.*

*On Monday 15 March this year, on instructions received from Melissa Campbell, senior partner at PCMG, I undertook a search of the photocopier room that is situated on the tenth floor of the banks' London headquarters.*

*With the assistance of a janitor, I moved the photocopier away from the wall and behind it found a number of sheets of paper. I took these away and identified them as papers for a RoyalBank board meeting the previous week.*

*The sheets contained information about forthcoming corporate mergers that would, if made known outside board level, have affected share prices. This constitutes a major breach of security, and would normally result in serious disciplinary action against the individual responsible.*

*Signed Allan Forsyth"*

And then –

*"I am Lord Michael Phillips of Kidwelton, Chairman of RoyalBank.*

*On Monday 8 February this year, when I arrived at work I was confronted by one of our secretaries, Helen Laker, who appeared to be agitated. She insisted on seeing me, and to avoid a scene in front of her colleagues I allowed her to come into my office. I sat her in an armchair and called for refreshments in the hope that I could get her to settle down and tell me what was the matter.*

She told me that on the previous Friday we had announced the promotion of one of her colleague secretaries and that she should have been promoted instead. She was clearly very angry and used some quite unprofessional language.

Then she said that Sir Gordon Gordon, one of the bank's clients, had indecently assaulted her on the bank's premises the same evening. I told her that if this was so, she should report it to the police.

She said Sir Gordon would deny it but didn't matter if it was true or not as her complaint would cause the bank a lot of embarrassment, but she would drop it if I would give her written confirmation of promotion right now. I asked if her allegation against Sir Gordon really was true and she told me she would say it was, and that no-one could disprove it.

From her answers and her manner, I strongly suspected that her allegation was false. However, I told her that as it was a serious complaint, I was duty bound by the bank's internal rules to appoint an independent investigator.

She repeated her demand that I promote her in return for her dropping her complaint. I refused, then she had a tantrum and kicked the tray of refreshments off the coffee table onto the floor and barged out of my office.

That morning, I secured the services of Melissa Campbell of PCMG as an independent investigator. Subsequently, in light of her findings, I convened a disciplinary panel and dismissed Helen Laker for gross misconduct.

Signed Phillips of Kidwelton."

The last statement in the bundle was from Judy —

"My name is Judy McConnell and I am the recently-retired personal assistant to Lord Phillips, chairman of RoyalBank.

At 8.15 am on Monday 8 February, Helen Laker, who was then one of the secretaries at the bank, came into my office and demanded to see the chairman immediately. He had just arrived for work and I told her that she did not have an appointment. Helen was clearly in an emotional state and the chairman took it on himself to invite her into his office, where I brought them refreshments.

211

*I was unable to hear what took place in his office as there was the usual noise of a busy morning going on around me, but shortly afterwards I heard a crash from inside. I went to his door and entered just as Helen came out pushing past me. Inside I found the chairman picking the contents of the coffee tray off the floor. Several items of his best china had been broken and I cleaned up as best I could before he continued his meetings for the day.*

*Signed Judy McConnell (Miss)"*

Finally Janie turned to the Independent Investigator's report. In it Melissa Campbell recounted being contacted by Lord Phillips and asked to conduct an independent review, her interview with Helen, Gordon's denials and the work she did to find witnesses and take statements.

Melissa Campbell recorded that in addition to interviews with Lord Phillips, Sir Charles Borden, Sir Gordon, Allan Forsyth and Judy, she had held one-to-one meetings with ten other tenth-floor women picked at random, and none of them had made any complaints about Sir Gordon.

She described the note from a 'well wisher and fellow victim' that Helen had sent her and said that, "In the complete absence of any corroboration, I conclude that it was fabricated by Helen Laker in a belated attempt to promote her own case."

Janie read on until she reached the section that Mike Phillips had used to condemn Helen:

*"In summary, the allegations made by the complainant Helen Laker as recorded in her statement to the independent investigating officer are entirely unsupported by the evidence. It is the firm conclusion of this investigation that she is a mendacious individual who has fabricated her story for the purposes of her personal advancement and financial gain. In doing so, Helen Laker has placed herself entirely at variance to the values and ethical standards of her employer, RoyalBank. Formal disciplinary action for gross misconduct is recommended.*

*Signed Melissa Campbell, managing director, PCMG, Independent Investigator."*

Janie put the papers down, and looked up John Murphy's phone number.

## CHAPTER 39  THE RECORDER

John Murphy was in his office. "Finished already Janet?" came his voice.

"I have. Did you read them?"

"I did, while you were on your way down to collect them. And I knew you'd be back pretty soon."

"And what do you make of it all?"

"Janet, as your solicitor I have to ask you a question. There can either be the truth according to Helen or the truth according to Gordon, Phillips, Borden and Campbell. There is no other truth. One party or the other is telling the truth and the other is lying. Now please forgive me Janet, but it is my duty to ask you - who do you believe is telling the truth?"

"I know Helen is telling the truth."

"Then there is an old fashioned word for it, Janet. Stitch-up. They've all got their heads together and they've stitched her up. And when it comes to the Employment Tribunal they will do the same. It will be your daughter, painted as a jealous, underperforming and drunken secretary, against a titled bank chairman and chief executive, a captain of British industry and a director of a top four accountancy firm who is also a champion of women's rights in the workplace. Who do you think will win?"

"Not Helen."

"That's what I think too."


Janie needed to talk it over with someone, but Helen still refused and Sam was out all night dealing unpaid with the death of an elderly resident who had been left untended for too long at an under-staffed home that the council was trying to rescue. Jess was home that evening and Janie could have sought her opinion, but she chose to leave her alone as she had spent another fruitless day at the Jobcentre with Harry on her knee being reminded that she was not the only unemployed former owner of a failed business who was now looking for work. So Janie spent the night lying awake alone talking to herself.

She phoned John Murphy again in the morning.

"John. We haven't got the money to fight it. It's option one. Give in."

"You didn't ask my advice, Janet, but that would have been it. But for what difference it makes, I too know that Helen is telling the truth."

That evening Janie was just settling down to catch some TV when Helen came in and dumped herself on the sofa next to her. "Mum, I've found something you've got to read." She waved two pieces of paper in front of her face.

"Now? East Enders is starting."

"Now. It's important."

"More important than East Enders?" Helen rose to stand in front of the TV screen with her arms folded. Janie turned the remote to silent. "OK Helen, what is it?"

"Read this." Helen handed her mother one of the pieces of paper. "Since I lost my job I've been listening to some recordings I made of meetings I went to at RoyalBank. A couple of years ago, there was due to be a meeting on a Friday afternoon, Charles Borden, Melissa Campbell and Gordon were all about to arrive, so as usual I tucked away a little recorder on Mike Phillip's shelf and switched it on ready."

She showed Janie a little silver-coloured device that was smaller than her thumb and clicked it on and off for her to see, then continued.

"Just then Mike took an urgent call from New York, and when he put the phone down he said he needed to go there the next morning. He told me to get on and book his flights straight away and rearrange all his next week's appointments, so I went back out to my desk. 'We'll just have to manage on our own this time,' he said to me."

Janie still had half an eye on the screen. Helen switched the TV off and put the remote out of her reach. "Anyway, by the time the meeting broke up I had all his tickets and itineraries in his folder ready for him to take away. Gordon put his hand on my leg while I was packing Mike's briefcase but I didn't say anything, we used to just have to put up with it, nobody could rock the boat. Look what happened to me when I did!"

"Yeah."

"Anyway, when they'd all gone, I popped back into Mike's office to tidy up and get my recorder back, then I locked up and went home. Nothing happened the next week to make me have to listen to the recording, so I just forgot about it until it came up on my recorder today. I've typed up what they said. You could do with reading it."

Janie picked up the first sheet and this is what she read:

*Phillips: You know, I never thought I'd hear myself say this, but I'm rather enjoying this recession. Look at the extra bank loans people have had to take out just to get by. Second mortgages. All those maxxed out credit cards with interest at top whack every month. Fees for handling redundancy payments. Our business has never been better. How about you Melissa?*

*Campbell: Our bankruptcy people are doing a roaring trade. And our tax advisers are rushed off their feet helping clients get their money out of Britain in case taxes go up again to pay for your banking crisis.*

*Gordon: I saw in the papers that a load of car workers got made redundant and that they're being fleeced by reps from finance firms buying their company pensions off them cheap using an up-front cash lump sum as bait, and flogging them rubbish pensions in their place. Any of them from RoyalBank by any chance?*

*Borden: Absolutely not. RoyalBank is all about Honest British Banking, not ripping off British workers. In any case, if we got found out and it went public then it'd do our reputation no end of harm.*

*Gordon: So?*

*Borden: So Melissa's set us up a special company to do it, it's offshore and can't be traced back to RoyalBank.*

216

Gordon: *Everyone's a winner then?*

Borden: *Everyone except the redundant workers. But then they aren't paying our wages, are they?*

"Charming!" Janie said.

"Now read this next one," Helen told her. She did.

Phillips: *And on the subject of profiting from this unfortunate recession, that other little project of ours starts today, how's it going?*

Borden: *Our team's up and running. We're calling them the Local Business Support Unit, it makes them sound all warm and friendly.*

Phillips: *I hope they're not.*

Borden: *They're anything but. I've hand-picked some of the toughest and greediest guys we've got - no women, they're too nice, sorry Melissa - and briefed them on what to do. When I told them the size of the bonuses they'll get if they meet their targets, they nearly fell off their chairs. They are hauling in a hundred businesses a month, telling them all that they going down the pan even if they aren't, and getting them signed up for an independent business review by our favourite accountants, PCMG.*

Campbell: *OK, I've got my people stood by ready, every company that you put in our direction will be reviewed and all the review reports will say that the business is now valued at less than the amount they owe RoyalBank.*

Phillips: *And PCMG's charge for these reviews?*

Campbell: *Ten percent of the loan value, the customer pays, not the bank. We'll split that between us.*

Borden: *Then when the business's owners get brought back a few months later to see the Local Business Support Unit again, they get told that as a result of the recession and their own bad management the value of their business has gone down and the loan is cancelled. RoyalBank seizes the business and hands it over to Melissa's insolvency people . . .*

Campbell: *. . . who will sell the plant, grab the customer receipts, auction the stock, fire the staff, till all that's left is the buildings and land, which we'll transfer to you Gordon at half their true market value.*

217

*Gordon: Then I sell them at full market value.*

*Borden: And tax free from Monaco.*

*MelissA: And you hand the profit back to me, Gordon, it's not yours to
keep. I'll split it four ways and put each of your shares wherever
you want it. I recommend Panama these days, it's cheaper than
Switzerland and has a lot fewer rules.*

*Gordon: You know what's ironic? Banks caused the recession, and now
the recession is going to make two bankers, an ex-banker and their
accountant very rich.*

*Phillips: You know what they say? When the sharks smell blood, it's
time to make a killing. More Findlays anyone? Gordon's left us
a bit for a change.*

Janie was alone. Helen had slipped out without her noticing,
presumably to bed to watch TV, leaving Janie's own TV
remote on the sofa arm, where it remained untouched. Janie
re-read the transcripts. She has no recollection of how she
spent the rest of that night, but the next morning Sam found
her still sitting on the sofa, still awake, and still clutching the
papers. For the first time since she stepped off that train in
Brighton all those years ago and walked along the High Street
looking for 'Situation Vacant' and 'Room To Let' notices, she
felt lost. Rootless. Adrift. Alone. The urge to go back and
walk the old cobbled lanes of Bethnal Green swept over her.
She made up an excuse, phoned Minnie, and took the train to
London.

# CHAPTER 40  THE CEMETERY

Minnie was waiting for Janie at the top of the steps at Bethnal Green underground station and suggested walking round to her place. She headed Janie up Cambridge Heath Road.

"Where are we going, Minnie?  This isn't the way to yours."

"I'm back in my old council flat," she said.  "Lost my nice house, didn't I."

"How did that happen?"

"The bank repossessed it.  They sent round some bailiffs, leather jackets, shaved heads, tattoos, but they're just local boys doing their job, I know their mums.  They were supposed to take all my stuff off to auction to pay the bank arrears, but they let me pick out anything I wanted to keep and then dropped it all off round at my old flat for me in their van.  They wouldn't take any money for it either.  There are still people like that round here, Janie, don't you know."

"I'm sorry Minnie," Janie said, "You loved that house."

"Oh, no need to be sorry, Janie.  Things come, things go.  Our parents got bombed in the war, so we're the lucky ones really.  Thank goodness I'd kept the council flat in my name, at least I still have a roof over my head even if I've lost all my savings."

"What happened to your savings?"

"They all went into my house.  I still can't work out how it happened, but for the first two years I could afford the monthly mortgage payments no trouble, but then the interest suddenly went through the roof and I couldn't pay.  You're right, I loved my house, it's the first thing I've really had that's all my own, and it was going to be my security when I get old, so when the monthly payments went up I paid them out of my savings till the savings ran out.  Then it got repossessed, like I said."

"I'm sorry, Minnie."

"I cried a lot but I'm over it now. There are plenty of people in this world much worse off than I am, that's how I look at it."

"Tell me, Minnie, when you signed the mortgage agreement did you read the small print?"

"Oh come off it Janie, don't tease me, you know reading's never been my thing. I got the man from the bank to read it all out to me."

"Did he read out anything about the interest rate going up after two years?"

"No, I'm sure of that. I wouldn't have taken his mortgage if I thought that was going to happen."

They walked on in silence until they reached the foot of the stairway to Minnie's flat. It smelt of urine, there were needles and a condom on the floor and an 'OUT OF ORDER' sign on the lift. "Which bank was it, Minnie?"

"RoyalBank."

It was the answer that Janie did not want to hear but fully expected.

Three flights up and safely behind the triple-bolted front door of her flat, Minnie made a pot of tea and dug out her well-stocked tin of biscuits.

"Do you see anything of Nutter these days, Minnie?"

"He's just moved back actually, I bumped into him in the park, he's got a room over that way."

"How is he?"

"Not a happy man, Janie, I can tell you that. He told me that because of the recession he got made redundant from that car factory. He got a pension from working there nearly thirty years, but he's lost it all."

"How?"

"Apparently some cowboy financial adviser got his claws into Nutter and told him he could do him a better deal if he handed over his pension and redundancy money for him to manage. Nutter's not the only one to get fleeced like that, a whole lot of them did. I wouldn't want to be in that fellow's shoes if Nutter ever meets him on a dark night."

"And Rudy? How's his pub?"

"The pub's still there, and he's still there too, only now he's not behind the counter, he's a customer, at least on benefits day."

"What happened to him?"

"He was doing just fine too. Rudy kept the Oak Barrel like a proper old East End pub, complete with a piano against the wall and each regular's own glass hanging on its hook above the bar. He was there every day, being the traditional East End pub landlord, knew all his customers, had their favourite drink served and onto the bar ready as they walked in."

"I can picture it. It's making me thirsty already."

"Yes, and he'd stand you a free drink if you were skint, then overcharge some tourist to make up the difference in the till. He drank enough of his own stock to be good company but not so much as to drink all his profits. All of us old-timers flocked there, and he was doing just lovely."

"And then?"

"Rudy tried to explain what happened, Janie, but in truth I don't really understand and I'm pretty sure he doesn't either. Apparently someone from the bank came to see him and told him he could lose a lot of money if interest rates went up, and signed him up to some sort of dodgy deal to protect him if that happened. But the interest rate went down instead and Rudy suddenly owed the bank a fortune, more than his pub was bringing in."

"RoyalBank?"

"I'm pretty sure it was, how did you know? Anyway, he struggled along for a while, but the stress was doing him in and making him drink too much and I could see it was going to kill him, and in the end I just went down there and marched him off to that branch of RoyalBank that's in Hackney and made him chuck the pub keys over the counter and walk away. Which he did."

Janie fell silent for a minute, remembering Rudy and Nutter and Minnie and the old times. And then Maxie.

"Do you think much about Maxie these days?" she asked Minnie.

"Sure, most days."

"And did Maxie ever say anything about me to you?" Janie asked.

"Sometimes, yes. She was very fond of you, you know. Then towards the end, when she was ill, she used to talk about how she looked after you when you were a baby. I told her not to though, it made her cry. Are you staying for tea, Janie?"

Janie was getting up to go. "No thanks Minnie,"

"Yes you are. Sit down." Janie sat down again.

Minnie left the kitchen, returning with an old shoe-box tied with brown string.

"Since you and Maxie go back all that time, why don't you have a root through this to keep you out of my hair while I get the tea ready? It was in Maxie's flat when she died, so it ended up in the back of my wardrobe at my house and I forgot all about it until I had to move out. She doesn't need it any more, so if you find anything you'd like to keep I'm sure that's fine by her."

"OK," Janie said, "If there's nothing I can help you with in the kitchen?"

"The best way you can help in this kitchen is by getting out of it and taking that box with you," Minnie said, turning to face Janie with the breadknife raised menacingly, "There's gin in the lounge sideboard, here are two glasses, bring one back full for me then clear off there till I call you."

While clattering sounds came from the kitchen, Janie sat on Minnie's sofa, sipped gin and went through Maxie's shoe-box. The jewellery did not mean anything to her, she recognised none of it and put it all back as she found it. There was a bundle of 1950s postcards with stamps of the old king or the very young queen, addressed to Maxie and with hurried messages from girlfriends mostly along the lines of 'sun is shining, wish you were here'.

Beneath these there were some bits of ribbon and buttons that looked as if they might have fallen out from a sewing kit, a single medal inscribed PTE 178665 J F MARTENS whom she took to be Maxie's father or an uncle from the First World War, and a battered brown envelope which she tipped out onto the sofa seat next to her.

The envelope contained photographs, about twenty in all. None was labelled, but she assumed that the faded photos of fierce-looking ladies in Edwardian dress were grandmothers or aunts, and that the young soldier in uniform was Private 178665 Martens. The child in dresses and curls, at different ages in successive pictures, was undoubtedly Maxie as she progressed from infancy to womanhood.

And then there was one more photograph. It was in black-and-white and quite worn, and from the trees and skyline must have been taken on a summer's day out in Victoria Park which adjoins Bethnal Green. Janie pocketed that photograph and still has it in a little frame by her bed, next to her Buckingham Palace group picture.

The photograph is of a young couple with an old pram and a baby. On the left is her Dad, younger than she remembers him, in baggy trousers and a jacket a size too big for him. Next to him is Maxie, in a cotton summer dress and headscarf, also younger than Janie remembers her but older than in the photos of her growing up. And in Maxie's arms there is a baby, about a year old, which she takes to be herself, as it looks just like her own children at the same age.

Janie wondered, not for the first time, if there was not some important detail that Maxie had omitted from her account of her mysterious mother.

"Tea's up!" called Minnie. "Did you find anything?"

"No, nothing. I've tied the box up again for you."

Tea at Minnie's was never just tea, it was ham sandwiches, fresh scones and home-made jam, while Janie brought her up to date with her latest news - David in gaol, Helen sacked, Sam out of work, Jess's business gone bust, and the debts and the house to be sold to pay for them. Minnie was sympathetic and sweet and a good listener and it did Janie good to get it off her chest. When she had finished, Minnie tidied up.

"You've still never visited your father's grave, have you Janie?"

"No, the last time I saw it was when I was throwing the first handful of soil down and hearing it clatter on top of his coffin."

"Then it's time you did. Get your coat on, I'll come with you."

In the gathering grey of the late afternoon they walked together along streets that Janie found at once familiar and strange, until they reached the gates of Bethnal Green Cemetery. Minnie took them first to Maxie's grave where they both paid their respects.

"Do you know where your Dad's grave is?" Minnie asked.

"Roughly, I'll find it."

"OK, I'll wait for you by the gates, you can have some time alone with him. Take as long as you like, it's been a while."

Walking through the cemetery brought back memories of the funeral. It had been a sad affair, but not as sad as Janie had expected. Half the manor turned out, and from all the kind things that the mourners said to her she grasped for the first time just how much her father was respected and admired among his peers. She knew that he was generous, but before that day she had not realised just how much of his money he gave away or, to spare the personal pride of the recipient, 'lent' with no expectation of repayment.

He had been there for his people when hardship struck and at the times of life's crises such as rent arrears, unemployment, business failure, illness, bail, incarceration, bereavement, and most expensive of all, daughters' weddings. He had robbed the rich, as they saw it, and given to the poor for thirty years of unstinting armed robbery. Janie had been proud to be the bank robber's daughter. And she wondered then, and still does now, whether the Guvnor raised his gun at the armed policeman on purpose, so that he would never have to live to be a witness to his first and only failure.

Janie knew where to look, the far left corner, where the trees are so old that their trunks have wrapped themselves round the old iron railings. She followed the rows of stones searching for the right one, all the time wishing that she too had given away her own share of the proceeds of their robberies long ago, and been able to live her life free of the curse of Jennifer Harding and her millions. She wondered if it was not too late, and resolved to ask the Guvnor for his advice when she found him.

His stone was there, in grey marble, discoloured by nature and the weather but still standing upright, unlike many of those around it. There were flowers, real or plastic, on a few of the graves, ornaments or trinkets on others, and fresh childrens' toys on one, very sad. There was nothing to adorn Dad's of course.

She read the inscription, a little worn but still readable all these years on –

HERE LIES FRANK ARTHUR LAKER
BORN 7 SEPTEMBER 1895, TAKEN FROM US 5 JANUARY 1951

and beneath, slightly less worn –

AND HIS BELOVED ONLY SON
GEORGE LAKER
6 MARCH 1931 TO 5 JUNE 1981

Janie had seen the stone before of course, when Dad used to take her as a child to put winter flowers on the grave of his own father every fifth of January. But she had left for good well before Dad's own inscription could be added.

She stood in the cool afternoon air and listened to the starlings that were already gathering for the evening in the trees that lined the cemetery. Minnie was at the gates and Janie was about to turn and go back to join her, when on an impulse she decided that she ought at least to tidy up around Dad's long-neglected grave. She bent over to clear away the weeds and as she did so she saw that they lay over an inscription near the base of the stone. In the gathering gloom, she crouched to read it.

"ITS TIME, TAKE'EM"

"It's time, take'em!" Someone from the old gang must have convinced the stonemason that this was a message for the Almighty. One last little blag, on Dad's behalf. He would have approved.

Janie stayed kneeling by the stone and pondered the irony of it. All those years ago, she used to rob banks. Then, when she turned her life around and made herself into an honest woman, a bank robbed her of everything. Dishonest bankers took her son, her business and her home, and stole from the honest lives of her family and her friends too.

And they had not just robbed her. They and their like had plunged the whole country into the banking crisis, the Credit Crunch and a recession that unleashed the years of austerity which had hurt everyone she knew.

And what happened to the people responsible? A few bank chiefs had to retire early, taking their gold-plated pensions with them. She read that one of them lost his knighthood, poor thing. And that was it. Not a single boss prosecuted, let alone gaoled. Others just carried on, bailed out with public funds for tens of billions of pounds, while finding yet more ways to line their own pockets. Not a single apology from even one of them.

There had been nothing she could do about it, so like everyone else she just had to let it go and get on with her life. Until now. She read again.

## "IT'S TIME, TAKE EM"

Janie could hear the Guvnor's East End accent in her head. "It's time, Janie Laker, take'em." She put a hand on the stone to steady herself as she stood up, then headed back along the gravel path towards Minnie. Minnie put her arm in Janie's to walk her back to the station, but Janie did not say much, she was too deep in thought. Minnie was not to know it, but while she was waiting at the cemetery gates, the Guvnor had told Janie what to do with the money.

"I'll do it, Dad," she had said, to his name on the stone. "I'll take'em."

# CHAPTER 41  THE PINK POST-IT

David's prison life hung heavily over the Lockwood household. The fact that they had Harry to run around after and the rest of the family back together under one roof was welcome in its own way but only served to emphasise the gap that David's absence left.

At random moments in the day and at night, Janie brought up mental images of him in his cell, at his meal bench, in the exercise yard. Sam took it even more badly, and often when Janie stirred in bed she would find him crying silently, trying not to wake her up.

"Promise me something, Janie," he would say every day, "That we'll find a way to get David back."

"I can't promise that," she used to reply, "But I promise to try."

Which is why, the morning after she visited Minnie and her Dad's grave, Janie went looking for Helen. She found her getting her coat on to walk down to the JobCentre.

"Never mind that, Helen, you and I have to talk."

"OK Mum, with the answer I have to put in the 'Reason for Leaving Previous Employment' box on the application forms, I'm wasting my time anyway. So what is it?"

Janie made them coffee in the kitchen.

"You know you recorded Mike Phillips' meetings with his crooked pals?" she began.

"Uhuh."

"Well from the extracts you showed me there's some pretty juicy stuff in there."

"I should say so," said Helen. "Maybe we could send it to the newspapers. Let's do that."

"No, let's not do that," Janie replied. "It might cause a bit of a stir but those types and their friends in high places will deny it and destroy the evidence and we still won't get David back. And for Sam and me, getting David out of prison is the single most important thing in our lives."

"In my life too, actually. So what do you want?" said Helen.

"A way forward. That's why I want you to think. Is there anything you can remember about the bank and its dirty dealings that could help us to expose them for the crooks they are? Do you have any documents or files or anything else, anything at all, that you can dig out for David's sake?"

"I saw and heard plenty when I worked there, but nothing's written down. I didn't keep a diary and I certainly didn't take any paperwork home with me, it wasn't allowed and I had no reason to anyway."

"What about the other staff on the tenth floor, would any of them come over to us and be witnesses?"

"Not a chance, Mum," Helen said, "They aren't going to stick their necks out, especially now they've all seen what happened to me when I did."

"Isn't there anything, Helen?" Janie begged her. "For David's sake. Think back over everything you did at RoyalBank. Just in case there's some little thing . . .?"

Helen thought for a minute.

"There might be something."

"What sort of thing?"

"It's a long shot, Mum, but there was one weekend when there was a big flap on and the directors needed a load of computer files deleted urgently by Monday. The Financial Conduct Authority were about to launch an investigation into something they'd been up to, I never found out what, and they had to make sure there was nothing for them to find. I volunteered to work the weekend to help out, Mike Phillips was being nice to me then. To do it I needed access to all the bank's most secure systems, including archives, diaries and customer accounts."

"You didn't have access normally?"

"Absolutely no way Mum, this was seriously confidential stuff. It was limited to a handful of senior system administrators so one of the system administrators had to work the weekend with us. She was called Terri. But then

229

her kid had toothache and she had to slide off for an emergency dentist's appointment, so she gave me the access codes and asked me to cover for her while she was away."

"And you've remembered the codes?" Janie said, hopefully.

"Of course not. There were about twenty numbers and letters in each one, they're scientifically designed in a way you'd never be able to memorise them. So she wrote them down for me. I remember it now. She typed them on a pink post-it note."

"And you've got that?"

"I might. I know I didn't throw it away, just in case I needed it again, which it turned out I never did. If I haven't lost it or chucked it out by mistake, it would still have been in my desk, and everything in my desk went in those bin sacks when I got fired."

"So it could still be in one of the sacks now?" Janie asked. "Let's go look."

The three sacks were still in the back of the garage, and Helen poked around inside them. She picked out the fullest one.

"If it's here at all, it's going to be in this one," she said. "I packed my personal stuff away carefully in two of the sacks, but that took most of my fifteen minutes and the security man was tapping on his watch, so for the third sack I just tipped whatever was left in the drawers straight into this sack while he held it open for me."

Janie fetched a sheet from the airing cupboard and laid it out on the lounge floor. Helen tipped out her sack and on hands and knees they sifted through its contents, looking for any pink papers among the assorted desk detritus.

They found a dozen pink post-its and checked them all, twice. None bore anything like a twenty-digit code. Then they ploughed through the heap again and found three more screwed-up pink post-its that they had missed on their first search, but these bore no codes either.

Defeated, they started to scoop everything back into the sack to take out to the bin. Janie was about to dump a big handful of screwed-up yellow post-its into the sack when she noticed that one of them, unlike the others, was folded tightly into quarters. She opened it up out of curiosity. On it were four sequences of twenty-four numbers and letters, in what looked to her like Helen's handwriting. "This wouldn't be it, would it?"

Helen peered at it, turned it over, and turned it back again. "This would be it, actually," she said.

"Are you sure?" Janie asked. "It doesn't look very pink or typed to me."

"No it isn't. I remember now," said Helen. "Terri did give me a pink post-it, but she told me I'd have to give it back to her to destroy when she returned from the dentist. So just in case I did need the codes again some other time, I copied them onto another post-it, yellow this time, and folded it up tight to tuck into a crack in my bottom desk drawer where compliance checks wouldn't find it. Then I forgot all about it. It must have fallen out when I tipped the drawer into the sack."

"And where did these codes get you into?"

"Everywhere, Mum. Everywhere in the whole bank."

"But surely they won't still work? Won't the bank have changed them by now?"

"I'll go check." With that, Helen was off to the study leaving Janie to finish clearing up the lounge floor. She was back in five minutes, with a print-out of Mike Phillips' electronic diary page for the next week. "Thought so, they still work. Terri's people were always getting on at us to make sure we were changing our passwords, but it was nobody's job to check they were following their own rules."

"Well, these could be the keys to David's cell." Janie said. "And to taking down some bankers on the way. So don't lose them this time."

"I won't."

"And is there any way you'd be able to find out where Melissa Campbell, Charles Borden and Mike Phillips live?"

"Right now?"

"Right now."

"OK Mum, Mike and Charles will be no trouble, their addresses will be on the payroll system. Melissa's isn't as straightforward, she doesn't work for RoyalBank, but I've got an idea, hold on Mum . . ."

Helen went back to the computer and tapped away.

"Yup, here they are Mum, I thought so. Mike Phillips couldn't be bothered to do his own Christmas cards, Judy always had to do them for him and Melissa's address is on her list."

She jotted down the addresses while Janie tied up the sack and carried it back outside.

Family meeting.

Seated round the dining-room table were: Janie, former well-to-do businesswoman, now a nearly million pounds in debt and searching for a little flat to rent once her lovely house by the Downs was sold; Sam, redundant former finance manager at British Care, now exhausted, stressed-out, unemployed and pensionless; Helen, former executive personal assistant, now rejected by anyone who asked for a reference from her last employer; Jess, until recently a successful entrepreneur and owner of an expanding homecare business, now the out-of-work former boss of a failed company; and Harry, not yet old enough to participate, but wise enough to know that something important was going on and sit quietly looking at his picture book. David was missing, in gaol, but they left him a space at the table.

Janie looked around them all. "OK, let's get started."

"And the topic is?" asked Jess.

"Getting David out of gaol." Silence. Puzzled looks.

Helen generally broke any silences in the Lockwood household. "You mean an appeal to a different judge?"

"No, I don't mean an appeal to a different judge. Mr Clarence says there's no chance with twenty-three unanimous guilty verdicts for international bank fraud."

"So what then?" said Jess. "I don't suppose you're going to rock up with some gun-toting gang to bust him out, are you Mum? Hardly your style, is it?"

"Well actually, I thought about that Jess." Janie had, too. "But it wouldn't work. I have a different plan though, and it involves us all. But first, there are some things you don't know about me because I've never told you. It's time you knew the truth about your mother."

And so Janie told them the truth about their mother. She told them all about her Dad, the Guvnor of the sharpest gang of bank robbers ever to come out of the East End. She told them about Janie Laker, alias Hulk, gun in one hand, holdall in the other, Rudy getting all the customers down on the floor, Nutter with the staff reaching for the sky. Minnie the lookout. The getaways. The share-outs. The money. The life.

She told them about the young Mike Phillips in Hackney counting out and banking her stolen money in Jennifer Marie Harding's false name, Gordon telling her how to hide it and Charles Borden making it disappear in Jersey. She told them about the Guvnor's last raid, her escape, and everything about her and Maxie and Minnie. The funeral. The one-way train ticket to Brighton and to Sam and to her new and better life. And she told them about the five million pounds.

Sam was sitting opposite her, and as she spoke she watched him closely and waited for the moment when he must surely explode with fury at all the lies she had told him and all the truths she had withheld from him, starting on the Saturday morning they first met in the shop and then going on every day of their lives together since. Janie had no plan for what to do when he did react, as he surely must, except to be ready to say "If you need to divorce me I will understand and I will do nothing to stop you, but I love you and I don't want you to." But what Janie least expected from Sam was what she got - a frozen silence, from the beginning of her story all the way to its end.

When Janie finished, there a very long silence from everybody else too, even Harry. She did not know what reaction to expect, but she was sure it would take the form of anger for living such a monstrous lie within her own family for so long. If Sam was not going to say anything, surely Jess or Helen would? She waited for one of them to turn on her, and eventually it was Jess who broke the silence. But not quite how Janie expected.

"Hey cool, Mum, did you ever shoot anybody?"

"No. I never even fired my gun." Jess seemed disappointed.

Helen's turn. "If we are going to shoot people, can I do Gordon? Please?"

"We aren't going to shoot anybody," Janie said. "If I thought it would get David out, then I would. But it won't. But I do have a plan to free David and take down Charles Borden, Mike Phillips, Melissa Campbell and that creep Gordon while we're at it. Do you want to hear it?"

Sam finally spoke, quietly and calmly, and looking Janie straight in the eye.

"Janet Lockwood," he said, "Or Janie Laker. Or Jennifer Harding. Or Hulk. Or whoever the hell you are today. Get us our son back. And while you're at it, make those people who took him pay for what they've done. Do that and I might forgive you. Fail and you are history. Got that?"

Janie nodded. She got that. Sam continued.

"That's all I'm going to say on the subject, at least until I've had a bottle of wine and I'm ready to say some more to you. Now bloody well stop wasting everyone's time and tell us the plan."

Janie told them the plan, and when she finished they all wanted to be part of it. She had the first half of the gang she needed. She put Helen to work straight away, with a shopping-list of the information that she needed her to dig out from RoyalBank's files. Shaken out of her listlessness,

Helen was still hard at work on the computer when Janie turned in for the night.

In bed, and draining the last half-glass of wine from the bottom of the bottle, Sam said, "Janet, you know I always thought there must be things I didn't know about you. I don't know why I thought that, but it turns out I was right. That was a pretty unforgiveable thing to do to me. But I'll forgive you if you rescue our son."

"Is that all you're going to say to me?" Janie asked.

"For the moment. The rest can wait."

He put the glass down, turned over and went to sleep, facing away from her, all night. Janie is still waiting.

When she came down early the following morning Helen was still at the study desk printing off the fruits of her night's labours. She stapled and bundled the pages and then headed to bed while Janie set off to Bethnal Green to recruit the rest of her gang.

A little out of breath from climbing all the stairs, Janie was on Minnie's doorstep before eleven and seated at her kitchen table a minute later.

"Well, well, Janie," Minnie said, sorting out tea and cake, "We don't see you here for thirty years, then we get you twice in three days.  We are honoured."

"I just can't keep away from your cakes, Minnie."

"Ha! So what do you really want?  I know you of old, don't forget.  You wouldn't be here this quick if there wasn't something you wanted."

"I want to show you this."

From her bag Janie pulled out the bundle of papers that Helen had left on her desk, and spread several printed sheets on Minnie's table.

"What's that lot?" asked Minnie, looking slightly offended.

"This is a copy of the mortgage application form you signed when you bought your lovely house that RoyalBank took off you once they'd had all your life savings.  You don't need to read it because I'm going to read just one section of the small print out to you."

"OK," said Minnie, still a little doubtful, "I'm listening."

Janie turned to page sixteen, and from a block of script so small and dense that even with her passably good eyesight she struggled to make out the words, she read - *"Paragraph 57(b).  On the second anniversary of the date of commencement of this mortgage the introductory interest rate of 2% will be substituted with a rate of whichever is the greater of 10% over the Bank of England Base Rate or 12% for the remainder of the term of the mortgage."*

"Minnie, when the mortgage salesman read out the terms and conditions of your application, do you remember him reading out that section?"

"I can tell you he absolutely damn well didn't!  I may not be much of a reader, but I'm not stupid and if he'd read that out I would have twigged straight away that it was a con. He never read that out. That's a definite."

Janie put the sheet down in front of Minnie and pointed out the box where the words '*I confirm that I have read, understand and accept all the above terms and conditions of this mortgage*' were followed by a scribble.

"Is that your signature, Minnie?"

"No, that's not how I sign at all." Minnie picked up the form, squinted at the signature, ran her fingers over it, and put it back in its place on the table. "The bastards. The absolute bastards. I loved that house, it was where I was going to grow old. Look at this shit-hole - sorry Janie, but let's be honest, it is - I try to keep it nice, but every time I step past the wee and needles in the corridor it reminds me of what I've lost. Bastards. OK, me and you and the rest of your Dad's gang robbed banks, but we never stole anything from the little people and we certainly didn't rob anyone of their house." She stood up and turned away to look as if she was washing up at the sink, too late to hide tears that Janie had already seen.

"I'm sorry, Minnie," Janie said, standing behind her with a hand on her shoulder, "I didn't come here to make you cry. I came here for something else."

"What?"

"You. For a bank job. The biggest bank job we've ever done. I want to put the old gang back together. Me, Rudy, Nutter, and you too Minnie, plus Sam, Helen and Jess. Together I think we can to take down RoyalBank and get David out of gaol. And get you your house back. I want to know if you're in?"

Minnie dried her hands and picked up the page with 'her' signature on it. She held it up facing Janie and said, "Oh I'm in, Janie, believe me I'm right in. You're the Guvnor's daughter after all. I'm all the way in. When do we start?"

"Right now." So over lunch Janie told Minnie about her plan and the parts she had in mind for Nutter, Rudy and herself. Minnie added some very useful suggestions that they were later to act upon. Then Janie told her how much money there was in it for her, half up front and the rest on completion, as is the custom in that part of the world. Minnie put down her knife and fork.

"I'll accept the money, thank you, that's very kind of you, it'll set me up on my feet again. But you're a rubbish businesswoman Janie, Maxie's friends will always be my friends, I'd have done it for nothing if you'd asked me." For the services that Minnie was subsequently to render, Janie would have given her double if she had asked for it.

Minnie told Janie that she would probably find Nutter in the park talking to the pigeons and, it being early afternoon, Rudy would almost certainly be in the pub.

Nutter was sitting on a bench in Bethnal Green Gardens, surrounded by pigeons that were pecking at the seeds he was throwing down for them by the foot of the 'Do Not Feed The Pigeons' sign. Janie walked slowly towards him, not wanting to startle him or his pigeons. As she got closer, she noted that although he was only a little older than her, he had not aged well. His hair, which when she last saw it was tousled and clumped, was now all gone. His eyes sat under sagging lids, and the expressionless white face that used to stare into bank tellers' eyes and strike fear into every nerve in their body was now creased and blotched with age and wear.

His clothes were about as shabby as clothes can get, and inside those clothes his whole frame seemed to have collapsed in on itself. From the footpath opposite his bench, Janie paused to watch the shrunken old man formerly known to his friends as Nutter, and concluded that she would have to drop him from her team, and therefore have to drop the plan itself.

But it did not seem right just to walk away from one of her oldest of old pals without even a 'hello'. So Janie moved to sit down on the same bench while the pigeons bustled along obligingly to make a space for her.

"Hello Hulk," he said, without looking up, "I knew you'd come back one day, I've been waiting. I recognised you as soon as you came round the corner. It's been a long time."

"It certainly has been a long time. How are you, Nutter? Is it still OK to call you that?"

"People still do so I suppose it still is. I'm alright. Getting along."

"What happened?"

They sat together for an hour with the pigeons waiting patiently around them while Nutter told his story. Like her, he had made it away from the Guvnor's last raid and he was still in one of Maxie's secret hiding places at the time of the funeral. He told Janie that when the police did eventually find him they interrogated him for weeks on end, even roughed him up, but he had just sat and taken it all without flinching or uttering a word.

Released without charge for lack of evidence and in the absence of any admission, he was in demand from other gangs but turned down their offers and found himself a job at a car factory out in Dagenham.

He told Janie that for years he moonlighted as an enforcer and worked for anybody he liked, and for nobody he didn't like. Collecting debts, retrieving goods not paid for, inviting rival operators to get off his paymaster's patch, encouraging runaway spouses to return lovingly to their doting partners, advising prosecution witnesses to become forgetful in the box, reminding jurors that their homes and families were being watched, that sort of thing.

In time he settled down to his day job on the assembly line and, like Janie, moved away from Bethnal Green and never expected to come back. However, car sales fell during the recession and production was cut back. The older workers were offered redundancy money if they would go on their way.

Nutter told her he had no need for the money, he had enough to live on and breed pigeons with, but the factory would not be the same with most of the people he knew gone, so he took the offer. He told her that he was then robbed of his money and pension by a conman. Janie did not need to ask him how - she already knew.

He had to give up his home and pigeon shed and returned to Bethnal Green, where he knew he could get a cheap room. For the past five years he had lived on welfare and charity from old friends, and this life had inflicted much of the visible damage on him that Janie could now see close up. But for a person who has done some very unpleasant things to creatures of his own species, he spoke fondly of the cats with which he shared his rented room, and he told Janie his address when she asked him.

"I know you can't have been just passing through the park for no reason," said Nutter when he'd finished his story. "What have you really come for?"

"I came to recruit you."

"What for?"

"A gang I'm putting together to do a bank."

He shook his head. "Not me, Hulk. I don't do that now."

Nutter watched the pigeons around his feet. Janie said nothing. It was only after several minutes that Nutter broke their silence.

"You see, Hulk, I had good money twice in my life, and what good did it do me? The first time was when we were robbing banks, and all it got was your Dad killed, you gone away and my other friends in prison. Then I worked in that car factory all those years and when I got made redundant I had money again, but that pension man took it all. Sure, I was angry at the time, but do you know what? If I bumped into him now I'd let him walk on by, he was only doing what we used to do but without a gun." He lapsed into silence while a black-and-white pigeon with a club foot hopped onto his lap to check the folds of his jacket for spilt seeds.

Nutter continued. "I've grown old Hulk, look at me. And I've changed. I don't get angry with people any more, and I'm too weak to do anything about it if I did. And I've changed inside too. I forgive, I forget, I walk past. I don't want to know. So whatever you're planning, Hulk, don't tell me because I don't want to know about that either."

"I gathered as much, Nutter," Janie said, "I'll leave you in peace and wish you well. Goodbye, it was nice to catch up with you." She put her hand out to shake, but Nutter, who had never once looked at her, stared down and followed the movement of the pigeons under his bench. She put her hand away.

Janie was twenty yards distant when she heard the sound of Nutter's flock of pigeons taking flight in agitation. Nutter was standing up and facing her.

"Which bank?"

She walked back over to him. "RoyalBank."

"Which branch?"

"No branch, Nutter. The whole bank. I want to take the whole bank. For what they've done to my family."

"Well good luck with it." And with that he picked up his bags and shuffled away towards the park gates.

Janie stayed on Nutter's bench for a while. His pigeons soon got the message that she had nothing for them and drifted away. She was re-thinking her plan to see if there was any way that they could pull it off without Nutter. And whichever way she looked at it, there was not. The plan needed Nutter. And with no Nutter there was no plan, and with no plan there was no bank job, and with no bank job there was no freedom for David.

Janie's next port of call was going to be the Oak Barrel, where Minnie had told her she would find Rudy, but she had second thoughts. She walked back to Bethnal Green Road and drew £100 from a cashpoint and, having nothing to write with, bought a biro at the little newsagents by the station. Then she walked over to Nutter's place.

Nutter's address was an old four-storey tenement block that had survived the Blitz but did not look likely to survive for much longer the spread of redevelopment that had crept from the tower blocks of the City of London nearly a mile into Bethnal Green in the years she had been away. The half-open front door led into a grubby hallway and an unpainted stairway, which she ascended. Each room off the stairwell had a number and she found Nutter's and knocked. There was no reply, except the scuffle and miaow of a cat. She tried the handle. Locked.

So she sat on the bottom step of the next flight, took out her wallet and the biro, and searched in her bag for the only piece of paper that she had on her. It was blank on one side, on the other was some text that she had asked Helen to print out for her to show to Nutter if the occasion arose. It read -

EXTRACT OF SECRET RECORDING OF ROYALBANK DIRECTORS AND ASSOCIATES DATED FRIDAY 23 OCTOBER 2015

*Sir Gordon Gordon: I saw in the papers that a load of car workers got made redundant and that they're being fleeced by reps from finance firms buying their company pensions off them cheap using an up-front cash lump sum as bait, and flogging them rubbish pensions in their place. Any of them from RoyalBank by any chance?*

*Sir Charles Borden: Absolutely not. RoyalBank is all about Honest British Banking, not ripping off British workers. In any case, if we got found out and it went public then it'd do our reputation no end of harm.*

*Sir Gordon Gordon: So?*

*Sir Charles Borden: So Melissa's set us up a special company to do it, it's offshore and can't be traced back to RoyalBank.*

*Sir Gordon Gordon: Everyone's a winner then?*

*Sir Charles Borden: Everyone except the redundant workers. But then they aren't paying our wages, are they?*

Janie scribbled it out with the biro, then turned over to the blank side and wrote:

*Dear Nutter, It was good to see you again after all these years. Here is some money for your cats. I am off to find Rudy now to see how he's getting on, All the best, Janie/Hulk*

Janie reckoned that Nutter would be too proud to take money for himself, but might let her help with his animals. She folded her note around the £100, pushed the bundle under Nutter's door, and left leaving the street door open as she found it.

With no Nutter, Janie's plan was done for, but since she had come all this way she decided to look Rudy up anyway. He was, as Minnie had said he would be, in the Oak Barrel, at a corner table by the fireplace. His glass was empty so she bought them both full ones, then went over to him.

"I was hoping you'd call by, Hulk," he said, after a handshake that turned into a huge hug and a slurp of beer that became nearly a pint. "I heard you were back in town."

"From Minnie?" she asked.

"No, actually it was one of the gardeners at the cemetery who clocked a stranger visiting the Guvnor's grave a couple of days ago. Nobody ever visits it and he was curious. He mentioned it to his uncle who knew your Dad and put two and two together and he told me."

"I'm impressed," she remarked.

"And so you should be, Hulk, there's not much goes on here I don't get to know about." His beer was already gone, Janie went for more, and on her return she asked him how he had been getting on all these years.

As Rudy spoke, Janie looked him over. He had aged of course, but not as much as Nutter. The face was still Rudy, round, fleshy, less hair on top but still plenty, a beard that was not there before, spectacles ditto. But now all of his face was pretty much red, so it would not matter too much what his nose chose to do.

Janie could see that his torso still had bulk and strength, but the shirt that housed it was gone at the collar and the jacket over it was fraying at the cuffs and elbows. He did not look as if he had much money and he did not stop her when she later offered to buy his third and fourth pints.

Rudy had been caught with his gun in his hand on the pavement next to the security truck, by police who poured out of the vehicle's side doors and jumped on him. While the Guvnor lay dead under a blanket on the pavement and Nutter and Janie were off on their toes, he was on his way to

Leman Street police station in handcuffs, with evidence preservation bags taped over his hands. He pleaded Guilty to armed robbery, was sentenced to twenty years, and with good behaviour served twelve.

He told her about his life in prison. People who have never seen inside a prison read and often believe what the papers about what a cushy existence it is, with snooker and TV, a well-equipped gym and three square meals a day. That is not how Rudy found it. It was horrible. Ghastly. Violent. Dangerous. Degrading. And particularly humiliating for a man whose nose goes red any time he is anxious, annoyed or embarrassed. Janie could not help thinking of her own son David, enduring all of that even as they spoke.

Rudy confirmed the snippets of news that Minnie had given Janie over the years. He told her how on release he had worked all hours and saved until he could scrape up the deposit on a loan to take over the Oak Barrel, which was going cheap because nobody wanted to run the old-time pubs any more.

"When I was stood behind there," Rudy said, waving his glass in the direction of the bar, "I felt like I was the King of the World. And I was making a go of it too, taking enough money to keep my head above water, till that fellow from the bank came in with his loan swap thing."

"RoyalBank?"

"Yes, it was. The ones that have "Honest British Banking" on all their adverts. We'll I'll tell you just how honest they are, Hulk." And he told Janie the story, though she already knew it, of his loan swap, and how the man from RoyalBank came a year later and told him that if he did not quadruple his loan repayments they would take his pub. He could not afford the increase and when his money ran out, they took his pub.

"I'll confess this," he said, "I was a mug. I didn't read the forms, I just took the man's word for it that I'd be protected from increases in the interest rate. And it was free,

I didn't even have to pay anything for it. Even now I don't really understand quite what happened and how I fell for it."

Rudy told her about his pleasure and pride in rescuing the old pub, and his heartache at having to leave the last time. He praised the new landlord, who had kept the pub going the way Rudy had set it up, and who gave Rudy a generous slate. In return, Rudy more-or-less lived at his table by the fireplace and ensured that a stream of his old friends and regulars kept up their patronage of the Oak Barrel to catch up with and share the local gossip, scandals and rumours and spend their money buying the new landlord's drinks.

"But it's good to have you back, Hulk," Rudy continued. "I think a lot about the old times, you and me and Nutter and Minnie, and the Guvnor's jobs. Do you know, every night in prison I used to go over all those jobs in my head, every little detail, reliving them, he was a perfectionist was your father, he ran perfect jobs that never went wrong till that last time. It kept me sane all those twelve years. Then maybe I got off to sleep, maybe I didn't. But he's gone now and none of that will ever happen again."

No, Rudy, Janie thought, but there is one job that might still have happened, if only Nutter had not gone soft .

"Do you see anything of Nutter these days, Rudy?" she asked, over Rudy's third pint.

"He's mostly in the park, entertaining the pigeons. You'll probably find him there now if you go that way."

"I already did, Rudy. He was covered in them. What do you make of him?"

"He's still a nutter."

"He doesn't look too good though, does he?" she said. "And he's changed. He says he doesn't want a fight with anyone, he even forgives the guy who robbed him of his redundancy money. He told me he just walked away from it all. That's not the Nutter I once knew."

"Yeah, he tells everybody that. It's just a little act he puts on for people. Don't be taken in by it, Hulk, it's just how he deals with things that upset him, you know, he just blanks them out. I told you, Nutter's still Nutter and he's still a nutter."

Janie looked across the table at him. Rudy must have thought she doubted him. Which she did.

"Listen Hulk, there's a story going round about what he did to a guy recently who was giving him hassle over his cats."

"What story?"

"Well, his landlord is some Asian feller who rents this old condemned block from the council in a false name but doesn't live there. He lets it out by the week and by the room to whoever can pay cash on the nail, and turfs out onto the street anyone who can't. Nutter lives there with a bunch of cats someone dumped in the park as kittens in a cardboard box."

"I've been round there, he was out but one of his cats said hello."

Rudy paused for a long draught of beer. Janie could see that another pint would soon be needed.

"Anyway," said Rudy, "Apparently his landlord told him the cats had to go and Nutter told him to go away and leave him alone, only a bit stronger than that, if you get my drift. It went on for months but Nutter wouldn't answer the door to him. Then it appears that a couple of weeks ago, while Nutter was out at the park with his pigeons, the landlord got in the room with his master key and was scooping all the cats into a bag to go and throw them in the canal when Nutter got home."

The beer was gone. Janie bought him another and Rudy picked up his tale.

"Well, I heard Nutter went nuts. Forget how he looks, that man's made of steel wire and springs. I'm told he jumped the landlord, trussed him up in his belt and shoe laces, strapped him to the bed, and pushed a screwdriver deep into the thick muscle of his thigh. Slowly. The type with the flat end. Apparently they hurt more, especially if you push it in then twist it. That's what I'm told, anyway."

"Didn't he scream?  Didn't the other tenants call the police or anything?"

"Oh that landlord screamed all right.  A lot.  Quite loud too, I should think.  I would, wouldn't you?  Nobody called the police though, the sort of people who live in week-to-rent rooms in an illegally sublet council block tend to have lives which aren't improved by any sort of contact with the police. Anyway, the landlord's disappeared and according to my reliable source, if he does come back Nutter will refuse to pay any rent until his mattress is replaced because now it's got blood stains on it."

"I can believe that, it sounds more like Nutter.  But how reliable is your reliable source?"

"Pretty damn reliable, Hulk.  Here comes my source now, you can ask him yourself."

Janie looked up.  Nutter was threading his way past the bar in their direction, and was soon at their table.

"Hello Hulk," he said, "The cats say thank you for their money.  And another thing," he said, placing Janie's note unfolded and with the printed side up in front of her on the table next to her glass, "When do we start?"

Janie, Rudy and Nutter spent what was left of the day at Rudy's table in the Oak Barrel, talking about times gone by, what RoyalBank had done to them all, and the job to come. When Janie told them how much money was to be put their way they both, like Minnie, said they would do it for free, Rudy so he could relive the glories of old times and Nutter, she suspected, for the opportunities it might bring to frighten and hurt people he did not like in ways he had not yet tried. But Janie insisted they both be paid, and had set aside an appropriate portion of Jennifer Harding's wealth in order to do so.  The idea of using money stolen from banks to finance an attack on a bank that stole from her, quite appealed to Janie.

# CHAPTER 44  THE LIST

Sam, until recently the Brighton area finance manager for the British Care group and now an unemployed job-seeker, took readily to his new job of running the money side of Janie's operation. He went through the plan with her and then turned out a set of spreadsheets with estimates and costings for all the necessary purchases, rentals, expenses, payoffs and bribes. Allowing a ten percent margin to be on the safe side, the cost came to two and a half million pounds.

"No problem," Janie told him, "Minnie's just sent me the latest statement for Jennifer Harding's account in Jersey, and with another year's interest it's just short of six million, so we'll have plenty left for if you've got it wrong."

Sam went off in a temporary huff at the suggestion that he might have got anything wrong, but he was soon back.

"It's all very well having that money in the account in Jersey," Sam said, "But it's not much use to us over there. For what we've got to do it needs to be here, preferably in the form of a suitcase full of cash up in the attic. How's that going to happen exactly?"

"I don't actually know," Janie replied. "I've never taken any money out of the account before. When I opened the account in Jersey I was in a bit of a hurry to make my flight home without you knowing I'd been there, so I never even asked about how to make withdrawals."

"Well maybe it's time you did."

Janie looked up RoyalBank's number in Jersey and called it.

"RoyalBank, can I help you?"

"Hello, my name's Jennifer Harding, I have an account with you and I'd like to talk to someone about making a withdrawal please."

"Putting you through, madam."

Twenty seconds of irritating bank telephone music and then "Ms Harding, good afternoon, David Holmes speaking, I understand you would like to make a withdrawal?"

"Yes please."

"Do you have your account number to hand?" She did, and read it out.

"And if I may ask you some security questions, can you tell me the balance as at the date of your last statement?" She told him that too.

"And your date of birth?"

"Eleven one fifty-five."

"Thank you, and how much are you looking to withdraw?"

"A million pounds, please. In cash"

"That's quite a large amount, Ms Harding. The simplest way would be for you to pop over here and see us, bring your passport as proof of your identity, and we can have the money waiting for you. And as one of our most valued customers, we'd be delighted to sort you out your visit, hotel, meals, drinks, taxis, see the sights all with our compliments. Bring Mr Harding, if there is one, or someone else if you fancy, what happens on the island stays on the island, as they say."

"I see some things haven't changed then," Janie said.

"I beg your pardon madam," said Mr Holmes.

"Nothing, sorry. But actually I'm a bit too busy to come over to Jersey," she said. Nor did Jennifer Harding have a passport, but Janie was not going to mention that. "I was rather hoping I could collect the withdrawal somewhere a bit closer to home."

"I quite understand, Ms Harding. To do that I'll need further verification of your identity."

"Of course. What do I need to do?" Janie hoped he was not about to ask her for a driving licence and utility bills, because Jennifer Harding had none of those either. But he didn't.

"Well let's try this," he said. "I have your file in front of me. It goes back to well before my time of course, but it's got the date on it when you opened your first account with us. Can you tell me the year?" Janie told him not only the year, but the actual date, and the branch.

"But it wasn't called RoyalBank then, it was Royal London Bank in those days," she added.

"Very good," Mr Holmes said, "Just one more check. Do you by any chance recall the name of the person in Jersey who opened your account here?"

Janie made a show of struggling to remember. "It was something like Bourne, I think. Or Brandon. No, I remember, it was Borden. Charles Borden. He told me his wife is French and he likes shooting. I don't suppose he's still with you after all this time, though."

"Actually, he is still with us, though no longer here in Jersey. I've never met him so I couldn't tell you about his wife, but I do know he still likes shooting. Well done for remembering his name."

"We got on well, I remember. I even gave him a nice bottle of Champagne to say thank you for his help, but I shouldn't think he will have mentioned that in the file."

"Indeed not madam," said Mr Holmes. "Now, let's discuss how to get this money to you. I've got a suggestion."

Janie liked his suggestion and three days later she packed Helen off for a day trip to London to cheer her up a bit. First class seat with an empty suitcase on the train up, lunch with a couple of girlfriends there, then over to one of RoyalBank's branches in Knightsbridge, where on production of the twelve digit reference number Mr Holmes had furnished Janie with, she was taken to the vault and given a key to one of the deposit boxes there.

She opened the deposit box and transferred the contents into her suitcase. She and the suitcase made it safely home where Sam, being an accountant by profession and mistrustful of banks by experience, counted every note and confirmed that the money was all there. The suitcase and the million pounds found refuge in a section of the loft that Jess had cleverly boarded off to look like part of the chimney breast.

The upstairs room at the Oak Barrel had not changed a great deal since the Guvnor's last briefing there. There were still metal and plastic chairs stacked untidily in the corner, folding trestle tables on their sides next to them, and uncleared debris from an old Christmas party.

If you wanted to hire the room using a credit card and get a VAT receipt it was fifty pounds an hour, but if you just slipped the landlord a twenty in cash it was yours for as long as you liked, and he gave you the key to lock the door from the inside too. Just like in Dad's day, reflected Janie, except that then it was ten shillings.

Janie arrived early with Jess and forked out her twenty, plus twenty more for the barman in return for his assurance that they would not be disturbed. They went up to the room where Janie drew the curtains right across all the windows and put on the lights, then set out chairs round a central table while Jess tidied up tinsel and broken crackers.

Helen, Sam, Nutter, Rudy and Minnie came trooping up the stairs together. Janie locked the doors and was going to start with introductions until they pointed out that while waiting they had met downstairs so she did not need to. So she began the briefing. "Helen, our targets please."

Helen unrolled four large sheets of wallpaper, one for each of Melanie Campbell, Mike Phillips, Charles Borden and Gordon, each sheet filled with photographs that Helen had collected up from the internet. She sellotaped them to a wall and everyone went over to have a good look at them.

As they stood around each sheet of pictures, they talked about everything that Phillips, Borden, Gordon and Campbell had done to their lives; David gaoled for a fraud they told him to commit, Helen sexually assaulted and then fired for reporting it, Jess's business stolen, Sam's job and pension sold for a pound, the Lockwoods' home soon to go to pay the bills for it all; Nutter's pension money stolen too, along with Rudy's pub and Minnie's house; and all the other people they knew for whom austerity and the recession were the personal price they paid for the greed and deceit of Phillips, Borden, Campbell, Gordon and all the other bankers like them.

Then they all threw in ideas. Minnie's were often the best and the ones they eventually went with. Nutter had some good suggestions too, but all of them were deemed too cruel even for their chosen prey, so Janie had to rule them out, reluctantly. It took half the day, but by the afternoon they had a plan for each of their targets.

Next, Janie briefed Helen on what information they needed her to find out about the targets using her access to RoyalBank's computers, and Rudy and Nutter on the surveillance work to be done of the homes and movements of Phillips, Campbell and Borden.

Then she passed round a list. It read –

1. *Transport*
2. *Gun*
3. *Clothes*
4. *Lock picking*
5. *Computer*
6. *Phones*
7. *Girl*
8. *Money*

Transport was first, and she gave this job to Rudy, confident that he would know somebody who could meet their needs. Rudy knows a lot of people.

"We're going to want vans for the next few weeks," Janie told him. "A different one every day, plain ones, no markings but all properly taxed and insured." She insisted on this. "Too many criminals have come to grief over simple things like that. Even the Yorkshire Ripper got caught because he had false plates on his car."

Rudy was onto it. "Good as done, Hulk."

"You can call me Janie if you like, Rudy." she said, "I haven't been Hulk for quite a lot of years."

"Rudy isn't my name either," Rudy pointed out. Janie had forgotten that. "And I don't know about you, but I don't think I can remember now what Nutter's real name actually is."

Nutter shrugged and clearly was not going to enlighten them. Janie moved on.

"Nutter, we need a gun."

"No problem, Hulk. I used to do some jobs for the Turkish boys and they owe me a favour. How much ammo?"

"We aren't going to fire the gun, it's just for us to wave around, Nutter," Janie said, "No shooting, so no ammunition, OK?"

"Got that Hulk, no shooting, no ammo," said Nutter. Janie detected a hint of disappointment in his voice.

Sam was next. "Sam - clothes?"

"I'll take Rudy and Minnie to Stratford on Tuesday to choose their outfits, I'll pick up the bills." Janie nodded approval. Much though she loved Rudy and Minnie, she also knew them of old and did not fancy the idea of letting them go shopping with an unlimited amount of Jennifer Harding's money and no supervision.

Lock-picking next. "Jess, what about getting into Melissa's place?"

"Rudy and Nutter need to get me photographs of her doors and windows, then I'll borrow whatever tools I need from one of the girls who used to work on my lock-fitting crew."

Janie moved on to Helen, "Computers and printing?"

"I'm all set up in the study at home, Mum. Nothing as exciting as lock picks or guns though. Just my laptop and a mountain of printer paper, ink and envelopes. And coffee."

"OK. Phones. Jess?"

"I've got a six dozen pre-paid mobiles. They are to be used for all calls, I'll dish them out when we split up today. Each time you use one, chuck it away and get out another one. Not very environmentally friendly, I know. But that way nobody can be traced."

Next item on the list - item seven, the girl.

"Minnie, getting us a girl's going to have to be your department."

"I've got a niece called Louise, she's smart with big ambitions and I'm sure she'd do the job on Gordon if the money's right."

"Do you think a quarter of a million would be the right money?"

"I should think so, Janie."

"Thank you everybody," Janie said, "That brings us to the finances. Sam, over to you."

Sam passed out an envelope each to Rudy, Minnie and Nutter. "Here's a thousand pounds cash each for any expenses. Use it to pay for everything you need. Let me know if you're running short and I'll top you up. And here's something that I have never said before in all my years as a professional accountant - don't keep any receipts."

Janie nodded in agreement. On this job, the less paper the better.

Sam continued, "And Minnie, Nutter and Rudy, if you'd like to see me in the car park when we've finished up here, I've got a holdall in the car for each of you with the first half of your money. I'll give you the rest on completion, I'm told that's how things are done round here."

It was time to get to work. "OK everyone, are we ready to start the watch on Melissa's house tomorrow morning?"

"We're ready, Guvnor," replied Rudy.

# CHAPTER 45 THE RECONNAISANCE

Even if the old Guvnor was robbing a bank that he walked past every week, he took his reconnaissance seriously. He would watch the comings and goings, look round the back, observe the staff routines, and check the approach and escape routes. He never tired of reminding his gang about the careless getaway driver who parked with the passenger door right next to a concrete bollard, and the unfortunate gang who failed to do their homework and were caught while trying to escape by pushing on an exit door that was marked 'PULL'. He left nothing to chance. So, as the new Guvnor, nor did Janie.

Back home from London, she set Helen to work.

"Helen, I'd like you to take a good look at Mike Phillips. Using your access codes, how much do you think you can find out about him?"

"Give me time and I'll find you everything the bank's got."

"Such as?"

"His diary, all his appointments, his expenses and travel, minutes of all the meetings he goes to. All his letters and e-mails, except those ones we deleted for him when the Financial Conduct Authority came calling that time. Even his bank accounts and credit cards. What are we looking for?"

"I don't know yet, Helen. But Mike Phillips is a big man and also a crook, and every big man has a weakness and every crook leaves a trail. Just go through everything RoyalBank's got on him and see what you can find."

"Yes Guvnor," said Helen. She was teasing Janie, but Janie quite liked it.

"And while you're at it, do the same for Gordon?"

Helen shook her head. "Not possible for Gordon, he doesn't work for RoyalBank, remember?"

"OK, then just concentrate on Mike Phillips, but if Gordon does pop up anywhere let me know."

Helen evicted Janie from the study and started work that same evening, and while Sam made the supper, Janie turned her attention to tomorrow.

Very early the next morning Janie was at Clackett Lane services on the M25, where Rudy and Nutter picked her up in a small white van. They headed off together to take a peek at the Campbell and Phillips residences.

Melissa Campbell's place turned out to be a large and well-kept detached house on the edge of Epsom in Surrey in the Millionaire Row of England's premier stockbroker belt, set in immaculate gardens backing onto woods, with no neighbours for a quarter of a mile on either side. There was a red van parked on the gravel drive, and they drove past just once so as not to draw attention to themselves, then moved on to their next observation.

The Phillips' abode was twenty miles away, still in Stockbroker Surrey, and like Melissa Campbell he had equipped himself well. Sited down a side road in a little wooded valley, an old stone gateway opened onto a driveway leading to a half-timbered Elizabethan-style mansion surrounded by an acre of lawn and a paddock and then a forest of oak trees.

"These rich bastards make it too easy for us," observed Nutter. "Back home we all lived in upstairs flats where there weren't any trees for anyone to hide behind and watch us from."

As they drove back past the house for a second look, a woman came out of the front door and made for a yellow Ferrari that was parked on the front drive. She appeared to be around thirty, tall, blonde and dressed in a short padded jacket over tight jeans and knee-length riding boots.

"That must be the new Lady Phillips," Helen was to tell Janie when she was back home and asked about the woman. "We heard he'd traded wife number three in for a newer model. But there were rumours going round the tenth floor that all is not well in the Phillips household and she's just

257

waiting to dump him and take half his money when she gets the chance."

Back at the motorway services Janie treated Rudy and Nutter to a pie and chips lunch and they dropped her back at her car. From then on Rudy and Nutter were in Surrey almost daily, in a different vehicle for each visit.

Mostly they worked on Melissa Campbell, using routines from Nutter's old enforcer days. Observing from the woods behind her house, they established that she lived alone, and that if she was not staying in London or away on business travel she left home at seven fifteen each morning in her Lexus. Unobserved, they trailed her the mile to Epsom railway station where she parked in a reserved space and caught the seven thirty-five, first class, to London.

A man-and-woman housekeeper-and-gardener team arrived at her house daily in their red van at eight and let themselves in, departing around four before Melissa was home. If the recycling bins were due out the following day they put them by the front gate as they left, convenient for Nutter and Rudy to empty into a sack in their van as they drove past. Then once a fortnight when Janie was visiting the London half of her gang, they tipped the sack out on Minnie's table and went through it.

They were not looking for anything specific in Melissa Campbell's recycling, it was just part of building a picture of her life and probing for vulnerabilities. She was careful, there were no bank statements, bills or letters, so presumably she took them to the office and put them in the confidential waste there. For several weeks they drew a blank and found nothing to suggest any secret love interest, dodgy dealings or any other way to get to her.

One afternoon after the red van had gone, Rudy kept watch while Nutter crept out of the woods and worked his way round the sides and back of Melissa Campbell's house taking photographs of the doors, windows and alarm box. Janie met up with them afterwards, collected the camera and took it home to Jess who went to see her locksmith friend.

Jess came home unimpressed. "That Melissa woman's got all that money yet she's too tight to spend a penny of it on security! Those patio doors were withdrawn from production ten years ago, you can open them from the outside with a screwdriver if you know the trick."

"And do you know the trick?" Janie asked.

"I do now."

"Won't the house be alarmed?" Janie asked. Her own knowledge of burglar alarms, though comprehensive in its time, must surely have been overtaken by technological progress, and she told Jess so.

"It isn't alarmed," Jess told her. "The alarm box on the front of the house is a dummy, it's the same make that we used to put up for customers who wanted to deter burglars but who didn't want the hassle of setting alarms every time they went out."

"I suppose with a housekeeper there every day Melissa doesn't expect anyone to break in," Janie said. "How are you at burglary, Jess?"

Since Jess knew how to get in and was so confident that there was no alarm, Janie gave her the job. One afternoon when the hired help had gone home, Jess applied a screwdriver expertly to the exact right spot on Melissa Campbell's patio window frame, then she and Nutter went for a snoop around the house while Rudy kept watch from the van. They spent an hour searching all the places where, from Janie's past experience of doing what they were doing now, she told them people keep things they do not want burglars to find. For good measure Jess took photographs of every room. Then they let themselves out the way they had come in, with Jess putting the patio door fittings back as she found them.

Back home, Jess told Janie what they had found and showed her the photographs. All Janie learned from them was that Melissa Campbell lived alone in a very nice five bedroomed house, and that it was clean and tidy and contained expensive furniture with smart clothes inside and tasteful ornaments on top. She had old prints and modern paintings on the walls, and framed photographs everywhere of her receiving awards and shaking hands with famous people. There was no sign that she shared her home or life with anyone, no alcohol or drugs, no safe or locked cupboards or drawers, and no sign of any secret hiding place or illicit wealth.

As far as bringing Melissa Campbell down or rescuing David was concerned, they had drawn a blank. Janie told Rudy and Nutter to be patient and keep watching.

One evening Helen called Janie in to the study.

"Hey Mum, you know you asked me to look out for anything about Gordon in the bank's files and I said he wouldn't be in there because he doesn't work for RoyalBank? Well, he's just turned up!"

"Where?"

"In the expenses system. It turns out the bank's been paying his hotel bills when he comes over from Monaco. Look, I've run them off for you."

Helen showed her some printed sheets with, each month, the name G. Gordon against a bill from the London Hatton Hotel. "I've cross-checked with Mike Phillips's diary, and it turns out the hotel bills are for the Thursday evenings before Gordon comes in for his Friday afternoon Findlays meetings with Mike Phillips and the rest of that crowd."

"Should I read anything into that?" Janie asked.

"Not really," Helen told her, "Gordon flies over from Monaco on Thursday afternoons to do business on Friday including having his Findlays with Mike, Charles and Melissa at four, then he meets up with Lady Gordon when she flies in to hit Harrods and Selfridges over the weekend. Gordon's one of the bank's most important clients so fixing him up with a free hotel would be no big deal. But look at this."

Helen showed her the file on her screen.

"For the same nights as the hotel bills, RoyalBank have also paid out another charge of £1000 to something named 'Foxhill Services'. I've never heard of them."

"Nor me," said Janie. "It sounds like a stopping point on the M1. And what sort of service costs £1000?"

Helen looked up Foxhill Services on the internet. Their website announced them as "London's premier corporate entertainment specialists" who promised "your business clients the best treatment in the capital" with access to "sold-out theatre and sporting event tickets, exclusive clubs, the best tables at London's top restaurants", and "whatever special welcome package you would like us to customise for you and your guests" with "absolute discretion and confidentiality".

Janie pursed her lips. "Sounds like it could be for something Lady Gordon might not approve of if she knew about it."

On her next weekly trip up to see Minnie, Janie asked her if 'Foxhill Services' meant anything to her.

"Oh, I know them, Janie," Minnie told her. "Foxy owns it, Mark Fox, he was at our school a few years after us. He started out as a street corner ticket tout, then got concessions on left-over discount West End theatre tickets, and after that he's never looked back. If you want something special and you've got the right money he can get you anything. And I mean anything. Tickets, VIP passes, introductions, drugs, girls, boys, you name it, Foxy's at your service."

"So if our friends at RoyalBank are paying your mate Foxy a grand for some sort of services every time Gordon spends a night in a hotel in London, am I right in thinking there are no prizes for guessing what services Foxy is providing?"

"No prizes at all. That'll be Gordon's prostitute for the night. A grand is about what Foxy would charge. Seven hundred for him, three for the girl. That's how it works."

"So how does it work, Minnie?

"Well, the girl Foxy sends round certainly won't join the client for dinner, it's too public, and it's sex not seduction that he's after. But before ten he'll finish eating and go to his room. She needs to arrive around ten fifteen. It's all quite early because they both have to go to work tomorrow. She walks into the hotel unaccompanied and the receptionists give her the room number and wave her past, they know the score. The hotel doesn't mind, satisfied hotel customers mean repeat business."

"And then?"

"And then he screws her, according to his budget and requirements. She may or may not stay the night, but if she does she leaves in good time for him to phone his wife to wish her good morning and tell her he loves her and how much he's missing her, then he has breakfast alone and gets back to the office. Where if he's a banker he can get on with screwing all the rest of us too."

"Thanks Minnie, you've educated me," Janie said. "And given me an idea."

Back in Brighton, Janie asked Helen to have another look at Gordon's hotel bookings. Helen took herself off for another trip into RoyalBank's computers and found that the bank had booked his rooms a year in advance, and for all except one of the dates there was also an order for the unspecified services of Foxhill at £1000. Janie was puzzled as to why Gordon would forgo his pleasure on that one occasion and made a mental note to see if she could find out why.

# CHAPTER 46  THE GOLD RUSH

It was time to turn some attention to Charles Borden, and as Janie set off for yet another visit to David she was still searching for a suitable way to bring Borden down.

After his trial and conviction David was only allowed one family visit a fortnight, and Janie timed her visits to Minnie, Rudy and Nutter so that she could see David on the same round trip.  Only two visitors were allowed on each prison visit so Helen, Jess and Sam took turns to come with her.

In some respects David bore up quite well.  He liked structure and had no difficulty adapting to the rules, procedures and routines that define daily prison life, and followed all the prison officers' orders diligently and without dissent or complaint.

He picked no arguments or fights with fellow prisoners, and finding a number of them to be illiterate he read them their letters from home and helped them compose suitable replies.  And Janie suspected that the prison food, however basic, was more regular and nutritious than whatever David had been feeding himself in his flat and on the hoof for the past decade.

But, she reflected sadly, it is no life to have to lead if you are innocent and have been framed by the people whom you admired and trusted.  And as she looked him over from the other side of the bolted-down metal table in the visitors' room, she reflected on another irony - that she, the guilty-as-sin bank robber, had lived her life at liberty while he, the innocent young victim of crooked bankers, would be behind bars until his best years were all gone.

Visiting times were strictly limited to an hour. Sometimes this hour was completely filled by David talking about his prison experiences and the visitors bringing him up to date with family news.  On other occasions there was time left over, and as Janie did not want to leave any of the allotted hour unused, she would ask David about the people he knew at RoyalBank. This might seem strange given that these were the men who had him gaoled, but David had enjoyed his time at the bank and liked to reminisce, so Janie encouraged him to talk freely.

It was on one of these visits, when Sam and Janie were using their last few minutes to hear David talk about his early years at the bank, that he mentioned the work he had done on gold prices for Charles Borden. The subject had come up at his trial but William Clarence QC had not pursued it.

"So you never read the letter that you took to New York to give to the American from NationBank?" Janie asked David.

"No, it was already sealed down when Mr Borden gave it to me and I just passed it on."

"And the American fellow didn't read it to you?"

"No, he just put it in his pocket."

"Then after you came back from New York, how did RoyalBank's gold trading go?"

"I checked half a half a dozen times over the next two years," he told her. "I saw that the bank started making a profit on its gold trades, but after that I was put on other jobs so I never looked at gold again."

While Sam drove them home, Janie broke her thoughtful silence only once.

"Sam, if there's one thing I know about gold it is that it attracts criminals. Always has, always will. Those Brinks Mat gold robbers back in the '80s got away with ten times more in gold than the Great Train Robbers took in cash, and most of it was never found. We need to look for gold."

Back home, Janie asked Helen to go prospecting for gold in RoyalBank's archives, starting with any hits on the word 'gold' in Charles Borden's personal correspondence file.

That is how Janie found herself reading the letter that had been marked 'For Deletion' but was missed, and that fourteen years previously had been addressed to *'My dear American friend',* and that told him that *'you will continue to manipulate the gold price as you have done to date, but from now on you will telephone Mr John Smith on that number the day before you fix the rate, so that he may have advance knowledge of the rates you are going to set, and trade profitably as a result'* and ended *'With best wishes, Your new English friend'.*

"Nice work, Helen."

"Thanks Mum. Is that it then?"

"Not quite. Can you work through RoyalBank's computer systems and find all the gold trades handled by the bank from the time of David's visit to New York right up to the present day?"

"What? That'll take weeks!"

"You'd better get started then."

Helen shrugged and was off, but she was back the next morning with a computer stick. "Got them, they're all on here." she said. "What next?"

"I thought you said it would take weeks."

"I'm a quick worker." It was good to see Helen back to her old chirpy self.

"OK Helen, now delete from your list, all the trades that were made by businesses that would have a legitimate commercial interest in buying and selling gold, such as mines, mints, electronics factories and jewellers."

Helen spent much longer on this task, because it meant matching hundreds of thousands of transactions against tens of thousands of clients. She found that she could not possibly do it by hand, so she had to write a computer programme to do it for her, but she managed it in the end and reported back a week later.

"Done it Mum, now what?"

"Right, from those deals that are left, delete all the ones that originate in countries with a functioning regulatory and tax regime, like the USA, Canada, Australia, the European Union countries, and even the United Kingdom just about. Then let's see what's left." And off Helen went again.

That task really did stretch her and it took her several weeks. Helen could not come up with a computer short-cut this time, and had to open up each gold transaction in turn, look at who was selling to whom, trace each of these parties and find out where they operated from. It was a laborious and repetitive job so she roped Sam in to sit beside her and help, and they got there in the end.

"Here's your list, Mum. All RoyalBank's dodgy gold deals."

"Exactly Helen, you now have the world's first database of all the gold deals that RoyalBank has done for people who are not in gold-related industries, and who operate from countries that don't check what you are up to. As you say, dodgy gold deals. Well done."

"Thanks, Mum, but I can tell from your voice that we haven't finished yet. Now what?"

"Analyse it and tell me what it says."

"How do I do that?"

"I've no idea, I'm a just a booted-upstairs hardware seller, remember. I'm seeing David tomorrow, why don't you come with me and we can ask him."

Armed with David's tips, Helen and Sam worked late into the night, and in the morning Helen told Janie what they had found.

"What it says, Mum, is that nearly a third of RoyalBank's iffy gold trades involve Russians. There are Russians moving gold out of Russia, Russians moving gold into Russia, and Russians who aren't in Russia at all selling gold back and forth between each other and to lots of other people who aren't in Russia either. What is it with Russians and gold?"

"I'm no expert on gold trading or Russia, Helen, but I do read the newspapers. I should think a lot of these trades are likely to be oligarchs and mafia types hiding their money and doing their dirty deals. Unpleasant characters, some of them, apparently."

Helen grimaced, then picked up and opened a ring-binder.

"Well in that case I do hope Royalbank are watching their own backs, because I think they're ripping these Russians off."

"Them too? How?"

"Sure. If you look here," Helen pointed to a row of figures that she had marked in yellow highlighter, "and here," she showed her another row, "and here," another row, "and all these," she showed Janie a whole page of lines of highlighter, "it's always the same thing. There are fluctuations in the world price of gold that match the exact times of the trades. There's something odd going on over and over again."

"What should I be seeing?" Janie squinted at the rows of numbers, unable to make out what Helen was telling her.

"Look. It's the same every time. The customer tells RoyalBank to buy gold. Just before the bank buys the gold, the gold price dips and the bank buys the gold at that cheaper price. A few seconds later, the gold price bounces back up and that's the higher price RoyalBank charges the customer." Helen ran her finger along the lines of numbers and now Janie could see it, all the numbers and times and prices matched up as Helen said.

"And that's not the end of it, Mum. When the bank's selling gold for a customer, the gold price dips just before the bank buys the gold off the customer, then jumps back to normal by the time they sell it on. I don't know how they do it, but it's such a consistent pattern that it can't be a coincidence. What do you make of that, Mum?"

"What I make of is that RoyalBank is skimming a bit off for itself every time it buys or sells gold for a customer. So the bank must either be fixing the gold price themselves, or being tipped off by someone else who is doing it. And with that letter you found, I know which it is." Janie took the letter out of its file and re-read it.

'*I am now in possession of a comprehensive file of evidence that implicates you . . . I am offering you the option of co-operating . . . to*

267

*indicate your willingness to co-operate with me, you will call the private United Kingdom number shown on the enclosed card . ."*

"There must be billions or maybe trillions in gold deals every year, with masses of them going through RoyalBank. And the bank fixes the deals and takes a slice every time. And then I should think the bank has the cheek to charge their customers a commission as well. Can you believe it?"

"Mum, you're forgetting I worked for them, I know what they're like, so yes I can believe it."

"Helen, last task, I promise you, weed the list until that it only shows the deals that involve Russians, and against each deal put how much money the buyer or seller lost to Charles Borden's little rake-off. Then it's job done."

"I'll bet it isn't," said Helen.


One afternoon Janie was at Minnie's place with Rudy and Nutter sorting through Melissa Campbell's latest paper recycling sack when they found an empty envelope addressed by hand to Melissa and bearing a postage stamp from Panama. It seemed out of place to Janie, and among the junk mail, newspaper and cardboard cartons there was no corresponding letter.

"Nutter," she said, "When you did Melissa's place did you spot anything that might have to do with Panama?"

"Nope."

"Sure?"

"Yep."

Janie had a similar response from Jess when she asked her the same question, and just to be sure she blew up all the photos Jess and Nutter had taken inside Melissa Campbell's house to see if they had missed some clue to her Panama connection. There was none.

So next she tried Helen.

"Helen, did any connection between Melissa Campbell and Panama ever come up in your Friday sessions at the bank?"

"Panama was mentioned once or twice as a handy place to send money to if you don't want to pay tax on it, but nothing specific was said that I remember, and I can't think of anything in the recordings I've listened to."

"Then would you be a treasure and listen to all the rest, unpleasant though that must be for you? I need to know what's going on with Melissa and Panama."

"Okay Mum, if you say so. What's the priority to do first, Melissa and Panama, or Charles Borden's gold deals?"

"Both."

"Thanks, Mum, I thought so."

# CHAPTER 47  THE BIG SPENDER

Janie took stock. Rudy's and Nutter's watch on Melissa Campbell's house drawing to a close, and Helen's work on Charles Borden's gold deals and Gordon's nocturnal entertainments was now complete. It was now time to turn the attention to "Call-Me-Mike" Phillips, or to be correct, now Lord Phillips of Kidwelton, Peer of the Realm, Chairman of the nation's biggest and most prestigious bank, and champion of Honest British Banking. Janie doubted that he had told anyone to call him 'Mike' for a long while now.

Helen used to work for him. Now Janie put her to work against him. Her mission was to crawl all over RoyalBank's records, systems and data and find where they might be able to gain some advantage over him. Janie thought it would be another weeks'-long long job for her, but to her surprise Helen was back to see her the same afternoon with a sheaf of print-outs in her hand.

"Tell me again who this man is, Mum?"

"You know who he is Helen, you've spent years in his delightful company, only now he's a Lord and the Chairman of the whole damned caboodle. Why do you ask?"

"And tell me how much you think he gets paid?"

"I don't know, you're the one who's got his bank statements. Five million a year? Am I anywhere near?"

"Not bad, but closer to eight million when you add in his bonuses and all his other directorships. And an extra £300 tax free for any days he signs in at the House of Lords, even if he just turns round and goes back out again. So how much money do you think he's actually got?"

"No idea. Shedloads? Is shedloads a recognised financial term?"

"Well, I've been through all his bank statements and credit cards. He does it all through RoyalBank, the top bosses have to use their own bank, it's stipulated in their contracts, it would be a bit embarrassing if it came out

270

publicly that the boss of the bank was using a rival bank for his accounts."

"And?"

"I think he may be skint."

"Skint?"

"Brassic."

"Brassic?"

"Broke. Done for. However you want to put it, he's got no money."

"Show me."

And Helen did. Sam came to join them and they all spent the evening poring over Lord Phillips' statements for his many current accounts, savings accounts and credit cards, trying to make sense of them.

Around eleven, a tired Sam made a valiant effort to get them all to go to bed and start again in the morning, but he failed and headed off upstairs alone. By then Janie and Helen were deep inside the world of this complicated man, and they were still at it at six in the morning when a rather tetchy Sam came down to complain about sleeping alone and bringing in toast and tea.

But what Helen said about Mike Phillips being skint seemed to be right. She and Janie had spent the early hours of the morning mapping the flow of his millions into, around and out of his accounts and plastic. They started with scraps of paper, then post-it notes stuck on the wall, and in the end Janie sneaked out to the garage at three in the morning, quietly so as not to wake Sam and draw his attention to the fact that she had still not come to bed, and brought in a roll of white wallpaper.

On this wallpaper they had drawn a tangled network of multi-coloured lines, shapes and numbers that always led them, by whichever route they took, to the same astonishing conclusion: Lord Phillips, Chairman of RoyalBank, pulled in well over half a million pounds a month but was, as Helen had put it, skint.

Their wallpaper showed huge sums of money going into his current account every month, his salary from RoyalBank and several other well-paid directorships.

"People in Lord Phillips' position never only have one job," Helen told Janie. "They have their full time paid main job and then they have lots of other positions as directors and chairmen of other big firms too. They get paid pretty well for those jobs too, for a day a week or a few days a month. Once, the girls in the office added up all the days he was being paid for in a year and it came to about five hundred days. So somebody's being had over somewhere."

The wallpaper showed that Lord Phillips had plenty of money coming in, over £500,000 a month after tax and national insurance which even bankers have to pay. But there was also a lot of money going out, and this is what took them the rest of the night to make sense of.

For a start there were some eye-watering outgoings that looked as if they must be maintenance payments. Helen recalled that even in the time that she worked on the tenth floor he had two divorces, and from his outgoings it looked as if he had racked up at least one more prior to that.

Then there were six sets of school fees - Helen had no idea that even minor boarding schools were so expensive. Big payments to credit cards. Four mortgages! Was this a mortgage for each house he had left a divorced wife in? Or multiple mortgages on his present house? They could not tell, but it all added up to a whole lot of mortgage.

Then there were assorted cheques, card payments and cash withdrawals that did not tell them much except that day-to-day living seems to be pretty pricey when you are a Lord with a trophy wife and you run a bank. Overall, every month at least as much money went out as came in, and his current account was usually overdrawn close to its £1,000,000 credit limit by payday.

Helen then took Janie through Phillips' savings accounts. A few hundred pounds here and there, that was all. This was a rich man who spent what he earned and had nothing left by the last week of the month, just like many of his bank's rather less affluent customers.

Then it was time to look at his twenty credit cards. Helen told Janie that whenever a bank launches a new card, its Chairman and directors all have to have one so they can be seen to use it. But the surprise was that most of these cards were continuously at their top limit, again like those of many of his humble customers, and he was only paying the minimum each month to avoid the penalty charges. Sometimes he missed even those dates and was hit, like his customers, with a hefty late-payment fee.

There was nothing unusual about the types of entries on his credit card statements - just clothes, restaurants, food, drink, trips, entertainments, house furnishings, and so on - but what was staggering to Janie and Helen, and what took up several feet of their wallpaper, was the size and frequency of the purchases. Lord Phillips certainly lived the high life, and by the looks of it the current Lady Phillips was a lady who liked to lunch, shop and get her hair done frequently, expensively and preferably in Paris, New York or Dubai.

"Helen, you've worked among these people, how do they get like this? What's going on? How can he pull in eight mill a year and still have no money?"

"It's not that unusual, Mum. To people like Mike Phillips, money isn't wages to live on, it's status and power. They measure their own importance by the money they spend, and compete with other men to out-spend them. Offer them the choice of a ten pound bottle of wine and one that tastes just the same but costs a thousand pounds, and they have to buy the thousand pound bottle, and make sure everyone sees them giving the wine waiter a hundred tip on top. Their whole way of judging their self-worth is by the money they spray around. Spending's like a drug addiction to them, they need to do it, they can't stop."

"If that's the case," Janie said, "I think we should give him a helping hand."

273

After breakfast Helen went off to get some sleep, and Sam sent Janie out to for a walk on the Downs to keep her awake. She was glad of that, because as she trudged wearily up to the viewpoint at the top her plan for Lord Mike Phillips took shape, and the next day she called in on John Murphy to ask for a little help. She did not tell him what she needed it for and he did not ask, but she left his office with what she went for - a sample of the standard letter that a solicitor sends to someone who is about to be taken to court and sued.

Janie went for another walk, by the beach this time, to clear her head for the work ahead, and when she arrived home there was a sheet of printed paper on the kitchen worktop next to the kettle. Helen's neat handwriting was across the top – '*Hi Mum, this is all I could find on Panama, hope it's enough, H. XX*'

Janie read on:

FRIDAY SESSION DATED 7 NOVEMBER 2014
Present: M. Phillips, C. Borden, G. Gordon
*Gordon: No Melissa this week?*
*Phillips: She's away. Sends you her best wishes Gordon.*
*Gordon: Where from?*
*Phillips: Panama.*
*Gordon: What for? I avoid Panama when I take Jubbly round the Caribbean, it's supposed to be a bit lawless there.*
*Phillips: She told me it's the best place on earth right now for keeping your money away from tax inspectors. They have law firms who fix it all up for you and apparently the money's just pouring in. One of the big-shot partners out there has useful connections with the Panama government and is also a pal of Melissa's so she's off to see him. Presumably there will a few more billions not going to the British taxman once they've hatched whatever plan they are up to.*
*Gordon: It makes what I'm doing in Monaco look like small change.*
*Borden: Perhaps you should up anchor and move to Panama, Gordon.*

*Gordon: I shouldn't think the shopping there is up to Lady G's standards.*

"That'll do nicely," Janie said, to nobody in particular.

# CHAPTER 48  THE DAME

The gang had been working flat-out for weeks. Helen and Sam were poring over computer screens and their stacks, literally, of print-outs. Rudy and Nutter were driving up and down country lanes and skulking around, come rain or shine, among trees and bushes. For her part, Janie was running back and forth between them all while keeping up with David's prison visits.

Jess meanwhile carted little Harry around with her while she called on her former staff doing her best to help them with their job applications and unemployment benefit forms, and from what personal funds her family still had she saved a few from bailiffs and evictions.

The sale of the house was going ahead. Sam and Janie accepted an offer that would cover what they had borrowed to pay for William Clarence QC's services and PCMG's Local Business Support review, leaving just enough for the rent of a small flat that Sam found for them around the corner from Janie's old bedsit.

Meanwhile, David was still in prison, the people who put him there were still free, and Janie was becoming impatient.

When Helen printed out her work on RoyalBank's Russian gold trades, it came to four hundred pages of numbers, spanning the entire period from when David arrived back from New York up to the present day - or to put it another way, for the whole time that Charles Borden stood to gain financially from bonuses linked to the profits of rigged gold prices.

At Janie's request Helen used the bank's personnel records to write up a short career profile of Charles Borden showing his links to the gold trading team and his annual bonuses, and ran it off along with another copy of the '*My Dear American Friend*' letter. She typed up a covering note that Janie dictated to her, then made thirty-one identical packs each containing the 400 pages, letter, profile and note.

Janie put each pack in a large envelope, sealed and addressed eleven of them and left the rest unsealed, then took them out to the garage to be ready to go in her car boot on a forthcoming trip up to London.

The next day Janie was back at Minnie's kitchen table with Rudy and Nutter, catching up on all the local chit-chat. Minnie had baked them a cake and while she cut it and handed it out, Janie asked, "Are there any Russians round here?"

"Russians?" said Minnie, "Not really. Most of the Russians in London are too well off to live in Bethnal Green."

"Yeah," said Nutter. "There's a few Russians settled in, they got to know about me somehow and I did a bit of work for them. But not the boss men, if that's who you're looking for. Just the workers, like me."

Rudy was of the same accord. "They come out of the woodwork when the World Cup's on and Russia are playing on the big telly screen down the Oak Barrel, then they go crazy, but otherwise you need to get over to Mayfair and look for the streets with the biggest cars, that's where they'll be."

The next task was to sort through Melissa Campbell's latest offering to the recycling industry. There was quite a lot that week, she must have been having a clear-out.

As they sorted through, it was Rudy who spotted it first.

"There's a bit missing," he said, holding up the business section of last Friday's Daily Telegraph, and sure enough there was a small neatly cut out space where an article ought to have been.

They spread the rest of the bag out on the floor, but whatever should have filled that space was not there. As curious as Janie, Rudy offered to go round later to all the local newsagents and get hold of a copy of Friday's Telegraph and phone her with the result, so they tidied up the kitchen and set about their next task, which was to discuss Mike Phillips.

Helen could now tell her exactly what he earned and how he spent it, but Janie needed to know more. She called Rudy and Nutter off from watching Melissa Campbell and switched them over to the Phillips residence, starting the next morning.

Rudy was on his way to Lord Phillips' home in Surrey, with Nutter at the wheel, when he phoned Janie on one of the disposable mobiles to tell her what he had found out about the cut-out space in the Telegraph, which was - nothing.

He told her that he had trailed round all the newsagents and there was not a copy to be had, they had bundled up all their unsold papers and sent them back to the distributor the next day. The public library had copies of all last week's papers and Rudy went there with the intention of filching last Friday's Telegraph but it was missing, presumably already taken by somebody else. "What's wrong with Britain today?" Rudy grumbled. "Now people are even stealing the newspapers from our public libraries."

The barbers' shops all had a pile of last week's papers on a bench or shelf, but these were the Sun and Mirror, not the Telegraph. And no chippie has served fish suppers in old newspapers for a generation, not even in Bethnal Green.

When she got home and told all this to Helen, Helen rolled her eyes in despair, pressed a couple of buttons on her phone, and found the article straight away.

"Just ask somebody my age next time," she said. "Newspapers are online now. Is this what you're looking for?"

"Oh," Janie said, as she stared at the little screen phone. "I think it must be."

### HONOUR FOR CAMPBELL.

*Melissa Campbell, a senior partner at PCMG, is to be honoured for services to the advancement of women in business, according to an announcement from Buckingham Palace yesterday.*

*Soon-to-be Dame Campbell said in a statement, "I am delighted to receive this great honour, and I sincerely hope that it will be a clear signal to other women in business that there is room at the top for them too if like me they have the drive and determination to get there."*

*Ms Campbell, 58, has been the Daily Telegraph businesswoman of the year a record three times, and her honour will mark the high point in a career marked by numerous other awards in recognition of her work in encouraging other women to climb the ladder to success.*

Below the article was a photograph of Melissa, looking very pleased with herself.

For security reasons most royal engagements are not published in advance, but when the Queen is at home presenting gongs the date cannot be kept a secret because all the recipients and their families and the press have to know. In any case she is secure in her own palace, so investiture dates are published well in advance in the Royal Gazette. Helen looked up her date - Monday 21 December, a nice Christmas present for Melissa. Janie had a rather different present in mind for her.

It was time to get back to Gordon. Janie asked Helen for her list of Gordon's hotel bookings.

"I'm interested in that one where he doesn't have a date with Foxhill," Janie said. "See what you can find out, will you?"

"Yes, Guvnor."

Helen was back with her an hour later.

"I think I've got it, mum," she said. "He has a hotel reservation and a Foxhill booking as usual for Thursday 10 December, look." She showed Janie the entries in the bank's booking system. "That's normal, it's the night before his monthly Friday meeting with Lord Phillips.".

"Then Gordon is back at the hotel a week later on Thursday 17 December, but there's no Foxhill booking for that night and no Findlays session on Friday 18 December," she said, "Which means he can't be coming over for that. I looked at all the other Directors' diaries for Thursday 17 December and for Lord Phillips and Charles Borden it says 'Chairman's Club Dinner'. I reckon Gordon's going there with them."

"What's the Chairman's Club Dinner?" Janie asked.

"I don't know," said Helen. "When I worked on the tenth floor all the top bosses used to go to it. It was for men only and they looked forward to it, but it didn't seem to be a topic for discussion afterwards."

"Can you find out where it takes place?"

"I should think so. The address will be on his chauffeur's itinerary." She tapped some buttons. "There it is. Grand Westminster Hotel, London, drop off 7.30, collect midnight. Happy Mum?"

"Happy is what I will be when David is out of prison, and Gordon is in. But good work anyway."

On her next trip to Minnie's flat, Rudy reported on the surveillance of Lord Phillips' place.

"He gets picked up early on work days, around six thirty in the morning," he told Janie. "His Rolls pulls up, the chauffeur jumps out to get his briefcase and do the door, and they're away."

Janie reflected that Phillips would have longer in bed if he just took the train like everyone else, but then she supposed that even first class would not offer the leather-seated comfort and tinted-glass status of a chauffeur-driven Rolls Royce.

"Then her ladyship gets up around nine," Rudy continued. "There's no sign of any kids, though she does have four Labradors, and some horses out back in the stables."

"And a cat," added Nutter.

"And a cat," said Rudy. "She doesn't go out to work, in the week she mostly spends her time riding or going out for lunch. There's a girl does the stables for her, arrives at eight, goes at three. Phillips gets brought home in his car at whatever time he finishes work or wherever he's been out to in the evening. Shall we do his bins and have a look around inside the house?"

"No thanks, I think we've got all we need now. Not just about Phillips. About all of them."

Janie gave Minnie, Nutter and Rudy their next instructions and topped up their expenses money courtesy of Jennifer Harding, then set off for her train.

On her way back to the station she made a detour to the cemetery. The grass had grown up again over the base of the stone and covered the inscription at its base. She pushed it aside with her foot.

"Thanks Dad. Like I said, we're going to take 'em. You'll see. Just watch."

She headed for home, feeling happier than she had done for a long time.

The following Thursday evening, after a final briefing crowded around Minnie's kitchen table, the gang moved out to take up their allotted positions.

Minnie and Rudy were, thanks to Jennifer Harding's bank account and their shopping trip to Stratford, now done up as a respectable married couple, which they both thought was hilarious. They decided to call themselves Bert and Nell Green, which they also thought was hilarious, and took themselves off to the London Hatton Hotel, where they had a reservation to celebrate their wedding anniversary with, in their words, a 'right posh slap up dinner'.

Sam was assigned to the up-market pizza restaurant next door to the London Hatton, alone at a table for two, picking at a starter that he had ordered while waiting for his dinner date to arrive and grumbling to the waiter that if she was late one more time she was going to find herself looking for someone else to buy her pizzas.

Janie herself took up position in the shadows of an alleyway across the road, from where she had a good view of the London Hatton's well-lit doorway. She was now the Guvnor and her gang were all in position. She glanced down at her watch. The date was Thursday 10 December, the time was seven forty-five in the evening, and Gordon, carrying a small case and a suit bag, was stepping out of a taxi that had pulled up in front of the hotel steps.

Even if she had not studied his face from the many internet photos that Helen had run off for her, Gordon was easily recognisable from his height and girth. He paused for a commissionaire to take his luggage and escort him through the doors.

Janie crossed the road to the Original Pizza Co, joined Sam at his table, and ordered. At eight fifteen there was a text message from Rudy, "He is having dinner". Then at nine forty-five, "He has gone to the lift. We are having drinks near reception". Then at ten past ten, "A girl has just gone up." Janie waited ten minutes, then picked up her mobile and dialled the hotel's number.

"London Hatton Hotel, can I help you?"

"Thank you, could you put me through to reception please?"

"This is reception madam, what can we do for you this evening?"

"I'm Lady Gordon, my husband is staying with you tonight. I've been up in town at the theatre so I've decided to pay him a visit. Would you just let him know, I don't want him gone to bed by the time I get there." Janie paused for effect. "Tell him five minutes, my cab's just pulled up."

"Of course, madam. Will that be all?" But Janie had already rung off.

Janie would love to have watched the scene in Gordon's bedroom when the hotel receptionist called up say his wife was on the way, but the following day Minnie phoned to report on what happened next.

Whatever the pandemonium in Gordon's room, Minnie told her that just four minutes after Janie's call the girl walked calmly, fully dressed and hair in place, out past reception and towards the street. "A good professional," Minnie told Janie later, clearly impressed.

Minnie followed the girl out and, as she left the hotel, stepped up beside her, took her arm gently, and said, "Don't worry dear, I'm in the same business as you. I know what happened, it used to happen to me too. Come with me and let me get you a coffee, I've got a financial proposition for you."

The girl went with her to a late coffee bar, and Rudy joined them at their table.

"My name's Tina," said Minnie, "and this is Richard Prendergast, he's from Prendergast Associates, a DNA tracing company."

"Good evening, miss, it's a pleasure to meet you," said Rudy, with his serious voice on.

Minnie continued., "I won't ask your name, I don't need it. But I can assure you Mr Prendergast is legit, unlike that pig of a man you were with just now in the hotel. Do you know, he's fathered children all over the place and refuses pay a penny to support any of them. One of the mothers is one of my girls. It's not right. Mr Prendergast needs a DNA sample to prove paternity. If you can get us one there's good money in it for you. How much are you getting paid tonight, if you don't mind saying?"

"He's one of my regulars. Three hundred."

"Cheapskate. I can get you a good bit more than that. And you know that man is a millionaire don't you? But anyway, Mr Prendergast has five grand for you . . .show her, Richard" - Rudy did - "if you can get him the DNA sample he needs."

"How?"

"Here's how." And, leaning over the table, Minnie told her how.

A few minutes later, Gordon heard a gentle knock on his door, and when he opened it, in came not his wife but the girl. "Your wife's not coming," she said softly, closing the door behind her, stepping into the room and unbuttoning her coat and then her blouse. "I spoke to a girlfriend of mine who works on reception. They're getting a lot of prank calls like that just now, somebody must think it's funny. Do you want to carry on where we left off? I think you do."

He did. When she took out a condom and started to put it on him, he protested, "You don't usually make me do this," and she replied, "I'm full of surprises, and anyway tonight you have to do whatever I tell you to, I think you might like that." She was right, Gordon did like that.

Afterwards, towards midnight, she dressed and slipped out of the room, down the stairs and out past reception back to the coffee bar. She passed the condom under the table to Rudy, who put it in a sealable bag and then into an insulated one-can-size drink cooler. He passed her back five thousand pounds in twenty pound notes in a padded envelope, and

Minnie slipped her own phone number into the girl's handbag. By this time Janie and Sam were nearly back in Brighton.

Next day Janie called on Minnie to check that the cooler bag and contents were safely stored in the back of her fridge. Janie was also going to collect whatever was left from the £500 extra expenses she had given Minnie out of Jennifer Harding's account to pay for last night's celebratory dinner but there was no change, she and Rudy had managed to spend it all.

From time to time Helen's old friends from London used to call her up to invite her out. Usually she did not return their calls, but Helen was not made for the life of a recluse and in the end she accepted an invitation to a pre-Christmas party. The rest of the household were asleep when she let herself in from the last train home, and were up well before her the next morning. When she did eventually emerge, she had something to tell them.

"Mum, Dad, I heard something odd last night at the party. There was a girl there who heard I used to work at RoyalBank and asked if knew an Allan Forsyth. I said I did, he was in charge of compliance, and I asked how she knew him, and she said he used to be her boyfriend. She said he was a total pain because he was always scrounging money off her, but then he ditched her when he suddenly came into a load of money of his own. She said she didn't know where it came from but it all seemed a bit dodgy. She said she didn't know any more than that. Seems odd though, doesn't it?"

"It does. Are you going to look into it?"

"I already did, when I got home. Read this, it was in Allan Forsyth's saved e-mails." She handed Janie two sheets of paper.

The first sheet was an e-mail chain between Allan Forsyth to Melissa Campbell. It began -

*Hi Melissa, as requested, Allan -*
*DRAFT STATEMENT FOR MELISSA CAMPBELL*

*My name is Allan Forsyth and I am a Compliance Manager for RoyalBank.*

*On Monday 15 March this year, on instructions received from Melissa Campbell, senior partner at PCMG, I undertook a search of the photocopier room that is situated on the tenth floor of the banks' London headquarters.*

*With the assistance of a janitor, I moved the photocopier away from the wall and behind it found a number of sheets of paper. I took these away and identified them as papers for a RoyalBank board meeting the previous week.*

*The sheets had no security classification so no security breach has taken place.*

*Signed Allan Forsyth.*

Melissa Campbell replied -

*Allan, Your statement is not what I wanted, please revise the third paragraph as discussed by phone just now.*
*Melissa Campbell.*

His response, sent ten minutes later -

*Hi Melissa, is this better? Allan*

*"The sheets contained information about forthcoming corporate mergers that would, if made known outside board level, have affected share prices. This constitutes is a major breach of security, and would normally result in serious disciplinary action against the individual responsible."*

*Signed Allan Forsyth.*

To which she replied -

*Allan, just right thanks, pop in and see me tomorrow, Melissa*

The second piece of paper was a print-out of a page of Allan Forsyth's RoyalBank bank account, on which Helen had highlighted a cash deposit of £25,000 made two days after the e-mail exchange.

It was Wednesday 16 December and Minnie's kitchen was again crowded. Minnie passed around plates and glasses to Janie, Helen, Sam, Rudy, and Nutter. Only Jess was missing, watching Harry's first Christmas play.

Rudy helped Sam to carry three holdalls containing ten parcels each from the car up all the stairways and into Minnie's bedroom.

"Sorry Minnie, it's only till Saturday," Janie told her, as she peered into Minnie's fridge and moved the jam and marmalade out of the way to make sure Gordon's condom, still in its plastic bag and cool-carrier, was safe. Minnie laid warm mince pies and a bottle of sherry on the table, and Janie made a rare exception to her and Dad's 'no alcohol' rule for briefings, though she left her own glass untouched.

Sharing the table were several rolls of duct tape, a dozen more pre-paid mobile phones and a revolver. It was nine days to Christmas and Janie was starting the final briefing. She went through each of those nine days, one at a time and in detail. How the attacks are to go in, who goes where, who does what, how, when and to whom. Starting tomorrow.

Three hours later and Janie was finished.

"If this all works," she said, "Then by Christmas Day Gordon will be in gaol, Melissa Campbell will on a long sea cruise, Charles Borden will be in hiding in fear of his life and Lord Phillips will not be enjoying his Christmas dinner one bit." She looked around her gang.

"Any questions?"

Nutter had a question.

"Is it still no ammunition, then?"

"No ammunition, Nutter. Any other questions?"

There were no other questions. Janie finally downed her sherry, in one gulp.

"Then it's time," said the new Guvnor, "Take 'em."

## CHAPTER 50  NINE DAYS OF CHRISTMAS

### THURSAY 17 DECEMBER

It was Thursday 17 December, the night of the Chairman's Club Dinner at the Grand Westminster Hotel. Gordon had his hotel room booked at the Royal Hatton but no Foxhill girl this time, and according to their diaries Sir Charles Borden and Lord Phillips were also due at the dinner, with Lord Phillips' Rolls Royce booked to collect them from the Grand Westminster at midnight.

The young lady from the DNA raid on Gordon at the London Hatton Hotel had left Foxhill to work for one of Minnie's friends and received her pay rise. It turned out that she had not believed a word of Minnie's and Rudy's cock-and-bull story about paternity and DNA, but for five grand it did not matter to her what their story was.

Dressed for the cold, Rudy and Nutter lurked in a shadowed doorway opposite the Grand Westminster, their throw-away phone at the ready. They were not alone - they shared their space with a few of London's many homeless, of both sexes and various ages, whose hungry night on a cardboard sheet and cold pavement would be in stark contrast to the stream of chauffeur-driven cars delivering their dinner-jacketed occupants to the feast on the other side of the street.

At two minutes before midnight, Rudy called Janie. "Targets Gordon and Phillips just left, Guvnor, got picked up in the Roller. Borden's not with them, he must still be inside."

Janie and Sam were also dressed for the cold, and also in a dark doorway, but opposite the London Hatton Hotel. "Thanks Rudy, you're stood down, say good night to Nutter for us."

She rang off and waited.

### FRIDAY 18 DECEMBER

A few minutes later, Janie watched as the Rolls Royce drew up opposite her and the large dinner-suited figure of Sir Gordon climbed out a little clumsily. As the car drew away and disappeared round a corner, he made his way unsteadily towards the steps and into the hotel.

Once he was out of sight Janie and Sam walked briskly over to the all-night coffee bar nearby. Minnie was seated at a table well away from the window with a young woman.

"Janie, Sam," said Minnie, "This is my niece, Louise."

Louise was in her late twenties, slim, attractive, long blonde hair tied up, tailored jacket buttoned over a well-filled low-cut top and a short skirt. Janie had not met her before and was not to meet her again, but she felt that Louise certainly looked the part that they had chosen her to play.

"Lovely to meet you Louise," Janie said. "He's in."

Louise extracted long stockinged legs and high-heeled shoes from under the table and headed for the café door.

When Janie and Sam eventually reached home in the small hours, there was a voice message on their phone. *"Hi Janie it's Minnie here. It all went to plan. Louise was as good as I said she would be. I'll take her to the police station on Sunday. This phone's going in the Regent's Canal right now, I'll leave it on so you can hear the splash."* Janie did not hear any splash, but she did hear the phone crackle and go dead five seconds later.

A good sleep and lunch out of the way, Janie put the specimen solicitors' letter that John Murphy had given her in front of Helen, then watched over her shoulder while Helen typed a copy onto the screen and made a few tweaks at her request.

Helen searched around the internet for small obscure law firms a long way from London until she found one that Janie took a liking to. She proceeded to lift their logo and address block from their website and add them to her letter, which now read as if it was from Rodgers Marshall of Darlington.

Rodgers Marshall is a real firm of solicitors and Helen put their real letterhead at the top of her letter, but Janie had her swap a couple of digits around on their phone numbers and e-mail address.

Helen then printed the letter on good quality paper with an envelope to match. In her time as a secretary she must have written thousands of letters for Mike Phillips, but this would be the first one she had done that would have his own name in the address box.

After that, they all had an early night, ready for a prompt start in the morning.

<u>SATURDAY 19 DECEMBER</u>

On Saturday morning Rudy and Minnie were up early, put on smart clothes, which in Rudy's case meant the suit he wore as Mr Green at the London Hatton Hotel as he had no others, and set off on the Central Line headed for Mayfair, each carrying a heavy holdall. Once there, they split up and between them spent the morning calling in at twenty different cafes and bars. At each they left one of Janie's packages behind a seat or under a table where it was sure to be found by staff or cleaners.

For the avoidance of any doubt the packages were marked on the outside, "THIS ENVELOPE CONTAINS INFORMATION ABOUT THEFT FROM RUSSIANS BY ROYALBANK OF LONDON" and the envelopes were unsealed to ensure that their contents were visible and accessible. Janie wanted the envelopes to be found and taken to the manager and then passed on to the manager's Russian friends, not blown up as suspected bombs by the police.

Nutter meanwhile took the other ten packages to a post office in a part of London where he was not known, and posted them at premium rate with guaranteed delivery on Monday. Unlike the others these packages were sealed, and addressed to the nation's major newspapers and TV stations.

Janie and Sam were also up early. They set their alarm for five thirty, were in the car at six fifteen, and pulled up outside Charles Borden's place at eight. It was a very large detached house in a smart suburb of West London, with trees all around and a driveway with in- and out-gates and space for at least ten cars. There were six cars on it, including a muddy Range Rover numbered CB 1 and another shiny clean new one numbered S1R CB.

"I think our friend Charles has bought himself an early Christmas present to celebrate his knighthood," Sam whispered to Janie as they pressed the entry buzzer.

The gate swung wide and they crossed the drive to the front door, which was opened by a dressing gown-clad and unshaven Sir Charles.

"Sorry," he said, "Bit of a party here last night, just clearing up, what is it?"

Then he looked at Janie more closely, as if trying to work out where he had seen her before.

"Good morning Sir Charles," she said, "I am Janet Lockwood, and this is my husband Sam, we've been looking forward to meeting you." Borden was still staring at her. "Our son David Lockwood used to work for you. He's in prison now. But you know that, because you put him there."

"Yes, I recognise you now," he said, "You were in court weren't you. Anyway, I have nothing to say to you, you are on private property and I order you to leave."

"We aren't staying, but let me give you this." Sam was carrying the last of the packages and held it out to Borden, who looked at it suspiciously but did not take it.

"It's not a bomb," Janie told him. "Though for what it's going to do to you it might as well be. It's a print-out from your own bank's computer records of every gold trade involving Russian clients that RoyalBank has fixed on your watch. Plus a copy of the secret letter you got our son to deliver to your contact at NationBank in New York to set it all up."

"That's ridiculous! Take your bloody envelope with you and clear off or I'll call the police." Borden turned to shut the door but Sam's foot was in the way. He opened it again, looked at Janie and the envelope, then over his shoulder into the house, and then said more quietly. "OK, so what do you want?"

"Nothing. We just came to tell you that as I speak, duplicates of this package are being put in places where they are likely to reach rich Russians in London, and some more are on their way to every news outlet in London to arrive on Monday morning."

Borden wobbled as if he was going to pass out, then steadied himself against the door frame. "Why are you telling me this?" he said.

"In case you feel there are any urgent measures that you feel you need to take with regard to your own personal safety."

Janie heard a woman's voice call out from the back of the house, "Is everything alright Charles?" He called back weakly that it was, then took the package from Sam.

"I don't expect we'll meet again", Janie said, "Do enjoy the rest of your weekend."

"Yes, and Merry Christmas," chipped in Sam, and they turned to leave the way they had come.

As the door closed behind them they heard the woman's voice call out "Who were they, Charles?" They did not catch Charles Borden's reply.

## SUNDAY 20 DECEMBER

Melissa Campbell did not attend her investiture, so she never became Dame. At nine o-clock on Sunday morning she heard a knock at her front door. It was Janie. In the absence of her housekeeper she went to answer it herself. There was a chain lock which prevented the door from opening fully but when she peered through the gap she saw only a respectable-looking and smartly dressed woman with a scarf pulled up to her nose to keep out the cold, so she opened up. As she did so, a figure stepped out from concealment beside the doorway and pushed the working end of a pistol into her chest. She looked down at it and then back up at the blotched head that housed Nutter's two dark staring eyes.

"Shall we all step into the house for a minute, Melissa," Janie said. They did.

Janie left the front door ajar for Rudy and Helen to join them from a white van that Rudy parked around the side of the house out of sight from the road. With the front door now closed behind them and with Nutter's gun in her face, Rudy lay Melissa Campbell on her sofa and tied her up. Hands behind her waist, then arms strapped to her sides, ankles lashed together, then feet pulled back and roped to her wrists so she could not move. Tape over her mouth but not her nose, the lady still had to breathe.

Melissa stared at Helen.

"Melissa, this is Helen, she used to work for Mike Phillips at RoyalBank," Janie said. "But I think you know that."

Melissa struggled and grunted but could speak.

"I am her mother, you've met me too, I know what you did to Helen and I am not too happy about it. These two gentlemen are my friends," she said, "The one with the gun is a nutter, he hurts people or kills them when I tell him to." Janie was rather enjoying pretending to be a proper gangster. "Or sometimes even if I tell him not to."

Melissa stared silently but defiantly at Nutter. Nutter glared back at her.

"In a moment," Janie continued, "I will loosen one of your hands and put a pen in it." She held up a pen and a pad of paper.

"Then, Melissa Campbell, you are going to write down for me the computer passwords and codes that will give us access to all the details of every client for whom PCMG has ever arranged tax avoidance. And I mean every single one, in every country in the world."

Melissa made no movement or sound.

"Once you have given us that information you will be removed from here to a place where you will be kept safe until we decide to release you. But if it turns out that you've given us false codes then Nutter will hurt you a lot then shoot you dead. Do you understand?"

Melissa nodded. Rudy untied her right hand and Helen held a pad up to it while Nutter idly spun the chamber of his revolver.

With her pen hand at an awkward angle, Melissa wrote clumsily "I DO NOT KNOW THE CODES" and Helen held it up for the rest of the gang to view.

When Nutter saw it, he broke his revolver open and reached into his coat pocket. He drew out a handful of pistol shells and, in front of Melissa's nose, inserted five of them into the revolving cylinder leaving just one chamber empty. He showed her the five full chambers and the one empty one, then closed the cylinder.

Janie distinctly remembered telling Nutter 'no ammunition'. He looked at her with a shrug and said, "They came free with the gun, Guvnor."

Nutter then turned back to Melissa and said, "Lady, have you heard of Russian roulette? Well I've invented a special version, just for you. It's special because there are five bullets in my gun and only one empty chamber."

Melissa stared back, still burning with defiance.

"Mate," said Nutter to Rudy, "Do me a favour and open the back door."

Rudy did so. Nutter spun the cylinder, raised the revolver, took aim down the garden and squeezed the trigger. There was a bang so loud that even Melissa jumped, trussed up as she was, and the rim of a flowerpot flew off in a shower of terracotta splinters. Rudy closed the door and Nutter knelt down next to Melissa's head.

"There's another reason why my game of Russian roulette is special," he told Melissa. "Each time I fire a bullet I load a fresh one in." Which he did. He touched the warm gun barrel on Melissa's cheek, making her flinch, pointed at her forehead, then stared into her eyes from nine inches away, and started to squeeze the trigger. She shut her eyes tight and squealed through the tape.

"Now be a good girl and write the codes like the Guvnor said," he whispered into her ear. With her eyes still closed, she nodded her head vigorously. Helen again held the pad up to Melissa's pen hand, and this time shakily-written sequences of numbers and letters appeared.

When Helen had the codes, Rudy fetched the van and reversed it up to the side door. Leaving Nutter and Helen to watch over Melissa, Rudy and Janie collected a trunk from the back of the van. They all lifted Melissa into it, then put the trunk and its contents back into the van. They left the house, shut the front door, and Rudy drove them crunching across the gravel drive and up the road in the direction of the motorway and London.

Helen sat on a bench in the back of the van with Melissa's codes on the seat next to her, tapping away at her laptop computer and complaining every time Rudy drove over a bump or round a sharp bend. By the time the van pulled up at the motorway services where they had left Janie's car, Helen was satisfied that the codes were genuine. She and Janie went for a late breakfast while Rudy and Nutter took their cargo on the next leg of its journey.

## MONDAY 21 DECEMBER

"What does Her Majesty do when one of her loyal subjects doesn't turn up for her Damehood and stands her up without even an apology," Sam asked Janie.

"How would I know, I made sure I got there on time when I went to see her. But if she has any sense she takes a well-earned afternoon off and catches up on some telly with a corgi on her lap, while one of her flunkeys adds Melissa Campbell's name to the list of people who will never be invited back for another go."

There being nobody to deceive, intimidate or kidnap on Monday 21 December, and as Janie was busy packing up the house, Sam had time to take a stroll down to the newsagents and buy one of each of the daily papers to see if there was any mention of Sir Gordon's imminent troubles.

There was nothing about Gordon, but Sir Charles Borden had succeeded in getting his name into a piece that was all over the front page of the Financial Times. *"THE SECRET CHARITY FUNDRAISER: MEN ONLY!"* ran the headline. While Janie wrapped ornaments in the inside pages, Sam read the story out to her for the amusement of them both.

*"At 10pm last Thursday night, television and sporting personality Chris Ambrose stepped up to the microphone on the ballroom stage at London's Grand Westminster Hotel and announced "Send in the girls!"*

*He was there to launch one of the most prestigious – and secretive – events of the annual social calendar, the Chairman's Club Dinner.*

*The event's organisers claim that they are raising money for charitable causes through a dinner and auction, black tie of course, attended by over 300 VIPs from the worlds of British business, politics and finance. But you can't apply for tickets, the event is by invitation only. And you can't come at all if you are a woman – it is strictly men only. The only way you can get there as a woman is as one of the 140 'hostesses'.*

*As the dinner began, and to the applause of the standing men, the stage curtains opened to reveal the hostesses, none over twenty-five years old and all wearing skimpy black outfits. To thunderous cheers they dispersed to the tables to take up position and commence their duties for the evening.*

*The event has been an annual fixture for over forty years, but for the first time the hostesses included two undercover reporters.*

*The agency who recruited them and all the other hostesses told them to dress as if 'going out for a high class sexy evening' with 'nice hair' and a 'revealing' dress with 'matching black underwear and high heels'. Many of them were students trying to earn some extra money and the* pay was good, £150 for one evening's work. Their task, they were told, was simple: 'engage with the men, pour their drinks and keep them happy'. Unusually for table staff at a function, they were expected to drink if the men at their table encouraged them to, which they certainly did.

As the dinner got under way and the alcohol flowed, many of the hostesses were subjected to touching of their legs, bottoms and breasts, comments about their appearance, invitations to sit on laps and repeated demands to come up to the hotel bedrooms.

Hostesses told our reporters of guests putting their hands up their skirts and one said an attendee had exposed himself to her whenever she went past to pour his drink.

The guest list includes senior figures from the worlds of advertising, betting, real estate, investment banking, accountancy and motor racing, a hedge fund founder, a government minister, peers, party fundraisers and donors, a famous comedian, and a TV presenter."

"Then there's a list of some of the characters who were on the guest list," Sam told her. "Gordon and Mike Phillips have somehow stayed below the radar, but Charles Borden gets a name-check." He read on.

While all this was going on, an older woman and two men, all in matching suits, patrolled round the ballroom, encouraging the more reluctant hostesses to drink more and make more of an effort to comply with their tables' increasingly ribald demands.

The dinner finished at midnight and many of the guests moved on to a party in the same hotel, taking their table hostesses with them. Our reporters went with them but left after one society figure said to them, "You pair look far too sober," filled their and his glasses with Champagne, grabbed one of them round the waist, rubbed his stomach against her and said "Come on, knickers off and get dancing on that table."

"Sounds to me like a bunch of sad old men," observed Janie when he finished reading.

"Well at least Mike Phillips and Gordon are in the clear on this one, they have witnesses that they both left at midnight. Though I don't imagine they'll be on the guest list for next year's bash."

"I hope Charles Borden made the best of it," said Janie, "He won't be spending too many more nights like that either. Anyway, pass me that paper, I need it to wrap these vases."

## TUESDAY 22 DECEMBER

Tuesday's newspapers still brought no news of Gordon, and Janie wondered how he was faring.

She was also curious as to what Sir Charles Borden might be doing. She asked Helen to have a peep at his office diary, and she reported that all his meetings were still shown in it. Janie doubted very much though that he would be at any of them.

"I'm sure that an organisation as big as RoyalBank, with people all over the world, has a security department and all resources it needs to protect its executives from kidnappers," she said to Helen, "But how does Charles Borden tell the bank, 'There is a dossier of how we've been secretly ripping off our Russian customers for years, the Russians have got it, and the newspapers too, and now I'm in danger so please help me.'?" Helen and Janie had fun trying to picture it.

Nor was there any news on Melissa Campbell, but she was going to be the subject of a trip up to Bethnal Green tomorrow so she could wait till then.

Janie and Sam had planned to spend the run-up to Christmas going round their house deciding which of their remaining belongings they could take with them to the flat and what they would have to sell or give away. These should have been some of the saddest days of their life together, but the thought of what was going to happen to Lord Phillips on Christmas Eve kept them both in good spirits. And their Christmas cheer took another boost when Janie turned on the radio to hear the lunchtime BBC news.

*"There are shocked reactions in the City to the news of billionaire businessman Sir Gordon Gordon's arrest yesterday on unspecified criminal charges.*

*Sir Gordon is the Monaco-based former owner of the British Care group, which he sold for a pound just a year before it collapsed disastrously leaving tens of thousands of British workers unemployed and without pensions.*

*A controversial and colourful figure, known for his lavish lifestyle and usually residing on a luxury yacht in Monaco, Sir Gordon was arrested at London City Airport yesterday evening as he boarded a Monaco-bound flight.*

*Police are making no comment and will only state that a man is currently helping them with their enquiries."*

The story headed the news bulletins on all channels for the rest of the day, but none of the newscasters had any idea what Sir Gordon was supposed to have done. The police must, for once, have managed not to leak.

But Janie knew. When Louise followed Gordon into the London Hatton Hotel she had asked at reception for his room number, 302, then headed for the lifts. She took a ride up to the top floor, judging it to be the quietest, and found an unlocked cleaners' room where she hid for the next fifteen minutes while she ruffled her hair, smeared her make-up, ripped her stockings and pulled her clothes out of place. Then she went back down to the ground floor, hurried out past the dozing receptionist and met up with Minnie a couple of streets away.

She tidied herself up in shop doorway and then the pair of them took the late bus back to Minnie's place, where Louise changed her clothes and underwear. After a nice cup of Minnie's tea, Minnie emptied the contents of the fridge condom onto Louise's pants, stockings and skirt and put them safely away. Louise then closed her eyes and gritted her teeth while Minnie slapped and punched her arms and legs several times as hard as she could.

Minnie walked a somewhat bruised Louise home to her own flat, where her latest live-in boyfriend was woken by Louise and made by her to have sex of a vigour and duration that both surprised and exhausted him.

Then on Sunday morning, still bruised and with her soiled clothes in a bag and accompanied by Minnie, Louise walked into Bethnal Green Police Station to report that she had been raped shortly after midnight last Friday morning by the tall drunk man staying in bedroom 302 at the London Hatton Hotel.

## WEDNESDAY 23 DECEMBER

Putting Melissa Campbell into the trunk was the last time Janie saw her. She stayed in her trunk as Rudy and Nutter whisked her round to the East End of London, and was still inside when, behind an abandoned garage, they transferred her into a hidden compartment in a lorry belonging to one of Turkish Ali's boys. Then Rudy and Nutter went their separate ways, no celebrating, that was the old Guvnor's rule and a good one.

Turkish Ali had settled in Bethnal Green after Janie left so she had never met him, but when Nutter had told her Ali was lending them a gun for free, she had asked Nutter how he knew him.

"I've done work for him, freelance," Nutter had told her. "I helped him out when he was first getting set up. When there were rivals to see off or arrears to be sorted out, his own Turkish boys were pretty good, but when it had to be better than that they used to come to me and I did some specials for them."

"What sort of 'specials'?"

"Best you don't ask, Hulk, then I won't have to tell you. Turkish Ali paid me the going rate and I gave him what he paid for, that's all you need to know."

"Do you think he'd do a job for me?"

"If it makes him money, then that's what he does, Hulk. And if you mean, can you trust him, then you can. He was always straight with me, always paid on time, generally we did our business over a nice bit of his wine. Decent honourable villain, I'd say. Would you like to meet him?"

So a few weeks back Nutter had fixed Janie up a meeting with Turkish Ali, over a meal in the private back room of one of his restaurants in Shoreditch. Nutter came too to make the introductions, after which Turkish Ali said,

"Mrs Hulk, a friend of Mr Nutter's is a friend of mine. What brings you here?" Janie did just wonder whether Turkish Ali thought Nutter's name really was Mr Nutter and hers was Mrs Hulk.

"I have a specialist job that needs doing, and I was hoping you could advise me as to who are the best people to do it."

"Tell me Mrs Hulk, I am listening."

"Would you know anyone who deals with the export of special products from the Central American region, Columbia perhaps, to Britain?"

"Perhaps I could find them if I needed to."

"And would any of this trade take place by sea, perhaps making use of the sort of large containers that we see piled high at Tilbury docks?"

"Compared to air freight, containers are slower but bigger and a lot less expensive and a great deal more difficult to search, if searching is a complication that needs to be avoided."

"And presumably if containers are bringing Columbian produce to us here in Britain, then there must be empty space in the ones going back the other way."

"One would think so, Mrs Hulk. It would stand to reason"

"Would any of that shipping go via Panama by any chance?"

"Panama is very close, and a ship goes wherever its master is paid to take it. Let me help you to some more coffee, Mrs Hulk, then why don't you stop being mysterious and tell me what you actually want?"

Janie told him her proposition, he named his price, and they agreed both over a handshake. Ali made a few tweaks to the arrangements based on his practical knowledge of the Central American import-export business, and in time-honoured East End fashion, Janie gave him half the money up front - £100,000 cash, courtesy of Jennifer Harding - with the remainder on proof of completion.

With two days to go to Christmas, Sam and Jess were still busy packing with Harry's 'help'. To be out from under their feet and to satisfy her growing curiosity as to how Melissa Campbell was faring, Janie arranged to have another lunch with Turkish Ali.

"It all went off no trouble, Mrs Hulk," he told her, "My boys took the trunk off Mr Nutter and his big friend with the red face and moved her out along one of our routes, you don't need to know how or where, some of the time they tied her up and locked her in, other times there was nowhere for her to run to and they let her go loose and get some fresh air. A sea breeze is good for the lungs, much better than this city air."

"She's unharmed then?" Janie asked. That had been one of her stipulations.

"She's in good hands and has suffered no bodily harm, Mrs Hulk. She didn't want to try anything silly anyway, she seemed just confused. My boys didn't inject her with anything, you told us not to, but they gave her some sleeping pills and she was drowsy a lot of the time. When she came to, she kept going on about being late to see the Queen, can you believe that Mrs Hulk?"

"Actually I can."

"Anyway Mrs Hulk, it will take three weeks to get her to where she's going, but it's all set up and my friends in Panama are looking forward to giving her a good reception when she gets there."

After a meal at which she lost count of the courses, and reluctantly declining any more than a single glass of Turkish Ali's finest Dolucan wine, Janie called in on Rudy to check the plans for tomorrow and to give him the envelope containing the letter headed Rodgers Marshall of Darlington, then made her way home through the late shopping traffic.

## CHRISTMAS EVE

Janie woke on Thursday 24 December with David on her mind, trying to picture what his Christmas would be like in a prison cell. It was the day of his fortnightly visit, and since only two visitors were allowed and Jess had not seen him for a while, they left young Harry with his Auntie Helen while she and Janie set off for the haul up to Reading.

Noticing her mother's silence in the car, and correctly identifying it as brooding over David, Jess tried to get Janie talking.

"So how's it all going, Mum?"

"Not bad. All on track."

"Anything new on Sir Gordon, is he still under arrest?"

"Better than that, he's been charged with rape," Janie told Jess. "It was on the news this morning, he'll be appearing in court today."

"Sounds good, Mum. What about Melissa Campbell?"

"I saw Turkish Ali yesterday, he couldn't tell me exactly where she is, but by now I should think she will be in a shipping container enjoying a free cruise to the Caribbean."

"Won't people be looking for her?"

"I doubt it, not yet anyway, maybe after Christmas when she doesn't turn up at work in January," Janie said. "We left no trace of our visit to her house, the only thing we broke was a flowerpot and that would look like frost damage if anyone even notices it. Other than that we left her place just as we found it, all tidy and locked up."

"What about her gardener and housekeeper?"

"They'd have come along as usual on Monday morning and found her not there, but they would be expecting that anyway. By Tuesday they'd twig that she hadn't been home, but they're only paid to keep the place clean and tidy, not to worry about her whereabouts. There must have been plenty of other occasions when she was called away on business at short notice."

"What about tyre marks on her drive?"

"Her driveway's gravel, by the time her staff's van and the postman have been over them a few times there will be nothing to see."

"Won't they miss her at work?"

"They would have known she wasn't coming in on Monday, then if she's a no-show on the next four days to Christmas they'll think she's just taking a longer break. No, I don't think anyone will start to worry about her till they all get back to work after New Year and she still hasn't turned up."

Janie grinned across at Jess.

"And by then she'll be somewhere nice and warm, and the trail will be cold."

"What if someone at PCMG gets nervous about her absence and changes the computer access codes that you got Melissa to give us?"

"Too late. Helen downloaded everything on Monday. And I mean everything. Every single client that PCMG have ever hidden money offshore for, whether it's in secret bank accounts, fake charities, non-existent trusts, bogus companies, film-making scams or whatever other contortions Melissa Campbell and her pals have gone through to save their tax-dodging clients the inconvenience of paying for their own country's hospitals, schools and pensioners."

"You really don't like her, do you Mum?" said Jess.

"She fitted up your sister, and made me cry." Janie told Jess the story of Melissa Campbell and the Institute of Chartered Accountants awards night. Jess had not heard it before.

They were halfway to Reading already. Jess left her mother in peace for a while, then picked up again.

"What about Sir Charles Borden? Where's he now?"

"That I couldn't tell you, because I don't know," Janie replied. "He'll be hiding somewhere where angry Russian mafiosi can't find him. In a friend's house I should think, he has a lot of friends."

"Don't the police do witness protection, you know, make you disappear, then give you plastic surgery and a new identity? I've seen it in movies."

"I'm sure the police can do that, but the clue's in the name, Jess - witness protection. Borden isn't a witness, he's a thief. If he takes his story to the police they will be only too pleased to put him somewhere nice and safe, which is behind prison bars. And he wouldn't even be safe there, if the Russians were angry enough."

"So why didn't we just give all the evidence about his gold trading frauds to the police and let them do that?"

"It would have been too easy for him. With his background he would have got himself into a cushy open prison pretty quickly, and then fooled a doctor that he was in poor health and needed leniency and early release. That's standard procedure for his sort of people. He'd be out years before David. But instead, we've given him a life sentence."

"A life sentence?"

"Yes, a sentence to spend the rest of his life on the run." Janie relished the thought. "He can't answer the door or the phone. He can't use the internet. He can't meet his friends in case they get tailed to where he's hiding. He can't work, or go anywhere. Or go shooting. Or do anything else. Ever again."

She paused to negotiate a busy roundabout, then carried on.

"He'll have to wear disguises and watch out for everyone around him. Every car parked nearby and every footstep outside. At night every sound will wake him in a cold sweat, if he sleeps at all. His shooting parties and hunting trips are history now, all replaced by sneaking and hiding and moving and packing a suitcase and unpacking and repacking and moving on. He was the Killer Banker who put my son in gaol, now he'll find out what it's like to be that giraffe and rhino and all those other animals he hunts."

"Mum," said Jess, "I do believe you've got a smile on your face."

"A little one maybe, I'm saving the big smile for when David gets out."

"What's going to happen to Charles Borden's job?"

"RoyalBank will have to dump him and walk away holding their noses. The story of his gold frauds must get out eventually, and when it does they can't exactly be seen to condone what he's done, so they'll have to put all the blame on him and get him out of the way. After that he'll have no job and no money, and pretty quickly no friends either."

"I can see that, Mum," said Jess. "The way you put it, life on the run doesn't sound much fun."

"It isn't, believe me," Janie said. "I was only ever in hiding for three days and that was bad enough. He's going to live like that for the rest of his life." She pulled off the road into the prison car park and walked to the visitor entrance humming 'We wish you a merry Christmas' to herself.

The visit to David went as well as could be expected in the circumstances. He looked pale and had lost weight, and despite knuckling down to prison life he admitted to crying every night when he was alone in his cell. For security reasons he was not allowed any presents, but the guard turned a blind eye to a Christmas hug.

In the car on the way home they learned from the radio news that the remand judge had refused Gordon bail because was deemed likely to flee the country and not come back. He would be joining David in prison for Christmas.

"That's a downside to being a rich tax exile and owning an ocean-going yacht that I bet Gordon didn't think of," Jess observed.

The traffic was thinning out as people headed home for Christmas. Janie kept glancing at the car clock as it neared five o'clock, because that was when Lady Phillips was due to get a surprise caller on her doorstep.

Her surprise caller would be Rudy, in his London Hatton Hotel suit. The next time Janie and he met, for a quiet after-Christmas drink that was not a celebration, he told her how it went.

Rudy rang the bell and Lady Phillips came to the door.

"Is this the residence of Lord Phillips, madam?" said Rudy, holding an envelope in his hand.

"It is, but who are you?"

"Might you be Lady Phillips then, madam?"

"I am, but as I said, would you mind please telling me who you are and what you are doing here, it's Christmas Eve you know?

"I am a bailiff and I have been instructed by Rodgers Marshall Solicitors to serve this letter on Lord Phillips."

"Lord Phillips is not at home," said Lady Phillips, though of course Rudy already knew that, otherwise he would not have been calling at that time.

"I can accept the signature of a member of his household." Rudy was good at being officious when the occasion arose. "Or I can wait outside madam, or even inside if that is not inconvenient for you?"

"Lord Phillips will not be home until later this evening. And I'd prefer it if you didn't wait, either outside or inside. So shall I take your envelope for you?"

"If you would, madam, it's been a long day and it would be good to get home." He gave her a form marked 'Acknowledgement of Service' and made a show of having her sign it, write her name under the signature, and enter the time and date. He handed over the envelope and headed off into the gloom to the layby round the corner where Nutter was waiting with the van to take them both home for Christmas.

Janie had left the envelope unsealed, in the confident expectation that the minute Rudy was out of sight Lady Phillips, being only human, would want to read its contents. This is what she would have read, on paper headed 'Rodgers Marshall Solicitors', with an address in Darlington and a telephone number and fax and e-mail to match, dated 23 December:

*Dear Lord Phillips*
*Preliminary Notice Before Action*
*We have been instructed by Miss Melanie Jane Eagle of Darlington to commence proceedings in the Darlington County Court, in respect of breach of promise in that you did, from January 3 to March 17 this year, purporting to be unmarried and to have the firm intention of marrying her, thereby and in that genuine belief induce her to consent to have sexual relations with you on a number of occasions, in London and elsewhere.*

*Our client will be seeking damages, compensation and costs to the value of £10,000,000.*

*In accordance with the County Courts Practice Direction on Pre-Court Action, we as her legal representatives in this matter are required to serve on you this our preliminary notice before action.*
*Rodgers Marshall*

It was Janie who came up with the storyline. It was a little corny, but in her lifetime she knew of least two Government ministers who had successfully deployed that same line to seduce their secretaries, so she thought it ought to work.

She chose Christmas Eve to have the letter delivered because all solicitors would be away from work for the Christmas and New Year break and uncontactable for a fortnight. If anyone checked, they would find that the firm of Rodgers Marshall is genuine and the letterhead apparently authentic. If they tried to make contact with the firm the numbers and e-mail address on the letterhead would look right but they would not get through, and it would appear that there was a connection fault somewhere.

Even if they did get the right phone number, nobody would pick up because nobody would be in the office. And if they did somehow dig up one of the solicitors off-duty somewhere, John Murphy told her that each partner will have his own client case-load, and will not want to get involved with a colleague's case and will suggest calling back after the break.

Janie wished she could be in the Phillips household to watch what happened when Lord Phillips staggered in merry from his Christmas Eve drinks. But she did get a clue. When Jess and she arrived home, Helen was in front of her computer watching the Phillips' bank accounts. At seven thirty a flurry of transactions started. Half an hour later, every remaining penny in every joint bank account had been moved into an account that was in Lady Phillips' name only. Practical girl, that young Lady Phillips, thought Janie.

The Lockwood household agreed on a family rule for Christmas, that nobody would mention Phillips, Campbell, Borden or Gordon, the forfeit being to have to do all the clearing away and washing up for a full twenty-four hours.  It was permissible to talk about David, and they did so a great deal, but the others were strictly off limits for the duration.

They made a good job of keeping them out of Christmas Day and Boxing Day, but when Janie came down early the next morning to make herself some breakfast to take back to bed, she found Helen already dressed and at her computer. She was immediately suspicious.

"Hello Helen, and what might you be up to?"

"Oh, hi Mum, I'm seeing what sort of Christmas Lord Phillips is having."

"You do know this means that I will have to report you to the rest of the family and get you posted to washing up duties."

"You do that, Mum, and you won't get to see what I'm seeing here.  Come and have a look!"

Janie quickly pulled up a chair next to her and squinted at the screen.

"What can I see?"

"I've got his credit card accounts open," Helen said. "There was no activity on Christmas Eve, but presumably when he got home he and Lady Phillips were getting their blazing row out of the way."

She scrolled down the bank transactions and said, "But look at what happens on Christmas Day.  Up comes a big credit card charge for a hotel.  I think she threw him out of his own house on Christmas Eve."

"Good," Janie said.  "Anything else?"

"Nothing else on Christmas Day, but on Boxing Day it gets busy.  There are credit card charges for another hotel night, then restaurants.  And a lot of taxis.  When she threw him out, it looks like he forgot the car keys."

"Even better," Janie said. "I'll do your washing up, you just sit here and tell me anything else that happens."

Helen watched the Phillips' bank accounts and credit cards all that day and the days that followed, and whenever there was a new development the whole family abandoned their 'no mentioning the bad bankers' rule and gathered round her screen for a communal viewing.

Phillips' credit cards popped up daily at restaurants at breakfast times, lunchtimes, dinner times and at hotels each morning. Lady Phillips certainly had thrown him out. As family Christmas entertainment it certainly beat charades and Morecambe and Wise repeats.

"Look," Helen said, "Now he's using his credit card for lots of small transactions, he must have run out of cash." Within days Phillips had loaded another five thousand pounds onto credit cards that were already close to their very substantial limits.

From then on it was like one of those disaster movies where a little piece of the dam crumbles, then a bit more, then a small crack, then the crack spreads, then chunks of masonry are falling, and then suddenly the whole dam bursts and unleashes a devastating torrent that sweeps away all in its path. To the watchers gathered around Helen's screen, it felt like that.

On New Year's Day Lord Phillips' credit cards showed that he had moved into a hotel suite in London, presumably to be near the office ready to go back to work.

"Look," said Helen, "He's spending money in tailors and shoe shops. He must have left home with only what he was wearing, and now he needs clothes for work."

"Happy New Year, Call-Me-Mike," Janie said.

Three days later there were two very large hits on his card, for five thousand and ten thousand pounds, from big legal firms in London. Janie surmised that these must be retainers for solicitors, his n' hers. And the other bills continued to rack up - hotels, food and drink for Lord

Phillips and some eye-watering charges from Knightsbridge stores as Lady Phillips hit the January sales.

By the middle of January, credit cards that were due for payment started to miss their dates, and penalty and interest charges were kicking in.

"Lady Phillips is out shopping," Helen told Janie. "Look, that's thirty thousand last week alone."

"I've heard of comfort shopping and revenge sex, but is there such a thing as revenge shopping?" she asked.

"I don't know, but it's pushing Lord Phillips over the edge. Look."

Helen showed her that their current account, which Lady Phillips had emptied before her husband came home on Christmas Eve, was now overdrawn by more than three times what Lord Phillips was paid in a month. Another massive lawyer's fee for Lady Phillips again, and the current account was swiftly yet another £200,000 beyond its overdraft limit.

Janie did wonder how long it would take for the Phillips' to realise that the letter that Rudy delivered was a fake, and she hoped that by the time they did, any damage that had been done to their fragile finances and their strained marriage would be irreversible. And so it proved. Helen called her in again.

"Come quick, Mum, you'll want to see this." Janie pulled up a chair once more as Helen flicked pages across the screen.

"What am I looking at now?"

"He's going round all his old savings accounts and has scraped up a couple of thousand altogether. It's like a rich man's version of searching down the back of the settee, but with the fees he's now paying for his overdrafts it will be gone in a couple of days. The bank's computerised system is now sending him automatic chase-up letters and directing default alerts to his branch manager, poor man, that'll rather put him on the spot."

"So it's all going rather well then," Janie said, sitting back to rest her eyes.

"It certainly is going well," said Helen. "For us, that is, not for him."

Then a week later Helen was trawling about late at night when she spotted something so interesting that she woke Janie up and made her come downstairs to hear about it.

She had noticed that some of Lord Phillips' directorships of other companies were due for renewal but a month after the reappointment dates there was no pay shown for a couple of the them and then in the month that followed the others also all disappeared from his bank statements.

Janie discussed this with Helen and they surmised that word must be getting around that Lord Phillips, Chairman of RoyalBank and champion of Honest British Banking, was fast heading for bankruptcy and was therefore not the sort of person other corporations wanted gracing their boardrooms or letterheads. They watched and waited nervously, as February slipped into March and then March into April.

In contrast to Lord Phillips, Janie knew nothing at all about Sir Charles Borden. There was no mention of him in the papers, so presumably his absence was explained by the bank in terms of some temporary incapacitation.

The Russian gold story did not go public either. Janie knew that newspapers can no longer afford the sort of investigative teams they used to employ, and with hindsight 400 pages of detailed spreadsheet were quite daunting and perhaps they should have summarised it for them to make their job easier. Or maybe it was because newspapers which benefit from lucrative advertising from companies like RoyalBank have to be careful about upsetting their paying clients.

Helen kept an eye on Borden's personal bank accounts but they showed no activity, and his office appointments diary went blank from New Year's Day onwards. Then in February RoyalBank made a low-key announcement that Sir Charles Borden had retired quietly on health grounds and that a successor would be appointed in the near future.

Nor did they know any more about Melissa Campbell. Turkish Ali sent Janie a message via Nutter that he was away visiting his suppliers in Central America and would check up on Melissa while he was out there, then collect the rest of his money when he was back.

But Gordon made up for it by giving them all plenty to enjoy. In the weeks following the news of his remand to prison, a dozen women went to the newspapers and the police to report him for indecent assaults and rapes. Some of them were former RoyalBank colleagues of Helen's, presumably emboldened by the fact that he was in gaol and no longer in a position to do them any more harm. Janie hoped one of them was the author of the *from a well wisher and fellow victim* note left under Helen's blotter.

The papers loved it of course. Sir Gordon was already something of a public hate figure for his part in taking a billion pounds out of British Care before selling it for a pound with nothing in the pension fund. They ran photos of him on his yacht on the front pages, alongside the 'here's what he did to me too' accounts of his female accusers, and as he did not buy any advertising from them, the papers had nothing to lose by tormenting him and calling for him to be stripped of his knighthood.

So in some respects it was indeed a Happy New Year. But it would have been a great deal happier if David was home, and it was a very sad day indeed when Sam and Janie said goodbye to their house by the Downs with views of the sea, and moved into their little rented flat. They almost left behind the suitcase in the concealed compartment in the loft, but Jess remembered it at the last minute and their cash in the attic went into the removal van in order to become their wad in the wardrobe.

Louise did not turn up for Sir Gordon Gordon's trial at the Old Bailey. She failed to answer her witness summons and neither the Crown Prosecution Service nor the police could find any trace of her until a check of airport computers showed that she had left the country in January bound for the Far East. In her absence her case was dropped, but that was of no benefit to Gordon because all his other accusers turned up at court and stood firm against him.

Sir Gordon applied for reporting restrictions, but the lady judge turned him down flat and said that as he was a major public figure there was no point trying to hide the case from public view. Janie thought that maybe she did not like Gordon much either. Gordon's trial was in the same courtroom as David's a year earlier, and although Janie did not qualify for a ringside seat this time the story contained all the elements that attract front page newspaper attention and she had no trouble following the action from the comfort of her armchair at home.

When it came to selecting a jury there was no hope of finding twelve men and women who had not seen a newspaper or the TV news for the last six months, so the judge just had to tell them to disregard anything they had read about Sir Gordon. Janie did not see much chance that they would do that. They must have been one of the best-nobbled juries ever to grace the Old Bailey.

With the jury sworn in, Gordon entered a 'not guilty' plea to all the charges and the trial began. It lasted six weeks, with Gordon denying the accusations of one woman after another and his barrister challenging each of them to admit that she had made up her story. But emboldened by each other, his accusers stuck to their guns and in the end it all boiled down to a question of 'who will the jury believe?'.

Janie knew who she believed, and the jury did too. When Sir Gordon's barrister tried to convince them that as a senior figure in the financial world and someone who has been honoured by the Queen, Sir Gordon was a man of integrity whose word as a gentleman the jury should trust, the press reported that some of the jury actually appeared to suppress laughter.

On an afternoon towards the end of the trial Janie was up in London and managed to find a seat in the public gallery when some people had gone home. Watching Sir Gordon's defence team's body language she gained the impression that they did not have a great deal of confidence in their own client's innocence either.

At the end of the trial the jury found Sir Gordon guilty of all the charges, the judge gave him eight years, and he was carted off that that worst of all prisons, a sex offenders' prison. There was immediate outrage in the press at the leniency, as they saw it, of the sentence, and yet more women came forward to denounce him. The police confirmed that these fresh allegations were being investigated, and the Crown Prosecution Service announced that they would be appealing for a longer sentence.

For most of the news of Sir Gordon's subsequent downfall, Janie had only to follow the papers over the next few months. He was indeed charged with more rapes and assaults, and further convictions added another seven years to his sentence. His knighthood was annulled. Now just plain Mrs Gordon, his wife left him, taking with her the billion pounds and the yacht. Putting them all in her name to avoid tax turned out not to have been such a smart move. His many victims came together and sued him, and his own lawyers took every penny that they left behind.

To fill in the gaps in what the papers told her, Janie had to rely on Rudy who, seated at his table by the fireplace in the Oak Barrel, knew everybody and heard everything. A friend who had a cousin who is a prison officer told him that Gordon became depressed in the company of the other sex-offender inmates among whom he was incarcerated, and the prison authorities twice tried to move him to general prisons in the interests of his own welfare. However, the inmates there recognised Gordon from his newspaper pictures and to protect him from serious injury at their hands he had to return to the sex offenders' prison, where he chose solitary confinement in preference to the company of his fellow prisoners there. According to Rudy's friend's cousin, he is now on permanent suicide watch.  Nutter says he hopes they are not watching too carefully.

Jennifer Harding's funds paid Louise £250,000 for her trouble.  Minnie told Janie that Louise has dumped her boyfriend and is now doing rather nicely for herself running a recreational establishment for discerning gentlemen of means in a sunny and exotic ocean-side city that is nowhere near the United Kingdom.

# CHAPTER 52  THE HONOURABLE MAN

It was early June before word reached Janie from Nutter that Turkish Ali was back in town with news of Melanie Campbell and would like to see her for the rest of his money. A week later, Janie was seated at a table in a corner at the back of one of his bars, with Nutter next to her and a bulky holdall on the floor by her feet.

"So how was your trip, Mr Ali," she asked.

"Good, good," he said. "In my line of work deals are sealed with a handshake. The upside is no paper with my name and signature on. The downside is that I sometimes have to travel half way round the world to make the handshake."

"And on the subject of paper-free deals sealed with a handshake, how are things with Melissa Campbell?"

"That's what I wanted to see you about. I've got some photos for you, I think you'll like them."

He called over to one of his staff who brought him an ornate mother-of-pearl inlaid Turkish Delight box from behind the counter. He lifted the lid and took out a small photograph album which he opened on the table in front of her.

"I brought these back from my trip," he said. "One of my boys took the ones on the ship and the prison governor took the rest." Nutter and Janie pulled their chairs forward and leaned over to get a better view. Turkish Ali took them through his album.

There were several flash photographs of Melissa in overalls sitting on a grubby mattress. "That's her on the ship," said Turkish Ali. "She was troublesome to start with so they had to tie her up, but when she learned to be more co-operative they set her loose and let her out of her container as long as she behaved herself. She couldn't exactly run away."

Janie thumbed through photos of her on deck, looking at the horizon or with grinning and gesturing Filipino crewmen posing around her. "They let her get exercise and fresh air. You wanted her to arrive at her destination in good health. There was nothing to stop her jumping over the side, but as you can see she didn't. She kept saying that she's very important and the British government would find her and bring her home, the Queen wanted to give her a medal. Is that true, Mrs Hulk?"

"Not any more, I shouldn't think."

There were photos of her tied up again, being put in a van. "She's landed now. On her way to her new home. She wasn't too happy, my man who went with her says she was biting and swearing until they taped her mouth up."

"Yes, she's been in a van before," Janie said. "I don't suppose she likes how it turns out."

"And here's where she is now, in her new home. I picked these photos up for you last week."

Janie turned over the photographs one at a time. Melissa Campbell in a tatty once-orange prison uniform with a prison haircut, lying on a bottom bunk in a squalid eight-bunk cell with a row of buckets in the corner. Melissa eating from a tin bowl among a row of other prisoners at a long bench. Melissa walking hunched over in a small barbed-wire exercise cage. Melissa in a narrow corridor carrying latrine buckets. Melissa kneeling down scrubbing a filth-covered floor.

"The prison governor took these for me," said Turkish Ali. "He's called Simeon, he's a very good friend of mine."

"You seem to have a lot of very good friends," Janie said.

"I generally find that they are the best sort to have," he replied.

"How did you get to be such good friends with Simeon?"

"A few years ago one of my employees was transporting a rather valuable cargo for me from Colombia via Panama, when he was unfortunate enough to be arrested at the airport. I am a responsible employer and it was my duty to go over there and arrange his release. Simeon was most helpful. Prison governors in Panama are not paid well, and a friend who helps him out financially is a very good friend indeed. He will take good care of your lady."

"What if someone finds out about her?" Janie asked. "Doesn't the Panama government have prison inspectors?"

"Of course it does, Mrs Hulk. The prison inspector is also a very good friend of Simeon's, and on inspections they go together to see your lady, it's their favourite part of the inspection. She shouts and screams and says she wants to see the British Ambassador and threatens them with all sorts of things. They even have a name for her, they call her 'la perra inglesa presumida' which means 'the stuck-up English lady dog'. They think it's really funny."

"So do I," Janie said. "Don't you think so, Nutter?"

"There's no photos of her being tortured," was all Nutter had to say on the subject.

"No, Mr Nutter, there are no pictures of her being tortured," said Turkish Ali. "Panama is a civilised country and a member of the United Nations, they don't torture people. Unless Mrs Hulk here wants to pay extra of course?"

"No thank you, Mr Ali, I am fully satisfied with the service I am already getting. And how long can she stay there?"

"No limit, Mrs Hulk. She stays there just as long as you keep giving me the money to pay Simeon to look after her. Or until she escapes, which she can't, it's maximum security. Or until she gets to see the British Ambassador, which she won't because all requests have to be approved in person by the prison inspector."

"Mr Ali, you have yourself a very satisfied customer. Would you like your money now?"

"Where money is concerned there is never a better time than the present, Mrs Hulk."

He handed her the photo album and with her foot she pushed the holdall and contents to him under the table. Like the true East Ender that he had become, he did not count it or even look inside.

They all shook hands and Turkish Ali announced that they should celebrate with Champagne, which he called on the waiter to bring over along with four glasses.

When the bottle arrived Turkish Ali opened it and then passed it, still fizzing from the neck, carefully over to Janie.

"Best Turkish Champagne," he said, beaming proudly.

Janie looked at label and read it out. "It says Lauren-Poirrier, Fine Vintage Champagne, Made in France."

"Well of course it does, that's how we sell it."

"And there are only three of us, why the four glasses?" she asked.

"It's an old tradition from my home country. The fourth glass is for la perra inglesa presumida and we will not fill it. It signifies that unlike us, she has nothing to celebrate."

They left the fourth glass empty.

While people puzzled about Melissa Campbell's disappearance and what to do about it, her house in Surrey had been standing empty for the best part of a year when Nutter let himself in through the patio door and set fire to it.

The roof and all the floors were so completely burnt that the fire service could not find the seat of the fire or establish the cause, but they suspected arson. The house could not be saved and what was left had to be demolished. The fire investigators were puzzled by the back patio door that they found lying covered in ash fragments but otherwise intact on the rear lawn.

Janie did not tell Nutter to do it, but she did ask him why.

"Now she hasn't got a house either," he said. "Though if she'd had a cat living there I wouldn't have done it."

Nutter is just Nutter and is still a nutter.

For a while Janie bought all the newspapers every day to see if they would break the story of RoyalBank's Russian gold and Sir Charles Borden's part in it, but there was no word. After all Helen's hard work she was a little disappointed, but she consoled herself by imagining how he must now be having to live his life as a fugitive.

But in the end the story was too good not to tell and the Guardian broke it, and once they did all the other papers were safe to pile in too. For days the headlines told of Sir Charles Borden's rise, crooked deals and sudden disappearance. On the inside pages there were reproductions of entries from Helen's gold trade dossier, and clever graphics to explain them to the readers.

Helen uploaded the entire dossier to Wikileaks, who placed it on-line worldwide, and the Financial Conduct Authority and the Serious Fraud Squad issued a joint statement announcing a combined investigation into RoyalBank and all its trading activities, not just gold. "That should keep them busy for a decade or two," thought Janie.

"Where's Charlie?" was the tabloid headline take on it all, with photographs of Sir Charles Borden on all front pages accompanied by police appeals for sightings and information as to his whereabouts.

Janie hummed 'Nowhere to Run' to herself as she strolled chirpily back to her flat with the newspapers under her arm.

What happened next was not part of her plan. On reflection, Janie felt that she should have anticipated it and regretted not having done more to avoid it, but by the time she found out it was much too late and out of her hands.

The police did find Sir Charles Borden in the end. According to the news reports, walkers on a quiet forest track in rural mid-Scotland had become used to seeing a scruffy bearded man living alone in an old camper van tucked away among the trees, and when they found it burnt out it was several days before they reported it. It took the authorities several more days to attend to remove the remains of the vehicle, but when they did they found inside it an incinerated body that was confirmed by DNA testing and dental records to be that of Sir Charles Borden, previously Chief Executive of RoyalBank but more recently a registered missing person.

It had taken some time for the police to establish the cause of death, but reconstruction of what was left of his skull after the fire indicated the track of a bullet passing through it, fired from inside the vehicle and exiting through a window into the trees somewhere, yet to be found.

The police's statements, then and on subsequent days until the papers lost interest and moved on, indicated that they had a fairly good idea of his killers' motive but that their investigation, which centred on the Russian ex-pat community, was making no progress in identifying who they actually were.

Janie wondered if Nutter had a hand in this somehow, she wouldn't put it past him, and she knew that if she asked him he would tell her honestly. But she has not asked him, because if she does he will tell her and she would prefer not to know.

It was around this time that Janie had a more pleasant surprise. Turkish Ali called her up and asked her to meet him at one of his restaurants, and when she did he gave her a large envelope stuffed with money.

"What's this for?" she asked.

"It's for you, Mrs Hulk," he replied. "There has been an unexpected development in Panama."

He spotted Janie's look of concern.

"No, Mrs Hulk, not a bad development, a good development. My very good friend Simeon called me to say someone has recognised your lady in his prison."

Janie must have looked even more concerned.

"No Mrs Hulk, I tell you it is good news."

And it was good news too. Simeon had told Turkish Ali that the Panama government was coming under pressure from the United States to do more to crack down on international money laundering and a number of crooked local lawyers and accountants had been arrested and lodged in his gaol. One of them was in the exercise yard when he and Melissa Campbell recognised each other and spoke through the wire, with Melissa demanding that he get a message to the British ambassador that she is incarcerated there.

The man has influential friends and was released within a few days but did not pass any messages for Melissa. Instead, and concerned that she knew too much about his and his associates' financial affairs, he preferred her to stay where she was. His wealthy friends were of the same opinion, so they all agreed to club together to pay Simeon the cost of keeping her locked away in his prison for the next ten years.

"Half up front, the rest on completion," said Turkish Ali, "Your strange East End custom seems to have crossed the ocean. So here is your money back, I don't need it."

"That's very kind of you, Mr Ali," Janie said, "Especially as I wouldn't have known if you hadn't told me, and then you could have kept it all."

"Then perhaps I am not such a good businessman either, Mrs Hulk. But then you are a very good friend."

# CHAPTER 53  THE NEW HOME

Helen and Janie had watched the cracks appear and the masonry crumble, but when the dam burst on Lord Phillips the newspapers were there first. The front pages led with the bankruptcy of the man who was "Lord Phillips, chairman of Britain's leading bank" in the smarter papers and "Failed Phillips" in the tabloids.

According to newspaper reports he was declared bankrupt at the London County Court, and therefore lost his banking licence, and so was immediately disqualified from working in banking in any capacity, and therefore unemployed and unemployable. He was immediately sacked by RoyalBank and then stripped of all his stock options by a vote of shareholders who were furious at the harm he had done to RoyalBank's share price.

Wife number four got her divorce, but none of his money because there was none. The papers love it when the mighty are humbled and reported gleefully when his house was repossessed along with Lady Phillips' Ferrari.

He would not have been friendless, he still had friends, but they would have been one-way friendships where they gave him a roof and food and money and he had nothing to give back. Janie imagined that his friends would eventually need to move on with their lives, unencumbered by their inconvenient guest.

When Janie is out and about she generally buys a copy of The Big Issue from a street-seller. It sometimes has interesting articles on off-beat topics, and buying it is her own little act of constructive charity towards the homeless.

That autumn Sam just happened to flick through a copy that Janie had brought home. He was about to toss it into the recycling bin when he stopped.

"Janet, take a look at this."

There was a photograph of a man who bore quite a resemblance to Lord Phillips. The Big Issue often carries features on homelessness, and as part of a 'keep warm for winter' campaign it was running photographs of people sleeping rough in cities around Britain.

"Do you think it could be him?" he asked.

The picture was in black-and-white, taken at night with a flash under an archway in London, and its subject was in a sleeping bag, bearded and looking away from the camera, but Janie had to agree that he looked very much like Mike Phillips. She went straight back into town and bought all the remaining copies from the delighted seller.

The following day Janie took a trip to London and found Rudy at his usual table in the Oak Barrel, where she showed him the picture.

"Do you reckon you could find him?" she asked.

"Maybe. I know some people who can look out for him. That's if he's still in London and still alive." In three weeks they did find him, wrapped in cardboard in a corner of an old railway arch near Waterloo Station.

Sam said they should leave Phillips where he was as he did not want anything more to do with the man, but Janie decided that they should intervene in his life once more. London's streets are rough where the homeless people have to go, so she gave Nutter the job of keeping a protective eye on him. A couple of nights a week Nutter took himself over to Waterloo to give Phillips food and a little money.

Then one evening, dressed up against the cold, Nutter led Rudy and Janie over to Phillips' railway arch.

Rudy had brought a torch and he shone it around in the gloom. Overshadowed by graffiti-sprayed walls and among a detritus of bottles, litter, empty cans and shredded polythene shopping bags were half a dozen squalid piles of old sleeping bags and flattened cardboard panels. Nutter led them over to one of them and Rudy shone his torch onto it. It did not move so he poked it with his foot. A head emerged and two eyes blinked at the torchlight.

"Get up, Phillips" said Nutter, "You're coming with us."

Phillips sat up. Filthy, bearded, long greasy grey hair, lips cracked from malnutrition and cold. But without doubt, Lord Phillips of Kidwelton.

Rudy and Nutter hoisted him out of his unpleasant-smelling nest. He did not resist, and did not look as if he would have had the strength had he wanted to. He had that look of animal fear on his face that you often see if you look a homeless person straight in the eye.

"Where are you taking me?" was all he could say.

"To your new home," was all Nutter replied. "Now shut your face."

They lifted Phillips onto the back seat of the car, on a big plastic sheet that they had brought to try to protect the upholstery, and drove out to Bethnal Green where they pulled into an alleyway that runs between a row of old garages and a disused section of railway track. Janie stopped the car and they led Phillips through a gap in the railings and under bushes that had started as weeds and were now ten feet high, to a derelict trackside hut.

The hut presumably once housed railwaymen's tools. It was built of bricks with a flat concrete slab roof, about seven feet long by five feet wide. The windows were now boarded up, the frames and glass gone decades ago. Until the day before, the floor had been knee-deep in the same sort of rubbish that littered Phillips' archway, but Rudy and Janie had cleared it out and it now contained all the home comforts and soft furnishings that Phillips would need for his new life, namely a clean sleeping bag on a fresh layer of cardboard, a pack of yesterday's sandwiches and a bottle of water.

"Your new home," said Nutter, as he pushed Phillips through the doorway and Rudy shone the torch around. "I'll be back in the morning and you'd better still be here."

Phillips was still there in the morning and Nutter had a nice long friendly chat with him. The gist of it was:

"This is where you live from now on, and if you ever so much as think about leaving I will find you like I found you before and break your neck, do you understand me?"

"Yes I understand you."

"And don't think I don't know who you are, because I do. If you ever go anywhere near the House of Lords I will also kill you, but first you will suffer a great deal of pain. Do you understand that too?"

"Yes I understand that too."

Nutter had raised the subject of the House of Lords at Janie's request. Her plans for Lord Phillips certainly did not include him pocketing £300 a day from the taxpayer just for turning up for a free lunch and a kip on a comfy leather bench. Lords do not lose their seat if they are disgraced or go bankrupt. If they did, half the nation's peerages would by now be vacant.

# CHAPTER 54 THE BIG ISSUE SELLER

John Murphy may only be a provincial family solicitor who had never been to the Old Bailey and who upset Mr Clarence QC over David's police confession, but in his secret negotiations on Janie's behalf with a very senior government official he showed a different side.

The upshot is that Janie now has a letter of indemnity, signed by the Home Secretary herself, for she is the only person who in law may sign such a thing. It indemnifies Janie and all of her family and associates against, to quote from the text *"any charge, criminal or civil, or any other legal action or liability, connected with or arising from"* her pursuit of RoyalBank and PCMG. Nice to have, there are not a lot of those around. It is not on gold leaf parchment, but it might as well be.

Yet again, the country is in financial difficulties. The economy faltered as the world's investors bet against us, the public purse was even more empty than before, and the government responded by increasing the top band tax rate - "The Rich Tax" as the papers immediately entitled it. Predictably, the nation's rich immediately got busy moving money and assets out of the country and into the usual tax havens and scams, with well-remunerated help from the banks and accountancy firms of course.

Enter Janet Lockwood, in possession of a computer memory stick furnished by her clever daughter Helen, containing files, formerly in the possession of RoyalBank and PCMG, that list the identity of every customer whom they had ever helped to hide their wealth or avoid their tax, or usually both, together with full particulars of all their secret accounts, investments and properties and where to find them.

The sums involved are colossal. Helen's stick contained all the information on where to find at least £1500 billion of illegally stashed money and missing tax. That is enough to fund the entire National Health Service for ten years.

Through John Murphy, Janie traded the stick and its contents to our cash-strapped government in return for the Home Secretary's indemnity.

Helen was included in the indemnity, provided she handed over all her other files and stays out of RoyalBank's hair from now on. They have changed all their administration codes anyway, Helen did just check. Helen decided to take a new name and move up north in case she gets death threats from some of the people she has helped to expose, but she still phones her mother for a long chat on Sunday evenings, and Janie passes on to Sam as much of Helen's news as she thinks he should know. Helen is taking a business studies course with a view to becoming a woman in business, so something positive of Melissa must have rubbed off on her.

Janie tried to secure a pardon for David too, but in the end the Home Secretary turned it down, she said that even though Charles Borden put him up to it, David was still guilty of the crimes that he was tried for. However, John Murphy negotiated early parole and David will keep his freedom as long as he stays out of trouble from now on.

Surprising as it seems, he is still in touch with most of his worldwide network of rate fixers and is close friends with some of them. He is just back from a trip to Tokyo to watch the Melbourne Demons on an exhibition tour, and is making plans to spend the summer with Dirk Krueger visiting obscure Dutch family archives in South Africa. After that, with no likelihood of getting his old job back, he is thinking of putting his talents and contacts to use as a self-employed general trader.

Jennifer Harding's bank account gave Jess enough money to set herself up in business again, and she now runs a successful company in Brighton installing burglar alarms - real ones, not dummies. She and Simon bring Harry over to see Grandma and Grandad once a month, and she is now expecting Simon's first child, due towards Christmas.

Jennifer Harding also paid off Minnie, Rudy and Nutter. Minnie used her money to buy herself another house just along the row from her old one, and is very happy there. Rudy bought back the Oak Barrel, but he no longer toils behind the bar. He has moved himself to a better table, in the big front bay window, and entertains the crowd from there while keeping an eye on the bar staff from his prime vantage point. Nutter gave most of his money to animal charities and the rest is in the bank, where Sam watches over it to see that he doesn't get fleeced again.

Janie is now back in Bethnal Green, living with Sam a few streets away from Minnie. She felt it was time to leave Brighton, as she knew she would not be too popular there when some of her erstwhile south coast neighbours and business colleagues found out that their financial shenanigans were on Helen's stick. And Sam has surprised her, as he always does, by becoming quite the East End gentleman.

From time to time Janie has a long lunch with Turkish Ali. He usually has some new photos for her of la perra inglesa presumida going about her chores. Janie accidentally knocked over Melissa's glass one time, but it didn't matter, there was nothing in it.

Jennifer Marie Harding's bank account probably still exists, but Helen collected all that was left in it a while ago and the latest statement was returned to Jersey marked "Unknown - not at this address". After everyone was paid off, the remainder of the cash was inside a holdall that was left on the counter of the Salvation Army hostel in Whitechapel when the receptionist was away from his desk.

Sam asked Janie the other day if there has been anything yet in the papers about Helen's stick.

"Nothing so far," she said. "I guess there must be so much information on it that the government's taking ages to go through it all."

"Or else they've found it's got so many of themselves and their pals on it that it's gone in the same canal as our phones," said Sam.

"Now you're just being cynical," said Janie. "They wouldn't do that. Would they?"

Saturday is Janie's favourite day of the week. It is the day when she and Sam meet up with Minnie and Nutter and head into town together to do Bethnal Green market, followed by a proper old-fashioned pie, mash and eels lunch at the Oak Barrel, which is now the last place for miles around that still serves that sort of fare. Rudy keeps them seats at his big table in the front bay window and joins them there with a full tray of drinks.

From that table they can see Lord Phillips. He stands outside in all weathers near the old water fountain, stooped, scarved, shabby, face veined, clutching a plastic carrier bag. When the pub is not too rowdy they can hear his call.

"Big Issue! Get your Big Issue!"

On the way out Janie likes to buy a copy. He looks at her, as if trying to work out where he knows her from. Maybe she'll tell him, maybe she won't, she hasn't decided.

Printed in Great Britain
by Amazon